TRIPLICITY

TRIPLICITY

ECHO ROUND HIS BONES
THE GENOCIDES
THE PUPPIES OF TERRA

Thomas M. Disch

NELSON DOUBLEDAY, INC.
Garden City, New York

Contents

ECHO
ROUND HIS
BONES

To my brother Gary,
who read it

CONTENTS

No more shall Walls, no more shall Walls confine
That glorious Soul which in my Flesh doth shine:
  No more shall Walls of Clay or Mud,
    Nor Ceilings made of Wood,
  Nor Crystal Windowns, bound my Sight,
  But rather shall admit Delight.
    The Skies that seem to bound
      My Joys and Treasures,
    Of more endearing Pleasures
    Themselvs becom a Ground:
While from the Center to the utmost Sphere
My Goods are multiplied evry where.

Hosanna, THOMAS TRAHERNE

Chapter 1

NATHAN HANSARD

The finger on the trigger grew tense. The safety was released, and in almost the same moment the gray morning stillness was shattered by the report of the rifle. Then, just as a mirror slivers and the images multiply, myriad echoes returned from the ripening April hillsides— a mirthful, mocking sound. The echoes re-echoed, faded, and died, but the stillness did not settle back on the land, the stillness was broken.

The officer who had been marching at the head of the brief column of men—a captain, no more—came striding back along the dirt track. He was a man of thirty-five or perhaps forty years, with fair, regular features, set now in an expression of anger—or, if not anger quite, irritation. Some would have judged him a handsome man; others might have objected that his manner was rather too neutral— a neutrality expressive not so much of tranquillity as of truce. His jaw was set and his lips molded in the military cast. His blue eyes were glazed by that years-long unrelenting discipline. They might not, it could be argued, have been by nature such severe features: without that discipline the jaw might have been more relaxed, the lips fuller, the eyes brighter—yes, and the captain might have been another man.

He stopped at the end of the column and addressed himself to the red-haired soldier standing on the outside of the last file—a master-sergeant, as may be ascertained from the chevron sewn to the sleeve of his fatigue jacket.

"Worsaw?"

"Sir." The sergeant came, approximately, to attention.

"You were instructed to collect all ammunition after rifle practice."

"Yes sir."

"All cartridges were to be given back to you. No one should have any ammunition now therefore."

"No sir."

"And this was done?"

"Yes sir. So far as I know."

"And yet the shot we just heard was certainly fired by one of us. Give me your rifle, Worsaw."

With visible reluctance the sergeant handed his rifle to the captain. "The barrel is warm," the captain observed. Worsaw made no reply.

"May I take your word, Worsaw, that this rifle is unloaded?"

"Yes sir."

The captain put the butt of the rifle against his shoulder and laid his finger over the trigger. He remarked that the safety was off. Worsaw said nothing.

"May I pull the trigger, Worsaw?" The rifle was pointed at the sergeant's right shin. Worsaw still said nothing, but beads of sweat had broken out on his freckled face.

"Do I have your permission? Answer me."

Worsaw broke down. "No sir," he said.

The captain broke open the magazine and removed the cartridge clip. He handed the rifle back to the sergeant. "Is it possible then, Worsaw, that the shot that brought us to a halt a moment ago was fired by this rifle?" There was, even now, no trace of sarcasm in the captain's voice.

"I saw a rabbit, sir—"

The captain's brow furrowed. "Did you hit it, Worsaw?"

"No sir."

"Fortunately for you. Do you realize that it is a federal offense to kill wildlife on this land?"

"It was just a rabbit, sir. We shoot them around here all the time. Usually, when we come out for rifle practice or that sort of stuff—"

"Do you mean to say it is *not* against the law?"

"No sir, I wouldn't know about that. I just know that usually—"

"Shut up, Worsaw."

Worsaw's face had become so red that his reddish-blond eyebrows and lashes seemed pale in comparison. In his bafflement, his lower lip had begun to tic back and forth as though some buried fragment of his character were trying to pout.

"I despise a liar," the captain said blandly. He inserted his thumbnail under the tip of the chevron sewn on Worsaw's right sleeve and ripped it off with one quick motion. Then the other chevron.

The captain returned to the front of the column, and the march back to the trucks that would return them to Camp Jackson was resumed.

This captain, who will be the hero of our history, was a man of the future—that is to say, of what would seem futurity to us, for to the captain it seemed the most commonplace present. Yet there are degrees of living in the future, of being contemporary there, and it must be admitted that in many ways the captain was more a man of the past (of his past, and even perhaps of ours) than of the future.

Consider only his occupation: a career officer in the Regular Army—surely a most uncharacteristic employment in the year 1990. By that time everyone knew that the army, the Regular Army (for though the draft still did operate and young men were compelled to surrender their three years to the Reserve Army, they all knew that this was a joke, that the Reserves were useless, that they were maintained only as a device for keeping themselves out of the labor force or off the unemployment rolls that much longer after college) was a career for louts and nincompoops. But if *everyone* knew this . . . Everyone who was with it; everyone who was truly comfortable living in the future. These contemporaries of the captain (many of whom—some 29 per cent—were so far unlike him as to prefer three years of post-graduate study in the comfortable and permissive prisons that had been built for C.O.'s—the chonchies, as they were called—rather than submit to the ritual non-activities of the Reserves) regarded the captain and his like as—and this is their most charitable judgment—fossils.

It is true that military service traditionally requires qualities more of character than of intelligence. Does this mean then that our hero is on the stupid side? By no means! And to dispel any lingering doubts of this let us hasten to note that in third grade the captain's I.Q., as measured by the Stanford-Binet Short Form, was a respectable 128—certainly as much or more as we can fairly demand of a hero in this line of work.

In fact, it had been the captain's experience that he possessed intelligence in excess of his needs; he would often have been happier in his calling if he had been as blind to certain distinctions—often of a moral character—as most of his fellow officers seemed to be. Once, indeed, this overacuteness had directly injured the captain's prospects, and it might be that that long-ago event was the cause, even this much later, of the captain's relatively low position, considering his age, in the military hierarchy. We shall have opportunity to hear more of this unpleasant moment—but in its proper place.

It may just as plausibly be the case that the captain's lack of advancement was due simply to a lack of vacancies. The Regular Army of 1990 was much smaller than the army of our own time—partly because of international agreements, but basically in recognition of the fact that a force of 25,000 men was more than ample to prosecute a nuclear war—and this, in 1990, was the only war that the two great powers' blocs were equipped to fight. Disarmament was a *fait accompli,* though it was of a sort that no one of our time had quite anticipated; instead of eliminating nuclear devices it had preserved them alone. In truth, "disarmament" is something of a euphemism; what had been done had been done more in the interests of domestic economy than of world peace. The bombs that the pacifists complained of (and in 1990, *everyone* was a pacifist) were still up there, biding their time, waiting for the day that everyone agreed was inevitable. Everyone, that is to say, who was with it; everyone who was truly comfortable living in the future.

Thus, the captain, though he lived in the future, was very little representative of it. His political opinions were conservative to a point just short of reaction. He read few of what we would think of as the better books of his time, saw few of the better movies—not because he lacked aesthetic sensibilities, no (for instance, his musical taste was highly developed), but because these things were made for other, and possibly better, tastes than his. He had no sense of fashion—and this was not a small lack, for among his contemporaries fashion was a potent force. Other-directedness had carried all before it; shame, not guilt, was the greater shaper of souls, and the most important question one could ask oneself was: "Am I with it?" And the captain would have had to answer, "No."

He wore the wrong clothes, in the wrong colors, to the wrong places. His hair was too short (though by present standards it would have seemed rather full for a military man); his face was too pale (he wouldn't use even the discreetest cosmetics); his hands were bare of rings. Once, it is true, there had been a gold band on the fourth finger of his left hand, but that had been some years ago. Unfashionableness has its price, and for the captain the price had been steep. It had cost him his wife and son. She had been too contemporary for him—or he too outmoded for her. In effect, their love had spanned a century, and though at first it was quite strong enough to stand the strain, in time it was the times that won. They were divorced on grounds of incompatibility.

At this point it may have occurred to the reader to wonder why in a tale of the future we should have chosen a hero so little representative of his age. It is an easy paradox to resolve, for the captain's position in the military establishment had brought him (or, more precisely, was soon to bring him) into contact with that phenomenon which, of all the phenomena of his age, was most advanced, most contemporary, most at the forefront of the future— with, in short, the matter transmitter—or, in the popular phrase, the manmitter—or, in the still more popular phrase, the Steel Womb.

"Brought into contact" is perhaps too weak and passive a phrase. The captain's role was to be more heroic than such words would suggest. "Came into conflict" would do much better. Indeed, he was to come into conflict with much more than the Steel Womb—but with the military establishment as well, with society in general, and with himself. It could even be said, without stretching meanings too far, that in his conflict he pitted himself against the nature of reality itself.

One final paradox before we re-embark upon this tale: It was to be this captain, the military man, the man of war, who was, at the last minute and by the most remarkable device, to rescue the world from that ultimate catastrophe, the war to end wars, the Armageddon that we are all, even now, waiting for. But by that time he would not be the same man, but a different man, a man quite thoroughly of the future—because he had made it in his own image.

At twilight of that same day on which we last saw him the captain was sitting alone in the office of "A" Artillery Company. It was as bare a room as it could possibly be and yet be characterized as an office. On the gray metal desk were only an appointment calendar that showed the date to be the twentieth of April, a telephone, and a file folder containing brief statistical profiles of the twenty-five men under the captain's command: Barnstock, Blake, Cavender, Dahlgren, Doggett . . .

The walls of the room were bare, except for framed photos cut out of magazines, of General Samuel ("Wolf") Smith, Army Chief of Staff, and of President Lind, whose presence here would have to be considered as merely commemorative, since he had been assassinated some forty days before. As yet, apparently, no one had found a good likeness of Lee Madigan, his successor, to replace Lind's photo. On the cover of *Life,* Madigan had been squinting into the sun; on *Time*'s cover he was shown splattered with the president's blood.

There was a metal file-cabinet, and it was empty; a metal wastebasket, it was empty; metal chairs, empty. The captain cannot be held strictly to account for the bareness of the room, for he had been in occupancy only two days. Even so, it was not much different from the office he had left behind in the Pentagon Building, where he had been the aide of General Pittmann.

. . . Fanning, Green, Horner, Lesh, Maggit, Norris, Nelsen, Nelson . . . They were Southerners mostly, the men of "A" Company. In the Southern states 68 per cent of the Regular Army was recruited from the backwoods and back alleys of that country-within-a-country, that fossil society that produced fossil men . . . Lathrop, Perigrine, Pearsall, Pearsall, Rand, Ross . . . Good men in their way—that cannot be denied. But they were not, any more than their captain, contemporary with their own times. Plain, simple, honest men—Squires, Sumner, Truemile, Thorn, Worsaw, Young— but also mean-spirited, resentful, stupid men, as the captain well knew. You cannot justly expect anything else of men who have been outmoded, who have had no better prospect than *this,* who will never make much money or have much fun or taste the sparkling elixir of being With It, who are, and always will be, deprived—and who know it.

These were not precisely the terms with which the captain regarded this problem—though he had been long enough in the Army (since 1976) to realize that they did not misrepresent the state of affairs. But he looked at things on a reduced scale (he was only a captain, after all) and considered how to deal with the twenty-five men under his command so as to divert the full force of their resentment from his own person. He had expected to be resented—this is the fate of all officers who inherit the command of an established company—but he hadn't expected matters to go to such mutinous extremes as they had this morning after rifle drill.

Rifle drill was a charade. Nobody expected rifles to be used in the next war. In much the same way, the captain suspected, this contest of wills between himself and his men was a charade—a form that had to be gone through before a state of equilibrium could be reached, a tradition-sanctioned period of mutual testing-out. The captain's object was to abbreviate this period as much as possible; the company's to draw it out to their advantage.

The phone rang, the captain answered it. The orderly of Colonel Ives hoped that the captain would be free to see the colonel. Certainly—whenever it was convenient to the colonel. In half an hour? In half an hour. Splendid. In the meantime perhaps it would be possible for the captain to instruct "A" Company to prepare for a jump in the morning?

The captain felt his mouth grow dry; his blood quickened perceptibly. He was hardly aware of answering or of hanging up the receiver.

Prepare to jump . . .

He seemed for a moment to fission, to become two men—an old man and a young man, and while the old man sat behind the bare desk the young one stood crouched before the open hatch of an airplane, rifle in hand (they *had* used rifles in that war), staring out into the vast brightness and down, far down, at the unfamiliar land, the improbable rice paddies. The land had been so *green*. And then he had jumped, and the land had come rushing up against him. The land, in that instant, became his enemy, and he . . . Did he become the enemy of that land?

But the captain knew better than to ask himself such questions. A policy of deliberate and selective amnesia was the wisest. It had served him in good stead these twelve years.

He put on his hat and went out through the door of the orderly room into a yard of unvigorous grass. Worsaw was sitting on the steps of the brick barracks building, smoking. The captain addressed him without thinking:

"Sergeant!"

Worsaw rose and stood to attention smartly. "Sir!"

"That is to say—" (Trying to make the blunder seem a deliberate cruelty, and not—which is inadmissible—an error). *"Private* Worsaw. Inform the men that they are to be prepared to make a jump in the morning at eight hundred hours."

How quickly the clouds of resentment could overcast the man's pale eyes! But Worsaw replied, in an even tone, "Yes sir."

"And shine those shoes, Private. They're a disgrace to this company."

"Yes *sir.*"

"You're in the Army now, Private, don't you forget it."

"No *sir.*"

As though, the captain thought wryly, as he walked away, *he had any choice. Poor devil. As though he* could *forget it. As though any of us could.*

"This will be your first jump, won't it, Captain?"

"Yes sir."

Colonel Ives laid a forefinger upon the soft folds of his chin. "Let me caution you against expecting much, then. It will be no different there than it is here at Camp Jackson. You breathe the same air, see the same dome overhead, drink the same water, live in the same buildings, with the same men."

"Yes—so I've been told, but even so it's hard to believe."

"There are *some* differences. For instance, you can't drive in to D.C. on the weekends. And there are fewer officers. It can become very boring."

"You wouldn't be able to tell me, I suppose, to whom I'll be reporting?"

Colonel Ives shook his head aggrievedly. "I don't know myself. Security around the Womb is absolute. It would be easier to break into heaven, or Fort Knox. You'll receive your final instructions tomorrow, just before you go into the Womb, but not from me. I only work here."

Then why, the captain wondered, *did you have me come to see you?*

The colonel was not long in answering the unasked question: "I heard about the little to-do you had this morning with the men."

"Yes—with Sergeant Worsaw."

"Ah—then you mean to say his rank has been restored already?"

"No. I'm afraid I was only speaking loosely."

"A shame that it had to happen. Worsaw is a good man, an absolutely top-notch technician. The men respect him—even the, um, colored boys. You're not a Southerner yourself are you, Captain?"

"No sir."

"Didn't think so. We Southerners are sometimes hard to explain to other folks. Take Worsaw now—a good man, but he does have a stubborn streak, and when he takes a notion into his head—" Colonel Ives clucked with dismay. "But a good man—we can't let ourselves forget that."

Colonel Ives waited until the captain had agreed to this last statement.

"Of course these things will happen. They're inevitable when you're taking over a new command. I remember, in my own case— did I tell you that I was once at the head of "A" Company myself? Yes indeed!—I had a little trouble with that fellow too. But I smoothed it over, and soon we were all working together like clockwork. Of course it was easier for me than it will be for you. I hadn't gone so far as to strip him of rank. That was a very strong gesture, Captain. I imagine you must have regretted it since?"

"No sir. I was convinced at the time, and still am, that he merited it. Amply."

"Of course, of course. But we must remember the Golden Rule, eh? Live and let live. The Army is a team, and we've all got to pull together. You can't do your work without Worsaw, Captain, and I can't do my work without you. We can't let *prejudice*—" Colonel Ives paused to smile. "—or *temper* affect our judgment. Mutual cooperation: that's the Army way. You co-operate with Worsaw, I co-operate with you."

The captain's attitude throughout this speech had been one of almost Egyptian stiffness. Now there was a long silence, while Colonel Ives waited, bobbing his head up and down into his chins, for the captain to agree with him.

"Is that all, sir?" the captain asked.

"Now isn't that just like a Northerner? Always in a rush to be off somewhere else. Well don't let *me* slow you down, Captain. But if I might offer a word of advice—though it's none of my business—"

"By all means, Colonel."

"I'd restore Worsaw's rank by the end of the week. I'm sure that will have been punishment enough for what he did. I seem to recall, in my day, that a little poaching wasn't unheard-of after rifle drill. Nothing official, of course, but then everything isn't always done in official ways, Captain. If you take my meaning."

"I'll consider your recommendation, sir."

"Do. Do. Good-night, Captain—and *bon voyage.*"

Outside the captain wandered about for some time to no apparent purpose. Perhaps he was considering the colonel's suggestion; more probably he was only considering the colonel. His wanderings brought him to the center of the unlighted parade grounds.

He looked about him, scanning the sky—forgetting, since he had lived so many years beneath it, that this was not the real sky but a simulation, for Camp Jackson, Virginia, was nestled under the western edge of the Washington D.C. Dome. The dome was studded with millions of subminiaturized photo-electric cells which read the positions of the revolving stars and re-duplicated their shifting pattern on the underside of its immense canopy.

There, low in the east, in the constellation of Taurus, was Mars, the red planet, portent of war. It was very strange, it almost exceeded belief, that in less than twelve hours, he, Captain Nathan Hansard of "A" Artillery Company of the Camp Jackson/Mars Command Post, would be standing with his feet firmly planted upon that speck of reddish light.

Chapter 2

THE STEEL WOMB

It measured, on the outside 14.4ft.$\times$14.14ft.$\times$10.00ft., so that an observer regarding it from the floor of the hall in which it stood would see each face of it as a golden rectangle. The walls were two feet thick, of solid chrome-vanadium steel. They were covered with banks and boards of winking colored lights; the play of these lights, itself an imposing spectacle, was accompanied by nervous cracklings and humming sounds vaguely suggestive of electricity, or, at least, of Science. There was a single opening to this sanctum—a portal some four feet in diameter set into the center of one of the golden rectangles, like the door of a bank vault. Even when this portal was open, though, it was not possible for onlookers to glimpse the awesome central chamber itself, for a mobile steel antechamber would hide it from view at such times. No one but the men who had made the jump—the priests, as it were, of this mystery—had ever seen what it was like inside the Steel Womb.

And it was all fakery, mere public relations and stagecraft. The jump to Mars could have been made with the equivalent of four tin cans full of electronic hardware and a power source no greater than would have been available from a wall socket. The lights winked only for the benefit of the photographers from *Life;* the air hummed so that the visiting Congressmen might be persuaded that the nation was getting its money's worth. The whole set had been designed not by an engineer but by Emily Golden, who had also done the sets, a decade before, for Kubrick's *Brave New World*.

Superfluous it might be, but it was no less daunting for all that. Hansard was given ample time to savor the spectacle. Once "A" Company had arrived at the outer, outer gate of the security complex of which the transmitter was the navelstone, there had been a continuous sorting-through of passes and authorizations, there had been searches, identity checks, telephone confirmations—every imaginable kind of appetizer. It was an hour before—they reached the heart of the labyrinth, the hall that housed the Holy of Holies, and it was another hour before each man had been cleared for the jump. The hall they waited in was about as big as a small-town high school auditorium. The walls were pale, unpainted concrete, the better to focus all eyes upon that magnificent Christmas tree at the center of the room. Large as it was, however, the hall seemed crowded now; there were guards everywhere.

There were guards before the portal of the Womb—a dozen at least. There were guards at the doubly-locked door that led out of the hall. There were guards all around the Christmas tree, like so many khaki-wrapped presents, and there were guards, seemingly, to guard the presents. There was a whole cordon of guards around the men of "A" Company, and there were also guards behind the glass partitions halfway up the walls of the hall. It was there, in the booths behind those windows, that the technicians adjusted the multitude of dials that made the Christmas tree glow and bubble—and operated the single toggle switch that could send the contents of the transmitter from Earth to Mars in, literally, no time at all.

The lights were reaching their apotheosis, and the countdown had already begun for the opening of the portal (countdowns being the very stuff of drama), when the door that led into the hall opened, and a two-star general, under heavy guard, entered and approached Hansard. Hansard recognized him from his photograph as General Foss, the chief of all Mars operations.

After the formalities of introduction and identification, General Foss explained his purpose succinctly: "You are to present this attaché case, containing a Priority-A letter, to the commanding officer, General Pittmann, immediately upon arrival. You will witness him remove the letter from the case."

"General Pittmann—the C.O.!"

General Foss made no further explanations; none were necessary, and he did not seem disposed to practice conversation for its own sake.

Hansard was embarrassed at his outburst, but he was none the less pleased to be enlightened. That General Pittmann was now heading the Mars Command Post explained the otherwise inexplicable fact of Hansard's transfer from the Pentagon to Camp Jackson. It was not Hansard who was being transferred so much as Pittmann; the General's aide had simply been swept up in his wake.

They might have told me, Hansard thought, though it did not surprise him that they had not. It wouldn't have been the Army way.

Already the first squad of eight men, concealed in the belly of the mobile antechamber as in some streamlined Trojan horse, were approaching the portal of the transmitter. The antechamber locked magnetically into place, and there was a pause while the portal opened and the eight men, all unseen, entered the Womb. Then the antechamber moved back, revealing only the closed portal. The multitude of lights ornamenting the surface of the transmitter now darkened—with the exception of a single green globe above the portal, indicating that the eight men were still visible within. The hall had grown hushed. Even the guards, themselves a part of the stagecraft, regarded this moment of the mystery with reverence.

The green light turned to red: the men were on Mars.

The Christmas tree lit up again, and the process was repeated three more times for three more squads of men. Nine, ten, even a dozen men, might have occupied the inner chamber without discomfort, but there was a regulation to the effect that eight (8) was to be the maximum number of men to be allowed in the manmitter at any one time. No one knew why such a regulation should have been made—but there it was. It was now a part of the rites surrounding the mystery and had to be observed. It was the Army way.

After the four squads had made the jump, there remained a single soldier, a Negro private whose name Hansard was uncertain of (he was either Young or Pearsall)—and Hansard himself. A warrant officer informed Hansard that he had the option of making the jump with this soldier or going through alone afterward.

"I'll go now." It was more comfortable, in a way, to have company.

He tucked the attaché case under his arm and climbed up the ladder and into the antechamber. The private followed. They sat up on a narrow ledge and waited while the Trojan horse rolled slowly and smoothly toward the portal of the manmitter.

"Made many jumps, Private?"

"No, sir, this is the first. I'm the only one in the company that hasn't been there before."

"Not the only one, Private. It's my first jump too."

The antechamber locked against the steel wall of the transmitter, and the portal opened inward with a discreet *click*. Crouching, Hansard and the private entered. The door closed behind them.

Here there were no special effects, neither rumblings nor flashing lights. The noise in his ears was the pulse of his own blood. The feeling in his stomach was a cramped muscle. As he had done in the practice session he stared intently at the sign stenciled with white paint on the wall of the vault:

CAMP JACKSON/EARTH
MATTER TRANSMITTER

Then, in an instant—or rather, in no time at all, the sign had changed. Now it read:

CAMP JACKSON/MARS
MATTER TRANSMITTER

It was as simple as that.

The instantaneous transmission of matter, the most important innovation in the history of transportation since the wheel, was the invention of a single man, Dr. Bernard Xavier Panofsky. Born in Poland in 1929, Panofsky spent his youth and early adolescence in a Nazi labor camp, where his childhood genius first manifested itself in a series of highly ingenious, and successful, escape plans. Upon being liberated, so the story goes, he immediately applied himself to the formal study of mathematics and found to his chagrin that he had, independently and all ignorantly, re-invented that branch of mathematics known as *analysis situs,* or topology.

In the late Sixties and already a middle-aged man, Panofsky masterminded his final escape plan: he and three confederates were the last men known to have got over the Berlin Wall. Within a year he had obtained an Associate Professorship in mathematics at a Catholic University in Washington, D.C. By 1970 topology was an unfashionable field, and even Game Theory, after a long heyday, was losing favor to the newer science of Irrationality. In consequence, though Panofsky was one of the world's foremost topologists, the research grant that he received was trifling. In all his work he never used a computer, never employed more than a single assistant, and even in building the pilot model of the transmitter spent only $18,560.00. There wasn't a mathematician in the country who didn't agree that Panofsky's example had set the prestige of their science back fifty years.

It is an almost invariable rule that the great mathematicians have done their most original work in their youth, and Panofsky had been no exception. The theoretical basis of the transmitter had been laid as long ago as 1943, when the 14-year-old prisoner, in fashioning his own topological axioms, naïvely evolved certain features discordant with the classical theories—chiefly that principle that became known as the Paradox of the Exploding Klein Bottle. It was to be the work of his next forty years to try to resolve these discrepancies; then, this proving impossible, to exploit them.

The first transmission was made on Christmas Day of 1983, when Panofsky transported a small silver crucifix (weight: 7.4 grams) from his laboratory on the campus to his home seven blocks away. Because of the circumstances surrounding this event, Panofsky's achievement was not given serious attention by the scientific community for almost a year. It did not help that the press insisted on speaking of the transmission as a "Miracle," or that a shrewd New York entrepreneur, Max Brede (pronounced Brady), was selling replicas (in plated nickel) of the Miraculous Hopping Cross within weeks of the first newspaper stories.

But of course it was a fact, not a miracle, and facts can be verified. Quickly enough Panofsky's invention was taken seriously—and taken away. The Army, under the Emergency Allocation of Resources Act (rather hastily drawn up by Congress for the occasion) had appropriated the transmitter despite all that Panofsky and his sponsors (which now included not only his university, but General Motors and Ford-Chrysler as well) could do. Since that time Panofsky found himself once again a prisoner, for it was obviously contrary to the Nation's best interests that the mind that harbored such strategic secrets should experience all the dangers of freedom. Like the President and ten or twelve other "Most Valuable" men, Panofsky lived virtually under house arrest. To be sure, it was the most elegant of houses, having been specially constructed for him on a site facing the university campus, but the gilt of the cage did little to cheer the prisoner within, whose singular (and inadvertent) manner of escaping from those circumstances we shall have opportunity to consider later in this history.

The invention suffered a fate similar to the inventor's. The transmitters, as we have already seen, were even more fastly guarded than he, and they were used almost exclusively for defense purposes (though the State Department had managed to have its chief embassies provided with small, one-man models), to the despair of Panofsky and a minority of editorialists, both right and left, and to the secret relief of every major element of the economy. Understandably the business community dreaded to think what chaos would result from the widespread use of a mode of transportation that was instantaneous, weighed (in the final, improved model) a mere 49½ ounces, and consumed virtually no power.

Yet even in its military application the transmitter had changed the face of the earth. In 1983, the year of the Miraculous Hopping Cross, the Russians had established a thriving and populous base on the moon, while the United States had twice suffered the ignominy of having lost the teams of astronauts they had tried to land in the Mare Imbrium. More than prestige was involved, for the Russians claimed to have developed a missile that could be launched from the moon with 50 per cent greater accuracy than the then presently-existing ICBM's, a boast made more probable by Russia's unilateral Earthside disarmament. International pressures began to mount that the U.S. follow suit, ignoring the fact that the Russian disarmament was more apparent than real. With the advent of the transmitter, the situation was reversed.

By 1985, thanks to its transmitters, the U.S. manpower on Mars exceeded Soviet lunar manpower by 400 per cent. All American nuclear weapons were removed to the neighboring planet, and by 1986 world disarmament was a fact, if not a very significant one. For the sword of Damocles were still poised above the earth, and the thread by which it hung seemed more frayed than ever.

The missiles that were stockpiled on Mars were not, strictly speaking, to be launched from that planet, but rather they were to be transmitted thence to satellites in permanent orbit above enemy territory and these satellites, in turn, would relay them to their destinations. The satellites were clap-trap affairs, their only purpose being to keep aloft the 49½ ounces of receiving equipment—and a miniature radar that could trigger the self-annihilation of the receiver should any object approach it nearer than fifty feet—i.e., should the Russians try to kidnap one. Once at the satellite, each missile was programmed to home in on its target by itself.

If only the receivers could have been dispensed with! The strategists of the Pentagon sighed for that millennial possibility, but it was not to be: all their mathematicians confirmed Panofksy's assurance that transmission could only be made from one machine *here* to another machine *there*. If the necessity for that second machine, the receiver, had not existed, anything might have been possible. Anything—but particularly a conclusive end to the Cold War. A victory! For, with a means of delivering bombs *directly and instantaneously* from Mars to Russian soil . . .

From Mars? From anywhere—from the other end of the galaxy, if need be. Without the necessity of sending a receiver on ahead to one's destination, distances were meaningless. Mars could be dispensed with; the satellites could be dispensed with; in the long run, with the universe at one's disposal, even Earth could probably be dispensed with.

But the receivers, alas, *were* necessary. The relay satellites were necessary. And Mars—or some such storehouse—was necessary.

And finally there was that necessity which all the other necessities took for granted—the necessity for Armageddon. Bombs, after all, are made to be dropped.

"Welcome to Mars, Nathan."

"It's good to be back, sir."

"To be—Oh, well, thank you. It's good to *have* you back. Sit down and tell me about the trip." General Pittmann sat down in one of two facing easy chairs, crossing his legs so that his ankle rested on his knee. He might have been a store mannequin, so perfectly did his tailored uniform drape itself about him while preserving immaculate its crease. Perfect, too, were the manicured nails, the thick hair just starting to gray, the deeply tanned and artificially weathered complexion, the unemphatic, slightly mocking smile.

"The trip was uneventful but never dull for a moment. This case, sir, contains a letter for you. Priority-A. I was instructed by General Foss to see you take it out of the case."

"Old Chatterbox Foss, eh? Here's the key, Nathan. Will you open it up for me? I've been expecting something on this order."

As General Pittmann read the letter the smile disappeared from his face, and a slight frown creased his brow, but even this seemed somehow decorative. "As I feared," he said, handing the letter to Hansard, who regarded it doubtfully. "Yes, read it, Nathan. It will ease my mind if someone else knows. I'll take my chances that you're not a security risk.

The letter directed that the total nuclear arsenal of Camp Jackson/ Mars be released upon the enemy, who was unnamed, who did not need to be named, on the first day of June, 1990, according to existing Operational Plan B. It was signed by President Lee Madigan and sealed with the Great Seal.

Hansard handed the letter back to his superior. "It hardly gives a person chance to breathe," he commented with calculated ambiguity.

The smile ventured a tentative return. "Oh, we have six weeks of breathing—and I'm certain that before the deadline falls due the order will have been rescinded. Yes, surely it will. This is mere brinkmanship. The news of the order will be leaked through the usual channels, and the Russians will negotiate whatever issue has brought the matter up. Jamaica, I should imagine, in this case. Also, Madigan has to show he isn't soft. How will they know to dread our bombs unless we're ready to drop them? We are ready to drop them, aren't we, Nathan?"

"The command isn't mine to give, sir."

"Nor mine. It is the President's. But it *is* ours to obey. It *is* our finger—mine or yours—" As if in demonstration, Pittmann lifted a single manicured finger in the immemorial gesture of the young Baptist. "—which must be prepared to press the button. But don't you feel, for instance, that such an action would be, as I've somewhere seen it called . . . genocidal?"

"As you've said, sir—the whole concept of a deterrent force is valueless if we refuse to employ it."

"Which doesn't quite answer my question."

"With your permission, sir—I don't think it's my place to answer such a question."

"Nor is it, indeed, mine to ask it. You're right, Nathan. Sometimes it is the wisest course to step back from too precise a knowledge of consequences. That is part of the rationale, I'm sure, of our being on Mars and the Russians on the moon. We can take a more disinterested view out here."

"Out here . . ." Hansard echoed, gliding away from a subject he had little taste for. "It's strange, but I have no feeling yet of being out *here* at all. Camp Jackson/Mars and Camp Jackson/Virginia are so much the same."

"The sense of their difference will come all too quickly. But if you're in a hurry, you might visit the viewing dome and look out at the dust and the rocks and the dusty, rocky craters. Otherwise, we have few tourist attractions here. The sense of difference lies more in the absence of Earth than in the presence of the dust and rocks. As you will find. Tell me, Nathan, have you wondered why you've been chosen for this assignment?"

"As your aide, sir."

"Of course—but I had upward of a dozen aides in Washington, several of them closer than you, as chance would have it."

"Then I appreciate that you've chosen me from among them."

"It wasn't I who chose you—though I approve the choice—but the psychologists. We're here, you and I, mostly on account of our latest Multi-Phasics—those tests we took in December with all those dirty questions. It seems we are very solid personality types."

"I'm glad to hear it."

"It hasn't always been the case with you, has it, Nathan?"

"You've seen my file, sir, so you know. But all that happened in the past. I've matured since then."

"Maturity, ah yes. Undoubtedly we're mature enough for the work. We can do what has to be done, even if we don't quite like to give it a name."

Hansard regarded the general curiously, for his speech was most uncharacteristic of the terran Pittmann that Hansard had known. Mars was having an effect upon him.

"But all that is neither here nor there, and you must be anxious to see your quarters and look over the lovely Martian landscape. You'll be disillusioned quickly enough without my help. The great problem here is boredom. The great problem anywhere is boredom, but here it is more acute. The library is well-stocked though not exactly up-to-the-minute. The army usually seems to regard books less than ten years old as subversive. I suggest that you try something solid and dull and very long, like *War and Peace*. No, I forgot— they don't have that here. For my own part, I've been going through Gibbon's *Decline and Fall*. Some day, when the time lies heavier on your hands, remind me to tell you the story of Stilicho, the barbarian who was the general of the Roman Armies. A paragon of fidelity, Stilicho-Honorius, the Emperor he served, was some kind of cretin and spent all his time breeding poultry. The Empire was falling apart at the seams, there were Goths and Vandals everywhere, and only Stilicho was holding them off. Honorius, at the instigation of a eunuch, finally had him assassinated. It was his only definitive act. It's a wonderful allegory, but I see you're anxious to sightsee. Officers' Mess is at thirteen hundred hours. As we two are the only officers here, I shall probably see you then. And, Captain—"

"Sir?"

"There's no need for you to frown so. I assure you, it's all brinkmanship and bluff. It's happened ten times before, to my sure knowledge. In a week or two it will be over."

"Or," the general added to himself, *sotto voce,* when Hansard had left the room, "in six weeks at the very limit."

Chapter 3

THE ECHO

The antechamber locked against the steel wall of the transmitter, and the portal opened inward with a discreet *click*. Crouching, Hansard and the private entered. The door closed behind them.

Here there were no special effects, neither rumblings nor flashing lights. The noise in his ears was the pulse of his own blood. The feeling in his stomach was a cramped muscle. As he had done in the practice session, he stared intently at the sign stenciled with white paint on the wall of the vault:

CAMP JACKSON/EARTH
MATTER TRANSMITTER

For the briefest of moments, he thought the EARTH had flickered to MARS, but he decided his nerves were playing tricks, for EARTH, solidly EARTH, it had remained. He waited. It should have taken only a few seconds for the technician in the glass booths outside to flick the switch that would transfer them to Mars. Hansard wondered if something had gone wrong.

"They sure do take their own sweet time," the Negro private complained.

Hansard watched as the second-hand of his wristwatch moved twice around the dial. The private seated across from him rose to his feet with an uncanny quietness and walked over to the portal, which here seemed no more than a hairline-thin circle drawn upon the solid steel. As a preventive measure against claustrophobia, however, a massive, functionless door handle ornamented its surface.

"This son-of-a-bitch ain't working!" the private said. "We're *stuck* in this goddamn tomb!"

"Calm down, Private—and *sit* down. You heard what they said at the practice session about touching the walls. Keep your hand away from that handle."

But the private, thoroughly panicked, had not heard Hansard's words. "I'm getting *out* of here. I'm not gonna—"

His hand was only centimeters away from the door handle when he saw the other hand. It was freckled and covered with a nap of red hair. It was reaching for him through the wall.

The private screamed and stumbled backward. Even these clumsy movements were performed with that same catlike quietness. A second disembodied hand, differing from the first in that it held a revolver, appeared. Then, bit by bit, the plane of the door surrendered the entire front of the body, so that it formed a sort of bas-relief. The private continued his muted screaming.

Hansard did not at first recognize the apparition as Worsaw. Perhaps, after all, it was not Worsaw, for Hansard had seen him only minutes before, in uniform and clean-shaven—and this man, *this* Worsaw, was dressed in walking shorts and a tee-shirt and sported a full red beard.

"Hiya, Meatball," he said (and certainly it was Worsaw's voice that spoke), addressing the private, who became silent once more. "How'd you like to be integrated?" A rhetorical question, for without waiting for a reply, he shot the private three times in the face. The body crumpled backward against—and partly through—the wall.

Hansard had heard of no other case of insanity produced by transmittal, but then he knew so little about it altogether. Perhaps he was not mad but only dreaming. Except that in dreams the dreamers should not be discountenanced by the bizarreness of the dreamworld.

"That takes care of *one* son-of-a-bitch," the spectral Worsaw said.

Before the man's murderous inference could be realized, Hansard acted. In a single motion he threw himself from the bench and the attaché case that he had been holding at Worsaw's gun hand. The gun went off, doing harm only to the case.

In leaping from the bench Hansard had landed on the floor of the steel vault—or, more precisely, in it, for his hands had sunk several inches into the steel, which felt like chilled turpentine against his skin. This was strange, really very strange, but Hansard had for the time being accepted the logic of this dream-world and was not to be distracted from his immediate purpose—which was to disarm Worsaw—by any untimely sense of wonderment. He sprang up to catch hold of Worsaw's hand, but found that with the same movement his legs sank knee-deep into the insubstantial floor.

Hansard's actions would have been fatally slow, except that when the attaché case had struck him Worsaw had staggered backward half a step. Mere inches, but far enough that his face vanished into the wall out of which it had materialized. But the gun and the hand that held it were still within the vault, and Hansard, lunging and sinking at once, caught hold of the former.

He tried to lever the weapon out of Worsaw's hand, but Worsaw held fast to it. As he struggled, Hansard found himself sinking deeper into the floor, and the drag of his weight unbalanced Worsaw. Hansard gave a violent twist to the arm of the falling man. The gun fired.

And Worsaw was dead.

Hansard, waist-deep in chrome-vanadium steel, stared at the bleeding body before him. He tried not to think, fearing that if he ventured even the smallest speculation, he would lose all capacity for action. It was hard to maintain even the most provisional faith in the dream-world.

He found that if he moved slowly he was able to raise himself out of the floor, which then supported the full weight of his body in the customary manner of steel floors. He picked up the attaché case (even here in the dream-world a Priority-A letter commands respect) and sat down carefully on the bench. Avoiding the sight of the two corpses, he stared intently at the sign stenciled on the wall of the vault:

CAMP JACKSON/EARTH
MATTER TRANSMITTER

He counted to ten (no better strategy suggested itself), but the corpses were still there afterward, and when he poked the toe of his shoe at the floor, he punctured the steel with his foot. He was stuck in his dream.

Which was only a polite way of saying, he realized, that he was mad. But damn it, he didn't *feel* mad.

There was no time for finer flights of epistemology, for at that moment another man entered through the wall of the vault. It was Worsaw. He was bare-chested and wearing skivvies, and Hansard was glad to see that his hands were empty. The living Worsaw looked at the dead Worsaw on the floor and swore.

Now Hansard did panic—though in his panic he did a wiser thing than he could have conceived soberly. He ran away. He turned around on the bench where he had been sitting and ran away through the steel wall.

Coming out of the wall, he fell four feet and sank up to the middle of his calves in the concrete floor. Directly in front of him, not two feet away, was one of the M.P.'s that guarded the manmitter.

"Guard!" he shouted. "Guard, there's someone—" His voice died in his throat as the hand that he had placed upon the guard's shoulder sank through his flesh as through a light mist of sea-spray. The guard gave no sign that he had felt Hansard's hand nor heard his voice.

But others did—and now Hansard became aware that the hall was filled with unauthorized personnel. Some of them Hansard recognized as men from his own company—though like the two Worsaws they were all bearded and dressed as though they were on furlough in Hawaii—and others were complete strangers. They moved about the hall freely, unchallenged by the guards to whom they seemed to be invisible.

Worsaw stepped out of the steel wall behind Hansard. He was holding the gun that had belonged to his dead double. "All right, Captain, the fun's done. Now, let's see what you got in that briefcase."

Hansard broke into a sprint, but two of Worsaw's confederates blocked his path in the direction he had taken.

"Don't waste bullets, Snooky," one of these men shouted—a scrawny, tow-headed man that Hansard recognized as Corporal Lesh. "We'll get him."

Hansard veered to the right, rounding the corner of the manmitter. There, in a heap before the door of the Steel Womb, were half the men of "A" Company—all eight of the Negroes and five whites —in their uniforms and either dead or dying. Nearby was another, more orderly pile of bodies; here the remaining men of the company were bound up hand and foot. A second Lesh and a man unknown to Hansard stood guard over them with rifles.

Worsaw—the same Worsaw that Hansard had seen enter the man-mitter with the last squad that morning—struggled to his feet and shouted, "Don't kill that bastard—you hear me. Don't touch him. I want him for myself."

Lesh, who had been raising his rifle to take aim at Hansard, seemed uncertain whether to heed his prisoner's request or kick him back into the heap. His doubt was resolved by the other Worsaw—the Worsaw with the revolver—who commanded Lesh to do as his double (or would it be triple in this case?) had ordered. "If the fourteen of us can't take care of a goddamn fairy officer, then he deserves to get away."

Hansard was encircled, and each moment the circle narrowed. He stood with his back to the wall of the transmitter (upon which the Christmas-tree lights were festively a-burble once more) and considered whether to make a dash to the right or to the left—and then realized that his encirclement was only apparent, that there was a clear path to the rear.

He turned and leaped once more through the steel wall of the vault. Forgetting that the floor of the inner chamber was raised two feet above the floor-level of the hall, he found himself standing knee-deep in steel again.

Like a wading pool, he thought, and the thought saved his life. For, if he could wade in it, should he not be able equally to swim in it?

Filling his lungs, he bent double and plunged his whole body into the yielding floor. With his eyes closed and the handle of the attaché case clenched between his teeth (Priority-A is, after all, the ultimate security rating), he went through the motions of swimming underwater. His limbs moved through the metamorphosed steel more easily than through water, but he had no way of knowing if these motions were propelling him forward. There was no sensation, as there would be for a swimmer, of water flowing over his skin, but only a feeling through his entire body, internally as well as externally, of tingling—as though he had been dipped into a mild solution of pure electricity, could such a thing be.

He swam until he was sure that, if his swimming was having an effect at all, he was out of the hall. Then he changed directions, angling to the right. At last, starved for oxygen, he had to surface.

He came up inside a broom closet. It was as good a place as any to catch his breath and gather his wits.

He rested there, only his head projecting out of the floor (his body, cradled in its substance, showed no tendencies either to rise or sink), fearful that his labored breathing would betray his presence to the . . . What *were* they: mutineers? phantoms?

Or phantasms, the product of his own paranoia?

But he knew perfectly well that he was not mad, and if he ever were to become mad he would not have inclined in the direction of paranoia. He had taken an MMPI only last December, and Pittmann had shown him the results. It was scarcely possible to be more sane than Nathan Hansard.

In the dim light that filtered into the closet through the crack under the door, Hansard could see motes of dust riding in the air. He blew at them, but his breath did not affect their demure Brownian movements. Yet he could feel the movement of that same air against his fingertip.

Conclusion? That he, and the crew that had come baying after his blood, were of another substance than the physical world they moved in. That he was, in short, a spirit. A ghost.

Was he then, dead? No—for death, he had long ago decided, was mere insentience. Or, if he had died inside the transmitter and this *were* some sort of afterlife, the system of Dante's inferno was evidently not going to be of any use as a guide.

Whatever had happened had happened during the time Hansard was in the transmitter. Instead of going to Mars at the moment of the jump, there had been a malfunction and his new immaterial condition (for it was simpler to assume that it was himself that had changed and not the world about him) was its result.

And all the other wraiths—the three separate Worsaws, the two Leshes, the pile of corpses—were *all* of them the result of similar malfunctions? The bearded Worsaw, he who had first stepped into the vault and would now step out of it no more, was probably, by this theory, the product of some earlier transmission breakdown—but what then of the two *other* Worsaws? Where had they come from? From subsequent breakdowns, presumably. But this would mean that the original Worsaw who had gone through the machine —the *real* Worsaw—had continued the course of his own life in the real world, served his term of duty on Mars, and returned to Earth —had made the Mars jump again. Twice again, counting today's

jump. And this *real* Worsaw went on with his life in complete ignorance of the existence of the doppelgangers splitting off from him.
And if all this were true . . .

Then there would be another Nathan Hansard too, on the Mars
Command Post, of whom he—the Nathan Hansard resting in the
concrete floor of the broom closet—was a mere carbon copy result-
ing from the imperfect operation of the transmitter.

Though for all he knew, this was its normal function.

In support of his theory, Hansard recollected that there had been
a moment within the transmitter when he had thought he'd seen the
word EARTH flicked to MARS. *Had* he made the jump to Mars and
then bounced back like a rubber ball in that briefest of moments
when the operating switch was flicked on?

Like a rubber ball, or like . . . an echo.

But this was not the time nor the place to elaborate ingenious
theories. Worsaw and his confederates were undoubtedly searching
the building and the grounds for him at this moment. He ducked
back beneath the floor and swam through the foundations, surfacing
only for air to get his bearings—now bobbing up into an office full
of silent, industrious clerks (for there were no noises in this dream-
world except the sound of his own breathing), then into an empty
corridor or unfurnished room (with which the building seemed to
abound, like some gigantic coral reef). It was several minutes before
he was outside the labyrinth of the security complex, in the sunlight
of the April noonday, where he saw—but was not seen by—two of
Worsaw's bearded friends.

It would not do to remain in Camp Jackson. He had lost the cap
of his uniform in the transmitter or in his flight from the hall, so that
he would be conspicuously out-of-uniform here. Among the throngs
of the city, however, he would be as good as invisible, since if he
refrained from walking through walls there were no visual evidences
of his dematerialized state.

He considered how he could travel the ten miles into downtown
D.C. most quickly. *Not* by swimming. Ordinarily he would have
taken the bus . . .

It felt strange to pass out the gate of Camp Jackson without showing a pass or I-D. The city-bound bus was waiting at the curb. Hansard got on, careful to walk lightly so that his feet would not pass
through the floor, and took an empty seat by a window. A moment

later a private sat in the same seat—and in Hansard. Hansard, much shaken, moved to the seat across the aisle.

The bus started up slowly, and Hansard was able to keep from sinking all the way through his seat. Each time the bus accelerated or decelerated Hansard was in danger of slipping out of the vehicle altogether. At a traffic light just before the bridge of the Potomac, the bus braked suddenly and Hansard somersaulted through the seat in front of him, down through the floor of the bus and the transmission, and deep into the roadway itself.

After that he decided to hike the rest of the way into the city.

Chapter 4

THE REAL WORLD

In witnessing the foregoing remarkable events, it may have occurred to the reader to wonder how he would himself have reacted in Hansard's circumstances, and if this reader were of a skeptical temperament he might very well question the plausibility of Hansard's so-sudden and so-apt adjustment to the enormous changes in the world about him. Yet this hypothetical skeptic shows the same ready adaptability every night in his dreams. Hansard, in those first perilous minutes, was living in a dream, and his actions showed the directness and simplicity of the actions of a dreamer. What had he done, after all, but flee from the face of danger? It can be objected that Hansard was *not* dreaming, but can we be sure of that yet? When else, in the usual course of experience, does one walk through steel walls? So that it is not really so wonderful that Hansard should have fallen into a half-dreaming state and been able to act so naturally amid so much that was unnatural. Perhaps our skeptical reader might even allow that, with wind in the right direction, he might not have acted entirely differently himself. At least he should not discount the possibility.

Hansard did not shake off this sense of unreality at once. Indeed, with the occasion for action past, with nothing to do but explore and reflect, this sense grew, and with its growth he felt the beginnings of dread, of a subtle terror worse than anything he had experienced in the hall outside the transmitter. For it is possible to flee the figures

of the nightmare, but there is no escape from the nightmare itself
but waking.

The worst of it was that none of the people that he passed on the
city's streets, nor the drivers of cars and buses, nor clerks in stores,
no one, would look at him. They disregarded Hansard with an
indifference worthy of God. Hansard stood between the jeweler and
his lamp, but the wraith's shadow was as imperceptible to the jeweler as was the wraith himself. Hansard grasped the diamond in his
own hand; the jeweler continued his careful cutting. Once, when he
was crossing a street, a truck turned the corner and, without even
ruffling Hansard's hair, drove straight through him.

It was as though he were a beggar or deformed, but in that case
they would at least have looked away, which was some sort of recognition. No, it was as though each one of them had said to him:
You do not exist, and it became increasingly difficult not to believe
them.

So that Hansard walked through this unheeding, intangible city as
through a dream-landscape, observing but not understanding it, not
even endeavoring as yet to understand it. He walked past the immemorial, unmemorable white stoneheaps of the capital buildings: the
unfenestrated mausoleum that housed the National Gallery, the
monumental Yawn of the Supreme Court, the Capitol's Great White
Wart, and that supreme dullness, the Washington Monument.
Though he had lived in the District of Columbia for the last eight
years, though he had passed these buildings almost daily, though he
even supposed that he admired them, he had never seen them before. He had always regarded them with the same unseeing, reveren-
tial eyes with which he would have regarded, for instance, his nation's flag. But now, curiously (for architecture was far from being
his immediate concern), he saw them as they were, with the veil of
the commonplace ripped away. Why, he wondered, did the capitals
of the columns burst into those Corinthian bouquets? Why, for that
matter, were the columns there? Everything about these buildings
seemed arbitrary, puzzling. Presumably they had been built for
human purposes—but what purpose can be served by a 555-foot
obelisk?

He stood beneath the blossoming, odorless cherry trees and tried
to argue against the horror mounting within him.

At those rare moments when the skin of the world is peeled away
and its substance laid bare before us, the world may assume either

of two aspects—benign or malignant. There are those sublime, Wordsworthian moments when Nature apparels herself in celestial light, but there are other moments too, when, with the same trembling sensibility, the same uncontrovertible sureness, we see that the fair surface of things—all flesh, these white and scentless blossoms, the rippled surface of the reflecting pool, even the proud sun itself— are but the whiting on the sepulchre, within which . . . it were best not to look.

Hansard stood at such a brink that first afternoon—and then he drew back. Once already in his life, long ago and in another country, he had stepped beyond that threshold and let himself see what lay there, so that this time he was able to foresee well in advance that such a moment threatened again. (The symptoms were clear: a minacious cold seemed to settle over him, followed by a feeling of hollowness that, originating in the pit of his stomach, spread slowly to all his limbs; his thoughts, like the music on a record played off-center on a turntable, moved through his consciousness at eccentric *tempi,* now too fast and now too slow.) He foresaw what was to be and he resisted it. This is not an easy thing to do. Most of us are passive before our strongest emotions, as before one of the Olympian gods. Even Medusa-headed horror has an allure, though we won't often admit it, and when we do surrender ourselves to her it is with averted eyes and the pretense that we are not helping out.

The same reader who may at first have tended to over-value Hansard's quick reflexes in the face of an immediate danger may now be inclined to value his struggle with the "Medusa" too lightly or not at all. Let such a reader be assured of the reality of this peril. Had Hansard succumbed to these feelings—had he, slipping into solipsism, let himself believe that the Real World was not any longer as real as it had been, then we would either have a much shorter and sadder tale to tell or we would have had to find another hero for it.

But for all that, it is true that a man in good health can bear a few hours of supernatural terror without lasting ill effect. The worst fear, after all, is of the known rather than the unknown—a truth that Hansard became aware of as soon as he realized, about sunset, that the hollow feeling in the pit of his stomach was a symptom of more than malaise, that it was simply hunger pangs. And worse than the hunger pangs was his thirst.

In restaurants he could see people eating, but their food—like all matter that belonged exclusively to the Real World—sifted through his fingers like vapor. He could not turn a water faucet nor lift a glass, and if he could have it would have availed him nothing, for the water of the Real World was as insubstantial as its solid matter. Hansard stood in a public fountain and let the water cascade through his body without dampening his clothes, or his thirst. It began to seem that his sojourn in the dream-world might not be of much longer duration than a dream. How long could one go without food or water? Three days? Four?

But what then of Worsaw and the others in Camp Jackson? To judge only by the length of their beards these men were veterans of the dream-world, from which it was only reasonable to suppose that there was someplace in this city ghostly food and ghostly drink to satisfy his most unghostly appetites. He had only to find it.

If the theory he had developed earlier that day concerning the cause of his changed condition were correct, there could be but one source of the food that sustained Worsaw and Co.: it had to originate from a transmitter, just as they themselves had. The "ghost" of food that had been transmitted to Mars would be, logically, the only food a ghost could eat; the "ghost" of water would be the only water a ghost could drink.

And would the same not hold true of air as well? Did Hansard breathe the same air that the residents of the Real World breathed— or another air, the "ghost" of theirs? If the latter were the case, that would explain the strange silence of the dream-world, in which the only noises audible to Hansard were the noises he made himself, and these, in turn, were inaudible in the Real World. The air that bore the sound waves Hansard produced was a different medium from the air of the Real World.

It was a theory easily confirmed or disproven. The transmitters that supplied the Mars Command Post with a constant fresh supply of both air and water were located beneath the D.C. dome, just outside the eastern perimeter of Camp Jackson itself.

As the simulated daylight of the domed city modulated from dusk to darkness, Hansard walked back toward Camp Jackson on the delicate snow-crust of the sidewalks, occasionally popping his toes through the thin membrane of the surface. He had discarded his military hat and jacket, depositing them with his attaché case inside the thick walls of the Lincoln Memorial, where, invisible to all eyes, Hansard was certain a Top-Priority secrecy could be preserved indefinitely. His tie was loosened, and his shirt open at the collar, despite the discomfort this caused him. Except for the officer's stripe down his pant's leg, he should pass for a pedestrian of the Real World—or so he hoped.

Hansard arrived at the barricade about the Mars "pipelines" an hour after the false twilight of the domed city had dimmed to extinction. The D.C. dome was composed of two shells: the inner was an energy-screen designed late in the 1970's as a defense against neutron bombs. Had it ever been put to the test, the unhappy residents of the city would have found it no more effective a defense than a magic pentagram drawn with the fat of a hanged man—an awesome but an empty symbol. Subsequent to its erection, however, this energy dome was found to have the pragmatic property of supporting a second outer dome, or skin, of plastic. Soon, from this single phenomenon, an entire technology had developed, and now it was possible to build outerdomes substantial enough to act as a weather shield over areas twelve miles in diameter and able to support a complex of lighting and ventilation systems as well.

The Mars pumps stood just outside Camp Jackson, since they were officially administered by NASA, though in fact by the Army. Accordingly it was Army guards who patrolled the barrier built about the pumping stations. Hansard need take no heed of either guards or barrier, but he did, if his theory was correct, have to be wary not to encounter any of the other men of Company "A," for this would be their only source of water as well as Hansard's.

Within the barrier the grounds sloping to the concrete pumphouse were attractively landscaped—for the benefit, apparently, of the inner guards, since the barrier prevented anyone else from seeing them. Hansard lowered himself into the earth and swam slowly up the hill through lawn and flowerbeds.

Reaching the pumphouse and having satisfied himself that he was alone, Hansard again assumed a standing posture and walked through the concrete wall of the building.

And found himself drowning.

The entire pumphouse was filled with water—real liquid water, or rather, unreal water of the sort that an unreal Hansard might drink, or drown in. Instead of floundering back through the wall, Hansard swam upward. The water rose to a height of fourteen feet, which was yet a few feet less than the high ceiling of the building. Surfacing, Hansard's ears popped.

The surface of the water was brightly lighted by the illuminated panels of the ceiling, and Hansard could see that the water in the center of this strange reservoir was bubbling furiously. Remarkable as these phenomena were, Hansard's first consideration was to quench his thirst and be gone. He could fit these facts to his theories at his leisure.

Regretful that he could carry back no water to the city except what was sloshing about in the toes of his shoes, Hansard returned on the bus—this time, without mischance. He got off outside the New St. George, a hotel that in the ordinary scheme of things he would have never been able to afford. At the reception desk he informed himself of the number of an unoccupied suite and found his way to it up the stairs (he suspected that the hotel's elevators would start and stop too quickly for him to be able to keep from popping out through the floor). Once in possession of his rooms, he realized that he might just as well have gone to a flophouse, for he was unable to turn on the light switch. Shivering in his damp clothes, he went to sleep in the midst of the suite's undoubtable, but darkened, luxury. He slept on a canopied bed, but he would have been just as comfortable, after all, in the floor.

He woke with a bad head-cold and screaming.

It had been so many years since he had had the dream that he had been able to convince himself that he had rid himself of it. The dream always concluded with the same image, but it might begin in a variety of ways. For instance:

He was there. Drenched. Mud up to his thighs. A buzzing somewhere, always a buzzing. Always wet. Always knowing that the enveloping greenness was made green by wishing for his death. Always bodies, scrapheaps of bodies along the muddy road. He was very young. He didn't always want to look. "I won't look," he said. Whenever he was there, in that country, in his dreams, he knew how young he was. But you could look at anything if you had to. And diseases, lots of diseases. And always something that buzzed.

The people of that country were very little. Little adults, like the children in the paintings of the Colonial period. Their faces were children's faces. He could see long rows of their faces pressed up against the wire. He was carrying pots of cooked rice. When they spoke it sounded more like screaming than speech. The compound always got fuller. Every part of the fence was filled with their faces.

They asked for "incendigel" which seemed to be the word for rice in their country. This part of the dream could never have happened, he knew, except in the unreal world of dreaming, because an officer would not have carried the pots of rice himself. A private would have done that. But in the dream it was always Hansard who carried the pots of rice, or "incendigel," and the little people stared at him hungrily, wishing for his death.

It was not a credible world, not in the sense that, for instance, Milwaukee or Los Angeles were real and credible. It was a dream-world of little half-people who could not speak unless they screamed.

And there was a lady in the middle of the road with most of her head missing. The medic cut open her belly and took out the baby. "It's going to live," he said.

"Thank God," said Hansard.

"Burn it all down," said the captain. The little men behind the wire fence began screaming when the interpreter told them what the captain was saying. They tried to get out, and the captain had to use tear gas, though he didn't want to, since supplies were limited this far inland.

He was there, in the fields. It was hot, windless noonday. The grains were swollen with their ripeness. The flamethrowers made a buzzing sound. Far across the blackened field a small figure waved at Hansard as though in greeting. "Welcome, welcome," he was screaming, in his strange language.

He was screaming. He found that he had fallen through the bed. He was looking up into the bedsprings. He stopped screaming and clambered up through the mattress into daylight.

"I've stopped dreaming," he said aloud. "That was all a dream, it never happened." Though this was not strictly true, it helped him to hear himself say it. "And now it's all over, and I'm back in the Real World."

But despite these reassurances and the good advice implicit in them that he should turn to daylight matters now, he could not keep from remembering that one moment of the dream—when he had been looking out through the wire fence at Captain Hansard carrying that big pot of rice. His mouth watered. He was hungry. He was so hungry and he had no food.

Chapter 5

THE VOYEUR

One of the minor provisions of the Emergency Allocation of Resources Act had been that the various transmitters built by the government were to be situated in different states. As soon as the first receiver had made the long rocket-journey to Mars and landed, materials for the construction of the Command Posts (of which there were six) were transmitted from Texas, California, and Ohio. Camp Jackson/Virginia, because it was under the D.C. dome, was an obvious choice for the location of the one transmitter through which the personnel staffing the Command Posts was provided. Food, nonperishable goods, and artillery, however, were still supplied through the California and Ohio transmitters.

It would have been a simple enough matter to stow away in the back of a Real World truck or train bound from Washington to Cincinnati, but it was certain that if he did he would arrive in a severe, not to say fatal, state of anoxic anoxemia. For the air that Hansard breathed here in the city was not the air of the Real World, but the dematerialized air created by the transmitters and kept from dispersing by the dome above the city. Outside the dome, on the open highway or in another city, his store of dematerialized oxygen would be quickly dissipated. The dome kept him alive—but it also kept him a prisoner.

Yet there had to be food of some sort coming through the transmitters, for the men of Camp Jackson were surely sustained by more than air and water. And since the greatest aid to solving a problem is knowing that it can be solved, Hansard need not and did not panic.

Whatever food they were eating had to be going through the Camp Jackson transmitter, and since only personnel went through the transmitters it must be that the men were bringing food with them to Mars—probably concealed in their duffels. Though this was against regulations, it was a commonplace practice since the Command Post lacked a PX. But how could they know to bring *enough?*

Unless there was a way, which Hansard had yet to discover, of communicating with the inhabitants of the Real World . . .

Reluctant to return to Camp Jackson during the day, Hansard bethought himself of some other way that he might put the day to good use—and remembered that the State Department had been provided with a small manmitter by means of which they were able to transport personnel to overseas embassies. If anyone were to go through this manmitter today, it would be well for Hansard to be on hand: Hansard could gain an ally for himself, and the new ghost would be spared considerable anguish in learning to cope with his changed condition.

It would be too much to hope that the possible State Department traveler would be bringing food with him. Nevertheless, Hansard hoped just that.

As he went out of the new St. George, Hansard stopped at the cashier's box and made out a personal check in the amount of $50.00, which he placed in the hotel's locked safe. It was not a wholly whimsical gesture, for Hansard had a highly-developed conscience and he would have suffered a pang of guilt to have skipped out on a hotel bill.

He did not know in which of the several State Department buildings the small manmitter would be located, but it was a simple matter to find it by searching through the various corridors for heavy concentrations of armed guards. When he did find it, at four in the afternoon, it was immediately apparent that he had not been the first to search it out.

The walls and floor of the small anteroom adjoining the manmitter were covered with delicate traceries of dried blood, which no cleaning woman would ever remove, for they were not of the Real World. When Hansard touched a fingertip to one of these stains, the thin film crumbled into a fine powder, like ancient lace. There had been murders here, and Hansard was certain that he knew the identity of the murderers.

And the victims? He hesitated to think of what distinguished men had used the State Department's manmitter during recent months. Had not even the then-Vice-President Madigan traveled to King Charles III's Coronation via this manmitter?

Hansard, rapt in these somber considerations, was startled by the sudden flash of red above the door of the manmitter's receiver-compartment, indicating that a reception had just been completed. There was a flurry of activity among the guards in the anteroom, of whose presence Hansard had been scarcely aware till then.

The door of the manmitter opened, and a strange couple came out: an old man in a power-wheelchair and an attractive black-haired woman in her early thirties. Both wore heavy fur coats and caps that were matted with rain. A guardsman approached the old man and seemed to engage him in an argument.

If only I knew how to lipread, Hansard thought, not for the first time.

His attention had been so caught up by this scene that he was not at once aware of the voices approaching the anteroom in the outer corridor. Voices: it could only be . . .

Hansard dodged first behind the couple in fur coats, then surveyed the room for a vantage from which he could eavesdrop without being seen. The guard who was addressing the man in the wheelchair had been sitting at a desk, and by this desk was a wastebasket. From the center of the room the contents of the wastebasket would be invisible.

Hansard lowered himself into the floor, careful not to allow his body to slip through the ceiling of the room immediately below, for it was only so—immersed in the "material" of the Real World—that gravity seemed to lose its hold on him. At last he was totally enveloped except for his head, which was out of sight in the wastebasket. And none too soon—for by the sudden clarity of the intruders' voices, Hansard knew he was no longer alone in the room.

"I told you this would be a waste of time," said a voice that seemed tantalizingly familiar. Not Worsaw's, though it had something of the same Southern softness to it.

A second voice that could only have belonged to the Arkansan

Lesh whined a torpid stream of obscenities in reply to the first speaker, to the general effect that he, being of an inferior nature, should shut up.

A third speaker agreed with this estimate and expanded upon it. He suggested that the first speaker owed himself and Lesh an apology.

"I apologize, I apologize."

"You apologize, *sir*."

"I apologize, sir," the first voice echoed miserably.

"You're goddamn right, and you'd just better remember it too. We don't *have* to keep you alive, you know. Any time I'd like, I could just saw your fat head off, you son of a bitch, and if it wasn't for Worsaw I'd have done it long ago. I should smash your face in, that's what I should do."

"Ah, Lesh," said the third speaker, "don't you ever get tired of that crap? What time is it anyhow?"

The first voice, which Hansard still could not place, said, "The clock over the desk says four-fifteen. And that means that Greenwich Mean Time would be ten-fifteen, and all the embassies in Europe will be shut down. There may still be a few people, like that old cripple, coming back *here*, but that isn't going to help *us* any."

"You think you're pretty goddamn smart, don't you?" Lesh whined.

"There's probably something to what he says though," the third voice put in. "There ain't any point sitting around here if nobody else is going through. Leastwise, *I* got better things to do."

Lesh, after a few more obscenities, agreed. Their voices faded, as they left the room.

Hansard decided to follow them. He risked little in doing so, for, in his present state, concealment took little effort, and escape perhaps less. He dropped through the floor into the room below, and his momentum took him through the floor of that room in turn— and so on, into the basement. This method of descent allowed him time to be outside the building and hidden from sight before the three men had exited from the front door. The man whose voice had seemed familiar to Hansard walked behind the other two (who carried rifles) and was bent under the weight of a field pack, so that it was not possible to see his face. The two armed men mounted a Camp Jackson-bound bus, leaving their companion to continue the journey on foot, for with the added weight of the pack and the consequent increase in momentum he would probably not have been able to stay inside the vehicle.

When the bus was out of sight, however, this figure removed his back pack and laid it in the middle of a shrub, then turned down a street in a direction that carried him away from Camp Jackson.

A canteen swung from his cartridge belt. Hansard needed that canteen for himself. He removed the field pack from the shrubbery and "buried" it hastily in the sidewalk, then set off after the vanishing figure in a soundless pantomime of pursuit: a lion padding after an inaudible quarry through a silent jungle.

After several turnings, they entered an area of luxury apartment buildings. The figure turned in at the main entrance of one of these buildings. Hansard, reluctant to follow him inside (for he might have joined more of his confederates within), waited in the doorway of the building opposite. An hour passed.

With misgivings—for he had never till now intruded upon the private lives of dwellers in the Real World—Hansard began his own exploration of the building, starting at the top floor and working his way down through the ceilings. He encountered families at dinner or stupefied before the television, witnessed soundless quarrels, and surprised people in yet more private moments. A suspicion of his quarry's intent in coming here grew in Hansard's mind, and in Apartment 4-E this suspicion was confirmed.

Hansard found him he sought in the apartment of an attractive and evidently newlywed couple. In the twilit room the man was sitting upon their bed and pretending to guide, with his intangible touch, the most intimate motions of their love. While the voyeur's attention was thus directed toward the lovers, Hansard approached him from behind, slipped his tie around the man's throat, and tightened the slip-knot. The voyeur fell backward off the bed, and Hansard saw now for the first time who his enemy had been: Colonel Willard Ives.

Hansard dragged Ives, choking, out of the bedroom. He wrested away the man's canteen and drank greedily from it. He had been all day without water.

While Hansard was drinking from the canteen, the colonel attempted to escape from him. Two evenings ago, in Ives' office, it would have been unthinkable that he should ever have occasion to assault his superior officer, but the circumstances were exceptional, and Hansard performed that unthinkable action with scarcely a scruple. Afterward he gave Ives his handkerchief to stop the bleeding of his nose.

"I'll have you court-martialed for this," Ives snuffled, without much conviction. "I'll see that you—I'll teach you to—"

Hansard, whose character had been made somewhat unpliable by fourteen years of military life, was not without retroactive qualms. "Accept my apologies, Colonel. But I can hardly be expected to regard you in the light of my superior at the moment—when I see you obeying the orders of a corporal."

Ives looked up, eyes wide with emotion. "You called me *Colonel.* Then, you know me . . . back there?"

"I was talking with you in your office only two nights ago, Colonel. Surely you remember?"

"No. No, not with me." Ives bit his lower lip, and Hansard realized that this was not, in fact, the same man. This Ives was a good seventy-five pounds lighter than his double in the Real World, and there were innumerable other details—the shaggy hair, the darker complexion, the cringing manner—that showed him to be much changed from his old (or would it be his other?) self. "*I* was never a colonel. I was only a major when I went through the manmitter two years ago. Sometimes he brings me to my office—to the Colonel's office—and humiliates me there, in front of him. That's the only reason he wants me alive—so he can humiliate me. Starve me and humiliate me. If I had any courage, I'd . . . I'd . . . kill myself. I would. I'd go outside the dome . . . and . . ." Choking with pity for himself, he was obliged to stop speaking.

"He?" Hansard asked.

"Worsaw. The one you killed in the manmitter. I wish you'd killed all three of him, instead of just one."

"How many men—of our sort—are there in Camp Jackson?"

Ives turned his gaze away from Hansard's. "I don't know."

"Colonel—or Major, if you prefer—I should not like to hurt you again."

"Wouldn't you? I doubt that. You're just the same as Worsaw. You're all the same, all of you. As soon as the discipline is gone, you lose all sense of what's right and decent. You betray your allegiance. You murder and rape. You act like . . . like jungle savages —all of you."

"It doesn't seem to me, Major, that you're in a good position from

which to offer moral instruction. Let me repeat my question: how
many—"

"Seventeen, twenty, twenty-four—the number varies. Oh, you
think you're so fine and upstanding, don't you! So damn *white!* They
always do when they're new here, before they've had to . . . had to
eat their . . ." He trailed off in vacancy.

"What, Major? What is it you eat here? Where do you get your
food?"

Ives' eyes dropped in a mockery of shyness to contemplate the
buttons of Hansard's shirt. His smile twisted with a slight, enigmatic
contempt for the man who held him prisoner. It was, in fact, the
characteristic smile of a prisoner—who, though powerless, knows
what distance separates himself, exalted in his guilt, from the common run.

With horror Hansard realized what the men of Camp Jackson
were living on. His horror was all the more potent because he also
knew that this realization had been with him from the first moment
he had seen the pile of corpses outside the portal of the manmitter.
For he had assessed the situation correctly: all the food that sustained Worsaw and his men would have to come to them through
the transmitter.

He knew this, yet even now he refused to believe it. "Then all
those men who went through the transmitter, *all* of them . . ."

"Those niggers, you mean? You're a Northerner, aren't you, Captain? Only a Northerner would call a bunch of niggers men."

"You foulness! You corruption!"

"You wait, Captain—wait till you get hungry enough. The day
will come that you'll wish you had a piece of nigger-meat to put in
your belly. You talk about us now, but just wait. Worsaw was the
one who saw the way it had to be. He had the strength . . . and the
. . . and the foresight to do what had to be done. So that we got the
niggers and the nigger-lovers before they got *us*. He's kept us alive
here. No one else was able to; only Worsaw. I was . . . afraid to
face facts, but Worsaw went right ahead and did it. He's a . . ." The
colonel began to choke again, but he finished his testimonial first.
". . . a good man."

"I recall that you said the same thing when last we met." Hansard
rose to his feet.

"Where are you going?" Ives asked anxiously. "You won't tell
him what I've been telling you? I'm not supposed to be here. I—"

"I'm hardly likely to have many conversations with your master, Ives. I'm going now, but you just stay here. Or go back in the bedroom if you like, and wallow in your filth. As long as you can't infect *them,* it can't matter."

Hansard was at the door when Ives called upon him in a strangely muffled tone. Hansard looked back. Ives was sitting on the floor, his face buried in his hands.

"Captain, please! I beg of you, Captain! Do this one thing—do it, I beg of you. I don't have the strength myself, but *you* could. Oh, for the love of God, *please!*"

"You want me to kill you—is that it, Major?"

"Yes," Ives whispered into his hands, "oh yes."

"You can go to hell, Major—but it will have to be under your own steam."

When Hansard left him, Ives was crying.

He proceeded back immediately to where he had hidden Ives' field pack. He pulled it out of the sidewalk; in the pool of light beneath a street lamp, he unbuckled it. The flesh that still adhered to the gnawed bones had a slightly carrion odor. Hansard dumped the charry remains into the ground and pushed them down beyond arm's reach. At the bottom of the pack there was a .45 automatic pistol and ammunition, wrapped in a plastic poncho. This Hansard kept for himself.

It was after sunset, time to return to the reservoir and fill his canteen. But when he began walking his legs betrayed him and he had to sit down. Likewise, his hands, as he put a clip of ammunition into the automatic, were trembling.

He was not terrified that the men at Camp Jackson would get him. He was confident that he could prevent that. He *was* terrified that he might get one of them—once he was hungry enough. And then? How much farther was it possible to sink then? He might have asked Ives while he had the chance.

Chapter 6

SCENE WITH A SMALL BOY

For a while food and sleep can replace each other. Knowing this, Hansard refrained from purposeless activities, went on no more idle walks, and found a residence for himself on the Virginia side of the Potomac, nearer to his water supply. After his encounter with Ives, the idea of intruding upon the privacy of residents of the Real World was more than ever distasteful to him; on the other hand, he valued his own privacy and did not want to make his home in a public concourse. The Arlington Public Library provided a happy compromise. When there were people there, they behaved sedately; it was open evenings, so Hansard did not have to spend the time after sunset in darkness; even the silence of this world, so unnatural elsewhere, seemed fitting here. At such times as Hansard could no longer pretend to himself that he was asleep (he had made the basement stacks his special burrow), he could come upstairs and read, over the shoulders of whoever was in the library that day, fragments and snippets of a variety of things, as Providence saw fit to furnish: the College Outline synopses of *A Farewell to Arms,* and *Light in August,* and diverse other Great Old Novels that were required reading in Arlington high schools; paradigms of Bantu verbs; back-number spools of the *Washington Post;* articles on how to develop hard, manly arms, on how to retire gracefully, on how to synthesize potatoes; and several graceful anecdotes from the lives of Christopher Robin and Pooh Bear . . .

It was a mistake to go into the children's room and read the Milne book, for it opened his heart wide to the temptation that he had all this while been strong enough to ignore. His wife and son lived beneath the D.C. dome. He could visit them with no more effort than it would take to get on an S-S-bound bus.

Since the divorce, Hansard's ex-wife had managed to make do on her meager alimony by moving into government-subsidized Sergeant Shriver Manors, popularly known as the S-S, a model development of the early 70's and now the city's most venerable slum. (*Really* poor people, of course, had to squat out in the suburbs, breathing the poisonous air of the megalopolitan landscape.) Hansard had been able to see his son, who was now eight years old, one weekend each month, but there had always been a constraint between father and son since the divorce, and Hansard still tended to think of Nathan Junior as the insouciant, golden-haired four-year-old who had listened with solemn attention to the adventures of Winnie the Pooh. The present Nathan Junior was therefore, in his father's eyes, something of a usurper—with very tenuous claims to the title of true son or to Hansard's affection. An injustice, surely—but an injustice that no amount of fair treatment could expunge; the heart listens to no reasons but its own.

With Ives' example before him, Hansard should have known better than to surrender to this temptation. *Only a glimpse,* he told himself. *I won't look at anything they wouldn't want me to see.* Could he really deceive himself so far as to credit these sophistries? Apparently not, for as the bus was passing near the Washington Monument, Hansard had second thoughts and dismounted.

He walked along the edge of the reflecting pool. He had grown so accustomed to his altered condition that as he debated with himself he did not dodge the lower branches of the cherry trees but passed through them unheedingly. He knew better than to believe the tempter's whispered *"Just this once."* No, there would be a second time, if he let there be a first—and a third time, and more. There is no food that can sate curiosity.

Curiosity? the tempter argued. *Merely that? Isn't there love in it too?*

Love is reciprocal, the conscientious Hansard replied. *What has a phantom like me to do with love? And besides* (and this was the crux of it) *there is no love there any more.*

It can be seen that the debate had insensibly shifted its focus from

Nathan Junior to Marion, and the tempter cleverly pointed this out. *Don't go for her sake, then, but for his. It is your duty as a father.*

The tempter's arguments became weaker and weaker, his true purpose more transparent. Hansard would surely have resisted him, had not a curious thing happened at that moment . . .

Across the reflecting pool he saw, among the many tourists and lunch-hour strollers, a woman—and this woman seemed for a moment to have been looking at him. She was a handsome woman, about Marion's age and, like Marion, a blonde. It was impossible, of course, that she had seen him, but for a moment he had been able to believe it. He strode up to the edge of the pool (but there he had to stop, for the water of the Real World did not sustain a swimmer's weight as the land would) and called to her: "Hello there! Hello! Can you see me? Wait—listen! No, no, stay a while!" But already she had turned away and was walking toward the Capitol and out of sight.

Then Hansard knew that despite all his good resolves he would become, like that man he had so much detested, a voyeur. He would trespass against his wife's and son's privacy. For it was not within him, nor would it be within any of us, to endure the unrelenting terror of his perfect isolation and aloneness amid the throngs of that city, where every unseeing pair of eyes was a denial of his existence. If that seems to overstate the case, then let us say, instead of aloneness, alienation. We will all agree that there is little chance of coping with *that*.

We have observed earlier that Hansard was very little a man of his own times and that even in ours he would have seemed rather out-of-date. Alienation, therefore, was for him a thoroughly unfamiliar experience, though the word had been dinned into his ears in every humanities course he'd ever taken (which had been as few as possible). So that, despite a well-developed conscience of the old-fashioned, post-Puritan sort, he was singularly ill-equipped to handle his new emotions. The bottom seemed to be dropping out—as though existence had been a hangman's trap which now was sprung. He felt a hollowness at the core of his being; he felt malaise; he felt curiously will-less, as though he had just discovered himself to be an automaton, as in a sense he had. In his innocence, he showed symptoms of a classic simplicity, like the dreams of some forest- or mountain-dweller, someone far beyond the pale, who has escaped even the mention of Freud's name. There is no need, therefore, to go into great detail here, except to remind the knowing reader that though Hansard experienced his first bout of the *nausée* at a rather advanced age (for that unfortunate experience that had required his presence some years before in an Army mental hospital could not fairly have been said to be "alienation" in the sense we employ here), it was no less devastating for that. Indeed, as is so often the case when an adult comes down with a childhood disease, it was rather worse.

The practical consequence was that he got back on the bus, but not without first resorting to his cache in the wall of the Lincoln Memorial and taking out the jacket of his uniform. Then, replacing the attaché case in the wall and very carefully straightening his tie (his concern with a good appearance was proportional to his intent to do wrong), he set off . . . downward.

She was sprawled on the living-room tuckaway—the tuckaway that had been their wedding gift from his parents—smoking and reading a personalized novel (in which the heroine was given the reader's own name). She had let herself grow heavier. It is true that a certain degree of stoutness had been fashionable for the last two years. Even so, she was beginning to exceed that certain limit. Her elaborate hairdo was preserved inviolate in a large pink plastic bubble.

There was a man in the room, but he paid little attention to Marion and she as little to him. His hairdo was likewise protected by a bubble (his was black), and his face was smeared with a cream that would give it that "smooth, leathery look" that was so much admired this year. A typical Welfare dandy. He was performing isometric exercises in a kimono that Hansard had brought back from Saigon for Marion, who had then been his fiancée.

The surprising thing was that he was not jealous. A little taken aback perhaps, a little disapproving—but his disapproval was more of her generally lax style of life than of the presence of another man. Adultery he could not countenance (and, in fact, he *had* not), but Marion was free now to do as she liked, within the limits of what was commonly accepted.

Love? Had he, so little time as four years ago, loved this woman? How can emotion vanish so utterly that even its memory is gone?

Marion rose from the tuckaway and went to the door to press the buzzer opening the downstairs entry (her apartment was on 28), then disappeared into the kitchen. She had left her book open on the table beside the couch, and Hansard bent over to read a passage from it:

> Marion Hansard, sitting up on the bed, glanced into the mirror of the vanity. There were times, and this was one of them, when Marion was startled by her own beauty. Usually she didn't think of herself as especially attractive, though she had never been and never would be drab. But how could Marion Hansard hope to compete with the dark-eyed beauties of Mexico City, with their raven hair and haughty, sensual expression?

Hansard looked away from his ex-wife's romance with the same embarrassment he would have felt had he walked in upon her in the performance of a shameful act. He made up his mind to leave the apartment.

Then his son came in the room.

It must have been to let him in that Marion had risen from the couch. His hair was darker than Hansard remembered, and he had lost another milk tooth. Also, he was dressed more poorly than when he went for a weekend expedition with his father.

The man in the black hair-bubble spoke to Nathan Junior in an equable manner, and Hansard was more than ever assured that he enjoyed resident status in his ex-wife's apartment. Marion returned from the kitchen and also addressed her son, whose cheeks were beginning to color. He seemed to be protesting what his mother had just told him or commanded him to do. More than ever Hansard was distressed by the vast silence of this world. It may be amusing for a few moments to watch a television with the sound cut off, but it is quite another thing when you see the words spilling soundlessly from your own son's lips. The man in the black hair-bubble concluded what must have been an argument by pushing Nathan Junior gently but firmly into the outer hall and locking the door behind him. Hansard followed his son into the elevator. He knew from experience that no elevator in S-S Manors could move quickly enough to be any danger to him.

S-S Manors had been so designed that children played on the high roof-tops instead of cluttering up the sidewalks and streets below. The architects had designed their lofty playground with considerable imagination and poor materials, and now the labyrinth, the honeycomb of playhouses, and the elaborate jumble-gym were all in the first stages of disintegration. Originally a cyclone fence had screened in the entire play area, but there were only a few shreds and tatters of that left. Even the guardrails were broken through in places.

As soon as Nathan Junior came out of the elevator he was herded into the labyrinth by an older boy. Hansard followed him inside. The twisting concrete corridors were jammed with children, all as small or smaller than his son. Any kind of games were out of the question here. The rest of the playground was monopolized by the older boys for their own games.

Nathan Junior fought his way to a group of his own friends. They stood together whispering, then the seven of them ran pell-mell out of the labyrinth toward that corner of the room where a game of isometric baseball was in progress. The leader of the escapees (not Nathan Junior) caught the ball and ran with it back to the labyrinth. Nathan Junior, not being a very good runner, lagged behind and was caught by one of the older boys.

This boy—he was about fourteen—took hold of Nathan Junior by the ankles, turned him upside down, and carried him to the edge of the roof where the fencing had been caved through. He held the smaller boy, twisting and screaming (though for Hansard it happened in dumb-show), out over that abyss. It was a sheer drop of thirty-five stories to the street. He let go of one ankle. Hansard had to turn away. He told himself that what he was seeing was a common experience, that it had probably happened to every one of the children up here at one time or another, that his son was in no real danger. It helped not at all.

At last the torture was brought to an end, and Nathan Junior was allowed to return to the little prison that the architects had unwittingly provided. *I'll leave now,* Hansard told himself. *I should never have come here.* But he was no more able to follow his own good advice than he had been to help his son. He followed him into the labyrinth once more. Nathan Junior pushed his way through to where his friends were, and immediately he struck up an argument with a slightly younger and smaller boy. The victim became the aggressor. A fight started, and it was clear that the smaller boy stood no chance against Nathan Junior, who was soon sitting on his chest and pounding his head against the concrete surface of the roof.

"Stop it!" Hansard yelled at his son. "For God's sake, stop it!"

But Nathan Junior, of course, could not hear him.

Hansard ran out of the labyrinth and down the thirty-four flights of stairs to the street. In his haste he would sometimes plunge through walls or trample over the residents of the building who used the stairwells as their community center, *faute de mieux*. But at street level he had to rest. He had not eaten for five days. He was very weak. Without having intended to, he fell into a light slumber.

And he was there again, in the country that was so intensely green. But now it was black, and a buzzing was in his ears. It was black, and the flame thrower was in his hands, his own hands. The little boy who had broken out from the stockade—he could not have been more than four years old—was running across the blackened field toward him. Such a small boy, such a very small boy: how could he run carrying that heavy carbine? His arms were too short for him to raise it to his shoulder, so that when he fired it he had to let the devastated earth itself receive the recoil. He ran forward, screaming his hatred, but for some reason Hansard could hear nothing but the buzzing of the flame thrower. He ran forward, such a very small boy, and when he was close enough Hansard let him have it with the flame thrower.

But the face that caught fire was no longer a little Chink face. It was Nathan Junior's.

When Hansard, considerably weakened by his exertions of the afternoon, returned to the reservoir that night to drink and fill his canteen, he found that the high barrier that had been built around the pumping station was being patrolled by Worsaw's men. Through the night the men kept doggedly to their posts. From a distance Hansard reconnoitered their position and found no flaw in it. The lamps of the Real World shone brightly upon the streets surrounding the barrier, and there was no angle from which Hansard might approach near enough unseen to the barrier to be able to swim the rest of the way underground.

At dawn the men surrendered their posts to a second shift. *They must be running out of meat,* Hansard thought. His canteen had given out. He had very little strength left. In a siege he had no doubt that they would outlast him.

And therefore, he decided, *I shall have to make my raid tonight.*

He returned to the library stacks to sleep, not daring to go to sleep within hearing range of his hunters, for it was only too likely that he would wake up screaming. He usually did now.

Chapter 7

SCIAMACHY

Since there was a danger that he might exhaust all his strength in re-
hearsals, after the second trial run he rested on the library steps and
basked in the warm airs of late April. He could not, so weak as this,
so hungry as this, take much satisfaction in mere warmth and quiet
—unless it could be called a satisfaction to drift off into cloudy,
unthinking distances. The sun swooped down from noonday to the
horizon in seeming minutes. The simulated stars of the dome winked
on, winked off.

Now.

He walked over to the Gove Street intersection. Half a mile further down, Gove Street ran past the pumping station. A number of
cars were stopped at the intersection for a red light. Hansard got
into the back seat of a taxi beside a young lady in a mink suit. The
taxi did not start off with too sudden a jerk and Hansard was able to
stay on the seat.

The pumping station came in sight. The taxi would pass by it
many feet nearer than Hansard would have been able to approach
by himself. He took a deep breath and tensed his body. As soon as
the taxi was driving parallel with the barrier Hansard leaped through
the floor and down into the roadway. He could only hope that he
had vanished into the pavement before either of the men guarding
this face of the barrier had had a chance to notice him.

He had rehearsed the dive, but not the swimming. Earlier he had
discovered that without the onus of necessity he possessed neither

the strength nor the breath for a sustained effort. This was not a clear guarantee that, given the necessity, he *would* find the strength. It is all very well to praise the virtues, but strength is finally a simple matter of carbohydrates and proteins. It was a chance he had to take.

A foolish chance—for already he could feel his strength failing, his arms refusing another stroke, his lungs demanding air, taking control of his protesting will, his arms reaching up, to the air, his body breaking through the surface, into the air, his lungs, the air, ah, ah yes.

And it was not after all a failure, not yet, for he had come up seven feet the other side of the barrier. Seven feet! He would have been surprised to find he'd swum that far altogether.

Ives had said there were at least seventeen men, probably more. Two men guarded each of the four faces of the barrier, and they worked in two shifts: that would account for sixteen. And the seventeenth, wouldn't he be guarding the reservoir itself?

He would be.

He would be Worsaw.

Reasoning thus, Hansard decided in spite of his weariness to swim up the hill. It wasn't necessary to go the whole distance in a single effort. He stripped for easier swimming, hung the .45 he had taken from Ives' pack in a sling fixed to his belt, then, inchmeal, keeping as much as possible within the interstices of flowerbeds and shrubs, he advanced up the slope. He could see guards about the station, but they seemed to be guards of the Real World.

Swimming, he thought of water, of the dryness in his throat, of water, the water filling the immaterial shell of the pumping station. He had since his first visit here developed a theory to account for what he had seen then. The ghostly water produced by the echo-effect of transmission was contained by the floor and walls of the station, just as the ground of the Real World supported the ghostly Hansard. (The *why* of this was as yet obscure to him, but he was pragmatist enough to content himself with the *how* of most things.) When the pressure of the mounting water became too great, the excess quantity of it simply sank through the floor of the station. Just so, Hansard could submerge himself in the ground by entering it with sufficient force. As for the turbulent bubbling he had observed, that was undoubtedly caused by the "echo" of the air that the other pump was producing as it transmitted air to the Mars Command

Posts. The air-pump was below the level that had been attained by the water, and so the ghostly air would be constantly bubbling up through the ghostly water and escaping through the skylight in the ceiling.

About thirty feet from the station, Hansard was confronted with a blank stretch of lawn from which the nearest cover—a plot of tulips, was eight feet distant. Hansard decided to swim for it underground.

He came up on the wrong side of the flowerbed and was blinded at once by the beam of a flashlight. He ducked back into the ethereal subsurface with Worsaw's rebel yell still ringing in his ears. Below the surface he could hear nothing, though he deduced, from the sudden stinging sensation in his left shoulder, that Worsaw was firing at him.

Without knowing it was stupid or cunning, only because he was desperate and had no better plan (though none worse either), Hansard swam straight toward his enemy, toward where he supposed him still to be. He surfaced only a few feet away.

Swearing, Worsaw threw his emptied pistol at the head that had just bobbed up out of the lawn.

Hansard had taken out his .45, but before he could use it he had to fend off Worsaw's kick. The man's heavy combat boot grazed Hansard's brow and struck full-force against the hand that held the automatic. The weapon flew out of his hand.

Hansard had drawn himself halfway out of the ground, but before he could get to his feet, Worsaw had thrown himself on top of him, grabbing hold of Hansard's shoulders and pressing them back into the earth. Hansard tried to pull Worsaw's hands away, but he was at a disadvantage—and he was weak.

Slowly Worsaw forced Hansard's face below the surface of the earth, into the airless, opaque ether below. Hansard grappled himself against the other man, not in an effort to resist him (he had too little strength for that), but to guarantee that when he went under Worsaw would go under with him. So long as they maintained the struggle, there was no force to prevent their sinking thus, together into the earth, eyes open but unseeing, down ineluctably, neither weakening yet, though surely the first to weaken would be Hansard. And then? And then, curiously, the chill turpentine-like substance of the earth seemed to give way to another substance. Hansard could feel the water—real and tangible—fill his nostrils and the hollows of his ears. The water within the building, seeping through the floor under its own pressure, had spread out to form a sort of fan-shaped water table beneath the station. It was to the edge of this water table that the two men had descended in their struggle.

Worsaw's grip loosened—he did not assimilate novelty so quickly —and Hansard was able to break away from him. He swam now into the water table and upward and in a short time he was within the transmitting station, though still under water. He surfaced and caught his breath. If only Worsaw did not too quickly realize where . . .

But already Worsaw, deducing where Hansard had gone, had entered the transmitting station and was swimming up after him, like the relentless monster of a nightmare that pursues the dreamer through any landscape that is conjured up, which even when it has once been killed, rises up again to continue the pursuit.

Hansard took a deep breath and dived down to confront the nightmare. He caught hold of Worsaw's throat, but his grip was weak. Worsaw tore his hands away. Improbably, he was smiling, and his red hair and beard waved dreamily in the clear water. Worsaw's knee came up hard against Hansard's diaphragm, and he felt the breath go out of his lungs.

Then Hansard was unable to see any more. His upper body was once more plunged into "solid" matter. Surely they had not already sunk as far as the floor in their struggle?

Suddenly Worsaw released his grip. Hansard fought free. He surfaced. The water was tinged a deep pink. Had his shoulder wound bled that much?

The headless corpse of ex-Sergeant Worsaw floated up lazily to the surface. Air was still bubbling out the windpipe.

Hansard did not at once understand: their fight had carried them into the transmitter itself. It was then that Hansard had found himself unable to see. Worsaw, pursuing his advantage unthinkingly, had entered the transmitter at a point several inches above Hansard's point-of-entry, and passed through the plane of transmission. The various molecules of his head had joined the stream of water that was being transmitted continuously to Mars.

Finding an area of water as yet untainted by the blood, Hansard drank, then filled his canteen. He dragged the decapitated body down through the water and outside the station. There he shoved it beneath a tulip bed. It was a better burial than he had received at Worsaw's hands.

He checked the wound in his shoulder. It was superficial.

It seemed strange, now that he thought of it, that Worsaw's confederates had not come in response to the shots that had been fired. More than strange.

He looked about desperately for the lost .45.

Then Hansard heard it.

It sounded like a marching band advancing down Gove Street. From the prominence of the hill Hansard could see much of Gove Street, and it was filled with nothing but its usual swift stream of headlights. The invisible marching band became very loud. It was playing *The Stars and Stripes Forever*.

Chapter 8

BRIDGETTA

The same afternoon that Hansard had waited out, drowsy, hungry, half-aware, on the steps of the Arlington Library witness elsewhere a dialogue that was to be of decisive consequence for our story. Herewith, a small part of that conservation:

"*We* are all in agreement."

"But when aren't you, popsicle? *We're* in agreement too, you know."

"If it's a question of food, then one of us is perfectly willing to go without. We're already overpopulated, or we will be by tomorrow. Besides, I should think you'd *enjoy* a new face around here."

"It is not a matter of largesse, and you are mistaken to think that I could prefer any face to your own. Your cheeks are like pomegranates. Your nose like a cherry. You are another Tuesday Weld."

"For heaven's sake—Tuesday Weld is pushing *fifty*, grandfather!"

"Grandfather, indeed! I'm your husband. Sometimes I think you don't believe it. Is that why you want that young stud around here? So you can be unfaithful to me? Frailty, thy name is—"

"I should like to have the *opportunity*. What good is virtue that is never tried?"

"I am deeply hurt." Then, after a suitable pause: "But it is so typically American a name, like Coca-Cola on the tongue: Tuesday Weld."

"The Army's also typically American. But you won't give him a chance."

"*You* will, I'm sure, my darling. Is it his uniform you love him for?"

"He cuts a handsome figure in his uniform, I can't deny it."

"Off! I hate uniforms. I hate people from the Army. They want to destroy the world. They are *going* to destroy the world. And they would like to keep me prisoner forever. God damn the Army. There is no justice. I am outraged."

She, calmly: "But if they're going to destroy the world, it seems all the better reason why, while there's still time, we might show some charity."

"All right then, you can have his head on a silver platter. I knew from the first you wouldn't stop till you'd had your way. If you can find him before *they* do, you can bring him home and feed him a meal. Like a stray dog, eh? But if he makes messes, or whines at night . . ."

"We get rid of him, my love. Of course."

"Kiss me, popsicle. No, not there—on the nose."

Hansard walked down the slope to where he had left his clothes, dressed, hesitated, then walked through the wall built about the power station. Worsaw's confederates had disappeared. A very few late strollers passed by on the sidewalk, taxis and buses sped past in the street, and all these soundless goings-on were accompanied by the incongruous Sousa march-tune, as though a film were being shown with the wrong soundtrack.

He was very weak. Indeed if it had not been for this supererogatory strangeness, he would very likely have let himself bed down for the night on the roof of the power station.

Among the strollers, a woman came down the street toward Hansard. Even worn down as he was, even knowing she was of the Real World and hence inaccessible, he could not help but notice her. In the lamplight her red hair took on a murky tinge of purple. And admirable eyes—what joke made them glint as they did now? The same, doubtless, that curled the corners of her lavender lips. And her figure—what could be inferred of it beneath the jumble of synthetic ostrich-plumes of her evening coat—that was admirable too. She reminded him . . .

The woman stopped on the sidewalk, not three feet away from Hansard. She turned to study the blank face of the wall behind Hansard. She seemed, almost, to be looking at *him*.

"I wish she were," he said aloud.

The smile on the woman's thin lips widened. The Sousa march was now very loud, but not too loud to drown the sound of her laughter. It was a discreet laugh, scarcely more than a titter. But he had heard it. She lifted a gloved hand and touched the tip of a finger to the end of Hansard's nose. And he felt it.

"She *is,* she *is,*" the woman said softly. "Or isn't that what you'd wished?"

"I—" Hansard's mouth hung open stupidly. Too many things needed to be said all at once, and the one that took priority was only a banal: "I—I'm hungry."

"And so, perhaps, are those other little men, who may still be watching our carcasses for all that John Phillip Sousa can do. And therefore I suggest that you follow me, keeping at a healthy distance, until we're well out of the neighborhood. You have strength left in you for another couple miles, I hope."

He shook his head, and with no more ado she turned on her heels (a low heel, out of keeping with the elegance of coat) and returned in the direction from which she'd come. Halfway up Gove Street she reached into a window recess and took out a pocket radio and two miniature amplifying units. She turned the radio off, and the music ceased.

"Good thing they were playing Sousa," she commented. "A Brahms quartet wouldn't have been half as frightful. On the other hand, a little Moussorgsky . . . And by the way, here's a chocolate bar. That should help for now."

His hand trembled taking off the tinsel wrapping. The taste of the chocolate exploded through his mouth like a bomb, and tears welled from his eyes. "Thank you," he said, when he had finished eating it.

"I should hope so. But this is still not the place to talk. Follow me a little further. I know a lovely little place on ahead where we can sit down and rest. Are you bleeding? Do you need a bandage? No? Then, come along."

As he followed her this time, the paranoid suspicion came to him that she was fattening him up on chocolate bars, as the witch fattened Hansel, so that when it was time to cook him he'd make a better meal. It did not, then, occur to him that if she had a source of chocolate bars she wouldn't have to cook *him.* But he was very weak and most of his attention had to be devoted, light-headed as he was, to the business of staying upright.

After a few turnings and shortcuts through opaque obstacles, she led him up the steps of a brightly-lighted Howard Johnson's. They sat across from each other in a green-and-orange plastic booth, where she presented him with a second candy bar and accepted his offer of a drink from the canteen.

"I suppose I should introduce myself," she said.

"I'm sorry. I seem to remember your face from somewhere, but I can't remember . . ."

"*But*—I was about to say—I *won't* introduce myself, not quite yet at least. Not until you've told me something about yourself."

With marvelous restraint Hansard pushed the remaining half of the candy bar aside. "My name is Nathan Hansard. I'm a Captain in the United States Army. Serial number—"

"Oh, for heaven's sake, this isn't a prisoner-of-war camp. Just tell me what's happened to you since you went through the manmitter."

When Hansard had finished his narrative, she nodded her head approvingly, making the high-piled hair (which was a much healthier shade of red under the incandescent light) to tremble becomingly. "Very noble, Captain. Really very noble and brave, as you realize full-well without *my* saying so. I see I was wrong not to have spoken to you yesterday."

"Yesterday? Ah, now I do remember. You were looking at me from the other side of the reflecting pool."

She nodded and went on: "But you can understand why we've had to be suspicious. Just because a man is good-looking is no guarantee he won't want to . . . put me in his cooking pot."

Hansard smiled. With the two candy bars eaten, he was able to concentrate more of his attention on the personal graces of his benefactress. "I understand. In fact I have to confess that I wasn't without suspicions of my own when I was following you up Gove Street a little while ago. You look so . . . well-fed."

"Ah, you have a smooth tongue, Captain. You'll turn my head with flattery, sure. Another candy bar?"

"Not just now, thank you. And I must also thank you, I think, for saving my life. It was your radio, wasn't it, that turned them away?"

"Yes. I had been waiting farther up Gove Street, hoping I could spot you before they did. I didn't know where else to look, but I was certain the transmitter would be your only source of water. But you got through the wall without my ever seeing you. When I heard the gunshots, I had to assume you were already inside, and I turned on the radio full-blast. Once one has become accustomed to the silences of this world, music takes on a rather dreadful intensity. Or rather, I suppose, we're able to hear it the way it was meant to be heard."

"Well, again I must thank you. Thank you, Miss . . . ?"

"Mrs."

"Excuse me. With your gloves on, I couldn't tell."

"But you can just call me Bridgetta. My husband calls me Jet, but I think that's vulgar. Of course, so does he—that's why he uses it. He thinks it's American to be vulgar. He doesn't understand that vulgarity isn't fashionable any more. It's because he first arrived in the States in the late Sixties that—"

"I'm afraid . . . I'm afraid you'll have to speak a bit more slowly. My mind isn't as quick as it would be if it had a full stomach."

"Excuse me. Panofsky."

"Panofsky?" He was more than ever lost.

"You asked my name, and that's what it is—Mrs. Panofsky, Bridgetta Panofsky, wife of Bernard. You've perhaps heard of my husband."

"God damn," Hansard said. "*God* damn."

There were many celebrities of that year—writers, actors, or criminals—who might have entertained as high an estimate of their own notoriety and of whom Hansard would have been as unaware as we today perforce must be, but the name Panofsky was known to everyone. Literally, to all. "I've heard of him, yes," Hansard said.

Bridgetta smiled coolly, allowing him time to reassemble his composure.

"Then that's why—" Hansard exclaimed, as he began to program himself with remembered data.

"Yes," she said, "that's why we're like you—sublimated."

"Eh? I'm afraid I never had time to read Freud."

"Sublimated is only Bernie's word for being *this* way." Illustratively, she brushed her hand through a bouquet of plastic flowers that graced the Formica tabletop. "You see, the powers-that-be have let Bernie equip the homestead with transmitters so he can carry on his research there. Bernie can do just about anything, if he tells them it's for research. Except drive out the front door. The existence of the transmitters in Elba—that's what we call the homestead—is strictly—what's the favorite word now for very, very private?"

"Priority-A."

"Just so. And for once the whole rigmarole has worked to his advantage. Since no one knows we have transmitters no one comes to bother us at Elba, as they do in the State Department."

"The State Department! I saw you there too—almost a week ago. I'm sure it was you, except your hair was another color. And the man with you, in the wheelchair, that would have been Panofsky."

"Panofsky-Sub-One, if any saw him in the State Department."

"Again, slowly?"

"We use numerical subscript to distinguish between our different levels of reality. For instance, there must be a Nathan Hansard on Mars now. He'd be Hansard-Sub-One, and you're Hansard-Sub-Two."

"But if you know the State Department manmitter is watched, why do you use it?"

"We only use it coming back from someplace, not going there. A week ago—where would we have been coming from? Moscow, I think. Borominska was premiering in a revival of Tudor's *Lilac Garden*. Bernie insisted on being there."

Hansard recalled now, from a long-ago article in *Time,* the fact that Panofsky was an ardent balletomane and made frequent—and instantaneous—excursions via manmitter to the world's ballet capitals throughout their seasons, these brief tours being the single concession that the government had agreed to make to Panofsky for the loss of his freedom. At any performance of significance Panofsky was to be seen in the box of honor, or, at the intermission, outside his box, presiding regally over a strange *mélange* of Secret Service guards and ballet enthusiasts, always the dominating figure in such groups—even in his wheelchair.

"Tell me," she asked after a pause, "do you like me better as a redhead?"

"It's hard to decide. There's something to be said on both sides of the question."

She cocked her head slyly, smiling. "Say, Captain Hansard, I'm glad you're here."

"The feeling is mutual, Mrs. Panofsky. I'd rather be having a steak dinner with you than with 'A' Company."

"We'll have some fun together, Captain."

"But some food first?"

"Mmm." Bridgetta Panofsky leaned forward through Howard

Johnson's Formica tabletop and, apropos of nothing, she laid a gloved hand on Nathan Hansard's throat and slowly, deliberately, and a little insistently kissed his lips.

"Hey, you're married, remember?"

Her laughter was too self-assured to be due to embarrassment. "Such an old-fashioned *pickle,*" she commented, as she stood to leave. "But I rather like that."

Jesus Christ, Hansard thought to himself. He thought it with such force that he wasn't quite sure he had not said it aloud. For Hansard's moral sense was too finely formed to tolerate a double standard; the notion of an adultery with another man's wife was as noxious to him as, years before, his own wife's adultery had been. In any case, moral sense notwithstanding, he had scarcely had an opportunity yet to be tempted, nor was he, given that opportunity, in condition to respond to it.

Perhaps this was what she had in mind when Bridgetta said to him, as they left the restaurant: "First thing, we'll get some chicken broth into your belly, and then maybe some soft-boiled eggs. But no steaks—not for a day or so. Do you like curries? Bernie can make very good curries."

"Don't know. Never had a curry."

"Lord, you *are* a military man! I've always liked men in uniform, but Bernie doesn't feel that way at all. Oh, now you've started blushing again. Really, you don't have the blood to waste on blushing, Captain."

"You'll have to excuse me," Hansard said stiffly.

"No, no," Bridgetta said, with an abrupt shift of mood, "you'll have to excuse *me*. You see, if the truth be told, Captain—if you would see what I'm feeling tonight, you'd see . . ." She broke off for a while, then, shaking her head as though in anger for her own awkwardness. "I'm afraid, that's all. And when a person is afraid, why then she reaches out. You know? Will you hold my hand at least? Like that. Thank you."

After they had walked on a way, he asked, "What are you afraid of?"

"Why, what is anybody afraid of, Captain?"

"I don't know."

"Of dying, certainly."

Chapter 9

PANOFSKY

"You'll have to admit," Bridie said, "that he's smart."

"Smart, smart, what is smart?" asked Panofsky. "A rat that runs a maze is smart. I'm smart. President Madigan is smart."

"And that he's polite and respectful," Jet added.

"At the moment, that is only a part of being smart," snapped the other Panofsky. "You might as well say that because he's good looking—"

"He does have an honest face," said Bridget firmly.

"Because he doesn't often smile," said the first Panofsky.

"He was humorous enough with *me,* love," Jet argued. "You forget at times how much you throw most people off balance. Captain Hansard didn't know what to make of you last night."

"Goulash or shish-kebab, eh?"

"That's being perfectly unfair," Bridget objected in her loftiest tone. "You heard everything the good captain said at Howard Johnson's over Jet's little transmitter. Not only is he not a *cannibal*—he's also the last of the Puritans, by the looks of it." The other two Bridgettas nodded their heads in glum confirmation.

"But there's no need to write him off *yet,*" Jet said, rallying. "He just needs to get his strength back."

"I think you're missing Bridget's point," Bridie said. "In her gentle way she was suggesting that you went after him too quickly. Why the poor man must suppose that he's escaped from a den of cannibals into a nest of vampires."

"Girls, girls," said both Panofskys together. Then the one who wore the knitted skull cap (possession of which gave its wearer priority at such times) continued: "I have no desire to engage in a debate on the merits of different strategies of seduction. I only wish to counsel you not to set your hearts too much on keeping him. Remember, he is in the Army, and while you're admiring the uniform watch out for the iron heel. Perhaps Bridie is right about going slow with him. He's survived this long only by having a too-rigid character. If it cracks, there's no telling what will come out from the old shell. But I'm certain I'd rather not find out. Do you agree with me, Bernard?"

"Entirely, Bernard."

"Then to your posts—and may the best woman win."

"Did you sleep well, Captain?"

"Very well, thank you." Hansard sat up from the mattress on which he had spent the night. "How do you do it?"

"The mattress, you mean? Bernie has to take all the credit for provisioning us. In fact, you have Bernie to thank for this too. It's his breakfast, but he thought you'd appreciate it more." Bridget held out the tray she was carrying. It held a plate of three fried eggs, other plates of bacon and toast, a pint glass of orange juice, a silver scallop-dish of jam, and an antique coffee server from the Plaza Hotel. Steam rose from the spout of the server. "After you've eaten, I'll have some water ready for you to shave with. Unless you'd rather let your beard grow out."

"Amazing," said Hansard, oblivious for the first few moments of anything but the breakfast. After one egg, however, he looked up. "You're a different color today," he observed. For this Bridgetta's hair was not red but flaxen-blonde and braided into a tight crown about her head, Irish-peasant-style.

"I'm a different girl altogether. It was Jet who rescued you yesterday. She's the beauty of the family. I'm Bridget—I take care of household things. And you've still to meet Bridie, the intellectual one."

"But aren't you all the same person? I mean, you speak as though the others were your older sisters."

"In a sense they are. It's important, if only for our self-concept, that we should be able to tell each other apart. So we try, by division of labor, to split the old single Bridgetta-identity into three. The youngest always has to be Bridget, because obviously that's the least fun."

"The youngest?"

"The one to have come out of the manmitter most recently is the youngest. You understand how it works, don't you. It's sort of like an echo. Well, the echo that's me has only been here a week. Jet, who was Bridget before I came, has been here four months now. And Bridie has been around from the very start, two years ago. You can always tell which of us is which because I'm blonde and wear an apron, Jet is a redhead and dresses *à la mode,* and Bridie is a sort of ashy brunette and has a moldly old lab coat. It's remarkable how easily clothes can dictate one's behavior."

"And your husband—are there more than one of him?"

"Two, but we thought we'd only confront you with one of each of us last night to keep things simple. Bernard is always just Bernard. He doesn't bother to differentiate between his two selves the way we do. In any case, there's very little that could threaten *his* self-concept. Tell me, Captain, do you like me better as a blonde or as a redhead?"

Hansard shook his head, as though to clear away cobwebs. "For a moment there you really did have me believing you were a different person than the girl I met last night, but when you said that I knew better."

"Excuse me, Captain—it's not always easy to remember to keep in character as a drudge. Even Cinderella has moments, when her sisters are away . . . You ate all that so fast! Do you want more?"

"Not now."

"Then if you please, come with me. Bernard wants to have a word with you." It was like following a teacher to the principal's office Hansard wondered what he could possibly have done wrong already.

"I can't tell you how much I appreciate your hospitality, Doctor Pan—"

"Then don't make the attempt, Mr. Hansard. You will excuse me if I do not employ your proper title, but for me it would be a pejorative form. My experiences with the American military—and before that with the military establishments of East Germany and the Third Reich—have been on the whole unhappy experiences. You may use the same informality in addressing me. In America I have always felt that that 'Doctor' of yours always has a pejorative sense when it refers to someone outside the medical profession. Dr. Strangelove, for instance—or Dr. Frankenstein."

"I'll try and remember that, sir. I certainly didn't intend any disrespect."

"How old are you, Mr. Hansard?"

"Thirty-eight."

"Married?"

"Divorced."

"So much the better. You are just the right age for my Bridgetta. She is twenty-seven."

"Just the right age for your Bridgetta for *what,* sir?"

"For what!" The two Panofskys laughed in chorus. Then, pointing at his double, the Panofsky wearing the skull cap said: "Do you not see those wispy gray hairs? That shrunken chest? Do you not realize that that old man is paralyzed from the waist down?"

"Nonsense, Bernard!" said the double.

"Please to remember, Bernard," said Panofsky, laying his hand on the skull cap, "that I have the floor. And allow me a little poetic license in stating my case. Where was I? From the waist down, yes. Do you not see me here before you in a wheelchair? And you ask "For what?" Are you naïve, my good Captain?"

"It's not that exactly," Hansard mumbled, shifting his gaze uneasily from one Panofsky to the other.

"Or perhaps, though you're willing enough to go out and kill people or to push the button that will destroy the world, you have too fine a moral sense to think of a little hanky-panky."

"It may surprise you to learn that some of us military men *do* have a moral sense—*Doctor.*"

"Ah, he's got you there, Bernard," said the Panofsky without the cap. "Dead to rights."

"If you have an objection, Mr. Hansard, please do state it."

"Much as I admire the fine qualities of your wife—"

"My wives, rather. There are presently three women meriting the distinction."

"Lovely as all three are, they *are* your wives, sir. And I don't believe in, uh, promiscuity. Not with another man's wedded wife."

"Really, Captain?" Both old gentlemen leaned forward in their wheelchairs. "Excuse me, but is that your *sincere* objection?"

"I might have others, but I wouldn't know of them yet, since the one I stated is sufficient in itself to serve as a basis of decision. Why should you question my sincerity?"

"Ask him if he's a Catholic, Bernard," said the Panofsky without the cap.

"Bernard, if you want to take over this discussion, I will give you my cap. As it happens, I was about to ask him just that question. Well, Captain?"

"No, sir. I was raised a Methodist, but it's been a few years since I've been in any kind of church at all."

Both Panofskys sighed. "The reason we asked," the first explained, "is that it's so unusual to find a young man today of your convictions. Even within the church. We are both Catholics, you see, though that becomes a problematical statement at the present time. Are we in fact *two?* But that's all theology, and I won't go into that now. As for these scruples of yours, I think they can be cleared up easily. You see, our marriage is of a rather fictitious quality. Bridgetta is my wife in—what is that nice euphemism, Bernard?"

"In name alone."

"Ah yes! My wife in name alone. Further, we were wed in a civil ceremony instead of before a priest. We married each other with the clear understanding that there were to be no children. Even had we had such an intention, it is highly doubtful, considering my age, that it could have been accomplished. In the eyes of Holy Mother Church such a marriage is no marriage at all. If we had access to the machinery of canon law an annulment could be obtained with ease. But an annulment, after all, is only a formality, a statement that says what does not exist has never happened. Consider, if you prefer, that Bridgetta is my daughter rather than my wife. That is more usual in these cases, isn't it—that the wise old scientist, or the evil old scientist, as the case may be, should have a lovely daughter to give the hero? And I've never heard it to happen that the hero refuses her."

"What was the point in having married her at all, if what you say is so?"

"My civil marriage to Bridgetta, whom, you must understand, I dearly love, is a *mariage de covenance*. I need an heir, someone who can inherit from me, for I have earned, from the Government and through patent contracts, a fantabulous amount of money—"

"Fantabulous—how vulgar!" observed the double quietly.

"Yes, but how *American!* And so I married Bridgetta, who had been my laboratory assistant, so that she might inherit from me. Otherwise it would go to the Government, for whom I have no great love. Then, too, someone must carry on my legal battles in the courts after I'm dead—"

"Against the Emergency Allocations Act, you know."

"*I'm* telling this, Bernard. And finally I need someone to talk to in this gloomy prison beside the Secret Service guards and brainwashed lab technicians they assign to me. I'm not allowed to hold private conversations with my colleagues from the University any more, because they're afraid I'll leak their secret weapon. Which *I* invented! In just such a manner as this was Prometheus dealt with for giving man the gift of fire."

"Now, Bernard, don't over-excite yourself. Better give me the cap for a while now, and I'll straighten out matters with the captain. I think we can come to an understanding that will satisfy everyone—"

But before this happy accord could be reached, they were interrupted by Bridgetta—a fourth version, with black hair—who entered at the door at the farther end of the room. Bridget, Jet, and Bridie followed closely after.

"She's going through," Bridie announced. And indeed it was so, for the new, black-haired Bridgetta walked on relentlessly toward and then through her husband, who seemed not at all perplexed by the experience.

"That was Bridgetta-Sub-One, of course," his double explained to Hansard. "Otherwise, you know, she wouldn't go around the house opening doors instead of, like any proper ghost, walking through them. Bridgetta-Sub-One is leaving for Paris. *Candide* is at the Opéra Comique. It was in expectation of her departure that I wanted to speak to you down *here* instead of in my usual room upstairs, for that—on the other side of the second door Bridgetta opened—that is our manmitter-in-residence."

Bridgetta-Sub-One closed the door of what had seemed to Hansard no more than a closet behind her. The six people watched the closed door in perfect, unbreathing silence, and in a moment a hand appeared through the oak panel. One could sense in the startled gestures of that hand all the wonderment that must have been on the woman's face. Panofsky purred forward in his chair and lifted his own hand up to catch hold of hers, and how much relief and happiness there was in the answering clasp of her hand.

Now the woman who had lately been Bridgetta-Sub-One stepped

through the door, smiling but with her eyes tight shut, an inescapable reaction to walking through one's first door.

She opened her eyes. "Why then it's true! You were right, Bernie!"

The two Panofskys chuckled indulgently, as though to say, "Aren't I always right?" but forebore to be more explicit. It was her birthday party, not his.

The new Bridgetta-Sub-Two regarded her three doubles with an amused and slightly fearful smile, then for the first time lifted her eyes to see the figure standing behind them. The smile disappeared, or if it did not quite disappear, it changed into a much more serious kind of smile.

"Who is he?" she whispered.

Hansard wasn't able to answer, and no one else seemed about to rescue him from his difficulty. Hansard and Bridgetta stood so, regarding each other in silence, smiling and not quite smiling, for a long time.

In the following days it became a matter of dispute between them (but the very gentlest of disputes) whether what had happened could be legitimately said to be—in Hansard's case, at least—love at first sight.

After the curry dinner that Panofsky had prepared to welcome the new Bridgetta, after the last magnum of champagne had been emptied and the glasses tossed out through the closed windows, the two Panofskys took Hansard into a spacious library in one corner of which a third Panofsky (Sub-One) was leafing through a handsome folio volume of neo-Mondrian equations.

"Oh, don't mind *him*," Panofsky reassured Hansard. "He's really the easiest person in the world to live with. We ignore him, and he ignores us. I took you aside so that we might continue our discussion of this afternoon. You see, Mr. Hansard—may I call you Nathan?—we are living here under most precarious circumstances. Despite our sometime luxuriousness, we have no resources but those which the Panofsky and Bridgetta of the Real World—a nice phrase that, Nathan, I shall adopt it, with your permission, for my own—can think to send us. We have a certain store of canned foods and smoked ham and such set aside for emergencies, but that is not a firm basis for faith in the future, is it? Have you much considered the future? Have you wondered what you'll do a year from now?

Ten years? Because, as the book says, you can't go home again. The process by which we came into being here is as irreversible as entropy. In fact, in the largest sense, it is only another manifestation of the Second Law. In short, we're stuck here, Nathan."

"I suppose, in a case like that, sir, it's best not to think too much about the future. Just try and get along from day to day."

"Good concentration-camp philosophy, Nathan. Yes, we must try and endure. But I think at the same time you must admit that certain of the old rules of the game don't apply. You're *not* in the Army now."

"If you mean that matter about my scruples, sir, I've thought of a way my objection might be overcome. As a captain I have authority to perform marriages in some circumstances. It seems to me that I should have the authority to grant a divorce as well."

"A pity you had to go into the Army, Nathan. The Jesuits could have used a casuist like you."

"However I must point out now that a divorce is no guarantee that a romance follows immediately after. Though it may."

"You mean you'd like me to leave off matchmaking? You Americans always resent that kind of assistance, don't you? Very well, you're on your own, Nathan. Now, hop to it."

"And I also want it understood that I'm not promiscuous. Those four women out there may all have been one woman at one time, but now there's *four* of them. And one of me."

"Your dilemma puts me in mind of a delightful story in Boccaccio. However, I shall let you settle that matter with the lady, or ladies, themselves."

At that moment three of the ladies in question entered the room. "We thought you'd want to know, Bernie," said Jet, "that Bridget is dead."

"What!" said Hansard.

"Nothing to become excited about, Nathan," Panofsky said soothingly. "These things have to happen."

"She committed suicide, you see," the new Bridgetta explained to Hansard, who had not seemed to be much comforted by Panofsky's bland assurance.

"But *why?*" he asked.

"It's all in Malthus," said Bridie. "A limited food supply; an expanding population—something's got to give."

"You mean that whenever . . . whenever a new person comes out of the transmitter, you just *shoot* somebody?"

"Goodness no!" said Jet. "They take poison and don't feel a thing. We drew lots for it, you see. Everyone but Bridie, because her experience makes her too valuable. Tonight Bridget got the short straw."

"I can't believe you. Don't you value your own life?"

"Of course, but, don't you see?—" Bridgetta laid her hands on the shoulders of her two doubles. "—I have more than one life, I can afford to throw away a few as long as I know there's still some of me left."

"It's immoral. It's just as immoral as joining those cannibals."

"Now, Nathan," Panofsky said soothingly, "don't start talking about morality until you know the *facts*. Remember what we said about the old rules of the game? Do you think I am an atheist that I would commit suicide just like that, one-two-three? Do you think I would so easily damn my immortal soul? No. But before we can talk about right and wrong, we must learn about true and false. I hope you will excuse me from making such expositions, however. I have never enjoyed the simplifications of popular science. Perhaps you would care to instruct the good captain in some first principles, of, my dear Bridie, and at the same time you could instruct Bridgetta in her new duties."

Bridie bowed her head in a slightly mocking gesture of submission.

"Yes, please," said Hansard. "Explain, explain, explain. From the beginning. In short, easy-to-understand words."

"Well," Bridie began, "it's like this."

Chapter 10

MARS

I should never have joined the Justice-for-Eichmann Committee, he thought. *That was my big mistake. If I hadn't joined the Committee I could have been Chief-of-Staff today.*

But was it, after all, such a terrible loss? Wasn't he happier here? Often as he might denigrate the barren landscape, he could not deny, to himself, that he gloried in these sharp rock spines, the chiaroscuro, the dust dunes of the crater floors, the bleeding sunsets. *It is all so . . . what? What was the word he wanted?*

It was all so dead.

Rock and dust, dust and rocks. The sifted, straining sunlight. The quiet. The strange, doubly-mooned heaven. Days and nights that bore no relation to the days and nights measured off by the Earth-synchronized clocks within the station; consequently, there was a feeling of disjunction from the ordinary flow of time, a slight sense of floating. Though that might be due to the lower gravity.

Five weeks left. He hoped . . . but he did not name his hope. It was a game he played with himself—to come as near to the idea as he dared and then to scurry away, as a child on the beach scurries away from the frothing ribbon of the mounting tide.

He returned down the olive-drab corridors from the observatory to his office. He unlocked the drawers of his desk and removed a slim volume. He smiled—for if his membership on the ill-fated Committee had cost him a promotion, what would happen if it became known that he, Major-General Gamaliel Pittmann, was the

American translator of the controversial German poet Kaspar Maas? That the same hand that was now, in a manner of speaking, poised above the doomsday button had also written the famous invocation that opens Maas' *Carbon 14*:

> *Let us drop our bombs on Rome*
> *and cloud the fusing sun,*
> *at noon, with radium . . . ?*

Who was it had said that the soul of modern man, Maas Man, was so reduced in size and scope that its dry dust could be wetted only by the greatest art? Spengler? No, somebody after Spengler. All the other emotions were dead, along with God. It was true, at least, of his own soul. It had rotted through like a bad tooth, and he had filled the hollow shell with a little aesthetic silver and lead.

But it wasn't enough. Because the best art—that is to say, the art to which he found himself most susceptible and which his rotting soul could endorse—only brought him a little closer, and then a little closer, to the awareness of what it was that underlaid the nightingale's sweet tremolos, brought him nearer to naming his unnamed hope.

The fancy cannot cheat so well as she is famed to do.

Yet what was there else? Outside of the silver filling was only the hollow shell, his life of empty forms and clockwork motions. He was generally supposed to be a happily married man—that is to say, he had never had the energy to get divorced. He was the father of three daughters, each of whom had made a good marriage in the same manner. Success? Quite a lot of success. And by acting occasionally as a consultant for certain corporations he had so supplemented his Army income that he had no cause to fear for the future. Because he could make agreeable conversation he moved in the best circles of Washington society. He was personally acquainted with President Madigan and had gone on hunting trips with him in his native Colorado. He had done valuable volunteer work for The Cancer Fund. His article, "The Folly of Appeasement," had appeared in *The Atlantic Monthly* and been commended by no less a personage than ex-Secretary-of-State Rusk. His pseudonymous translations of Maas and others of the Munich "Götterdammerung school!" had been widely praised for their finesse, if not always for content. What else *was* there? He did not know.

He knew, he knew.

He dialed 49 on the phone, the number of Hansard's room. *I'll play a game of pingpong,* he thought. Pittmann was an extremely good pingpong player. Indeed, he excelled in almost any contest of wits or agility. He was a good horseman and a passing-fair duelist. In his youth he had represented the United States and the Army in the Olympics Pentathlon.

Hansard was not in his room. Damn Hansard.

Pittmann went back out into the corridor. He looked into the library and gamesroom, but it was empty. For some reason he had grown short of breath.

Darkling, I listen.

Ex-Sergeant Worsaw was outside the door of the control room. He came to attention and saluted smartly. Pittmann paid no attention to him. When he was alone inside the room he had to sit down. His legs trembled, and his chest rose and fell sharply. He let his mouth hang open.

As though of hemlock I had drunk, he thought.

He had never come into the control room like this, never quite so causelessly. Even now, he realized, there was time to turn back.

The control room was unlighted, except for the red ember of the stand-by lamp above the board, which was already set up for Plan B. Pittmann leaned forward and flicked on the television screen. A greatly-magnified color image of the Earth, three-quarters dark, appeared.

Love never dies. It is a mistake to suppose that love can die. It only changes. But the pain is still the same.

He looked at the button set immediately beneath the stand-by light.

Five weeks: was it possible? Would this be the time? No, no, surely the countermand would come. And yet . . .

Tears welled to Pittmann's gray eyes, and at last he named his hope: "Oh, I want to, I want to. I want to push it *now.*"

Hansard had seldom disliked his work so intensely. If it could be called work. For aside from the mock runthroughs of Plan B and the daily barracks inspections "A" Company had been idle. How are you to keep twenty-five men busy in a small, sealed space that is so fully automated it performs its own maintenance? With isometrics? Pittmann was right: boredom was the great problem on Mars.

Strange, that they didn't rotate the men on shorter schedules. There was no reason they couldn't come here through the manmitter on eight-hour shifts. Apparently the brass who decided such questions were still living in a pretransmitter era, in which Mars was fifty million miles from Earth, a distance that one does not, obviously, commute every day.

Hansard had tried to take Pittmann's advice and looked through the library for a long, dull, famous book. He had settled on *Dombey and Son,* though he knew nothing about it and had never before read anything by Dickens. Though he found the cold, proud figure of Dombey somewhat disquieting, Hansard became more and more engrossed with the story, but when a quarter of the way through the book, Paul Dombey, the "Son" of the title, died, he was unable to continue reading the book. He realized then that it was just that irony in the title, the implied continuity of generations from father to son, that had drawn him to the book. With that promise betrayed, he found himself as bereft as the elder Dombey.

A week had passed, and the order to bomb the nameless enemy had yet to be countermanded. It was too soon to worry, Pittmann had said, yet how could one not worry? Here on Mars the Earth was only the brightest star in the heavens, but that flicker in the void was the home of his wife and son. His ex-wife. Living in Washington, they would surely be among the first to die. Perhaps, for that very reason, they would be among the luckiest. The countermand would certainly be given, there was no need to worry, and yet, what if it were not? Would not Hansard then be, in some small degree, guilty of their deaths, the deaths of Nathan Junior and Marion? Or would he be, somehow, defending them?

It was of course misleading to consider two lives among the many millions affected. Strategy was global; the policy of optimum benefit was collected, a computer in possession of all the facts.

Guilt? A man may murder another man, or three or four, and be culpable, but who could assume the guilt of megadeaths? Ordinarily the answer would have been simply—the enemy. But the enemy was so far away and his guilt so engrained in the confusions of history— camouflaged, so to speak—that sometimes Hansard doubted that the answer was so simple and so convenient for his own conscience.

Unwholesome, purposeless speculations. What had Pittmann said? "Conscience is a luxury for civilians."

Hansard ate his dinner alone, then went to his room and tried to listen to music, but tonight everything sounded like German beerhall polkas. At last he took a mild barbiturate, standard issue for the men of the Mars Command Posts.

He was walking with Nathan Junior through a field of sere grass. The air was drowsy with the buzzing of flies. They were hunting deer. Nathan Junior carried the shotgun just as his father had shown him to. Hansard carried the lunchpail. Something terrible was going to happen. The color of the grass changed from yellow to brown, from brown to black. There was a loud buzzing in Hansard's ears.

He picked up the receiver of the phone. "Yes?"

"Ah, there you are, Nathan!"

"General Pittmann."

"I thought you might enjoy a game of pingpong."

"When?" Hansard asked.

"Right now?"

"That sounds like a good idea," said Hansard. And it did.

Chapter 11

THE NATURE OF THE WORLD

"You have to be very quick," said Bridie, "or it might happen that two objects will occupy the same place at the same time. A highly undesirable condition. That's why we're so careful always to be here from two to three in the afternoon, when transmissions are made."

Hansard snatched away the can of *pâté de foie gras* that the small transmitter had just produced as an echo. The lab technician reached into the right-hand receiver and placed the can_1 that he had just transmitted there into the right-hand transmitter. He pressed a button, transmitting the can_1 to the left-hand receiver and at the same time producing a can_2 which Hansard immediately removed from the transmitter. The pile of $cans_2$ that had been thus produced that afternoon filled a large basket at Hansard's feet.

"It seems to me," said Hansard judiciously, not interrupting his stockpiling, "that all this contradicts the laws of conservation. Where do these cans come from? How does a single can in the Real World produce a gross of cans here?"

"If you want an answer to your question, Nathan, we'll have to start with first principles. Otherwise it would be like explaining a nuclear reactor to someone who believes in the indivisibility of the atom. In a sense though, your question isn't far afield from what it was that gave Bernard the whole idea of sub-species of reality. He'd already built the first experimental model of the machine and the Press hadn't decided whether to treat him like God or like a maniac, when he realized that he'd overlooked the notorious fact that every action has an equal and opposite reaction. But there seemed to be no reaction corresponding to the action of transmission—nothing that could be measured. Of course it *was* there in the mathematics, and Bernard busied himself with that. Are you familiar with topological transformations? No? But you *do* know that there are non-Euclidean geometries, and that these have the same validity as the commonsense varieties? Well, matter transmission is essentially a topological transformation from our world of commonsense spaces to . . . somewhere else, and then back again. It is just at the moment that the transmitted body reaches that somewhere-else that the reaction takes place that forms the 'echo.' "

"Which tells you very little, I fear, that you haven't already figured out for yourself, but have patience, I will get to your question. The consequence, you see, of Bernard's *ex post facto* reasoning was an entirely new physics, a physics in which our universe is just a special case—indeed, a trivial case, as a point is a trivial case of the circle. There are, in this physics, progressive levels of reality, and matter can exist at each level. Now at the same time that there can be radical changes in the nature of the material world there need not be corresponding changes in *energetic* relationships."

"That is to say?" Hansard asked.

"That is to say that sub-two reality enjoys the same light of common day as sub-one reality, though that light issues from a sun composed of sub-one atoms. A fortunate consequence of the double nature of light, which seems to be both wave and particle—and highly beneficial for us."

"Highly necessary, too—I can see that for myself. But how much energy spillover is there? Sound, for instance, doesn't carry over from the sub-one to the sub-two world."

"Because it is produced by the collision of sub-one particles and carried in a medium of sub-one gases. Similarly, we can receive *radiant* heat from the sub-one universe, but not heat produced by conduction or convection. Magnetism and gravity still act upon sublimated bodies, but Bernard has proven experimentally that the gravitational attraction isn't mutual. But we'd best not go into that. It's an embarrassing notion for someone, like me, who wants to go on living in a comfortable old-fashioned Newtonian universe."

"And you receive radio and television broadcasts from the Real World. I've learned that much."

"Yes—if we possess a sub-two receiver."

"But in that case, why don't you communicate with the Real World by broadcasting to them? Tell them about your situation on short-wave radio."

"Have you ever tried shining a flashlight in the eyes of somebody in the Real World? No? Well, it's the same principle: we can see by *their* sunlight, but they're oblivious to light issuing from a light source constituted of secondary matter. The same would hold true of any radio broadcasts we might make. The Real World always remains real for we secondary creatures—all *too* real—but for primary beings, our secondary world might as well not exist, for all the difference it makes to them. No, there is no communication backward. As Bernard pointed out, the sublimation of matter that the transmitter causes is irreversible—another case of entropy, of the universal back-sliding of all things. So, no matter how much *pâté* we can pile up here, we must remain permanently second-class citizens."

"But in that case I don't understand why Panofsky—Panofsky-Sub-One, that is, back there in the Real World—keeps providing for you."

"Faith," said the new Bridgetta, who was helping Hansard to stack the cans in such a way that they did not become too heavy to keep on top of the floor, "it's all done on faith. We must be thankful that Bernard is a Catholic and has lots of experience believing unlikely things. Oh, I'm sorry," she said, glancing at Bridie. "It's *your* story."

"You needn't practice being Bridget yet, darling. Not until you've been able to dye your hair. Besides, as it's been two years since I was in the Real World, you're the better qualified to tell about that."

"Once Bernard had figured out the theory behind it," Bridgetta began, "he tried to extrapolate the problems that a sublimated being would have to face in an unsublimated world. None of the necessities would be available naturally to him: no food, no water, not even air. But he would definitely exist and be alive—for as long as one *can* stay alive under such conditions. The first problem was to provide a supply of sublimated air, and fortunately such a supply was at hand in the pumping station that was to be built to supply the Command Posts. Bernard invented all kinds of specious reasons for having that transmitter built here under the D.C. dome, instead of, as first planned, by Lake Superior. After only a month of transmitting, the dome would have been filled, and as long as the pumps keep pumping, the supply is more than adequate to compensate for what is lost through the traffic locks. Unfortunately, the locations of the general cargo transmitters were specified in the rider to the Emergency Allocation Act, so we couldn't look forward to having all the initial advantages of Robinson Crusoe."

"Though you do have cannibals," Hansard observed.

"That was something else Bernard could do nothing about. He wanted to have the Camp Jackson manmitter built outside the dome, which would have solved our problem neatly."

"And mine too."

"Excuse me, that was a rather careless statement. But he was right: those men do pose a threat. The best we can hope for is that they don't discover us. Fortunately, one doesn't leave footprints here."

"There'd be no problem at all, if you just told the government about this. Then those men could be supplied with the food—and officers—that they need."

"Bernard looks on the government in a different light than you do, Captain," Bridie said, rather coldly. "You forget that his relations with the government have not usually been of an agreeable nature. When it has not directly hindered his work, it expropriates and perverts it. No, don't try to argue about that with me—I'm only trying to explain Bernard's attitude. Furthermore, the government's scientists would not have understood the refinements of his theory, for they are still debating the validity of the mathematics on which the transmitter itself was based. Then, if the scientists could be convinced, try to imagine how you would go about explaining to an Army general that there are people just like you and me who are invisible, who can walk through walls, to whom we must send food, though it is probable that we will never be able to demonstrate, in any tangible way, that they exist."

"When you put it like that, I don't see how he's convinced *himself.*"

"Faith," Bridgetta said again earnestly.

"Faith and reason," Bridie corrected. "Don't forget that Bernard has spent his life as a mathematician. A balanced equation is tangible proof for *him.* Though our existence is abstract at best, he can believe in us just as readily as in the Pythagorean theorem."

"And out of that kernel of belief has come . . . all this?" Hansard waved his hand at the goods lining the shelves of the room. "What possible reason does he give this lab assistant for carrying on this idiot work? It certainly can make no sense to him, if he's unaware that he's producing groceries for us."

"In the case of food, Bernard tells them that he's concerned about possible nutritional losses that might be caused by excessive and repeated transmissions. Preposterous of course, but you must remember that the very idea of the machine is preposterous to most people. Remember, too, that the government will do all it can to humor Bernard so long as he remains tame. The mattress, for instance: have you heard the story of the mattress?"

Hansard shook his head.

"For a while," Bridgetta said, taking her cue from Bridie, "whenever I was transmitted anywhere, Bernard insisted that I wrap myself in a mattress. To keep myself from being *bumped,* he explained to the Secret Service guards. Of course, it was really to give *us* something besides a floor to sleep on. But it did make a spectacular entrance at the Paris Embassy. Madame Viandot thought it was a new fashion from New York and ordered three mattresses for herself the next day."

"And no one ever suspects? The things you transmit are so evidently survival items."

"No one has any reason to suspect, however, that survival is a problem for us. The lab assistants, of course, are constantly complaining about the meaningless tasks that Bernard sets for them, and once Bazeley of NASA came around to ask what Bernard was up to, but he only has to hint that he's doing research on a receiverless transmitter and they fall over themselves to be obliging. For all they know, Bernard's still good for another golden egg."

"Well, does that explain everything, Captain?" Bridie asked.

"Yes, thank you very much. I appreciate your giving me so much time."

Bridie smiled acidly. "But you've forgotten, you know, the biggest problem of all. You haven't learned how it is that you can walk."

"Christ, I've gone all this time without realizing it *was* a problem! How is it that I'm able to walk across the same floor I can swim through?"

"Don't feel dumb, Captain," said Bridgetta. "It's only natural to take for granted that things that you've always been able to do are possible. For Bernard, however, lacking any direct experience, this was the chief theoretical difficulty standing in the way of survival.

He could never be certain that as soon as we arrive here we just don't start sinking into the ground. That's why *I* was so relieved when I arrived this morning—because I found myself on *terra firma*. Firm enough, at least, if I don't wear heels."

"But *how* does it work? What keeps me from just sinking down, if gravity is acting on me, as you say?"

"Call it surface tension," said Bridie. "Though actually it is a form of potential energy that is inherent in all matter at whatever level of reality. Like static electricity, it forms an equipotential surface over all objects—a sort of "skin" of energy. What keeps sublimated objects above the ground—the cans on the shelves, for instance, or your feet—is the small repellent force generated by the two surfaces, a force that decreases in proportion to the distance between the two realities. Thus, a sub-four and perhaps a sub-three can, *would* sink through a sub-one shelf, but in two adjacent fields of reality the repellent force is quite sufficient for most purposes, though not so great that it cannot be overcome by an opposing force. And therefore second-degree matter can interpenetrate first-degree matter and you can swim through the floor. All this we've learned here. Panofsky-Sub-One has never been able to be sure, and so he keeps providing us with things we really don't need—boards and linoleum rugs. When we try to spread the rugs, they just curl up into the floor. Still, we can be grateful that he errs on the side of caution."

"I am afraid that I *am* sinking deeper and deeper now, though. Sub-three and sub-four cans. I'd never even considered the possibility."

"Imagine what would happen if one of us were transmitted. A sub-two person going through a transmitter would leave behind a sub-three echo of himself. Surely you've been in caves and heard the echo of an echo. As a matter of fact, you've already described such a case. When that unpleasant sergeant donated his head to Mars, the transmission would have produced a sub-three head. Though God only knows what's become of it. Sub-one water, as you may have found out, won't support sub-two bodies. A convenient rule-of-thumb is this: after sublimation, the solids of the unsublimated world appear to have the properties of liquids; liquids, the properties of gas and gas, the properties of that unfashionable commodity, an ether."

"But to return a moment to what became of Worsaw-Sub-Two: his head was taken off by a sub-one transmitter. How is that?"

"As I said earlier, energic relationships don't change as one descends the scale of reality. A sub-two transmitter, for instance, could not transmit a sub-one object, but a sub-two object, such as Worsaw's head, *will* be transmitted by a sub-one transmitter."

"Well, all this has convinced me of one thing."

"And that?" Bridgetta asked.

"I'm never going to be transmitted again."

"I don't understand," said Bridie.

"If I've been having a hell of a time surviving here, think what it would be like for Hansard-Sub-Three."

"Oh, you don't have to worry on that score. After all, if he didn't immediately begin to sink into the earth, he would very soon die of suffocation, since he would lack a supply of sub-three air. No, at *this* point, Hansard-Sub-Three—or Bridgetta-Sub-Three, for that matter —is not a viable form."

Panofsky entered the room then, driving his wheelchair through the wall. "Have you justified our little euthanasia program, my love?" he asked cheerily.

"I was just getting to that," Bridie said.

"It won't really be necessary now," Hansard said. "I can appreciate the need for some sort of measure, so long as you keep being transmitted regularly. It seems to me that you keep the population at a lower level than need be, but no doubt there are reasons for that."

"There are," Panofsky assured him. "And the reason that we must keep going through the transmitter and replicating ourselves is that back *there* I can't be sure that the population is *large* enough. Not all our losses are voluntary, you know. On more than one occasion I've driven this chair and myself into the ground and drowned. Not I, strictly speaking, but the equivalent, me. So then, Nathan, you understand everything, eh?"

"There's only one thing I still don't understand, sir."

"And that?"

"You."

"Oh, but that is always the great mystery. Even Bridgetta cannot penetrate to the essential Panofsky, but keeps peeling off layers like an onion. Not my metaphor, of course—Ibsen's. But what, particularly, puzzles you?"

"That you should try to do this all on your own. I'm sure if you spoke to someone in the government, though they might be skeptical at first, they would eventually believe you and aid you."

"I'm just as sure of that, Nathan, and so I have said nothing. One of the few consolations of being here is that I am, for the first time in my life, a free man. I have at last found a way of escaping successfully. The government's first act of assistance would no doubt be to send a crew of men through the transmitters who could supervise me here."

"If your luck turned and Worsaw were to discover you, you'd be thankful for such supervision."

"That's the chance I take."

Hansard shook his head disapprovingly, but by the set of his jaw it was evident that he had decided not to pursue the argument.

"Consider, Nathan, what I have already suffered at the government's hands, and then think if I could gladly invite them *here*. They have taken my invention—which could have made the world a paradise—and turned it into a weapon—as though the world wants for new weapons. I should despair if I thought it were possible for my achievement to be suppressed forever. Happily, as Norbert Wiener observes, the greatest guarantee that a thing will be done is simply the knowledge that it is possible. So that in the long run, unless they prefer annihilation—and they may, they may—my work will not have been for nothing."

There was a long pause during which Hansard considered how most tactfully to protest against Panofsky's apolitical attitude. Didn't the man see the moral necessity of the war? Was he not himself a refugee from the tyranny of East Germany? But before he could formulate these objections clearly, Panofsky had resumed speaking, in a rather more wistful tone.

"Imagine what it might be like. Think what a source of *power* the transmitter represents. The mind staggers. Even *my* mind staggers."

"Of power?" Hansard asked.

"Instead of moving something laterally, suppose one were to transmit it upward. Water, for instance. A circular waterfall could be created, which could power a dynamo, and only the smallest fraction of the dynamo's power would be needed to operate the transmitter itself. In effect, a perpetual motion machine."

"Then it *does* violate the laws of conservation!"

"At our level of reality, yes. But within the larger system, no. In other words, another universe somewhere is shortly going to experience a considerable power drain. Let us hope they have no means of plugging the hole, eh?"

"My God," said Hansard, who was still envisioning the circular waterfall. "It *would* change everything."

"Everything," Panofsky agreed. "And it will change our view of the universe as well. Not too long ago, in 1600, I regret to say that the Catholic Church burned Giordano Bruno as a heretic. The church will have to change its position now. The universe is infinite, after all, but there is no need for God to be embarrassed on that account. God can simply be *more* infinite. The bigger the universe, the vaster must be God's might. There are, just as Bruno envisioned them, worlds no telescope will ever see, worlds beyond those worlds, worlds still beyond, infinities of worlds. Imagine, Nathan, if the Earth itself were to be transmitted, and if Earth-Sub-Two were transmitted afterward, then Earth-Sub-Three . . . And not just once, but each a dozen, a hundred, numberless times, each transmission producing its own echo."

"Is it possible?"

"Much more is possible, though perhaps not just now. The solar system itself could be transported. We could take our sun with us as we journey about the galaxies. Is it possible? With a transmitter such as this, anything is possible. And what do *you* use it for? What is the only use the military mind can find for such a marvel? To dispense bombs with it!"

"Does the president know about that waterfall-machine you spoke of?"

"Of course he does. It was immediately evident to every scientist in the country that such a thing is possible now."

"Then why isn't it being built? Why, with a source of unlimited power, there never need be a war again. Or hunger, or poverty."

"You'll have to answer that question, Captain, for you represent the government, not I."

"You know," said Hansard, unhappily, "perhaps I don't."

Chapter 12

THE NATURE OF THE SOUL

"Then you still don't want to tell him about it?" Bridie asked.

"To what end?" Panofsky said. "Why call him back from vacation, when there's nothing he can do to alter the situation?"

"He might gather his roses a little more quickly if he knew," Jet said.

"I think we might best consult the tastes of the lady most directly concerned," said Panofsky, turning to regard Bridgetta, who was now a blonde and no longer, in fact, Bridgetta, but merely Bridget. Her smile spoke for her: *she* was satisfied.

"Any more objections?" Panofsky asked.

"It's best so, of course," said Jet. "It was only selfishness that made me want to share my fear with him. But it becomes harder and harder, as the time advances, to pretend to be lighthearted."

"The effort will be good for both of us," Bridie said. "Pretending makes it so."

"Furthermore," said Panofsky, "we have every reason to suppose it will be called off. The day is fully a month away."

"Not quite that long," corrected his double.

"Well, very nearly a month. After all, it's not as though this were being decided by merely human wit. The best computers in the world are blowing fuses this very minute to do something about it. It's all game theory and bluffing. I, for one, am not worried about it. Not in the least." But when Panofsky's eyes looked across the room and met the eyes of his double, his gaze faltered and his assurance failed.

"Well," said the double somberly, "I, for another, *am.*"

Toward the end of Hansard's second week at Elba, and five days after the preceding conversation had taken place, our hero found himself doing something he had promised himself never to do again —arguing with his host. Panofsky had made another passing reference to his "little euthanasia program," and Hansard had furrowed his brow just enough to show that he considered it a little murder program—but he refused steadfastly to discuss it.

"It's hardly fair, Nathan, for you to sit in judgment—and Minos himself could not more prominently sit in judgment than you—your face crinkles up like Saran Wrap—and never to allow the poor sinner a chance to justify himself, if he can."

"I'll allow that something of the sort has to be done. But . . ."

"But? But? Now it really isn't fair to stop at that *but,* is it?"

"I was going to say it seems a perfectly reasonable attitude, from the scientific point-of-view, but it seems strange in a Catholic."

"What a picture you must have of science, Nathan! You pronounce the word as though it were a euphemism for something unspeakable, as if science were the antithesis of the ethical—as, since the bomb, it has in part become."

"I have nothing against the bomb," Hansard protested hastily.

Panofsky allowed this to pass with scarcely the raising of an eyebrow. "But it is curious that you should imagine an opposition between science and Catholicism, which I am sure you regard as wholly irrational. No? Yes. A dismal prospect, if evil can only be opposed by unreason."

"Honestly, Dr. Panofsky, I don't follow you when you go off on figure-eights like that. What I had in mind was simply this: Catholics are supposed to believe in immortal souls and that sort of thing. In fact, you've already said that you do. But suicide is—I don't know the technical term for it."

"A mortal sin. And so it is, but fortunately I cannot commit that sin at this level of reality. Only Panofsky-Sub-One can commit suicide, in the sense that it's a sin."

"Well, if you take poison and die from it, what else are you going to call it?"

"First, Nathan, I must explain to you the nature of the soul. At conception, when the soul is created, it is unique, only one, indivisible. God made it so. Do you think *I* can create souls? Of course not. No more can the transmitter, which I invented, create souls. So that the apparent multiplicity of my selves means nothing in God's eyes. I would not go so far as to maintain that I am a mere *illusion*. Rather let us say that I am an epiphenomenon."

"But physically your existence on this plane of reality is just as . . . as existent as it ever was. You breathe. You eat. You *think*."

"Ah, but thinking is not a *soul*. Machines can think."

"Then you're no longer bound by any moral laws whatever?"

"On the contrary, natural law—the law derived from reason as opposed to that which is revealed to us divinely—has as binding a force here as in the Real World, just as the laws of physics work here. But natural law has always condoned suicide in certain circumstances: consider all those noble Romans throwing themselves on their swords. It is only in these Years of Grace that suicide has become an evil, since it is in contradiction to the second supernatural virtue, hope. It is not allowed for a Christian to despair."

"Then you've ceased to be a Christian?"

"I am a Christian perhaps, but not a man. That is to say, the fact that I no longer possess a soul does not prevent me from believing as I always have. I am the same Panofsky as ever—so far as you or I can see, for we are not given to see the soul. When Hoffmann sold his soul, he lost his shadow—or was it the other way around? In any case, it was a visible sign. But how much sadder to lose something which one cannot even be sure afterward that one ever possessed. Happily, I am prepared for this paradox by being a modern. Camus, you know, was troubled by a similar disparity between the strict atheism which he felt reason required and his feeling that it was wrong to do evil. But *why* was it wrong? For no reason at all. But still one must have some basis for action, for choosing. So one just tries to do the best one can, from day to day, without examining the ethical dilemma too closely. Which is more concentration-camp philosophy. I'm sorry I have nothing better to offer you."

"But if it's all meaningless—and isn't that what a soul is all about, meaningfulness?—then why does Panofsky-Sub-One keep providing for you? Why should he care?"

"That is a question that I hope he will never chance to ask himself. Happily, he has devoted all his attention up till now to our physical rather than our spiritual condition. If he were to convince himself that we are soulless, he might very well stop sending us supplies."

"I just can't believe that, Doctor."

"Only because you're not a Catholic."

"Look—if what you said that day in the transmitting room were to happen—if the whole damn world were to be transmitted, what then? With all the people on it, the Pope and everyone."

"Nathan, what a splendid question! I'd never thought of that. Of course the basic situation remains unaltered, but the *magnitude* of it! A whole *world* without shadows! Yes, and for a final paradox, what if such a transmission were to take place not tomorrow but two thousand years ago, and Christ Himself . . . Nathan, you *do* have an instinct for these things. You may have changed my mind, which is an almost unheard-of thing at my age. I will certainly have to give a good deal of thought to the question. But now that I've shown you my soul, such as it is or isn't—would you like to show me yours?"

Hansard's brow furrowed more deeply this time. "I don't understand."

"Why is it, Nathan, that you wake up screaming in the middle of the night?"

And—yet another week later:

"I'm sorry," Hansard said, "for flying off the handle with you like that."

"Not with me, I'm afraid," said Panofsky. "Though Bernard did tell me about that incident. As a matter of fact, Nathan, I scolded him on your behalf. Your dreams are nobody's business but your own. I think Bernard's let himself become something of a snoop since he left the Real World. That happens to all of us to some degree, but he could confine his eavesdropping to that world and leave *us* alone."

Hansard laughed uneasily. "It's funny you should say that, because I'd just come to tell you—to tell *him*—that he was right. Or perhaps not exactly right, but . . ."

"But you were going to answer his question anyhow? Confession does ease the soul, as they say. Especially, I've always observed, the souls of Protestants, in which category I would include those of your stamp. It's because they're so severe with themselves that the fact of mercy overwhelms them."

"I'm not looking for mercy," Hansard said dourly.

"Precisely my point: you'll be all the more surprised to find it. Tell me, Nathan, did you fight in Viet Nam back in the Sixties?"

Hansard turned pale. "I was just about to tell you about that. How did you know?"

"It's nothing telepathic—just a simple inference. If you're thirty-eight now, you would have come of age for the draft at the height of the whole mess. Some very nasty things happened in that war. We civilians with our heads in the sand probably got little idea of what went on, and even so the newspapers were full of stories almost every day. Women and children?"

Hansard nodded. "It was a child—a little boy—he couldn't have been much older than five."

"You had to shoot him in self-defense?"

"I incinerated him in self-defense."

They were silent together a long while, though it was not, on Panofsky's part, an unsympathetic silence.

Then Hansard said, reaching for a tone of ordinariness: "But you knew it all before I even told you. You anticipated everything I had to tell you."

"We sinners are never as unique as we suppose ourselves to be. When a boy of thirteen goes into the confessional with his nails bitten to the quick, the priest will not be surprised to learn that he has committed sins of impurity. When a grown man, an Army captain, who usually evidences the most straight-laced moral code, wakes up screaming in the night, one looks for a cause commensurable to the pain. Also Nathan, your case is not unique. There have been a dozen novels written about that war by other men who woke up screaming. But why is it, after all this time, you wanted to speak about it?"

"I haven't been able to tell Bridgetta. I tried to and I couldn't. I thought perhaps I'd be able to, if I told you about it first."

"And why were you anxious to tell her?"

"I've always thought that one of the reasons my first marriage never worked was because I didn't tell Marion about that boy. She wouldn't let me, the one time I tried. This time I won't make that mistake."

"This is news! You're marrying the girl then?"

"In another week. There's going to be a big society wedding at Grace Episcopal, and we thought we'd just sneak in and make it a double wedding. I hope you'll be able to be there to give the bride away."

But before Panofsky could commit himself, Bridie came into the room unannounced and wearing a look of grave concern. "You'd better come and see this, Bernard. We have them on the screen now, and it's just as we feared."

Hansard followed Bridie and Panofsky into the sitting-room adjoining Bridgetta's bedchamber. There Bridgetta-Sub-One, in a terrycloth bathrobe and her hair wound up in a towel, was standing a few feet back from the 12-inch screen of the videophone. The Sub-Two residents of Elba were crowded close about another receiver, apparently on an extension line from the first. The image on the screen that Bridgetta-Sub-One was watching was of Panofsky, but on the other screen there were *two* Panofskys, the second of them with what appeared to be a cloud of cellophane wreathing his head. With the two Panofskys crowded before the screen and the others pictured on it, there were a total of four functioning Panofskys visible to Hansard in a single glance. It was too much, by at least one.

"What in hell is—" he began, but Bridie silenced him with a peremptory gesture.

No sound came from either videophone, but this did not seem to dampen the interest of the spectators. While he waited for this strange charade to end, Hansard reasoned. He reasoned that (1) the videophone that Bridgetta-Sub-One was watching belonged to the Real World (which was confirmable by sticking a finger into it), that (2) the Panofsky pictured upon it must therefore be Panofsky-Sub-One (and hadn't there been talk lately of his having gone off for the Bolshoi's spring season?), and that (3) the *second* Panofsky, visible on the screen of the other videophone (which *was* tangible to Hansard's touch), must be a sublimated Panofsky.

When the call was concluded and the image had shrunk to a small dot of light, Panofsky congratulated Hansard on his reasoning. "One of our knottiest problems," the old man went on, "was establishing communications with the others of us around the world. You see, I've made as much provision as I can for the Sub-Two Panofskys produced by the transmissions from Paris or Moscow back to Washington. There is a gas mask and oxygen supply stored beneath the seat of my wheelchair at all times. It gives me—or him, whichever way you choose to regard it—twenty-four hours more or less—time enough for one last night at the Bolshoi and sometimes a visit to the Kremlin. But of what use is it to be a perfect spy, if one can't communicate what one has unearthed. The method that had to be employed was soon obvious to *us,* but we had to wait for Panofsky-Sub-One to think of it, and that man can be almost military in his thinking sometimes. But at last the solution occurred to him. What we do now is this: at a predetermined time to be indicated on my desk calendar, Bridgetta-Sub-One receives a call here at Elba from Panofsky-Sub-One who is in another city. Today it was Moscow. Once the connection has been established, it is a simple matter for the Panofsky-Sub-Two then in Moscow to be on hand and give his report at the same time. It requires a bit of hithering and thithering on Panofsky-Sub-One's part. Usually he goes from Moscow after the curtain falls at the Bolshoi, jumps to Paris for supper, and returns to Moscow next day for another performance—and to make the phone call. The sublimated Panofsky does not, of course, appear on the screen of Bridgetta's receiver, but on this one, which has itself been sublimated, he does appear. There is no sound, for the Panofsky-Sub-One on the other end has only the air he has brought with him. But we have learned to lip-read, so that is hunky-dory."

"Hunky-dory!" Jet whispered, with a shudder. *"Not* hunky-dory!"

While the first Panofsky sat back to savor his Americanism, the other sighed: "I wish there were some simpler way. This method is so wasteful of lives. There are none of the resources in those other cities that we have here at Elba. It is hard to bring everything one requires for even a short visit. The breathing equipment is bulky, and the Secret Service guards think it strange that Panofsky-Sub-One should always insist on bringing it along."

"Fortunately," the first Panofsky interrupted (they were neither wearing the skull cap at the moment), "he has a reputation for eccentricity. He has invented a delightfully paranoid theory concerning foreign germs."

The two Panofskys smiled in ironic appreciation of this theory.

"But there are compensations," said the second.

"Oh yes, there is usually time to see one last performance, and from a vantage better even than the conductors. Since being sublimated, *I* have seen nothing, less than nothing. Here we are in one of the chief cities of the world, the capital of the most affluent culture on Earth, and have you ever seen what is called ballet here? It is vomit! I protest against it vehemently. But in Moscow . . . ah! To-night, for instance, we were told that Malinova was extraordinary in the second act of *Giselle*."

The second Panofsky sighed more deeply. "Now more than ever does it seem rich to die. For *him,* that is."

"Exactly. *We* shall both be dead inside of two weeks. And *we* will never have seen that *Giselle*. I'd willingly give two weeks of my life to see that."

"Two weeks?" Hansard asked.

"Oh, Bernard!" Bridgetta cried out. "You promised not to say anything."

"My dear, excuse me. It just slipped out."

"Why should you be dead in two weeks? There's something you've been keeping back from me. I've felt it in the air ever since I came here."

"May I tell him?" Panofsky inquired of Bridgetta.

"What choice is there now? Nathan, don't look like that. I didn't want you to know, because . . . because we were so happy."

"In two weeks, Captain Hansard, all hell breaks loose. To be pre-cise, on the first of June. My double in Moscow just informed us that the Kremlin is being as foolishly resolute and resolutely foolish as Washington."

"I find that hard to believe," said Hansard.

"Nevertheless it is so. Bridgetta, may I show him the letter?"

"Try to understand, Mr. Hansard," Bridie said (for Bridgetta, in tears now, was able to do no more than nod her head yes), "that when Bridget followed you that day and took this out of its hiding place in the Monument, she was only concerned to find out who you were. We had no way to know if we could trust you. We weren't ex-pecting anything of this sort."

"You mean to say you opened that attaché case? But it was Priority-A!"

Panofsky removed a folded paper from his coat pocket and handed it to Hansard. "The case contained only this letter, Nathan. And since this letter was signed, a month ago, nothing has altered."

After he had digested the President's written order, after he had convinced himself of its authenticity, Hansard said: "But the diplo-mats . . . Or the U.N. . . . ."

"No," said Jet dismally. "I've been watching them here in Wash-ington every day. The President, the Secretary of Defense, the Russian Ambassador: none of them will unbend. Because CASS-9 won't. They've become the slaves of that computer. And now the President and the cabinet and all the important officers of the Pentagon have gone into hiding. They've been away a week. It bodes no good."

"I simply can't believe that if nobody *wants* the war—"

"Has anybody *ever* wanted the war? But it was bound to happen, you know. The whole effectiveness of our arsenal as a deterrent force was based on the possibility of their being used. Now that possibility will be realized."

"But there's been no aggression, no provocation . . ."

"CASS-9, apparently, does not need to be provoked. I'll confess that with respect to game theory I am naïve."

The second Panofsky, who had been listening intently the while, hit the arm of his wheelchair with his fist and swore.

"He is so especially distressed," his double explained, "because he knows he could stop it, if only there were a way for him to speak to Panofsky-Sub-One."

"If all that you say is true, though," Hansard said, deliberately, "it seems to be too late for the explanations of men of goodwill."

"You mistake my meaning, Nathan. He, Bernard Panofsky, single-handed, could stop the war—snap! like that. It is all written out on vellum, a splendid, magnificent, preposterous plan. But it cannot be carried through by any of us, only by someone of the Real World. And so it is all no good, a failure . . ."

"Single-handed?" Hansard asked, with a note of professional incredulity.

"Alas, yes," said both Panofskys in chorus.

Then one of them removed the skull cap from his pocket and put it on his head. "If you please, Bernard—*I* will tell him how."

Chapter 13

MARS

Here there were no usual measures of time. The Camp lived on a twenty-four hour Earth-day, but a complete rotation of Mars took thirty-six minutes longer, so that only once in forty days was the high noon of the sun in perfect agreement with the high noon dictated by the clocks on the wall. Five weeks of anxious waiting had slipped by in a twinkling, five weeks in a limbo of inactivity and the ritual gesturing of the run-throughs and inspections, five weeks going up and down the olive-drab corridors, eating tinfoil dinners, swilling the hot coffee, thinking the same well-worn thoughts, which through repetition (just as the food seemed to lose its flavor day by day) grew wearisome and were set aside. Like a spring brook in the dry season of the year, conversation subsided to a trickle. The enlisted men passed the long hours with endless games of poker. General Pittmann kept more and more to himself, and so, perforce, did Captain Hansard.

A strange condition, a condition difficult to describe except in negatives. Life was reduced to a minimum of automatic processes—waking, sleeping, eating, walking here and there, watching the time slip by, listening to silences. The Camp's narrow world of rooms and corridors came to seem somehow . . . unreal.

Or was it himself that seemed so? He had read a story once, or seen a movie, of a man who sold his shadow, or perhaps his reflection in a mirror. Hansard felt like that now—as though at the moment of the Mars jump, five weeks before, he had lost some essential, if intangible, part of himself. A soul perhaps, though he didn't exactly believe he had one.

He wished that the countermand to the President's order would come, but he wished even more that he might be called back to the fuller reality of Earth. Yet these were neither very strong wishes, for the reservoirs of all desire were drying up within him. He wished mainly for an ending, any ending, an event to accent this drear, uninflected, trickling time.

So perhaps there had been a sort of wisdom behind the decision to keep the men at the Mars Command Posts two months at a stretch, despite that there was no technical necessity for it, the same wisdom that is at the foot of all the compulsory dullness of military life. For boredom makes a soldier that much more able and that much more willing to perform the task that it is especially given a soldier to perform.

Ex-Sergeant John Worsaw sat in the guard bay before the door to the control room reading a tattered personalized novel. Because of his reading habits, Worsaw had a reputation around Camp Jackson/ Mars as an intellectual. This was an exaggeration, of course, but, as he liked to point out in his more ponderous moments (after about two beers), you couldn't get anywhere in the year 1990 without brains, and brains wouldn't do you much good either without an education. (Worsaw had earned a College Equivalent diploma in Technics.) Take Wolf Smith, for example—the Army Chief of Staff: that was a man who had more facts at his command than a CASS-9 computer. For a man like Smith, facts were like ammunition.

Facts: Worsaw had nothing but contempt for people who couldn't face hard facts. Like that fairy Pittmann in the control room now, worrying about the bombs probably, and afraid of the button. No one had told Worsaw of the President's order, but he knew what was in the air by the looks on the two officers' faces. What were they scared about, as long as they were here on Mars? It was the sons-of-bitches back on Earth who had to worry.

Thinking something to this effect, though rather more hazily, Worsaw found that he had read down a quarter of a page of the novel without taking any of it in. With a more concentrated effort, he returned to the last passage he remembered:

Worsaw lobbed another grenade in the bunker entrance and threw himself flat, pressing his face into the jungle dirt. Thunder rent the air, and thick yellow smoke belched from the crumbling structure.

"That oughta do it, Snooky!" yelled the corporal, thumbing the safety off his M-14. "Let's mop up now." And Corporal O'Grady leapt to his feet.

"Look out, Lucky!" Even as Worsaw screamed it was too late —the sniper bullets had caught O'Grady in a vicious cross-fire, spinning him and flinging him mudward, a dead man.

"The yellow-belly sons-of-bitches," Worsaw muttered. "They'll pay for this."

A few feet away the blood of Lucky O'Grady seeped out into the jungle soil. The man who had been Worsaw's best friend had run out of luck at last.

Strangely moved by this last paragraph, Worsaw laid his book aside. He had heard someone coming down the corridor, and it was likely, at this hour of the day, with the men playing cards in their barracks, to be Hansard. The captain spent a lot of his time roaming about in the corridors.

"General Pittmann?"

"Yes, he's inside, sir."

Hansard went into the control room, closing the door after him. Worsaw cursed him softly, but there was in that quiet obscenity a trace of respect, even affection. Despite the pressure to restore his rank that Worsaw had put on him through Ives (who owed Worsaw more than a few favors and could be counted on to pay his debt), Hansard wasn't backing down. Which showed guts. Worsaw admired guts.

But the deeper motive of Worsaw's admiration was simply that he knew Hansard to be a veteran of Viet Nam, the last of the big fighting-wars. Worsaw himself had been born four years too late to enlist for that war, and so he had never, to his chagrin, undergone a soldier's baptism of fire. He had never known, and perhaps now he never would, what it was like to look at a man through the sights of a loaded rifle, to squeeze the trigger and see that man fall dead. Life had cheated Worsaw of that supreme experience, and it had offered very little by way of compensation. Why else, after all, does a person go Army?

He fished the novel out of his back pocket and started to read again. He skipped ahead to the chapter he liked best, the burning of the village of Tam Chau. The anonymous author described it very well, with lots of convincing details. Worsaw liked a realistic-type novel, that showed what life was like.

Chapter 14

THE BRIDE

Love will intrude itself into places where it simply has no business being—into lives or stories that are just too occupied with other matters to give it its due. But somehow it can always be squeezed in. Marriage is an exemplary institution for this purpose, since conjugal love can usually "go without saying," whereas the more exotic forms of romance demand the stage all to themselves, scornful of the ordinary business of life. A married man can divide his life comfortably in half, into a private and a public sector, which need never, so long as both run smoothly along, impinge upon each other.

Thus, Hansard had fallen in love, paid court, proposed, been accepted, and now it is the very morning of the wedding—and all these things have already taken place, as it were, in the wings. We should not suppose, because of this, that Hansard's was a milder sort of love than another man's or that the romance was so ordinary and undistinguished as to be without interest for us—or even, perhaps, for the principals involved. We need only point out the singular circumstance that the rivals of the beloved were, essentially, her exact doubles to dispel such a notion. No, if there were time, it would be most interesting to linger over their month-long idyll, to document the days and nights, to smile at the follies, to record the quicksilver weathers of their growing love. Notice, for instance, how Hansard's expression has relaxed. There is a sparkle in his eyes that we have not seen there before. Or is it, perhaps, that they seem deeper? He smiles more often—there can be no doubt of that—and even when he is not smiling there is something about his lips . . . what is it? Do they seem fuller now? See, too, how his jaw has relaxed, and when he turns his head, how the tendons are less prominent. Small changes, but taken as a whole they give his face an altogether different stamp. Surely it is a change for the better.

Already it is May 26, the morning of the wedding—how quickly a month can go by! And is there no time left to tell how splendid a month it has been, of what has been happening back there in the wings? By all means, let us take the time—while the bride and her three bridesmaids (for Bridgetta-Sub-One had gone through the transmitter once more, increasing the Sub-Two population by one. The newcomer immediately assumed the role of Bridget, for the bride would now be neither Bridie nor Jet nor yet Bridget—but Mrs. Hansard). The two Panofskys, and Hansard, are walking down the May-morning streets to the church.

The month had gone by as though they'd been playing a game all the while: there had been such *fun*. Sometimes Hansard spent the day alone with "his" Bridgetta; at other times one or more of her doubles would come out with them to swim in the municipal police station or in the Senate buildings. He and Bridgetta had made love in heaps of flowers in a florist's window. They had taken picnic lunches to diplomatic dinners, where, since there was no room for them around the table, they had sat on top and dangled their legs through the tablecloth. They'd played tennis, singles and doubles, after spreading slices of the linoleum rugs about the court so that they wouldn't lose the tennis balls. The greatest lark, once Hansard got over his embarrassment at playing a children's game, had been Bridgetta's special version of hide-and-seek, which they played in the most crowded streets and offices of the city, while the sober workaday population milled about them. They'd sneaked into the most expensive theaters and left during the first act if they found the play not to their liking—left without any regret for the money wasted. (And more often than not, the plays were boring, since they had to be seen in dumb show.) At especially bad performances, Hansard and one or more Bridgetta would get up on the stage and ham it up themselves. Such fun, and much, much more, too—and gentler moments, which might be only a word, a caress, a glance, forgotten as quickly as it happened, but what, if not the sum of such moments, is love? A moment, a month—how quickly—and here they are already on the way to the church!

The bride was wearing a makeshift gown sewn together from damask tablecloths and synthetic lace plundered from various articles of lingerie, no one back in the Real World having had the forethought, or the occasion, to provide for such a contingency as this today. If only fashion were considered, the bridesmaids might have been thought a good deal better dressed than the bride—but the bride was wrapped in the glory of a myth that quite out-tops all that fashion can do. Both Panofskys were wearing formal clothes, since they had usually set off through the transmitters formally attired for the theater. Hansard, however, had nothing better than his everyday uniform, for which the hat was still missing.

The church was crowded when they arrived, and there was no room for the invisible intruders except before the altar. Bridie put a tape of the *Tannhäuser* wedding march on the portable phonograph and let it play at medium volume. There was a stir in the waiting crowd, and heads turned to regard the bride advancing down the center aisle, her train borne up by three children. "A pity we couldn't get orange blossoms for you, my dear," Panofsky whispered to the bride-to-be, who was holding a bouquet of yesterday's wilted roses, the transmitters of Elba having provided nothing more appropriate for the day.

Bridgetta took three steps forward to stand behind the other bride, her feet planted squarely in the billowing train. The two grooms came out of the sacristy to take the hands of their betrotheds. The minister began to speak the silent words of the ceremony, which Panofsky, reading his lips, repeated after him.

Hansard had to dodge out of the way when the groom reached around to receive the ring from his best man. Panofsky handed Hansard the ring that Bridie had made from a costume-jewelry ring of her own by removing the stone and filing away the setting until there was only a thin gold band. Hansard placed the gold circlet on Bridgetta's finger.

He leaned forward to kiss her. When his lips were almost touching hers, she whispered, "Say it again," and he said, "I do, I do." Then they kissed, man and wife now, till death should part them.

"I've written a small epithalamion for the occasion. Would anyone like to hear a small epithalamion?" Panofsky asked.

"Afterward. Epithalamions come with the dinner," Jet said.

The sub-one bride and groom turned around and, stepping to an inaudible music, descended from the altar and went out of the church. Bridie ran the tape ahead to the sprightlier Mendelssohn theme. Hansard and Bridgetta stopped kissing.

"Stand back and let me look at you," he said, smiling broadly.

She stepped back, and then, when the shot rang out, stepped back again. Blood stained the makeshift bridal gown just beneath her heart. Her mouth dropped open, and the smile was vanished from her lips, from her eyes. He caught her in his arms. She was dead.

"That's *one*," shouted a half-familiar voice. Hansard turned to see Worsaw standing in the midst of the wedding guests crowding into the aisle. "And this is two." The rifle fired again, but he missed Bridie, who had been his second target.

"Get down, out of sight!" Hansard shouted, though he did not think to take his own advice. Jet took hold of the wheelchair of one Panofsky and pushed him into the sacristy. Bridie and the new Bridget both dived into the floor. The other Panofsky had driven off under his own power, and Hansard could not see him, though indeed he could see very little beyond the widening circle of blood staining the damask of the bridal dress. Forgotten, the tape recorder continued to play the Mendelssohn march tune.

"Beast!" Panofsky's voice shouted. "Monstrous, loveless beast!" He was driving his wheelchair through the crush of people in the center aisle. He aimed a revolver at Worsaw, but even from where he was Hansard could see the old man's aim was wide. A third and fourth shot rang out, the pistol and then the rifle, and Panofsky pitched forward in his chair. The wheels penetrated the surface of the floor, but the chair scarcely slowed in its headlong motion forward. Soon the wheelchair, bearing the crumpled body, had passed out of sight downward.

Hansard realized that the moment demanded action, but he was reluctant to let his bride's still-warm body sink to the floor.

Another rifle shot—and the tape recorder was silenced.

"That was dumb, Hansard," Worsaw called out. "Playing that music was plain dumb. I wouldn't have known you were in here without that."

Gently, Hansard lowered Bridgetta's body, keeping his eyes always on her murderer.

"Oh, you don't have to worry yourself yet, Captain. I won't touch *you* till I've wiped out your friends. I've got a score to settle with you. Remember?"

Hansard reached inside the jacket of his uniform for the pistol with which Panofsky had provided him. He did not move fast.

"Don't be stupid, Captain. How can you pull that out, when all I have to do is squeeze a trigger? Now, put your hands up in the air, and tell those women and that other old man to come out from where they're hiding. If they're good-looking enough, I might not have to kill them after all. How about that?"

Hansard did not obey these commands, nor did he, by any deliberate action, disobey them. Indeed, his mind was too numb to produce the thoughts that would have led him to action.

Behind Worsaw a woman's voice let forth an incoherent cry; Worsaw spun to face the imagined danger, but it came not from behind him, as it first seemed, but from above. He had been standing at the back of the church, beneath the choir loft. When he turned, Panofsky's wheelchair dropped through the low-hanging ceiling on top of him. Hansard's wit thawed sufficiently for him to draw his pistol from its holster and empty it into Worsaw's back.

Jet dropped down from the choir loft and came running forward to Hansard. She spoke disjointedly—"I thought . . . are you hurt? . . . and then, around the outside of the church, and up the stairs to the choir . . . it was so heavy, and I could hear him . . ." He allowed her to embrace him, but he did not return her embrace. His body was rigid, his jaw tense, his eyes glazed with inexpressiveness.

Once she'd released him, he walked forward and turned over Worsaw's bleeding body. "Three times," he said. "First, inside the manmitter. Then, at the pumping station. And now here. I seem to spend all my time killing this one man."

Bridie and the new Bridget came in at the main door, where the last of the wedding guests were filing out. "Bernard is dead," Bridie announced. "We found him in the cellar. But where's the other Bernard?"

"In the sacristy," said Jet. "Hiding in the minister's clothes closet. It was his idea that I use his chair as a projectile. He felt that I would probably have just as poor aim with a pistol as his double had."

"I seem to spend all my *life* killing people," Hansard said aloud, though he seemed to be talking only to himself.

"Nathan, it isn't like that," Jet insisted earnestly. "What happened today could have happened any time, without your ever being around. It was an accident, a grotesque accident."

"Go away, please, all of you. I'd rather not see . . . your faces . . . when hers . . ." He turned away from the three women and walked back to the altar. There he took up the dead Bridgetta in his arms.

Jet would have protested again, but she was checked by Bridie. Instead she went with the empty wheelchair into the sacristy. Bridie and the new Bridget dragged the body of Worsaw out of the church. In five minutes Jet returned to ask when they would see him again.

"I want to spend the night here," Hansard said, "with my bride."

Jet went away. The cleaning people came into the church and began to sweep it out and mop up, though they did not see the blood-flecked book lying in the center aisle: *The Private War of Sergeant Worsaw.*

Afterward, the electric lights were turned off. In the semidarkness Hansard found himself able at last to cry. It had been many years since the tears had come from those eyes, and they did not, at first, flow freely.

Before the brute fact of death, nothing can be said. It would be best, if, like the three women, we leave Hansard to himself now. His grief, like his love, cannot take a very large part of our story, which is not very far from ending.

Chapter 15

WOLFGANG AMADEUS MOZART

And yet—what a curious, contradictory grief it was. For she who had died was not dead. She was alive; thrice over, she was alive. Though no one of the Bridgettas proposed this consolation in so many words, still the daily and unavoidable fact of their presence, of *her* presence, could not but have its effect on Hansard. In one sense it only made his loss more poignant by offering constant reminders of her whom he had lost. On the other hand, he could not very well pretend that his loss was irreplaceable.

The surviving Panofsky and three Bridgettas, for their part, accepted what had happened with great equanimity. They were, after all, accustomed to the idea of their own expendability.

Then too, there was the sobering consideration that in a week—in six days—in five days—they would *all* be dead. Bridgetta, Panofsky, Hansard, and the whole populace of the Real World. Even in the depths of his grief Hansard was aware of the minutes slipping by, of the dreaded day creeping up on them, like a fog bank rolling in from the river.

On the evening of the 27th, Panofsky called them all together. "The question arises, fellow citizens—how shall we pass the time? Bridgetta has a supply of LSD in our medicine cabinet, should anyone so desire."

Hansard shook his head.

"Nor do I. However, we may change our minds. If anyone starts to panic, it's a good thing to remember. I understand it's especially helpful for terminal cancer patients, and somehow I've always associated cancer and the bomb. There are also any number of bottles of good brandy and Scotch in the cellar, should the need arise. What I would suggest, most seriously, is what a defrocked priest advised in a clandestine religion class in the labor camp of my youth—that if one knows the Day of Judgment is at hand, one should just go about one's ordinary business. Any other course partakes of hypocrisy. For my own part, I intend to study the folio of equations that Bernard-Sub-One just sent me through the transmitter."

Though it was sensible advice, Hansard had difficulty following it. With Bridgetta dead, the ordinary fabric of his life had dissolved. He might still continue to mourn her, but as the time advanced, the magnitude of the impending catastrophe seemed to mock at the smallness of his own sorrow. Perhaps it was exactly this that goaded him to find a solution to the catastrophe—and thereby restore a measure of dignity to his own mourning.

Or perhaps it was just luck.

However that may be, he found himself more and more driven to listen to music. At first he gave his attention to the more fulsomely elegiac selections from Panofsky's library of tapes: *Das Lied von der Erde, Die Winterreise,* the *Missa Solemnis.* He listened to the music with an urgency more intense than he had known even at the depth of his adolescent *Sturmn-und-Drang,* as though some part of him already knew that the key he sought was concealed behind those silvery shifting tone-fabrics, hidden in the pattern but a part of it. Gradually he found the Romantics, even Beethoven, too heavy for his taste. He would have liked to turn to Bach then, but Panofsky's library provided only the Sonatas for Unaccompanied Violin and the Well-Tempered Clavier. Here, too, though indistinctly still, he felt the presence moving just beyond the veil, yet when he tried to touch it, to fix it firmly in apprehension, it eluded him, as when, reaching into a pool of water, the fish dart swiftly out of reach of the grasping hand. At last it was Mozart who gave it to him.

On the first play-through of the tape of *Don Giovanni,* he felt the veil tearing. It began during the trio of the three masquers at the end of the first act, and the rent widened steadily until the penultimate moment when Donna Elvira arrives to interrupt the Don at his carousal. He scorns her earnest warnings, she turns to go out of the

door . . . and screams, the great D-minor chord thunders in the orchestra, and the Statue bursts into the hall to drag the unrepentant
Don to hell.

Hansard stopped the tape, reversed the reel, and listened to the
scene again from the moment of Donna Elvira's scream.

The veil parted.

"The chord," he said. "Of course, the chord."

He tore himself away from the music to seek out Panofsky, but he
discovered the old man sitting only a few feet away, listening raptly
to the opera.

"Doctor Panofsky, I—"

"Please, the music! And no more of that foolish 'Doctor.'"

Hansard switched off the recorder during the height of the brief
electric scene between Don Giovanni and the Statue.

"I'm sorry, but I must tell you now. It concerns the music in a
way—but more than that—I've thought of how it can be done, what
you said could not be. How to communicate with the Real World!
Perhaps, just perhaps."

"The most awesome moment in all music, and you—"

"I'll form a chord!"

"It is true," Panofsky replied, in a more moderate tone, "that
Mozart can suggest to us a harmony embracing the world, but art is
sadly not the same thing as reality. You are wrought up, Nathan.
Calm yourself."

"No, no truly—*this is the way*. You *can* talk to Panofsky-Sub-
One, by becoming part of him again, by restoring the unity that was
disrupted. You'll mesh with his body—and with his mind. Probably
when he's asleep."

A light began to glow in Panofsky's eyes. "I am a fool," he whispered, then paused, as though waiting for Hansard to contradict him
—or perhaps for his other self to agree. He went on: "An idiot. A
chord—yes, it is a fine analogy, though, mind you, nothing *more*. I
can't be sure yet. There is a demonstrable relationship between a
man of the Real World and his echo, a sort of proportion, but
whether it is enough . . . I cannot, in the time we have left, develop
a mathematical model—"

"There's no need to. Just *do* it!"

"But what a lovely analogy." His eyes were closed, and his fingers
moved in pantomime before him. "You sound middle C on the

piano, and simultaneously the C an octave above. The ear can no longer sort out what it hears, and the overtones of the two notes resolve into a single chord."

"The fibers of the body would be the overtones," Hansard theorized eagerly. "The tone of the muscles, the memory-traces of the brain, the blood-type, the whole pattern of being. Place the two patterns together, and there'll be a sort of resonance between them, a knitting-together."

"Yes, a kind of understanding perhaps, a natural sympathy, a bond."

"A chord. And wouldn't communication be possible then?"

"Without evidence, Nathan, how can we know? But there's a chance, and I must try it. If it works, why then, Nathan, you and I may have saved the world at its last minute. You frown! What now, Nathan? Is it that you misdoubt my plan? Well, well, Napoleon had his skeptics too, and see how far he went. No, I'm perfectly confident that once I've been able to communicate with Panofsky-Sub-One, I can carry it off, grandiloquent as it must sound to you. But now I must find that gentleman out. And speak of the devil . . ."

For another Panofsky had just entered the library through the open door. "You *might* have been waiting outside the transmitter if you'd been expecting me. It wasn't very cheery coming into an empty house. Why are the two of you looking at me as though I were a ghost? And for that matter—" Turning to Hansard "—I don't believe we've been introduced."

"But you're not Panofsky-Sub-One," Hansard said.

"A sound induction. No, *he* just left for Moscow. Didn't you see where I'd noted it down on the memo calendar?"

"And Bridgetta?" his double asked.

"Went with him, of course."

"How long will they be gone?"

"Till June 2nd, when Malinova repeats her *Giselle*. Good heavens, Bernard, what's the matter? You look as though I'd just announced the end of the world."

But, a little later:

"You can't expect me to *build* it!" Hansard protested.

"Nonsense, Nathan—there's nothing to build. Just a trifle of rewiring. Surely there is a stock of spare elements at the Mars base.

With the equipment as it exists, it shouldn't take more than fifteen minutes' work to convert those elements to what we'll need."

"But the elements for the Camp Jackson manmitter are so small!"

"Size is no consideration, Nathan. Nor is distance. And you'll have all the power you need in a dry cell. No, my chief worry is not in your assembling the transmitter, but in your getting the co-ordinates down pat. I think we can afford a day of practice. Have you ever put together your own hi-fi?"

"When I was a kid."

"Then you should have no trouble. A hi-fi is more complicated. Let me show you what you must do. In the laboratory. Now. Quickly, quickly."

At twilight of the 29th of May, Hansard and Bridie stood once again on Gove Street and watched the men of Camp Jackson walking in and out of the wall about the pumping station. Their number had been much reduced: Hansard counted fewer than ten. It was necessary to use these transmitters, which were in continuous operation, rather than the manmitters within the camp proper, since there were no jumps scheduled to Camp Jackson/Mars for two more weeks. Had Panofsky possessed the co-ordinates for the Mars Command Post, Hansard might have foregone this sort of hitchhiking altogether.

Finally the last of the men that they had seen go in had come back out. They waited another half hour, then strolled down the street to the wall, and through, trundling an empty wheelchair before them. The door of the pumping house had been standing open during the day, and the great volume of sub-two water had spilled out, to run down the hill and form a shallow moat on the inside of the wall. There were only a few inches of water on the floor of the station, and the steady cascade pouring out of the transmitter, the echo of the water that had just been transmitted to Mars. A chilly breeze stirred their clothing, originating in the transmitting chamber of the air pump.

"Now," Bridie said briskly, "we shall just have to hope that we can discover to which of the Posts they're transmitting at any given moment. Follow the technicians about and see what they do. I'll look over the equipment meanwhile."

Within five minutes they had found the switch marked CJ that controlled air transmissions. They observed two full cycles of transmission, as the stream of air was routed to each of the Command Posts in turn. There was an interval between transmissions averaging five seconds. Only during this time would it be safe for Hansard to enter the transmitting chamber; a little earlier or a little later, and he would be transmitted piecemeal to Mars as Worsaw had been.

"It's not enough time," Bridie said unhappily.

"It's enough time," said Hansard.

They took turns blowing up the air mattress which was to serve as his cushion inside the transmission chamber. The cushion was not for the sake of comfort, but to prevent, as much as possible, any part of Hansard from projecting through the "floor" of the chamber and being left behind.

Hansard began to strap on the breathing equipment that had been stored on the underside of Panofsky's wheelchair. There would not be sub-two air on Mars, so he would have to bring his own supply. He pulled the flimsy-looking, clear plastic mask down over his head, sealed it about his neck, and opened the valve controlling oxygen input.

"Ready or not," he said, "here I come." Only after the words had left his lips did he realize that they had been an unconscious echo of his games of hide-and-seek with Bridgetta.

Bridie said something, but with the mask sealed over his head he could not hear her. She stepped directly before him and repeated the words, with exaggerated movements of her lips and appropriate gestures: "We . . . loVe . . . You."

Hansard nodded his head curtly. "Ditto," he whispered.

Bridie stood on tiptoe so she might kiss him. Their lips pressed against each other's through the thin film of plastic.

"Be . . . LucKy . . . CoMe . . . BacK."

He positioned himself before the transmitting chamber, and Bridie watched over the shoulder of the technician throwing switches. She nodded to Hansard, who carefully laid the rubber mattress on the bottom of the chamber, then sliding in through the thin metal wall spread himself out flat upon it in the darkness. In almost the same instant the mattress popped and the air rushed out. "Hell!" Hansard said aloud, but it was too late to turn back now. At almost any moment the switch would be thrown that would send him to Mars.

It was taking too long. He remembered the last time he had gone through a transmitter: the long wait, the hand coming through the door of the vault . . .

Then he realized that he was there, that the mattress had popped at the moment of transmission. Some part of it had been pushed down through the floor of the chamber, outside the field of transmission. It was fortunate for Hansard that it had been the mattress that had thus inadvertently punctured and not his gas mask.

He rose to his feet and walked forward in the darkness of the receiving chamber. He came to a wall and passed through it. There, not ten feet away, drinking coffee with General Pittmann, was Nathan Hansard, Captain in the United States Army. No man had ever seemed more strange to Hansard than he.

The mattress popped and the air rushed out. "Hell!" Hansard said aloud, but it was too late to turn back now. Then his sub-three flesh, too insubstantial to be supported by the "skin" of energy of the sub-one world (Mars, not Earth, since this transmitter, unlike the Camp Jackson manmitter, transmitted continuously, re-echoing endlessly the echoes thrown back by transmission) began to sink slowly into the ground. Realizing the hopelessness of his situation, Hansard-Sub-Three turned off the oxygen input valve.

An infinite series of Nathan Hansards, echoes of echoes, made the same decision, and each died clinging to the same hope: "I hope he makes it."

Chapter 16

THE CHORD

"You're not looking well, Nathan. Small wonder. I don't suppose I look very thriving myself."

As a matter of fact, though, that was just how one would have described General Pittmann at that moment: thriving. While Hansard had seemed to age a decade in these last weeks, the General's features had assumed a strange and unbecoming youthfulness, an effect exaggerated by an unaccustomed looseness in his manner. His tie was knotted lopsidedly, and his collar unbuttoned. His hair needed trimming and his shoes were scuffed. There was a lightness in his step, a nervousness in his gestures, a quickness in his speech, that had not been customary to him these many years. Just so, the weather of an October afternoon can sometimes be mistaken for spring.

Hansard looked down at the rainbow-banded swirls of oil coating his coffee. With great effort he moved his lips to say, "No sir."

"Perhaps you're not getting enough vitamins. I notice that you've been missing meals. We should always take care of our health. Good health is our most precious possession."

Hansard couldn't decide if the General was taunting him with these banalities, or if he really did have so little sense of their inappropriateness.

"Now if I were Julius Caesar, I would be wary of someone with that 'lean and hungry look' of yours."

A joke seemed to be called for, so Hansard roused himself to make an attempt. "I'd lose that look fast enough, if you could get us something to eat besides these everlasting frozen dinners."

Pittmann's laughter was out of proportion to the joke. He indulged himself in a short diatribe against Army food. It was quite funny. Despite himself Hansard had to smile. Since it had become evident, two weeks before, that the order was not going to be countermanded neither man had mentioned the bombs.

Hansard$_2$ regarded himself with something approaching horror. That wan smile, those furtive eyes returning ever and again to the coffee cup, the pallor and inertness of his flesh, and—overwhelmingly—his *falseness*. For though he could not understand what words Hansard$_1$ was speaking, he knew, beyond all doubting, that they were lies.

At 2130 hours Hansard$_1$ finished his coffee and went out into the corridor, Hansard$_2$ following, where he strolled idly and ill at ease. Hansard$_2$ experienced another moment of uncanniness when he passed, on his way out of the toilet, Worsaw, who, when he saw that Hansard$_1$ could no more see him, sneered and muttered a silent obscenity that one did not need to be a lipreader to interpret. How strange it seemed that this man, resenting him as deeply as he did, should yet be subservient to him here. How had society so been ordered that all mankind should accept the invisible restraints of custom—Hansard no less than Worsaw?

For it was evident that Hansard$_1$ for no more compelling reason than because it was expected of him, was prepared to assist at the annihilation of humanity, in violation of everything he knew to be moral. It was a paltry consolation to realize that a million others could have been found as pliable as he.

Eventually Hansard$_1$ went into his own small room, which, despite some few shards of blond wood tentatively posing as furniture, seemed less a habitation than a branch of the corridor that came here to a dead end. Instead of preparing for sleep, Hansard$_1$ took a book from the wall locker and began reading.

It was the Bible. Hansard had not looked into a Bible since he'd prepared for Confirmation a quarter-century before. This nervous, morose stranger seemed to bear less and less relationship with anyone Hansard$_2$ could recognize as himself.

It had seemed worth a try. Wasn't religion intended for just such times as this, when all reasonable hopes were daunted? Though I walk through the valley of the shadow of death, and all that.

But it wasn't working. For one thing, there was just so much of it, and none that he had found—neither prophets nor apostles nor yet the faded image of Christ, who seemed to live for Hansard, in a landscape of calendar art—seemed quite to the purpose. Here on death's brink he found it as hard to believe in the Ressurrection and the Life as he had at the age of fourteen, when, for his parents' sake (and had *they* really cared so much themselves?), he had been confirmed.

No, he had found no consolation here, but he did (as one will torment oneself by probing at a rotten tooth) take a kind of perverse pleasure in reading just those passages—in *Job,* in *Ecclesiastes,* in *Jeremiah*—that strengthened and confirmed his unbelief:

Then said I in my heart, As it happeneth to the fool, so it happeneth even to me; and why was I then more wise? Then I said in my heart, that this also is vanity.

For there is no remembrance of the wise more than of the fool for ever; seeing that which now is in the days to come shall all be forgotten. And how dieth the wise man? as the fool.

Therefore I hated life; because the work that is wrought under the sun is grievous unto me; for all is vanity and vexation of spirit.

In sleep the complex melodies of conscious thought would be dampened; there would be only the simple C of Hansard$_1$'s sleeping mind, and, an octave below, the C of Hansard$_2$. Such, at least, had been his hope. But he was impatient.

Now, he thought, *it may be possible . . .*

Carefully he lowered his frame into the seated body of Hansard$_1$. A curious and not quite pleasant sensation to feel his two legs, real and ghostly, slipping into alignment, to feel his breath stop for a moment and then return, synchronized with the breathing of Hansard$_1$. His vision blurred, and then, when it was restored, he found his eyes moving over the printed page, not reading, only seeing the print skitter past.

He concentrated on the meaning of the text and tried to bend his mind to the emotional state that he supposed must be Hansard$_1$'s. But though he could feel his larynx vibrating with the same subvocalized soundpatterns, the two minds maintained their distinct identities. Sometimes he would feel a memory stirring with strange autonomy, or he would feel, fleetingly, the most inexpressible sadness, but it was with these moments, as with night-vision, that whenever he tried to concentrate upon them they would retire into the obscurity whence they had come.

Reluctantly he disengaged himself from Hansard$_1$. It was no good. He would have to wait till he went to sleep.

Hansard could not sleep. Since he had made the Mars jump he had been taking heavier and heavier dosages of barbiturates. They no longer helped. He lay on his bunk in the darkness, remembering how, as a child, in another darkness, he had lain awake so, trying by sheer power of imagination to place himself outside his slum-suburban bedroom, far far off, on Mars perhaps; whispering—*If I pretend hard enough it will come true.*

And so it had, and so it had.

Now where? Now, what worlds could he wish himself away to? Madness perhaps—such a madness as seemed to have possessed Pittmann. Or sleep? But he remembered a tag from Shakespeare: To sleep, perchance to dream—aye, there's the rub.

He elbowed himself out of bed, smoothed the wrinkles out of his shirt, and went out into the corridor. Now where?

In the observatory he looked at the dead rocks of Mars. In his youth, he had been so sure that Mars had been teeming with life. Even when the first Mariner pictures had come back (he'd been thirteen) he refused to believe them. Nobody believes, at that age, that there can be such a thing as death.

Though the clocks inside the Command Post gave the time as only a bit after midnight, it was a bright, chiaroscuro morning outside. It hurt one's eyes to look too long upon it.

Sleep, you bastard, sleep! Hansard$_2$ thought angrily. He did not dare cease pacing the floor of the observatory, for he was himself so tired (having kept himself awake throughout the previous night just so that he would not be insomniac himself) as to be in danger of dropping off to sleep if he let himself sit down anywhere. Hansard$_1$, meanwhile, sat staring at the Mars noonday. What in that barren waste absorbed him so?

At length Hansard$_1$ did return to his room and lay down again, without undressing. In the utter darkness Hansard$_2$ had no way to know if his double had fallen asleep except by entering his body.

This time Hansard₁'s eyes were closed. His jaw relaxed, his mouth opened slightly, his lungs drew deeper breaths of air. His fist unclenched, and he accepted the case of ammunition that was handed to him. They were going hunting. "For what?" he asked, but the grownups went on chattering in their shrill buzzsaw voices, ignoring him. He walked through fields of sharp black rocks, stirring up swarms of buzzing flies with every step. The ammunition case was so heavy and he was so little—it wasn't fair! It was surprising how few people there were on Mars. He supposed they must all be locked up underground or somewhere. Why couldn't he carry the gun instead? But he was. He was all alone with the gun, in that burnt-over landscape. The ashes got into his eyes so that he almost had to cry. He walked toward the flame that burned at the horizon, holding the rifle on the ready. The man was shooting fire from a plastic garden hose, burning the rice, and so he planted the butt of the rifle into the ground, because he was too little shoot it any other way. He looked at the man with the garden hose, in his strange uniform. No man had ever seemed more hateful to Hansard than he. The man Hansard turned the flame thrower on the boy Hansard, and they woke, both of them, screaming a single scream.

"It wasn't right," he said, astonished that it had taken himself so long to learn what, as soon as it had been spoken, seemed so self-evident.

And then, from another and not quite familiar (as though, waking, he continued to dream) part of his mind. "It *isn't* right."

He shook his head sadly. Right or wrong, there was nothing *he* could do about it.

"But there *is*," the dream-voice insisted. The voice was his own and not his own. He relaxed and let himself smile. It was such a relief to have gone mad. It would be interesting to see what he did now. "Listen," said the voice, his own and not his own, and he listened.

Chapter 17

THE CATACLYSM

"Good morning, Nathan! You seem to have recovered your appetite."

"Yes, and then some. No matter how much I seem to eat this morning, my stomach still feels hollow as a drum. Can you beat that?"

"—and your good humor too. Welcome back to civilization. We've missed you."

"Just in the nick of time, eh?"

Pittmann regarded his subordinate uncertainly: had this been said in jest? He decided it had been, but limited his show of appreciation to the barest smile.

"And you already have the coffee perking."

"I'm afraid I made it a little strong."

General Pittmann poured himself a cupful from the electric percolator and sipped the hot coffee appraisingly. "Yes, just a bit." It was a choice between making do with this and waiting for another pot. He made do.

"I've been thinking . . ." Hansard said.

"We try to discourage thinking in the Army," Pittmann said placidly, as he pried apart two slices of frozen bread and put them into the toaster.

". . . about what you said the day I arrived here. I think you were right."

"I wouldn't be surprised." He grimaced over a second mouthful of the coffee. "But you'll have to refresh my memory, Nathan. I say so many right things."

"That it's genocidal to use the bombs."

"Did I say that? Surely only in the most hypothetical way, if I did. For my own part, I have little but contempt for people who warm their consciences over such words—and over that word especially. You can't win a war, you know, without making omelettes." Pleased with his timing, Pittmann cracked two eggs neatly into the electric skillet. "So I hope you're not taking such talk *too* seriously. At your age it isn't becoming to be that deadly earnest."

"But if the word has any meaning at all—"

"Exactly, Nathan: it has none. It's a red flag to wave at liberals."

"There is the classic example."

"Yes?" General Pittmann looked up, inviting—or daring—Hansard to continue. An impish grin played at the corner of his lips. "The example of Germany, you mean? Why do you bring up a subject if you then refuse to talk about it? Auschwitz was ill-advised, certainly. A terrible waste of manpower. Not to mention the prejudice involved. That is what *I* find most offensive. But nowadays prejudice doesn't enter into it. The bomb is the most democratic weapon man has ever devised. It draws absolutely no distinctions. You make lousy coffee, Nathan."

"You make filthy jokes, General."

"That borders on impertinence, you know. But I'll overlook that for the sake of having you making conversation again."

"It will taste better if you put milk and sugar in it."

"A barbaric custom," Pittmann complained, but he followed Hansard's advice.

"Since when have you let considerations like that stand in your way?"

Pittmann laughed in good earnest. "Better, much better. You see, it's all in having a delicate touch. Would you like a piece of toast? Isn't life . . ." He scarcely seemed to pay attention to the knife that slipped out of his fingers and clattered on the floor. ". . . a terrible waste of manpower?" He laughed weakly.

"Oh, put that gun away, Nathan! What do you think I'm going to do—attack you with a butter knife? I'm too weak to . . ." He closed his eyes. ". . . to finish sentences. It won't do you any good, Nathan, this noble gesture of yours. If you'd waited till the last minute, perhaps you might have prevented me—but then, this is only one post. What of the other? What of Russia? Foolish Nathan."

"Why did you poison me?"

Hansard stared at the General coldly. Pittmann had very delicately balanced himself in the spindly tubular chair so that he could not fall out of it when he was unconscious.

"I always wondered, you know . . . I always wondered what it would be like to die. I like it." He fell asleep, smiling

Hansard chuckled. He knew Pittmann would be mortified when he woke up next day. There had been nothing but Army-issue barbiturates in the coffee, which were guaranteed non-lethal in any quantity. Hansard left the Officers' Mess, locking the door behind him.

He returned to his cabin to work on what Panofsky had promised would be "a trifle of rewiring." The adjustments that had to be made in the standard transmitter elements that Hansard had rifled from storage taxed his manual abilities to the limit, but he had had the advantage of having performed the same task only hours before under Panofsky's superintendence. It was exasperating just now, at the moment of highest crisis, to have to work electronic jigsaw puzzles, but it was possible. He needn't even feel rushed. Indeed, with so much at stake, he did not dare to.

When all the assemblies were put together and they'd been checked and rechecked, Hansard fitted them into two overnight bags —all but the essential "fix." This he hid in the observatory ventilation shaft.

As fate would have it, it was Worsaw whom he found on duty before the entrance to the manmitter.

"Private Worsaw, the General asked me to tell you to report to him on the double in the observatory."

"Sir?" Worsaw looked doubtful. It was not likely Pittmann would be interested in seeing *him*.

"I shall stand duty for you here, of course. Better not keep him waiting. I suspect his request has something to do with those chevrons missing from your sleeves." Hansard winked, a friendly conspirator's wink.

Worsaw saluted briskly and took his leave. *Poor fool,* Hansard thought. *He too walks out of my life smiling.* He was happy that he had not been required once again—and this time definitively—to kill Worsaw. He never wanted to kill anyone again.

Hansard entered the manmitter with the key he had taken from Pittmann. After taking out the first of the devices he would need, he depressed the button that operated the manmitter. The letters stenciled on the steel wall flickered from MARS to EARTH. He was home again, but there was no time to kiss the Terran ground. His arrival would not have been unannounced; neither would it be welcome.

He looked at his watch. 2:18 p.m. He had, he estimated, another three minutes. He had found that he could hold his breath no longer than that. He made the last connections in the receiverless transmitter just as the door of the receiver sprang open and the guards burst in.

They opened fire on the man who was no longer there.

"Receiverless transmitters?" Hansard had objected, when first Panofsky had outlined his plan. "But you've said yourself that such a thing isn't possible. And it doesn't make *sense*."

"Sense!" Panofsky jeered. "What is sense? Does gravity make sense? Do wavicles? Does the Blessed Trinity? God glories in paradoxes more than in syllogisms. But I was quite sincere in what I told you: strictly speaking, a receiverless transmitter isn't possible. The receiver has to be where you want your bundles transmitted. Why not send it along *with* them?"

"Yes, and why don't I lift myself up by my bootstraps?" Hansard replied sourly.

"The heart of the matter," Panofsky continued imperturbably, "lies in that word 'instantaneous.' If matter transmission is truly instantaneous, and not just very very fast, like light, then at the exact instant of transmission, where is the object we're transmitting? Is it here, or is it there? And the answer, of course, is that it is both here and there. And thus—the receiverless transmitter, so-called. We just attach a set of three transmitters and three receivers to the object, posit the transmitters as being *here* and the receivers as being *there,* press the button, and *poof!* You see?"

Hansard shook his head glumly.

"But you've already seen it *work!* You traveled all over the house in it."

"Oh, I know it happened. But the state I'm in now, you could as easily convince me that it's magic that makes it work as the laws of nature. That's what it is—even down to the magic number three."

"Numbers *are* magic, of course, and none more so than three. But there is also a reason for that number. Three points establish a plane. It is the hypothetical plane that those three receivers define by which we can place the transmitted object at exactly that point in space where we wish it to be."

"Even I can call your bluff on that one, Doctor. It takes four points to define an object's position in space. Three will determine a plane, but for a solid body you need four. That's simple Euclidean geometry."

"And you'll get a good grade in that subject. In fact, there does have to be a fourth transmitter-receiver for the whole thing to work at all. And the fourth one doesn't travel along with the others. It stays behind and serves as the point of reference. The 'here' posit of the transmitter and the 'there' posit of the receiver can be considered to form two immense pyramids sharing a common apex at the 'fix' point."

"And where will my fix be?"

"On Mars, of course. Where else could it be?"

Naturally enough, the first point for which Panofsky had been able to obtain exact information concerning longitude, latitude, and altitude had been his own residence, and it was there, in the library, that Hansard came first after leaving Camp Jackson/Virginia. Panofsky and Bridgetta being away in Moscow, Hansard was conveniently alone. He placed the first transmitter-receiver at the agreed upon location behind the uniform edition of Bulwer-Lytton. Then, taking up the two bags with the rest of the equipment, he set off once again, a comfortable thirty seconds ahead of schedule.

It had been more difficult to find sufficiently detailed information concerning two other locations. The data on the Great Pyramid of Egypt Panofsky had discovered in a back number of *The Journal of Theosophical Science*.

Hansard arrived at the apex of the Great Pyramid at night. He had never seen a desert from such a height under moonlight before, and despite the urgency of his task, he had to pause to gaze down at the scene with awe. Someone—perhaps a tourist—glimpsed Hansard's silhouette against the moon and began shouting at him. The night wind carried his words off, and Hansard caught only scattered wisps of sound, not enough even to tell what language the man was speaking, much less his meaning. Hansard left the second of the transmitter-receivers atop the crumbling stone and moved on to the third, and last, point of the triangulation.

He found himself in the midst of a vast concrete expanse from which there projected, at wide intervals, the small knobs of the headstones. This was the eighty acres of the Viet Nam War-Dead Memorial erected outside Canberra by the new liberal government that had taken Australia out of the war. With a magnanimity unparalleled in history, the government had here commemorated the enemy's dead in equal number with its own.

Hansard set the last receiver-transmitter upon one of the headstones. Only one minute twenty-three seconds had passed since he'd made the first jump from Camp Jackson/Virginia. There was time, some few seconds, for reverence.

"It was wrong," Hansard said with great definiteness.

And, though he did not go on to say so, the wrong was irretrievable. The boy was dead forever. This very headstone might mark his grave.

That was all the time he could allow for reverence. He pressed down the button of the third transmitter-receiver. A delayed-action mechanism provided him with fifteen seconds' grace. He unzipped the second of the two bags and took out the neutralizer. It had an effective range of six feet.

"You'd better go now," he said to himself. It was Hansard$_2$ who said this, but there was no reply from Hansard$_1$.

Only then did Hansard$_2$ realize that he had been deceived all this while, that in an inviolable part of his mind Hansard$_1$ had formed his intention and kept it secret from his other self. It was too late to argue with him, for suddenly the ground under Hansard$_2$'s feet became solid, and he knew that the Earth had just been turned upside-down on its axis and transmitted to the other side of the solar system.

"Impossible!" Hansard had said. "And if it *could* be done, it would be a madness worse than the bombs."

"Fudge, Nathan! Haven't you learned yet that I'm always right?"

"What will become of all the people in the Real World? You should think of their welfare before you consider ours."

"The chief immediate consequence for them will be that people in the Northern Hemisphere will suddenly see the constellations usual to southern skies. There will, in consequence, probably be more than a few shipwrecks on the night-side of Earth. A small enough price to pay, considering the alternative."

"But how is it that this is to prevent the bombs? They'll be coming from Mars to their receiver-satellites in any case."

"But the receiver-satellites will lie outside the Earth's field of transmission. Earth-Sub-One will cross the solar system and leave the satellites behind."

"So they can drop their bombs on Earth-Sub-Two?"

"You forget that for anything constituted of primary matter, secondary matter seems not to exist. From the point of view of those bombs, Earth will seem to have disappeared. Moreover, they will cease to be satellites, since the echo of Earth remaining behind has no gravitational grip on them. They'll fly off tangent to their orbits and eventually be dragged down into the sun." Panofsky grinned. "Imagine, though, what your people on Mars will think when the Earth suddenly disappears from the sky! Will they blame it on the Russians?"

Hansard was not ready to make jokes on the subject. "But . . . the magnitude of it! The whole damn Earth!"

"Is that meant to be an objection? Great magnitudes often simplify an operation. Clock towers were built before wrist watches, and the solar system has often been called a celestial timepiece. Consider that in transmitting the Earth I waste none of its momentum. Placed properly and pointed in the right direction, it should proceed in its immemorial orbit about the sun without a hairsbreadth of wobble. I can't guarantee quite *that* exactitude, but my calculations show that nothing too terrible should result."

"And turning it upside-down?"

"To conserve the order of the seasons, which as you certainly should know are caused by the Earth's position along its orbit about the sun. In effect, I am advancing the Earth six months through time. Turning it topsy-turvy will compensate for that exactly."

There was no air for him to breathe.

You fool! Hansard$_2$ thought angrily. *Why did you stay inside the field of neutralization? Why?*

What difference, now? There was a sadness in the tone of the reply that Hansard$_2$ could not believe to be his own. The six weeks they had lived apart, had, after all, made them different men.

Do you suppose you're even *now? Do you think your lost life can make up for his? Fool!*

Not for his sake, no.

Then why? Why? What of Bridgetta?

Hansard$_1$ did not, or could not, reply. Perhaps for him, there would not have been a Bridgetta. Reluctantly, Hansard$_2$ disengaged his body from its sheath of fibers. The discarded and soon lifeless body did not sink to the ground (which was not ground for it) but slowly, ever so slowly, lifted into the air and drifted above the vast concrete field like a helium balloon, withered, at the end of a long day. The gravitational pull of the newly-created Earth$_2$ had no effect upon the primary matter of that body, and it was being pulled inexorably toward the Real Moon, low in the West, hidden behind clouds.

The moon, in turn, had begun its slow plunge toward the sun. There was no longer any force to hold it in place.

A residue at the back of Hansard$_2$'s mind told him why his sub-one self had gone willingly to his own death: he was ashamed of having, to his way of thinking, been guilty of that most heinous of crimes—mutiny.

Hansard$_2$ removed the breathing equipment he had been wearing since the night before. He did not need it, for now he had a world of air to breathe again, a world of ground to walk upon, and a world of men to give meaning to his own manhood. This, the echo of a world, was his Real World now.

And there would not be a war to destroy it.

Chapter 18

THE HAPPY ENDING

Hansard's taxi came to a stop outside the new St. George, a hotel that in the ordinary scheme of things he would not have been able to afford. He asked the man at the desk the number of Panofsky's suite. It was, perhaps not wholly by chance, the same that Hansard had occupied invisibly forty days before. He found the two Panofskys alone.

"Nathan! How good to see you, Nathan!" They drove their wheel-chairs toward him with one accord, braking just short of a collision.

"I was afraid," said the Panofsky in the skull cap, "that I would have to leave without seeing you."

"He's off to Rome, you know," the other Panofsky explained, "to see the Pope. For the time being, anyone who travels via transmitter is under Vatican interdict, so Bernard will fly. You flew yourself, didn't you, Nathan?" Hansard nodded. "But it took you such a long time!"

"The Egyptian emigration authorities were just a little upset to find me in their country. And then, when the moon began to disappear . . ."

"Ooof, the moon! I am so stupid, I deserve not to live. A kick in the pants I deserve."

Hansard was skeptical. "You can't mean that you actually *overlooked* that this would happen? That you thought of everything but that?"

The two Panofskys exchanged a guilty look. "Such at least," the first said mildly, "we have given the government to believe."

"But let's not speak of it, for though the government is treating us a little more civilly now, this room is surely bugged. Tell me, Nathan—do you think the end justifies the means? Once in a while perhaps? It is true that without the moon there will be no tides, either here or on Earth-Sub-One, the ocean currents will become confused, there will be terrible disasters, yes—disorders, tragedies. But on the other hand, there has not been a war. Besides, I have a plan in readiness—it is being explained now to the Russians—for recovering the moon. But you had better explain it to Nathan, Bernard, for I'm late for my plane. Is there anything I can do for you in Rome, Nathan? Arrange a wedding, perhaps, at St. John Lateran?"

"Off to His Holiness, busybody. You know the Captain dislikes to be nudged."

"The moon," he continued, when his double had departed, "is this moment populated by a number of very perplexed, not to say frantic, scientists, Russians, none of whom have an inkling of what is happening to the solar system. Similarly, on Earth-Sub-One, no one will have any notion of what's going on—no one but myself, Panofsky-Sub-One, and even he may be upset to think that someone else has, all unknown to him, developed a receiverless transmitter and put it to such apocalyptic use. Here, meanwhile, I have been explaining—to the President, to committees of every kind, finally even to the Press—what has been done, and why, and though they are all very outraged I think they are secretly glad—like a matador waking in a hospital, amazed at still being alive after his excesses of courage. They have listened to me, and a few have understood. Those who didn't understand believed. So—this is what is being done—a number of our military and scientific personnel have been transmitted to Earth-Sub-One, and there they will try to do what you did—to reintegrate with their sub-one selves. When any one of them has accomplished this, he will use a receiverless transmitter to travel to the moon, dealing with that body as you dealt with the Earth. The moon-sub-one will be returned to its proper orbit, leaving behind a sub-two echo, which can then be returned to *its* proper orbit, leaving behind a sub-three moon, which sad to say will have to fall into the sun. Unless its sub-three inhabitants, still equipped with receiverless transmitters, decide to take it somewhere else. And why shouldn't they? While their stores last they can travel anywhere in the universe. Perhaps that moon will be the first interstellar voyageur. It is all very complicated, isn't it? If you'd like to take a bath, our suite has three *huge* bathtubs. I always find a bath helps when things become too complicated."

"Thank you, not a bath. But I had hoped . . ."

"Of course, Nathan! Of course she is here. Enter! enter, Bridgetta!"

She rode in on ripples of laughter. He did not know which Bridgetta she was, Bridie, Jet, Bridget, any other, it made no difference, they were but a single woman, whom he loved, and he embraced her, saying, "Darling," and they kissed, a kiss that was like laughing still.

"Professor Panofsky," said Hansard stiffly (though there was a kind of grace in his stiffness now that had not been there before), "I would like to ask for the hand of your wife Bridgetta in marriage."

"You have my blessings, both of you, but first you had better come to an understanding with your rivals."

"No," Hansard said, "this time it is for *her* to decide how she wants to dispose of *me.*"

"Not Bridgetta's rivals, Nathan—yours." And with a flourish of laughter, of music, the two Nathan Hansards who had been waiting in the adjoining room entered, arm-in-arm with two more Bridgettas. They arranged themselves before him with the modest symmetry of a Mozart finale. He had known they would be here, he had known it these many days (since, after all, he was not the final, the Australian Hansard$_2$ but the penultimate Hansard$_2$ who had remained behind after the transmission to Canberra, an echo, atop the Great Pyramid), and yet he had not till now believed it. He grasped each of their extended hands in his own, and they stood there so a little while, as though about to begin a children's ring-game.

And here *we* are, quite at the end of our story—or very close to the end. Our hero is to be rewarded for his labors, the world is saved from annihilation, even the moon has been recovered, and Panofsky, for the first time in his life, is free. Now is the loveliest of June weathers, though (it is true) one has to go outside the dome to appreciate the young summer in all its glory. Now is the perfect time to take a boat out on the river or just go walking along country roads, though these (it is true) become harder and harder to find.

But perhaps for our hero it will not be hard at all. Love bathes all landscapes in a softening light. It is only ourselves, at our greater distance, with our cooler view, who may feel a little sad to think that the world's loveliness will not always and everywhere bear too close examination.

But even that is changing! Even the world will change now and become a better world, milder and mightier, and more humane. There will be power, and power to spare, to do all the things that were so hard to do till now. There will be no more boundaries but instead everywhere freedom and unconstraint. There will be no more war. There will be room to move about in, places to go, destinies—all the universe, in fact. What a splendid world! and what grand fun it would be to live there!

But it is too late, for we are now quite at the end of *our* story. The rest belongs to them.

It had been a wedding in the grand manner—cascades of white laces, orange blossoms, organ music, a minister with the broadest, the stateliest, of *A*'s—and now they stood, Hansard and Bridgetta and Hansard and Bridgetta and Hansard and Bridgetta, on the threshold of the transmitter. Each couple had chosen a different destination for their honeymoon—the first to Ceylon, the second a cruise up the Amazon, and the third—

"Are you ready?" Panofsky asked.

In reply Hansard lifted up his bride and carried her over the threshold. Panofsky pushed the button that would transmit them to the Vatican. Hansard had never before seen the Sistine Chapel. He gasped.

Hansard sighed, "It doesn't seem to be working, does it?"

Bridgetta laughed softly, without stopping to nibble at his ear.

He carried her back across the threshold, through the closed door. Hansard and Bridgetta and Hansard and Bridgetta were waiting for them outside the transmitter. They pointed to Panofsky, who was writing on a notepad on the worktable. Panofsky finished the note, turned, smiled, though it could not be said he smiled quite at them, and left the room.

Unthinkingly, Hansard tried to pick the piece of paper off the table. The tertiary flesh of his hand passed through the secondary matter.

It was now as it had been: the pumps that had been pumping air to Mars were pumping still, though they pumped air of second-degree reality, which left behind the echo of an echo, and this air the six lovers, themselves the echoes of their echoes, could breathe.

"What does it say?" asked Bridgetta, though she could read the note as well as Hansard. But she wanted to hear him say the words:

"Happy Honeymoon."

THE
GENOCIDES

To Alan Iverson

CONTENTS

The harvest is past, the summer is ended, and we are not saved

Jeremiah 8.20

THE END OF THE SPECIES:

The further process of incineration is expected to proceed less rapidly now that this, the last of the chief artifacts, has been levelled and sown. The remaining artifacts are small and widely spaced. Though our sample has shown that most of these are no longer inhabited, we will, pursuant to instructions of 4 July 1979, effect their entire incineration.

Estimated completion of project:
2 February 1980.

Chapter 1

THE PRODIGAL

As the lesser and then the greater stars disappeared in the advancing light, the towering mass of the forest that walled in the cornfield retained for a while the utter blackness of the night. A light breeze blew in from the lake, rustling the leaves of the young corn, but the leaves of that dark forest did not stir. Now the eastern forest wall glowed gray-green, and the three men waiting in the field knew, though they could not yet see it, that the sun was up.

Anderson spat—the day's work had officially begun. He began to make his way up the gentle incline toward the eastern forest wall. Four rows away on either side of him, his sons followed—Neil, the younger and larger, on his right hand, and Buddy on the left.

Each man carried two empty wooden buckets. None wore either shoes or shirts, for it was midsummer. Their denims were in tatters. Anderson and Buddy had on wide-brimmed hats woven of crude raffia, like the coolie hats you used to get at carnivals and state fairs. Neil had sunglasses but no hat. They were old; the bridge had been broken and mended with glue and a strip of that same fiber from which the hats had been made. His nose was calloused where the glasses rested.

Buddy was the last to reach the top of the hill. His father smiled while he waited for him to catch up. Anderson's smile was never a good sign.

"You're sore from yesterday?"

"I'm fine. The stiffness comes out when I get working."

Neil laughed. "Buddy's sore because he *has* to work. Ain't that so, Buddy?"

It was a joke. But Anderson, whose style it was to be laconic, never laughed at jokes, and Buddy rarely found very funny the jokes his half-brother made.

"Don't you get it?" Neil asked. *"Sore.* Buddy's *sore* because he has to work."

"We all have to work," Anderson said, and that pretty well ended what joke there had been.

They began to work.

Buddy withdrew a plug from his tree and inserted a metal tube where the plug had been. Below the makeshift spigot he hung one of the buckets. Pulling the plugs was hard work, for they had been in place a week and had stuck fast. The sap, drying about the plug, acted as a glue. This work seemed always to last just long enough for the soreness—of his fingers, his wrists, his arms, his back—to reassert itelf, but never to abate.

Before the terrible work of carrying the buckets began, Buddy stopped and stared at the sap trickling through the pipe and oozing, like lime-green honey, into the bucket. It was coming out slowly today. By the end of the summer this tree would be dying and ready to be cut down.

Seen up close, it didn't seem much like a tree at all. Its skin was smooth, like the stem of a flower. A proper tree this size would have split through its skin under the pressure of its own growth, and its trunk would be rough with bark. Farther back in the forest, you could find trees, big ones, which had reached the limit of their growth and begun at last to form something like bark. At least their trunks, though green, weren't moist to the touch like this one. Those trees—or Plants, as Anderson called them—were six hundred feet tall, and their biggest leaves were the size of billboards. Here on the edge of the cornfield the growth was more recent—not more than two years—and the highest stood only a hundred and fifty feet tall. Even so, here as deeper in the forest, the sun came through the foliage at noonday as pale as moonlight on a clouded night.

"Get the lead out!" Anderson called. He was already out in the field with his full buckets of sap, and the sap was brimming over Buddy's buckets too. *Why is there never time to think?* Buddy envied Neil's mulish capacity just to *do* things, to spin the wheel of his cage without wondering overmuch how it worked.

"Right away!" Neil yelled from a distance.

"Right away!" Buddy echoed, thankful his half-brother too had been caught up in his own thoughts, whatever they could be.

Of the three men working in the field, Neil surely had the best body. Except for a receding chin that gave a false impression of weakness, he was strong and well proportioned. He was a good six inches taller than his father or Buddy, both short men. His shoulders were broader, his chest thicker, and his muscles, though not so well knit as Anderson's, were bigger. There was, however, no economy in his movements. When he walked, he lumbered. When he stood, he slouched. He endured the strain of the day's labor better than Buddy simply because he had more material to endure with. In this he was brutish, but worse than being brutish Neil was dumb, and worse than being dumb, he was mean.

He is mean, Buddy thought, *and he is dangerous.* Buddy set off down the row of corn, a full bucket of sap in either hand and his heart brimming with ill-will. It gave him a sort of strength, and he needed all the strength he could muster, from whatever source. His breakfast had been light, and lunch, he knew, wouldn't be quite enough, and there'd be no dinner to speak of.

Even hunger, he had learned, provided its own kind of strength: the will to wrest more food from the soil and more soil from the Plants.

No matter how much care he took, the sap splattered his pants legs as he walked, and the tattered fabric stuck to his calf. Later, when the day was hotter, his whole body would be covered with sap. The sap would bake dry, and when he moved, the stiffened cloth would tear out the crusted hairs of his body, one by one. The worst of that was over now, thank heaven—the body has a finite number of hairs—but there were still the flies that swarmed over his flesh to feed on the sap. He hated the flies, which did not seem to be finite.

When he had reached the foot of the decline and was in the middle of the field, Buddy set one bucket down and began to feed the thirsty young plants from the other. Each plant received about a pound of thick green nutrient—and to good effect. It wasn't the Fourth yet, and already many plants were up over his knees. Corn would have grown well in the rich lake-bottom soil in any case, but with the additional nourishment they drew from the stolen sap, the plants throve phenomenally—as though they were in central Iowa instead of northern Minnesota. This unwitting parasitism of the corn served another purpose besides, for as the corn throve, the Plants whose sap they had drunk died, and each year the limit of the field could be pushed a bit farther.

It had been Anderson's idea to pit the Plant against itself this way, and every corn plant in the field was a testimony to his judgment. Looking down the long rows, the old man felt like a prophet in full view of his prophecy. His regret now was that he hadn't thought of it sooner—before the diaspora of his village, before the Plants had vanquished his and his neighbors' farms.

If only . . .

But that was history, water under the bridge, spilt milk, and as such it belonged to a winter evening in the commonroom when there was time for idle regrets. Now, and for the rest of that long day, there was work to do.

Anderson looked about for his sons. They were straggling behind, still emptying their second buckets over the roots of the corn.

"Get the lead out!" he yelled. Then, turning back up the hill with his two buckets empty, he smiled a thin, joyless smile, the smile of a prophet, and spat out, through the gap between his front teeth, a thin stream of the juice of the Plant that he had been chewing.

He hated the Plants, and that hatred gave him strength.

They worked, sweating in the sun, till noonday. Buddy's legs were trembling from the strain and from hunger. But each trip down the rows of corn was shorter, and when he returned to the Plant there was a moment (and each a little longer than the last) before the buckets filled, when he could rest.

Sometimes, though he did not like the vaguely anise-like taste, he could stick his finger into the bucket and lick off the bittersweet syrup. It did not nourish, but it allayed for a while the worst of his hunger. He might have chewed the pulp carved from the phloem of the trunk, as his father and Neil did, but "chewing" reminded him of the life he had tried to escape ten years before, when he had left the farm for the city. His escape had failed, as surely as the cities themselves had failed. At last, just as in the parable, he would have been content with the husks the swine ate, and he had returned to Tassel and to his father's farm.

True to form, the fatted calf had been killed, and if his return had been a parable, it would have ended happily. But it was his life, and he was still, in his heart, a prodigal, and there were times when he wished he had died during the famine of the cities.

But in a contest between the belly's hunger and the mind's variable predilections, the belly is likelier to win. The prodigal's rebellion had been reduced to catch-words and petty crochets: an obstinate refusal to use the word *ain't,* an abiding contempt for country music, a distaste for "chewing," and a loathing for the hick, the hayseed, and the dumb cluck. In a word, for Neil.

The heat and his body's weariness conspired to direct his thoughts to less troubled channels, and as he stood gazing into the slowly filling buckets, his mind surged with the remembered images of other times. Of Babylon, that great city.

He remembered how at night the streets would be swift-flowing rivers of light and how the brilliant, antiseptic cars had streamed down those rivers. From hour to hour the sound would not abate nor the lights dim. There had been the drive-ins, and when there was less money, the White Castles. Girls in shorts waited on your car. Sometimes the shorts were edged with little, glittering fringes that bounced on tan thighs.

In the summer, when the hicks had worked on the farms, there had been flood-lit beaches, and his parched tongue curled now remembering how—in the labyrinth of empty oil drums supporting the diving raft—he would have kissed Irene. Or someone. The names didn't matter so much any more.

He made another trip down the row, and while he fed the corn he remembered the names that didn't matter now. Oh, the city had swarmed with girls. You could stand on a street corner, and in an hour hundreds would walk past. There had even been talk about a population problem then.

Hundreds of thousands of people!

He remembered the crowds in the winter in the heated auditorium on the university campus. He would have come there in a white shirt. The collar would be tight around his neck. In his imagination, he fingered the knot of a silk tie. Would it be striped or plain? He thought of the stores full of suits and jackets. Oh, the colors there had been! the music, and, afterward, the applause!

But the words of it, he thought, resting back at the Plant again, *is that there isn't anyone to talk to any more.* The total population of Tassel was two hundred and forty-seven, and none of them, not one of them, could understand Buddy Anderson. A world had been lost, and they weren't aware of it. It had never been their world, but it had been, briefly, Buddy's, and it had been beautiful.

The buckets were full, and Buddy grabbed hold of the handles and made his way back to the field. For the hundredth time that day, he stepped over the cankerous knob of tissue that had formed on the stump of the Plant that had irrigated these rows last year. This time his bare foot came down on a patch of the slick wood where there was a puddle of slippery sap. Weighted down by the buckets, he couldn't recover his balance. He fell backward, the sap in the buckets spilling out over him. He lay in the dirt, and the sap spread across his chest and down his arms, and the myriad flies settled to feed.

He didn't try to get up.

"Well, don't just *lay* there," Anderson said. "There's work to do." He stretched out a hand, kinder than his words, to help Buddy up.

When he thanked his father, there was a just-perceptible quaver in his voice.

"You all right?"

"I guess so." He felt his coccyx, which had struck against a knob of the stump, and winced.

"Then go down to the stream and wash that crap off. We're about ready to go and eat anyhow."

Buddy nodded. Grabbing the buckets (it was amazing how automatic the work had become, even for him), he set off down a forest path that led to the stream (once, farther inland, it had been Gooseberry River) from which the village drew its water. Seven years ago, this whole area—fields, forest and village—had been under ten to fifteen feet of water. But the Plants had siphoned off the water. They were still at it, and every day the North Shore of Lake Superior moved a few inches farther south, though the rate of its retreat seemed to be lessening, as all but the newest of the Plants reached the limits of their growth.

He stripped and lay down full length in the stream. The tepid water moved languidly over his bare limbs, washing away sap and dirt and the dead flies that had caught on him as on flypaper. He held his breath and lowered his head slowly into the flowing water until he was totally submerged.

With the water in his ears, he could hear slight sounds more distinctly: his back scratching against the pebbles in the bed of the stream, and, more distantly, another sound, a low rumbling that grew, too quickly, to a pounding. He knew the sound, and knew he shouldn't be hearing it now, here.

He lifted his head out of the water in time to see the cow running full-tilt toward him—and in time for her to see him. Gracie jumped, and her hind hooves came down within inches of his thigh. Then she ran on into the forest.

More followed. Buddy counted them as they splashed across the stream: eight . . . eleven . . . twelve. Seven Herefords and five Guernseys. All of them.

The yearning bellow of a bull sounded in the air, and Studs came into view—the village's great, brown Hereford, with his flaring white topknot. He stared at Buddy with casual defiance, but there was more urgent business than the settling of old scores. He hurried on after the cows.

That Studs had got out of his pen was bad news, for the cows were all of them half-gone with calves, and it would do them no good to be mounted by an eager bull. The news would be even worse for Neil, who was responsible for Studs. It could mean a whipping. This was not a thought to sadden Buddy deeply, but still he was concerned for the cattle. He hurried into his overalls, which were still sticky with sap.

Before he'd got the straps over his shoulders, Jimmie Lee, the younger of Buddy's two half-brothers, came running out of the forest on the bull's trail. His face was flushed with the excitement of the chase, and even as he announced the calamity—"Stud's broke out!" —a smile touched his lips.

All children—and Jimmie was no exception—feel a demonic sympathy with those things that cause disorder in the grown-up world. The young thrive on earthquakes, tornadoes and escaped bulls.

It would not do, Buddy realized, to let their father see that smile. For in Anderson the secret sympathy for the powers of destruction had been metamorphosed by the agency of time into a stern, humorless opposition to those same powers, a magnificent, raw willfulness as ruthless in its way as the enemy it opposed. Nothing could more surely elicit that ruthlessness than seeing this hectic flush in the cheeks of his youngest and (it was commonly supposed) dearest.

"I'll tell Father," Buddy said. "You go on after Studs. Where's everyone else?"

"Clay's getting together all the men he can find, and Lady and

Blossom and the women are going out to scare the cows away from the corn if they go that way." Jimmie shouted the information over his shoulder as he trotted along the broad trail blazed by the herd.

He was a good boy, Jimmie Lee, and bright as a button. In the old world, Buddy was sure, he would have become another prodigal. It was always the bright one who rebelled. Now he'd be lucky to survive. They all would.

The morning's work accomplished, Anderson looked across his field and saw that it was good. At harvest the ears would not be large and juicy, as in the old times. They had left the bags of hybridized seed mouldering in the abandoned storerooms of old Tassel. Hybrids gave the best yield, but they were sterile. Agriculture could no longer afford such fripperies. The variety he was using now was much closer hereditarily to the ancient Indian Maize, the Aztec *Zea mays*. His whole strategy against the usurping Plants was based on corn. Corn had become the life of his people: it was the bread they ate and the meat as well. In the summer Studs and his twelve wives might get along on the tender green roughage the children scraped from the sides of the Plants or they might graze among the seedlings along the lake shore, but when winter came corn sustained the cattle just as it sustained the villagers.

Corn took care of itself almost as well as it took care of the others. It did not need a ploughman to turn over the soil, only a sharp stick to scratch it and hands to drop in the four seeds and the lump of excrement that would be their first food. Nothing gave the yield per acre that corn did; nothing but rice gave as much nourishment per ounce. Land was at a premium now. The Plants exerted a constant pressure on the cornfields. Every day, the smaller children had to go out and hunt between the rows of corn for the lime-green shoots, which could grow in a week's time to the size of saplings, and in a month would be big as grown maples.

Damn them! he thought. *May God damn them!* But this curse lost much of its forcefulness from the conviction that God had sent them in the first place. Let others talk about Outer Space as much as they liked: Anderson knew that the same angry and jealous God who had once before visited a flood upon an earth that was corrupt had created the Plants and sown them. He never argued about it. When God could be so persuasive, why should Anderson raise his voice? It had been seven years that spring since the first seedlings of the Plant had been seen. They had come of a sudden in April of '72, a billion spores, invisible to all but the most powerful microscopes, sown broadcast over the entire planet by an equally invisible sower (and where was the microscope or telescope or radar screen that will make God visible?), and within days every inch of ground, farmland and desert, jungle and tundra, was covered with a carpet of the richest green.

Every year since, as there were fewer and fewer people, there were more converts to Anderson's thesis. Like Noah, he was having the last laugh. But that didn't stop him from hating, just as Noah must have hated the rains and rising waters.

Anderson hadn't always hated the Plants so much. In the first years, when the Government had just toppled and the farms were in their heyday, he had gone out in the moonlight and just watched them grow. It was like the speeded-up movies of plant growth he'd seen in Ag School years ago. He had thought then that he could hold his own against them, but he'd been wrong. The infernal weeds had wrested his farm from his hands and the town from the hands of his people.

But, by God, he'd win it back. Every square inch. If he had to root out every Plant with his two bare hands. He spat significantly.

At such moments Anderson was as conscious of his own strength, of the force of his resolve, as a young man is conscious of the compulsion of his flesh or a woman is conscious of the child she bears. It was an animal strength, and that, Anderson knew, was the only strength strong enough to prevail against the Plants.

His oldest son ran out of the forest shouting. When Buddy ran, Anderson knew there was something wrong. "What'd he say?" he asked Neil. Though the old man would not admit it, his hearing was beginning to go.

"He says Studs got out into the cows. Sounds like a lotta hooey to me."

"Pray God it is," Anderson replied, and his look fell on Neil like an iron weight.

Anderson ordered Neil back to the village to see that the men did not forget to bring ropes and prods in their hurry to give pursuit. Then with Buddy he set off on the clear trail the herd had made. They were about ten minutes behind them, by Buddy's estimate.

"Too long," Anderson said, and they began to run instead of trotting.

It was easy, running among the Plants, for they grew far apart and their cover was so thick that no underbrush could grow. Even fungi languished here, for lack of food. The few aspens that still stood were rotten to the core and only waiting for a strong wind to fell them. The firs and spruce had entirely disappeared, digested by the very soil that had once fed them. Years before, the Plants had supported hordes of common parasites, and Anderson had hoped mightily that the vines and creepers would destroy their hosts, but the Plants had rallied and it was the parasites who had, for no apparent reason, died.

The giant boles of the Plants rose out of sight, their spires hidden by their own massive foliage; their smooth, living green was unblemished, untouched, and like all living things, unwilling to countenance any life but their own.

There was in these forests a strange, unwholesome solitude, a solitude more profound than adolescence, more unremitting than prison. It seemed, in a way, despite its green, flourishing growth, dead. Perhaps it was because there was no sound. The great leaves overhead were too heavy and too rigid in structure to be stirred by anything but gale winds. Most of the birds had died. The balance of nature had been so thoroughly upset that even animals one would not think threatened had joined the ever-mounting ranks of the extinct. The Plants were alone in these forests, and the feeling of their being set apart, of their belonging to a different order of things, was inescapable. It ate at the strongest man's heart.

"What's that smell?" Buddy asked.

"I don't smell anything."

"It smells like something burning."

Anderson felt small stirrings of hope. "A fire? But they wouldn't burn at this time of year. They're too green."

"It's not the Plants. It's something else."

It was the smell of roasting meat, but he wouldn't say so. It would be too cruel, too unreasonable to lose one of the precious cows to a party of marauders.

Their pace slowed from a run to a trot, from a trot to a cautious, stalking glide. "I do smell it now," Anderson whispered. He withdrew from its holster the Colt Python .357 Magnum that was the visible sign of his authority among the citizens of Tassel. Since his elevation to his high office (formally, he was the town's mayor, but in fact he was much more), he had never been known to be without it. The potency of this weapon as a symbol (for the village had a goodly stock of guns and ammunition yet) rested upon the fact that it was only employed for the gravest of purposes: to kill men.

The smell had become very strong; then at a turn in the path they found the twelve carcasses. They had been incinerated to ash, but the outlines were clear enough to indicate which had been Studs. There was also a smaller patch of ash near them on the path.

"How—" Buddy began. But he really meant *what,* or even *who,* something that his father was quicker to understand.

"Jimmie!" the old man screamed, enraged, and he buried his hands in the smaller pile of still-smoking ashes.

Buddy turned his eyes away, for too great sorrow is like drunkenness: it was not fitting that he should see his father then.

There's not even any meat left, he thought, looking at the other carcasses. *Nothing but ashes.*

"My son!" the old man cried. "My son!" He held in his fingers a piece of metal that had once been the buckle of a belt. Its edges had been melted by the heat, and the metal's retained heat was burning the old man's fingers. He did not notice. Out of his throat came a noise, deeper than a groan, and his hands dug into the ashes once more. He buried his face in them and wept.

After a while, the men of the village arrived. One had brought a shovel to use as a prod. They buried the boy's ashes there, for already the wind was beginning to spread them over the ground. Anderson kept the buckle.

While Anderson was speaking the words over his son's shallow grave, they heard the *moo* of the last cow, Gracie. So as soon as they'd said *amen,* they went running after the surviving cow. Except Anderson, who walked home alone.

Gracie led them a merry old chase.

Chapter 2

DESERTION

They had to abandon Tassel, the old Tassel that they still thought of as their proper home, the spring before last. The Plants had flung out their seedlings (though exactly how this was done remained a mystery, for the Plants exhibited not the slightest sign of flowers or fruiting bodies) over the surrounding fields with a profligacy that had finally conquered every human effort. They, the humans, had been extended too far: their town and the farms about it had not been laid out with a siege in view.

For the first three years, they held their own well enough—or so it had seemed—by spraying the seedlings with poisons that the Government had developed. Each year, for as long as the Government and its laboratories lasted, it was a new poison, for the Plant developed immunities almost as quickly as the poisons were invented. But even then they had sprayed only the fields. In marshes and along the wild lake shore, in forests and along the roads, the seedlings shot up beyond the reach of any enemy but the axe—and there were just too many Plants and too few axes to make that a conceivable enterprise. Wherever the Plants grew, there was not light enough, nor water enough, nor even soil enough for anything else. When the old trees and bushes and grasses were crowded out and died, erosion stripped the land.

Not the farmlands, of course—not yet. But in only three years the Plants were crowding the fields and pastures, and then it was only a matter of time. Of very little time, really: the Plants nibbled, they bit, and, during the summer of their fifth year, they simply overran.

All that was left was this shadowy ruin. Buddy took a certain elegiac pleasure in coming here. There was even a practical side to it: scavenging in the debris he was often able to find old tools and sheet metal, even occasional books. The time for edibles was past, though. The rats and marauders working their way up from Duluth had long ago cleaned out the little that had been left behind after the move to New Tassel. So he gave up looking and went to sit on the steps of the Congregationalist Church, which thanks to his father's continued efforts was one of the last buildings in the town to remain intact.

There had been, he remembered, an oak, a tall archetypal oak, over to the right of the Plant that had broken through the sidewalk at the edge of what used to be the town park. During the fourth winter, they had used the oak as firewood. And many elms, too. There had certainly been no lack of elms.

He heard, distantly, Gracie's lugubrious plaint as she was pulled back to town at the end of a rope. The chase had been too much for Buddy. His legs had given out. He wondered if the Hereford was now extinct. Perhaps not, for Gracie was pregnant, she was still young, and if she bore a bull calf, there would be hope for her race, though it were but a glimmer. What more could one ask than a glimmer?

He wondered, too, how many enclaves had held out as long as Tassel. For the last two years, captured marauders had been the village's only link with the outside, but the marauders had been growing fewer. It was likely that the cities had come to their end at last.

He was thankful he had not been there to witness it, for even the little corpse of Tassel could make him melancholic. He would not have thought he could have cared so. Before the advent of the Plants, Tassel had been the objectification of everything he despised: smallness, meanness, willful ignorance and a moral code as contemporary as Leviticus. And now he mourned it as though it had been Carthage fallen to the Romans and sown with salt, or Babylon, that great city.

It was not perhaps the corpse of the town that he mourned, but all the other corpses of which it was compounded. Once a thousand and some people had lived here, and all but a paltry two hundred and forty-seven of them were dead. How invariably the worst had survived and the best had died.

Pastern, the Congregationalist minister, and his wife Lorraine. They had been good to Buddy during the years before he'd left for the University, when life had been one long feud with his father who had wanted him to go to the Ag School in Duluth. And Vivian Sokulsky, his fourth-grade teacher. The only older woman in town with a sense of humor or a grain of intelligence. And all the others too, always the best of them.

Now, Jimmie Lee. Rationally you couldn't blame the Plants for Jimmie's death. He had been murdered—though how or by whom, Buddy could not imagine. Or why? Above all, why? Yet death and the Plants were such close kin that one could not feel the breath of one without seeming to see the shadow of the other.

"Hello there, stranger." The voice had a strong musical timbre, like the speaking voice of the contralto in an operetta, but to judge by Buddy's reaction one would have thought it harsh.

"Hello, Greta. Go away."

The voice laughed, a full husky laugh that would have reached the last rows of any balcony, and Greta herself came forward, as full and husky in the flesh as in her laughter, which now abruptly ceased. She stood herself before Buddy as though she were presenting a grievance before the court. Exhibit A: Greta Anderson, arms akimbo and shoulders thrown back, full hips jutting forward, her bare feet planted in the dirt like roots. She deserved better clothing than the cotton chemise she wore. In richer fabrics and brighter colors and given better support, the type of beauty Greta represented could excel any other; now she seemed just slightly overripe.

"I hardly ever see you anymore. You know we're practically next-door neighbors—"

"Except that we don't have doors."

"—yet I don't see you from one week to the next. Sometimes I think you try to avoid me."

"Sometimes I do, but you can see for yourself it doesn't work. Now, why don't you go fix your husband's dinner like a good wife? It's been a bad day all around."

"Neil's in a blue funk. I expect he'll be whipped tonight, and *I'm* not going to be around the house—or should I say the tent?—when he comes home from that. When he went back to town, he fooled with the rope on Studs's pen to try and make it look like it wasn't his fault—that Studs had jumped over the bar. I can just see Studs clearing an eight-foot fence. But it didn't do him any good. Clay and a half a dozen others saw him doing it. He'll just get whipped a little harder now."

"That idiot!"

Greta laughed. "You said it, not me."

With a feigned casualness, she sat on the step below his. "You know, Buddy, I come here a lot too. I get so lonely in the new town —it's not really a town at all, it's more like summer camp with the tents and having to carry water from the stream. Oh, it's so boring. *You* know what I mean. You know it better than me. I always wanted to go live in Minneapolis myself, but first there was Daddy, and then . . . But I don't have to tell *you*."

It had grown quite dark in the ruined village. A summer shower began to fall on the leaves of the Plants, but only a few droplets penetrated their cover. It was like sitting in spray blown in off the lake.

After a considerable silence (during which she had leaned back to rest her elbows on Buddy's step, letting the weight of her thick, sun-whitened hair pull her head back, so that as she talked she gazed up into the faraway leaves of the Plant), Greta let loose another well modulated laugh.

Buddy couldn't help but admire her laugh. It was as though that laughter was a speciality of hers—a note she could reach that other contraltos couldn't.

"Do you remember the time you put the vodka into the punch at Daddy's youth meeting? And we all started doing the twist to those awful old records of his? Oh, that was precious, that was such fun! Nobody but you and me knew *how* to twist. That was an awful thing to do. The vodka, I mean. Daddy never knew what happened."

"Jacqueline Brewster could twist well, as I recall."

"Jacqueline Brewster is a pill."

He laughed, and since it had become so much less customary for him, the laughter was rough-edged and a little shrill. "Jacqueline Brewster's dead," he said.

"That's so. Well, I guess next to the two of us she *was* the best dancer around." After another pause, she began again with a great show of vivacity. "And the time we went to old man Jenkins' house, out on County Road B—do you remember that?"

"Greta, let's not talk about that."

"But it was so *funny*, Buddy! It was the funniest thing in the world. There we were, the two of us, going at it on that squeaky old sofa a mile a minute. I thought it would fall to pieces, and him upstairs so dead to the world he never knew a thing."

Despite himself, Buddy snorted. "Well, he was *deaf*." He pronounced the word in the country way, with a long *e*.

"Oh, we'll never have times like that again." When she turned to look at Buddy, her eyes gleamed with something more than reminiscence. "You *were* the wild one then. There wasn't anything that stopped you. You were the king of the heap, and wasn't I the queen? Wasn't I, Buddy?" She grabbed one of his hands and squeezed it. Once her fingernails would have cut his skin, but her fingernails were gone and his skin was tougher. He pulled his hand away and stood up.

"Stop it, Greta. It won't get you anywhere."

"I've got a right to *remember*. It *was* that way, and you can't tell me it wasn't. I know it's not that way any more. All I have to do is look around to see that. Where's Jenkins' house now, eh? Have you ever tried to find it? It's gone; it's simply disappeared. And the football field—where is that? Every day a little more of everything is gone. I went into MacCord's the other day, where they used to have the nicest dresses in town, such as they were. There wasn't a thing. Not a button. It seemed like the end of the world, but I don't know —maybe those things aren't so important. It's people that are most important. But all the best people are gone, too."

"Yes," Buddy said, "yes, they are."

"Except a very few. When you were away, I saw it all happen. Some of them, the Douglases and others, left for the cities, but that was only at the very beginning of the panic. They came back, the same as you—those who could. I wanted to go, but after Momma died, Daddy got sick and I had to nurse him. He read the Bible all the time. And prayed. He made me get down on my knees beside his bed and pray with him. But his voice wasn't so good then, so usually I'd end up praying by myself. I thought it would have looked funny to somebody else—as though it was Daddy I was praying to and not God. But there wasn't anybody left by that time who could laugh. The laughter had just dried up, like the Split Rock River.

"The radio station had stopped, except for the news twice a day, and who wanted to hear the news? There were all those National Guard people trying to make us do what the Government said. Delano Paulsen got killed the night they got rid of the National Guard, and I didn't know about it for a week. Nobody wanted to tell me, because after you left, Delano and I went steady. I guess maybe you never knew that. As soon as Daddy got on his feet, he was going to marry the two of us. Really—he really was.

"The Plants seemed to be everywhere then. They broke up the roads and water mains. The old lake shore was just a marsh, and the Plants were already growing there. Everything was so terribly ugly. It's nice now, in comparison.

"But the worst part was the boredom. Nobody had time to have fun. You were gone and Delano was dead and Daddy—well, you can imagine. I shouldn't admit this, but when he died, I was sort of glad.

"Except that was when your father was elected mayor and really started organizing everybody, telling them what to do and where to live, and I thought: "There won't be room for me." I was thinking of Noah's ark, because Daddy used to read that one over and over again. I thought: "They'll take off without *me*." I was scared. I suppose everybody was scared. The city must have been scary, too, with all those people dying. I heard about that. But I was really *scared!* How do you explain that?

"And then your brother started coming to visit me. He was about twenty-one then and not really bad-looking from a girl's point of view. Except for his chin. But I thought: 'Greta, you've got a chance to marry Japheth.'"

"Who?"

"Japheth. He was one of Noah's sons. Poor Neil! I mean, he really didn't stand a chance, did he?"

"I think you've reminisced enough now."

"I mean, he didn't know anything about girls. He wasn't like you. He was twenty-one, just three months younger than you, and I don't think he even *thought* about girls. He said later it was your father who recommended me! Can you imagine that! Like he was breeding a bull!"

Buddy started walking away from her.

"What should I have done? You tell me. Should I have waited for you? Put a candle burning in the window?"

"You don't need a candle, when you're carrying a torch." Again the lyric laugh, but barbed with undissimulated shrillness. She rose and walked toward him. Her breasts, which had been noticeably slack before, were perceptibly less so.

"Well, do you want to know why? You don't. You're afraid to

hear the truth. If I told you, you wouldn't let yourself believe it, but I'll tell you anyway. Your brother is a two-hundred pound noodle of wet spaghetti. He is completely and totally unable to *move*."

"He's my *half*-brother." Buddy said, almost automatically.

"And he's half a husband for me." Greta was smiling strangely, and somehow they had come to be standing face to face, inches apart. She had only to stand on tiptoe for her lips to reach his. Her hands never even touched him.

"No," he said, pushing her away. "It's over. It's been over for years. That was eight years ago. We were kids then. Teenagers."

"Oh, brother, have you lost your guts!"

He slapped her hard enough to knock her to the ground, though in fairness it must be said that she seemed to co-operate and even to relish the blow.

"That," she said, the old music quite gone from her voice, "is all the best that Neil can do. And I must say that between the two of you he does that better."

Buddy laughed a solid, good-humored laugh and left her, feeling some of the old stallion blood rising in him. Ah, he had forgotten what a magnificent wit she could muster. Absolutely the only one left with a sense of humor, he thought. And still the best-looking. Maybe they *would* get together again.

Eventually.

Then he remembered that it was not a day to be in a good humor, and the smile left his lips and the stallion quieted and went back to his stall.

Chapter 3

A BUNDLE OF JOY

There was something of the mouse about Maryann Anderson. *Mouse* was the color of her hair: a lusterless gray-brown. There was a mousy tendency, when her mind was on other things, for her lips to part, revealing largish, yellowed incisors. Worse, she had, at the age of twenty-three, a faint, downy moustache. She was short, no more than five feet two, and thin: Buddy's thumb and middle finger could completely encircle her upper arm.

Even her good qualities were mousy: She was perky, industrious and content with scraps. Though she would never be a beauty, she might once have been thought cute. She was submissive. She did not intrude.

Buddy didn't love her. There were times when her very passivity infuriated him. He had been used, on the whole, to something more. Still, it was as hard to find fault with Maryann as it was to find anything particularly to admire. Buddy was comfortably sure that she would never be unfaithful, and as long as his wants were looked after, he didn't really resent Maryann for being his wife.

Maryann, for her part, could not reciprocate this indifference. She was slavishly devoted to her husband and hopelessly, girlishly in love with him. Buddy had always been able to elicit a species of self-sacrificing devotion, though he had usually called for a different sort of sacrifice, and his altars, so to speak, were dark with the blood of his victims. But he had never tried to exert his influence on

Maryann, who had only interested him for one brief moment and then not amorously but by her pitiableness.

It had been during the fall of the fourth year after the Plants had come, and Buddy had only just returned to Tassel. A party of marauders, Maryann among them, had somehow worked their way up from Minneapolis. Instead of raiding, they'd been foolish enough to come to the village and *ask* for food. It was unheard of. The invariable rule was for marauders to be executed (hunger could turn the lambs to wolves), but a small controversy arose in this case, because of the seeming good-will of the prisoners. Buddy had been among those in favor of releasing them, but his father—and the majority of the men—insisted on execution.

"Then at least spare the women," Buddy had pleaded, being still rather sentimental.

"The only woman that goes free is the one you take to wife," Anderson had proclaimed, extemporizing the law, as was his way. And quite unexpectedly and out of pure cussedness Buddy had gone and chosen one of them, not even the best-looking one, and made her his wife. The other twenty-three marauders were executed, and the bodies were properly disposed of.

Maryann didn't speak unless spoken to, but in their three years together Buddy had picked up enough bits and pieces of her background to convince himself that her depths were no more interesting than her surfaces.

Her father had been a bank clerk, scarcely more than a teller, and she had worked for one month in a stenographic pool before the world had entirely collapsed. Though she had gone to a parochial grade school and later to St. Bridget's, where she took the commercial course, her Catholicism had never been more than lukewarm at best, with hot flashes around the holidays. In Tassel she was able to adopt Anderson's homemade and apocalyptic brand of Congregationalism without a qualm.

But Maryann's special distinction was not her conversion from papistry: it was the new skill she had brought to Tassel. Once, almost by chance, she had taken a night course in basket-weaving at the CYO. Something in Maryann, something quite fundamental, had responded to the simplicities of that ancient craft. She experimented with the thicker rushes and with swamp grasses, and when the shortages began, Maryann went out on her own and began stripping the smooth green boles of the Plants and shredding their great leaves into raffia. Right to the end, to that day when the Government trucks failed to show up in the city for the morning dole, she went on making her baskets and bonnets and sandals and welcome mats. People thought it silly, and Maryann herself considered it a weakness. That it was the one thing that the poor mouse had ever done well or found more than passing satisfaction in escaped their attention and hers.

In Tassel, Maryann's light was no longer hidden, as it were, beneath a bushel. Her basketry quite transformed the village's way of life. After the fatal summer when the Plants invaded the fields, the villagers (the five hundred who were left) had picked up as many pieces as they could carry and took themselves to the shore of Lake Superior, a few miles away down Gooseberry River. The lake had been receding at a prodigious rate, and in several areas the water was two or three miles from the old, rock-strewn shore line. Wherever the water retreated, the thirsty seedlings sprang up, sank roots, and the process accelerated.

That fall and through the winter, the survivors (their number, like the lake, was always shrinking) worked at clearing as large an area as they could hope realistically to maintain for their own fields the next year. Then they begin to sink their own roots. There was little timber but what they could scavenge from the old town. The wood of the Plant was less substantial than balsam, and most of the trees native to the area had already rotted. The villagers had the clay but not the skill to make brick, and quarrying was out of the question. So they spent the winter in a great grass hut, whose walls and roof were woven under Maryann's supervision. It had been a cold, miserable November, but a person could keep his fingers warm weaving. There was a week in December when the panels of the commonroom were blown halfway back to the old village. But by January they had learned to make a weave that was proof against the worst blizzard, and by February the commonroom was downright cozy. It even had a welcome mat at each of the doors.

No one had ever regretted admitting the clever mouse to the village. Except, occasionally, the mouse's husband.

"Why isn't there any dinner?" he asked.

"I was all day with Lady. She's awful upset about Jimmie Lee. Jimmie was her favorite, you know. Your father didn't help much either. He talked all the time about the Resurrection of the Body. He must know by now she doesn't believe the same as he does."

"A person has to eat just the same."

"I'm fixing it, Buddy. As fast as I can. Buddy, there's something—"

"Father's feeling better then?"

"—I wanted to tell you. I never know how your father is feeling. He's acting the same as ever. He never loses control. Neil's going to be whipped tonight—I suppose you heard about that?"

"Serves him right. If he'd fixed the gate shut, that whole thing wouldn't have happened."

"What whole thing, Buddy? How can a person be burned to ashes like that in the middle of the forest? How can that be?"

"You've got me. It doesn't seem possible. And those cows and Studs, besides. Seven tons of beef turned to ash in less than ten minutes."

"Was it lightning?"

"Not unless it was the lightning of the Good Lord. I suspect it's marauders. They've invented some new kind of weapon."

"But why would they want to kill *cows?* They'd want to steal cows —and kill people."

"Maryann, *I* don't know what happened. Don't ask any more questions."

"There was something I wanted to tell you."

"Maryann!"

Glumly, she went back to stirring the suppawn in the earthenware pot that nestled in the hot embers; to the side, wrapped in cornhusks, were three sunfish that Jimmie Lee had caught that morning at the lake shore.

From now on, with neither milk nor butter to add to the corn meal, they'd have to settle for mush, with an occasional egg whipped in it. One of the nice things about being married to an Anderson had always been the extra food. The meat especially. Maryann hadn't questioned too closely where it all came from; she just took what Lady, Anderson's wife, offered her.

Well, she thought, *there are still hogs and chickens and a lake full of fish. The world hasn't come to an end.* Maybe the hunters could bring in enough after the harvest to make up for the Herefords. A couple of years ago, the hunting had been so good that there'd been talk of turning nomad and following the game, like the Indians used to. Then the deer started falling off. There was a winter of wolves and bears, and then it was just like old times. Except for the rabbits.

Rabbits could eat the bark off the Plants. Rabbits were cute, the way they wiggled their noses. She smiled, thinking about the rabbits. "Buddy," she said, "there's something I should talk to you about."

Maryann was talking about something, which was almost an event in itself, but Buddy's mind, after a day like this, didn't seem to focus on things very well. He was thinking of Greta again: the curve of her neck when she'd thrown her head back out on the church steps. The slight protuberance of her Adam's apple. And her lips. Somehow she still had lipstick. Had she worn it just for him?

"What'd you say?" he asked Maryann.

"Nothing. Oh, just nothing."

Buddy had always thought that Maryann would have made the ideal wife for Neil. She had the same chin, the same lack of humor, the same stolid industriousness. They both had front teeth like a rabbit's or a rat's. Neil, who was abject before Greta, would not have found fault with Maryann's passivity. With Maryann in bed, Buddy was always reminded of tenth-grade gym class, when Mr. Olsen had had them do fifty pushups every day. But apparently that aspect of things didn't mean so much to Neil.

It had been a shock to come back and find Greta Pastern married to his half-brother. Somehow he'd been counting on finding her waiting for him. She'd been so large a part of the Tassel he'd left behind.

It had been a touchy situation all around, those first weeks. Buddy and Greta had been anything but secretive during Buddy's last year in Tassel. Their carryings-on were discussed in every bar and over every back fence in town. Greta, the pastor's only child, and Buddy, the eldest son of the richest—and most righteous—farmer in the township, in all Lake County. So it was common knowledge that Greta was a hand-me-down in the Anderson family, and a common expectation that something bad would come of it.

But the prodigal who had returned to Tassel was not the same as the prodigal who had left it. In the meantime he had starved a third of his weight away, worked on the Government's pressed-labor crews, and butchered his way to Tassel from Minneapolis, joining the human wolf packs or fighting them as the occasion offered. By the time he got to Tassel, he was much more interested in saving his own hide than in getting under Greta's skirts.

So, besides being a humanitarian gesture, it had been prudent to marry Maryann. Buddy as a husband seemed much less likely to breach the village peace than Buddy as a bachelor, and he could pass Greta on the street without causing a storm of speculation.

"Buddy?"

"Tell it to me later!"

"The suppawn's ready. That's all."

Such a ninny, he thought. But a passable cook. Better, leastways, than Greta, and that was a consolation.

He shoveled the steaming, yellow porridge into his mouth, nodding to Maryann that he was satisfied. She watched him put down two bowls of the suppawn and the three fish, then she ate what was left.

I'll tell him now, while he's in a good mood, she thought. But before she could get a word in, Buddy was up off the mat on the floor of the tent and heading outside.

"It must be about time for the whipping," he said.

"I don't want to see it. It makes me sick."

"Nothing says a woman has to go." And with half a smile to cheer her up, he was out of the tent. Even if he had been squeamish (which he wasn't), he would have had to be there, as did every male in the village over seven years old. A good whipping could instill almost as much fear of the Lord in the hearts of beholders as in the single heart about which the lash curled.

In the square before the commonhouse, Neil was already strung up to the whipping post. His back was bare. Buddy was one of the last to arrive.

Anderson, with the whip in his hand, stood spraddle-legged in readiness. There was just a bit too much stiffness in his stance. Buddy knew that it must be costing the old man to carry on as though this were no more than an ordinary fiasco, a matter of some twenty lashes.

When Anderson had to whip Buddy or Neil, he meted out the pain impartially—no more and no less than he would have doled out to anyone else for the same offense. His touch was as precise as a metronome. But tonight, after the third stroke, his knees collapsed and he fell to the ground.

There was a gasp from the circle of spectators, then Anderson was on his feet again. The color had run out of his face, and, giving the whip to Buddy, his hand trembled.

"You continue," he commanded.

If the old man had handed him his Python—or a scepter—Buddy couldn't have been any more taken aback.

Maryann heard it all from inside the tent, while she licked the pot. When there was a pause after the third stroke, she hoped that might be the end. She understood of course that these things had to be done, but that didn't mean she had to like it. It wasn't good manners to enjoy someone else being hurt, even if you didn't like them.

The whipping started again.

She wished Buddy had left her more food. And now, with the Guernseys all dead, there'd be no more milk!

She tried to think of what she would say when he got home. She decided on "Darling, we are going to have a bundle of joy."

It was such a nice expression. She had heard it first in a movie a long time ago. Eddie Fisher and Debbie Reynolds had been the stars.

For *his* sake, she hoped it was a boy, and she fell asleep wondering what his name should be. Patrick, for his grandfather? Or Lawrence? She had always loved that name, for some reason. Joseph was a good name, too.

Buddy? She wondered if there was a Saint Buddy. She had never heard of one. Perhaps he was a Congregationalist saint.

Chapter 4

GOOD-BYE, WESTERN CIVILIZATION

On 22 August 1979, as per instructions of 4 July 1979, preparations were begun for the incineration of the artifact shown in the maps as "Duluth-Superior." Meteorological conditions were ideal: for 17 days there had been no rain, scarcely a dampness in the mornings. "Duluth-Superior" was quartered, and each of these Quarters was divided into three Sections, as shown in the accompanying photographs, taken from elevation 1.33 kms. Action began at 20.34 hours, 23 August 1979.

This artifact was constructed upon numerous low mounds of natural formation, topographically akin to the artifact "San Francisco." Here, however, the major construction element was wood, which burns quickly. Firing began in the lowest areas of each Section, and the natural up-draft of air accomplished almost as much as the firing devices.

With the exceptions of Sections II-3 and III-1 near the old lakeshore (here for some reason, the elements of the artifact were larger and constructed of stone and brick instead of wood), complete incineration was achieved in 3.64 hours. When the work in each Quarter had been accomplished to satisfaction, the equipment of that Quarter was transferred to Sections II-3 and III-1, and these Sections were incinerated by 01.12 hours, 24 August 1979.

There were two mechanical failures in Section IV-3. Appraisal of damages has been sent to the Office of Supplies, and a carbon of that appraisal is enclosed herewith.

Mammals dwelling in the periphery of Quarters I, II, and IV escaped into the adjacent fields due to the insufficiency of the equipment and the openness of the terrain. Current estimates are from 200 to 340 of the large mammals, constructors of the artifacts, and from 15,000 to 24,000 of the small mammals, within established limits of probable error.

All wood-burrowing insects were eradicated.

Operations have been begun to trace the escaped mammals and other mammals living beyond the limits of "Duluth-Superior," but equipment is limited. (Consul Requisition Form 800-B: 15 August 1979; 15 May 1979; 15 February 1979.)

Following incineration, ash was levelled into the concavities of the artifact, and seeding operations were begun 27 August 1979.

Based on the results of samples taken from 12 May 1979 to 4 July 1979, this unit was then removed to follow a route along the southern shore of "Lake Superior." (Consult map of "Wisconsin State.") Sampling had indicated that this area was most densely populated with indigenous mammals.

The obsolete Spheroid Model 37-Mg will be employed for this operation, due to the shortages of Models 39-Mg and 45-Mh. Despite their bulkiness, these models are adequate for the extermination of such mammalian life as they are likely to encounter. Indeed, their thermotropic mechanisms are more highly developed than those of the later models. However, in exceptional circumstances the operation of Model 37-Mg cannot, without undue delay, be assumed by the Central Intelligence Bank of this Unit.

The further process of incineration is expected to proceed less rapidly now that this, the last of the chief artifacts, has been levelled and sown. The remaining artifacts are small and widely spaced. Though our sample has shown that most of these are no longer inhabited, we will, pursuant to instructions of 4 July 1979, effect their entire incineration.

Estimated completion of project: 2 February 1980.

"What do you make of it, my dear?" he asked.

"It's very beautiful," she said. "And did you do it just for me?"

"Sweetheart, as far as I'm concerned, you're the only girl in the world."

Jackie smiled, her bittersweet smile, the one she reserved for hopeless disasters. She closed her eyes, not to shut out the scene, but because they were very tired, and shook the ash from her short, curling black hair.

Jeremiah Orville closed her in his arms. It wasn't chilly, but it seemed the right thing to do just then—a traditional gesture, like taking off one's hat at a funeral. Calmly, he watched the city burn.

Jackie was rubbing her bobbed nose in the scratchy wool of his sweater. "I never really liked that city anyhow," she said.

"It kept us alive."

"Of course, Jerry. I didn't mean to be ungrateful. I just meant—"

"I understand. That's just my well known sentimentality getting out of hand again."

Despite the heat and his enclosing arms, she shivered. "We'll die now. We'll die for sure."

"Chin up, Miss Whythe! Tally-ho! Remember the Titanic!"

She laughed. "I feel like Carmen, in the opera, when she turns up the Ace of Spades." She hummed the Fate theme, and when the last note proved too low, she mumbled: "In an amateur production."

"It's no wonder one feels depressed, with the world burning up about one," he said in his best David Niven manner. Then, in an authentic Midwestern accent: "Hey, look! There goes the Alworth Building!"

She turned around quickly, and her dark eyes danced in the light of the pyre. The Alworth Building was the tallest in Duluth. It burned magnificently. The whole downtown area was in flames now. To the left of the Alworth Building, the First American National Bank, after a late start, flared up even more splendidly due to its greater bulk.

"Ooowh," Jackie shouted. "Wheee!"

They had lived these last years in the safe-deposit vault in the basement of the First American National Bank. Their precious store of scavenged cans and jars was still locked in the safe deposit boxes, and the canary was probably in his cage in the corner. It had been a very cozy home, though there were few visitors and they had to kill most of those. Such luck couldn't last for ever.

Jackie was crying real tears.

"Sad?" he asked.

"Oh, not sad . . . just a little déracinée. And annoyed with myself, because I don't understand it." She snuffled loudly, and the tears were all gone. "It's so horribly like what they used to call an Act of God. As though God were the source of everything unreasonable. I like to know the reason for things." Then, after a pause. "Perhaps it was the termites?"

"The termites!" He looked at her unbelievingly, and her cheek began to show its tell-tale dimple. She was pulling his leg. They broke out laughing together.

In the distance, the Alworth Building collapsed. Beyond, in the dry harbor, a ship lay on its side and squirted flames out of its portholes.

Here and there, scuttling about the rubble, the incendiary mechanisms could be glimpsed attending their business. At this remove they seemed really quite innocuous. They reminded Jackie of nothing so much as of Volkswagens of the early Fifties, when all Volkswagens seemed to be gray. They were diligent, tidy, and quick.

"We should be getting on our way," he said. "They'll be mopping up the suburbs soon."

"Well, good-bye, Western Civilization," Jackie said waving at the bright inferno unafraid. For how can one be afraid of Volkswagens?

They coasted their bicycles along the Skyline Parkway from which they had viewed the burning city. When the Parkway went up hill, they had to walk the bicycles, because the chain on Orville's was broken.

The Parkway, unmended for years, was full of potholes and cluttered with debris. Coming down from Amity Park, they were in the dark, for the hill cut off the light of the fire. They went slowly with their handbrakes on.

At the bottom of the hill, a clear womanly voice addressed them out of the darkness: *Stop!* They jumped off the bicycles and spread themselves flat on the ground. They had practiced this many times. Orville pulled out his pistol.

The woman stepped into view, her arms over her head, hands empty. She was quite old—that is to say, sixty or more—and defiantly innocent in manner. She came much too close.

"She's a decoy," Jackie whispered.

That much was obvious, but where the others were Orville could not tell. Trees, houses, hedges, stalled cars stood all about. Each would have been an adequate cover. It was dark. The air was smoky. He had lost, for the while, his night vision by watching the fire. Determining to make a show of equal innocence, he reholstered his gun and stood up.

He offered his hand to the woman to shake. She smiled, but did not approach that near.

"I wouldn't go over that next rise, my dears. There's some kind of machine on the other side. Some sort of flame-thrower, I think. If you like, I'll show you a better way to go."

"What does it look like, this machine?"

"None of us have seen it. We've just seen the people who got crisped when they got to the top of the hill. Shocking."

It was not impossible nor even unlikely; it was equally possible and likely that he was being led into a trap. "One moment," he told the woman. He signaled to Jackie to stay where she was and walked up the gentle slope of the hill. He scanned the debris that the years had heaped there and selected a strip of lathing that must have dropped from a load of firewood. Halfway up the hill he stopped behind one of the Plants that had broken through the asphalt. He hurled the stick of lathing over the crest of the hill.

Before it reached the top of its arc it flared into flame, and before it fell out of sight, the flame was dead. The wood had been utterly consumed.

"You're right," he said, returning to the woman. "And we thank you."

Jackie rose to her feet. "We don't have any food," she announced, less to the old woman than to those she supposed were surrounding them. The habit of distrust was too strong to break in an instant.

"Don't worry, my dears, you've passed your first test, such as it is. As far as we're concerned, you've shown your mettle. If you only knew how many people walk right on up. . . ." She sighed. "My name's Alice Nemerov, R.N. Call me Alice." Then, almost as an afterthought: "The letters mean I'm a nurse, you know. If you get sick, I can tell you the name of what you've got. Even help a little, sometimes."

"My name's Jeremiah Orville, M.S. Call me Orville. My letters mean I'm a mining engineer. If you have any mines, I'll be happy to look at them."

"And you, my dear?"

"Jackie Janice Whythe. No letters. I'm an actress, for the love of God! I have thin hands, so I used to do a lot of soap commercials. But I can shoot, and I don't have any scruples that I know of."

"Splendid! Now come along and meet the other wolves. There are enough of us to make a tidy pack. Johnny! Ned! Christie! All of you!" Shards of shadows disengaged themselves from the static darkness and came forward.

Jackie hugged Orville about the waist delightedly. She pulled at his ear, and he bent down for her to whisper in it. "We're going to survive after all! Isn't that wonderful?"

It was more than they had expected.

All his life he had hoped, Jeremiah Orville, for better things. He had hoped when he started college to become a research scientist. Instead he had drifted into a comfortable job with more security (it had seemed) than San Quentin. He had hoped to leave his job and Duluth as soon as he had saved $10,000, but before the fabled sum, or even half of it, was put together he was married and the owner of a nice suburban home ($3,000 down, ten years to pay the balance). He had hoped for a happy marriage, but by then (he married late, at age 30) he had learned not to hope too hard. By 1972, when the Plants came, he was at the point of transferring all these choice hopes to the slender shoulders of his four-year-old son. But little Nolan proved unable to support even the burden of his own existence during the first famine that hit the cities, and Therese lasted only a month or two longer. He heard of her death by chance the next year: shortly before she had died he had deserted her.

Like everyone else, Orville pretended to hate the invasion (in the cities it was never considered anything but that), but secretly he relished it, he gloried in it, he wanted nothing else. Before the invasion, Orville had been standing on the threshold of a gray, paunchy middle age, and suddenly a new life—life itself!—had been thrust upon him. He (and anyone else who survived) learned to be as unscrupulous as the heroes in the pulp adventure magazines he'd read as a boy—sometimes, as unscrupulous as the villians.

The world might die about him. No matter: *he* was alive again.

There had been the intoxication, while it lasted, of power. Not the cool, gloved power of wealth that had ruled before, but a newer (or an older) kind of power that came from having the strength to perpetuate extreme inequity. Put more bluntly, he had worked for the Government. First, as a foreman over pressed-labor gangs; later (within only a few months, for the pace of events was speeding up), as the director of the city's entire labor operation. At times he wondered what difference there was between himself and, say, an Eichmann, but he didn't let his speculations interfere with his work.

In fact it was this, the strength of his imagination, that let him see the untenability of the Government's position and make suitable preparations for its collapse. The farmers could not be driven much further. They had the habit of independence and resented the parasitism of the cities. They would revolt and keep their little food to themselves. Without rations, the slaves in the city (for, of course, that's what they were—slaves) would either revolt or die. In any case, they would die. So (after suitable bureaucratic fictions and a few bribes had had the building condemned), Orville had provisioned his fortress in the basement of the First American National Bank and retired from his life of public service.

There had even been a romance, and it had progressed (unlike his marriage) exactly as a romance should progress: a strongly contested courtship, extravagant declarations, fevers, jealousies, triumphs —oh unceasing triumphs, and always the aphrodisiac of mortal danger that suffused the alleys and looted stores of the dying city.

Three years he had been with Jackie Whythe, and it seemed no more than a holiday weekend.

If it were true for him, would it not be true for the other survivors as well? Did they not all feel this clandestine gladness in their hearts, like adulterers together secretly in a strange town? It must be so, he thought. It must be so.

Past the Brighton Beach Tourist Camp, the Plants grew denser and the urban sprawl thinned. They had come to the wilderness, where they might be safe. As they moved northeast on Route 61, the dim light of the burning city faded behind them, and the dimmer light of the stars was blotted out by foliage. They advanced into perfect darkness.

They moved rapidly, however, for though the Plants had broken through the road wherever they wished, they had not obliterated it. It was not as though the hurrying band had to fight its way through one of the old scrub woods that had once grown around here: no branches tore at one's face; no brambles snagged one's feet. There were not even mosquitoes, for the Plants had drained all the marshes roundabout. The only obstructions were occasional potholes, and sometimes, where the Plants had broken the asphalt sufficiently to give headway to erosion, a gulley.

Orville and the others followed the highway until morning glowed greyly through the eastern mass of forest, then turned toward the light, towards the lake, which had once been visible to the cars driving along this road. It seemed dangerous to follow Route 61 any farther, as though it were an extension of the city and subject to the city's fate. Then, too, they were thirsty. If luck was with them, they might even get fish from the lake.

The route had been forced on them by circumstances. It would have been wiser, with the winter in view, to move south, but that would have meant circling the burning city, a chance in no way worth taking. There was no water to the west, and to the east there was too much. Lake Superior, though diminished, was still an effective barrier. Perhaps one of the lake-shore villages would have maintained serviceable boats, in which case they might turn pirate, as that fleet of tugboats had done three years before when Duluth Harbor ran dry. But the best probable direction was to continue northeast along the shore of the lake, looting the farms and villages. Worry about winter when winter came.

Lake Superior teemed with sunfish. Cooked over a driftwood fire, they were good even without salt. Afterward the group discussed, with some attempt at optimism, their plight and prospects. There was not much to decide: the situation dictated its own terms. The gathering was in fact less a discussion than a contest among the sixteen men to see who would assume leadership. Their band had been formed at hazard. Except for the couples, they did not know each other. (There had been little social life those last years; the only community that had survived in the cities had been the pack, and if any of these men had been in a pack before, he wasn't talking about it now.) None of the contenders for leadership seemed willing to discuss the details of his own survival. Such reticence was natural and becoming: at least they had not become so brutalized as to exult in their depravity and brag of their guilt. They had done what they had to, but they were not necessarily proud of it.

Alice Nemerov rescued them from this awkwardness by narrating her own story, which was singularly free of unpleasantness, considering. From the very first days of the famine she had stayed at the main hospital, living in the isolation ward. The hospital personnel had traded on its skills and medical supplies and got through even the worst times—except, apparently, for this last worst time of all. The survivors were mostly nurses and interns; the doctors had retired to their country houses when, after the failure of the Government, anarchy and famine had governed the city. In the last years, Alice Nemerov had gone about the city, armored in innocence and the certain knowledge that her skills would be a passport among even the meanest survivors, secure also in the knowledge that she had passed quite beyond the point where she need worry about rape.

Thus, she had come to know many of her fellow refugees, and she effected their introductions with aplomb and tact. She told too of other survivors and the curious expedients by which they had saved themselves from starvation.

"Rats?" Jackie asked, trying not to seem over-delicate in her disgust.

"Oh yes, my dear, lots of us tried that. I'll admit it was highly unpleasant." Several of her listeners shook their heads in agreement.

"And there were cannibals, too, but they were poor guilty souls, not at all what you'd think a cannibal would be like. They were always pathetically eager to talk, for all of them lived quite alone. Fortunately, I never came across one when he was hungry, or my feeling might be different."

As the sun mounted to noonday, weariness and sheer contiguity made the others drop their guards and speak of their own pasts. Orville realized for the first time that he was not quite the monster of iniquity that he had sometimes thought himself. Even when he revealed that he had been a foreman on the Government labor crews, his hearers did not seem outraged or hostile, though several of them had been impressed for labor in their time. The invasion had turned everyone into relativists: as tolerant of each other's ways, and means, as if they were delegates at a convention of cultural anthropologists.

It was hot, and they needed sleep. The breaking down of the barriers of solitude had tired their spirits almost as much as the march had tired their bodies.

The band did post sentinels, but one of them must have slept. The opportunity for resistance was already past before it was realized.

The farmers—their bones as ill-clothed with flesh as that flesh with tattered denim—outnumbered them three to one, and the farmers had been able, while the wolves slept (lambs, might not one better say?) to confiscate most of the weapons and prevent the use of the rest.

With one exception: Christie, whom Orville had thought he might grow to like, had managed to shoot one farmer, an old man, in the head. Christie was garrotted.

Everything happened very quickly but not too quickly for Jackie to give Orville a last kiss. When she was pulled away from him, roughly, by a younger farmer who seemed better fleshed-out than the majority, she was smiling the special, bittersweet smile which was reserved for just such occasions as this.

Chapter 5

BLOOD RELATIONS

Lady tucked Blossom into bed that night just as though she were still her little girl. She *was* only thirteen after all. Outside the men were still going at it. It was a terrible thing. If only she could shut her ears to it.

"I wish they didn't have to do that, Mother," Blossom whispered.

"It's necessary, darling—a necessary evil. Those people wouldn't have hesitated to kill us. Are you warm under that thin blanket?"

"But why don't we just *bury* them?"

"Your father knows best, Blossom. I'm sure it distresses him to have to do this. I remember that your brother Buddy——" Lady always referred to her stepson as Blossom's and Neil's brother, but she could never forget that this was a half-truth at best and she stumbled over the word. "——that he once felt the same as you."

"*He* wasn't there tonight. I asked Maryann. She said he'd gone out to the west field."

"To guard against the other marauders who may come." The steady rasping noise outside penetrated the light weave of the summer walls and hung in the air. Lady brushed back a strand of gray hair and composed her features to something like sternness. "I have work to do now, darling."

"Would you leave the light?"

Blossom knew better than to burn oil to no purpose—even this oil, which had been extracted from the Plant. She was only seeing how far she could go. "Yes," Lady conceded (for it was not just any night), "but keep it very low."

Before she lowered the curtain that partitioned Blossom's bed from the rest of the commonroom, she asked if Blossom had said her prayers.

"Oh, *Mother!*"

Lady lowered the curtain without either condoning or reproaching her daughter's ambiguous protest. Her husband, certainly, would have seen it as an impiety—and punishable.

Lady could not help being pleased that Blossom was not *so* impressionable (and if the girl had a fault, it was that) as to be led too fervently or too fearfully to adopt her father's fierce, unreasoning Calvinism. If one had to behave like an infidel, Lady believed, it was sheer hypocrisy to pass oneself off as a Christian. Indeed, she very much doubted whether the god to whom her husband prayed existed. If He did, why pray to Him? He had made His choice some eons ago. He was like the old Aztec gods who had demanded blood sacrifice on their stone altars. A jealous, vengeful god; a god for primitives; a bloody god. What was the scripture Anderson had chosen last Sunday? One of the minor prophets. Lady shuffled through the pages of her husband's great bible. There it was, in Nahum: "God is jealous, and the Lord revengeth; the Lord revengeth, and is furious; the Lord will take vengeance on his adversaries, and he reserveth wrath for his enemies." Ah, that was God all over!

When the curtain was down, Blossom crawled out of bed and obediently said her prayers. Gradually the rote formulas gave way to her own requests—first, for impersonal benefactions (that the harvest be good, that the next marauders be luckier and escape), then for more delicate favors (that her hair might grow faster so that she could set it in curls again, that her breasts would fill out just a little more, though they were already quite full for her age—for which she gave thanks). At last, snuggling back in bed, these formal requests gave way to mere wishful thinking, and she longed for the things which were no longer or which were yet to be.

When she fell asleep, the machinery outside was still grinding on.

A noise woke her, something woke her. There was still a little light from the lamp. "What is it?" she asked sleepily.

Her brother Neil was standing at the foot of her bed. His face was strangely vacant. His mouth was open: his chin hung slack. He seemed to see her, but she could not interpret the expression in his eyes.

"What is it?" she asked again, more sharply.

He did not reply. He did not move. He was wearing the pants he had worn all that day and there was blood on them.

"Go away, Neil. What did you want to wake me up for?"

His lips moved, as though in sleep, and his right hand made several gestures, emphasizing the unspoken words of his dream. Blossom pulled her thin cover up to her chin and sat up in bed. She screamed, having only meant to tell him to go away a little louder, so he would hear her.

Lady slept lightly, and Blossom did not have to scream more than once. "Are you having nightmares, my—Neil! What are you doing here, Neil?"

"He won't say anything, Mother. He just stands there and he won't answer me."

Lady grabbed her oldest son—now that Jimmie was dead, her only son—by the shoulder and shook him roughly. The right hand made more emphatic gestures, but the eyes seemed to stare less raptly now. "Huh?" he mumbled.

"Neil, you go to Greta now, do you hear? Greta is waiting for you."

"Huh?"

"You've been sleepwalking—or something. Now get along." She had already pulled him away from the bed and let the curtain drop, veiling Blossom. She was a few more minutes seeing Neil out the door, then she returned to the trembling Blossom.

"What did he want? Why did he—?"

"He's been upset by the things that happened tonight, darling. Everyone is nervous. Your father went out walking and he isn't back yet. It's only nerves."

"But why did he—?"

"Who knows why we do the things we do in our dreams? Now, you'd better get to sleep again. Have your own dreams. And tomorrow—"

"But I don't understand."

"Let's hope Neil doesn't either, love. And tomorrow, not a word of this to your father, do you understand? Your father's been upset lately, and it's best that we keep it a secret. Just the two of us. Do you promise?"

Blossom nodded. Lady tucked her into bed. Then she went back to her own bed and waited for her husband to return. She waited till dawn, and all the while, outside, the sausage machine kept up its dreary rasping song.

Waking was pain. Consciousness was consciousness of pain. Movement was painful. It was painful to breathe.

Eddying in and out of the pain were figures of women—an old woman, a girl, a beautiful woman, and a very old woman. The beautiful woman was Jackie, and since Jackie was dead he knew he was hallucinating. The very old woman was the nurse. Alice Nemerov, R.N. When she came it was more painful, so he knew she must be real. She moved his arms and, worse, his leg. *Stop that,* he thought. Sometimes he could scream. He hated her because she was alive, or because she was causing his pain. He was alive too, it seemed. Otherwise, would he feel this pain? Or was it the pain that kept him alive? Oh, stop it. Sometimes he could sleep. That was best.

Ah, Jackie! Jackie! Jackie!

Soon it was more painful to think than anything else, even than having his leg moved. He was no more able to stop or diminish this pain than those that had preceded it. He lay there, while the three women came and went—the old woman, the girl and the very old woman—thinking.

The girl talked to him.

"Hello," she said, "how are you feeling today? Can you eat this? You can't eat anything if you won't open your mouth. Won't you open your mouth? Just a little? Like that—that's fine. Your name's Orville, isn't it. My name's Blossom. Alice told us all about you. You're a mining engineer. It must be very interesting. I've been in a cave, but I've never seen a mine. Unless you call the iron pits mines. They're just holes, though. Open a little wider, that's better. In fact, that's why Daddy—" She stopped. "I shouldn't talk so much though. When you're better, we can have long talks."

"That's why what?" he asked. It was more painful to talk than to eat.

"That's why Daddy said to . . . said not to . . . I mean, both you and Miss Nemerov are alive, but we had to . . ."

"Kill."

"Yes, we had to, all the rest."

"The women too?"

"But you see, we had to. Daddy explains it better than I do, but if we didn't do that, then the others would come back, a lot of them together, and they're very hungry, and we don't have enough food, even for ourselves. The winter is so cold. You can understand that, can't you?"

He didn't say anything more for some days.

It was as though, all that time, he had lived only for Jackie, and with her gone he no longer had any need to live. He was drained of desire for anything but sleep. When she had been alive, he had not known that she had meant so much to him, that anything could. He had never plumbed the measure of his love. He should have died with her; he had tried to. Only the pain of memory could ease the pain of regret, and nothing could ease the pain of memory.

He wanted to die. He told this to Alice Nemerov, R.N.

"Watch your tongue," she counseled, "or they'll oblige you. They don't trust the two of us. We shouldn't even talk together, or they'll think we're plotting. And you'd better try and get well again. Eat more. They don't like you laying around not working. You understand what saved your life, don't you? I did. You're a damn fool to let them break your leg for you. Why wouldn't you talk? They only wanted to know your occupation."

"Jackie, was she—?"

"It wasn't any different for her than for the rest. You saw the machines. But you've got to get your mind off her. *You*—you're lucky to be alive. Period."

"The girl who feeds me—who is she?"

"Anderson's daughter. He's the one in charge here. The wiry old man with the constipated look. Watch out for him. And his son, the big one, Neil. He's worse."

"I remember him from that night. I remember his eyes."

"But most of the people here aren't any different from you and me. Except they're organized. They're not bad people. They only do what they have to. Lady, for instance, Blossom's mother, is a fine woman. I have to go now. Eat more."

"Can't you eat more than that?" Blossom scolded. "You have to get your strength back."

He picked up the spoon again.

"That's better." She smiled. There was a deep dimple in her freckled cheek when she smiled. Otherwise, it was a commonplace smile.

"What is this place? Does just your family live here?"

"It's the commonroom. We only have it for the summer, because Daddy's the mayor. Later when it's cold, the whole town moves in. It's awfully big, bigger than you can see from here, but even so it gets crowded. There's two hundred and forty-six of us. Forty-eight, with you and Alice. Tomorrow do you think you can try walking? Buddy, he's my brother, my other brother, made a crutch for you. You'll like Buddy. When you're healthy again, you'll feel better—I mean, you'll be happier. We aren't as bad as you think. We're Congregationalists. What are you?"

"I'm not."

"Then you won't have any trouble about joining. But we don't have a real minister, not since Reverend Pastern died. He was my sister-in-law's father—Greta. You've seen her. She's the beauty among us. Daddy was always important in the church, so when the Reverend died, he just naturally took over. He can preach a good sermon, you'd be surprised. He's actually a very religious man."

"Your father? I'd like to hear one of those sermons."

"I know what you're thinking, Mr. Orville. You think because of what happened to the others that Daddy's bad. But he's not cruel deliberately. He only does what he has to. It was—a necessary evil —what he did. Can't you eat more? Try. I'll tell you a story about Daddy, and then you'll see that you haven't been fair to him. One day last summer, at the end of June, the bull got out and started after the cows. Jimmie Lee—that was his youngest—went out after them. Jimmie Lee was sort of Daddy's Benjamin. He put great stock by Jimmie Lee, though he tried not to show it to us others. When Daddy found Jimmie Lee and the cows, they were all burned up, just like they say happened in Duluth. There wasn't even a body to carry home, just ashes. Daddy went almost out of his mind with grief. He rubbed the ashes into his face and cried. Then he tried to behave like nothing happened. But later that night he just broke down again, crying and sobbing, and he went off by himself to the grave, where he'd found him, and he just sat there for two whole days. He has very deep feelings, but most of the time he doesn't let them show."

"And Neil? Is he the same way?"

"What do you mean? Neil's my brother."

"He was the one who put the questions to me that night. And to the other people that I knew. Is he another one like your father?"

"I wouldn't know about that night. I wasn't there. You've got to rest now. Think about what I told you. And, Mr. Orville—try and forget about that night."

There was growing in him a desire and will to survive, but unlike any desire he had known till then, this was a cancerous growth, and the strength it lent his body was the strength of hatred. Passionately, he desired not life but revenge: for Jackie's death, for his own torture, for that whole horrible night.

He had never before felt much sympathy for avengers. The basic premises of blood vengeance had always struck him as rather improbable, like the plot of *Il Trovatore,* so that at first he was surprised to find himself dwelling so exclusively on one theme: Anderson's death, Anderson's agony, Anderson's humiliation.

Initially his imagination was content simply to devise deaths for the old man; then, as his strength grew, these deaths were elaborated with tortures, which finally displaced death entirely. Tortures could be protracted, while death was an end.

But Orville, having himself tasted the bitterest gall, knew that there was a limit beyond which pain cannot be heightened. He desired Anderson to endure the sufferings of Job. He wanted to grind ashes into the man's gray hair, to crush his spirit, to ruin him. Only then would he allow Anderson to know that it had been he, Jeremiah Orville, who had been the agent of his humbling.

So that when Blossom told him the story of how the old man had carried on over Jimmie Lee, he realized what he had to do. Why, it had been staring him in the face!

They had walked all the way to the cornfield together, Blossom and Orville. The leg had mended, but he would probably always have the limp. Now, at least, he could limp on his own—without any other crutch than Blossom.

"And that's the corn that's going to feed us all this winter?" he asked.

"It's more than we really need. A lot of it was meant for the cows."

"I suppose you'd be out there harvesting with the rest of them if it weren't for me?" It was the custom, during harvest, for the old women and the younger girls to take over the village duties while the stronger women went out into the fields with the men.

"No, I'm not old enough."

"Oh, come now. You're fifteen, if you're a day."

Blossom giggled. "You're just saying that. I'm thirteen. I won't be fourteen till January 31."

"You could have fooled me. You're very well developed for thirteen."

She blushed. "How old are you?" she asked.

"Thirty-five." It was a lie, but he knew he could get away with it. Seven years ago, when he had been thirty-five, he had looked older than he did now.

"I'm young enough to be your daughter, Mr. Orville."

"On the other hand, Miss Anderson, you're *almost* old enough to be my wife."

She blushed more violently this time and would have left him except that he needed her for support. This was the farthest he'd walked on his own. They stopped for him to rest.

Except for the harvesting, it was hard to recognize this as September. The Plants did not change color with the seasons: they just folded their leaves like umbrellas to let the snow pass to the ground. Nor was there any hint of autumn spiciness in the air. The cold of the mornings was a characterless cold.

"It's beautiful out here in the country," Orville said.

"Oh yes. I think so too."

"Have you lived here all your life?"

"Yes, here or in the old town." She darted a sideways look at him. "You're feeling better now, aren't you?"

"Yes, it's great to be alive."

"I'm glad. I'm glad you're well again." Impulsively she caught hold of his hand. He answered with a squeeze. She giggled with delight.

They began to run.

This, then, seemed to be the final stage of his years-long reversion to the primitive. Orville could not imagine a more unseemly action than the one he intended, and its baseness only heightened the bloody passion that continued to grow in him. His revenge now demanded more than Anderson, more than the man's entire family. It demanded the whole community. And time to savor their annihilation. He must wring every drop of agony from them, from each of them; he must take them, gradually, to the limit of their capacity for suffering and only then push them over the edge.

Blossom turned in her sleep and her hands clutched at the pillow of corn husks. Her mouth opened and closed, opened and closed, and beads of sweat broke out on her brow and in the dainty hollow between her breasts. There was a weight on her chest, as though someone were pressing her into the earth with his heavy boots. He was going to kiss her. When his mouth opened, she could see the screw turning within. Shreds of ground meat tumbled forth. The screw made a dreary rasping sound.

Chapter 6

THANKSGIVING

Gray clouds were massing overhead. The ground was dry, bare, gray; no grass, no trees, only the Plants, folded for the winter like parasols, grew here. The dull, autumnal light would thicken at times, and a breeze would pass through the park, picking up the dust. Sitting at the concrete picnic tables on the cold benches, a person could see his own breath. Bare hands grew numb and stiff in the cold. All through the park, people exercised their freezing toes inside their shoes and wished that Anderson would finish saying grace.

Across from the park stood what remained of the Congregationalist Church. Anderson had not let his own people cannibalize the wood from the church, but last winter marauders had stripped off the doors for firewood and broken the windows for fun. The winds had filled the church with snow and dust, and in the spring the oak floor had been covered with a lush green carpet of young Plants. Fortunately it had been discovered in time (for which they were to be thankful), but even so the floor would probably soon collapse of its own weight.

Buddy, wearing his single surviving suit, shivered as the prayer dragged out its slow length. Anderson, standing at the head of the table, was also wearing a suit for the occasion, but Neil, sitting on his father's left hand and facing Buddy, had never owned a suit. He was bundled in woollen shirts and a denim jacket, enviably snug.

It was the custom of the townspeople, like expatriates who returned home on brief visits to establish their legal residence, to celebrate all festive occasions except Christmas here in the old town park. Like so many of the unpleasant and disheartening things they had to do, it was necessary for their morale.

Anderson, having at length established the principle that God Almighty was responsible for their manifolded blessings, began to enumerate them. The most salient of these blessings was never directly referred to—that, after seven and a half years, they were all still alive (all of them that were), while so many others, the great majority, were dead. Anderson, however, dwelt on more peripheral blessings, local to that year: the abundance of the harvest, Gracie's continued health in her tenth month with calf (not referring to associated losses), the two recent litters of pigs, and such game as the hunters had come home with. Unfortunately, this had been little (one deer and several rabbits), and a surly, scolding note crept into the prayer. Anderson soon rallied and came to a graceful close, thanking his Creator for the wealth of his great Creation and his Savior for the promise of Salvation.

Orville was the first to respond. His *amen* was reverent and at the same time manly. Neil mumbled something with the rest of them and reached for the jug of whiskey (they called it whiskey), which was still three-quarters full.

Lady and Blossom, who sat together at the end of the table nearest the brick barbecue, began serving the soup. It was faintly reminiscent of rabbit and poorly seasoned with weeds from the lake.

"Dig in!" she said cheerily. "There's plenty more coming."

What else could you say on Thanksgiving?

Since it was an important holiday, the whole family, on both sides, was together. Besides the seven Andersons, there was Mae, Lady's younger sister, and her husband, Joel Stromberg, formerly of Stromberg's Lakeside Resort Cabins, and the two little Strombergs, Denny, age ten, and Dora, eight. There were, moreover, the Anderson's special guests (still on probation), Alice Nemerov, R.N., and Jeremiah Orville.

Lady could not but regret the presence of the Strombergs, for she was certain that Denny and Dora would only remind her husband more forcibly of him who was absent from the table. Then, too, the years had not dealt kindly with her dear sister. Mae had been admired as a beauty in her youth (though probably not to the degree Lady had been), but at forty-five she was a frump and a troublemaker. Admittedly, she still had her flame-red hair, but that only pointed up the decay of what else remained. The only virtue that remained to her was that she was a solicitous mother. Too much so, Lady thought.

Lady had always hated the brassy reverence of the holidays. Now, when there was not even the ritual gluttony of a turkey dinner to alleviate the gloom that underlay the holiday cheer, one's only hope was to be out of it as quickly as possible. She was grateful, at least, to be occupied with the serving. If she were carefully inefficient, she might get out of eating altogether.

"Neil," Greta whispered. "You're drinking too much. You'd better stop."

"Huh?" Neil replied, peering up at his wife (he had the habit, when he ate, of bending down over his food, especially if it was soup).

"You're *drinking* too much."

"I wasn't drinking at all, for gosh sakes!" he said, for the whole table to hear. "I was eating my *soup!*"

Greta cast up her eyes to heaven, a martyr to truth. Buddy smiled at the transparency of her purpose, and she caught his smile. There was a flicker of eyelashes, no more.

" 'N any case, it ain't any business of yours *how* much I drink or don't drink. I'll drink just as much as I want." To demonstrate this, he poured himself some more of the liquor distilled from the pulpy leaves of the Plant.

It didn't taste like Jim Beam, but Orville had testified to its purity from his own experience of it in Duluth. It was the first use, as food, that Anderson had been able to find for the Plants, and since he was by no means a teetotaller himself, he'd given the project his blessing. Anderson wanted to frown at the way Neil was swilling it down, but he said nothing, not wanting it to look as though he were taking Greta's side. Anderson was a firm believer in male supremacy.

"Anyone want more soup?" Blossom asked.

"I do," said Maryann, who was sitting between her husband and Orville. She ate all she could get now, for the baby's sake. For her little Buddy.

"And I do," said Orville, with that special smile of his.

"I do, too," said Denny and Dora, whose parents had told them to eat all they could at the dinner, which Anderson was providing.

"Anybody else?"

Everybody else had returned to the whiskey, which tasted unpleasantly like liquorice.

Joel Stromberg was describing the progress of his disease to Alice Nemerov, R.N. "And it doesn't really hurt—that's the funny thing. It's just that whenever I want to use my hands they start to shaking. And now my head's the same way. Something's got to be done."

"But I'm afraid, Mr. Stromberg, that nothing can be. There used to be some drugs, but even they didn't work very well. Six months, and the symptoms would reappear. Fortunately, as you say, it doesn't hurt."

"You're a nurse, aren't you?"

He was going to be one of *those!* Very carefully, she began to explain everything she knew about Parkinson's disease, and a few things she didn't. If only she could involve someone else in the conversation! The only other soul within speaking distance was the greedy Stromberg boy, who was snitching drinks from the glass of that foul liquor (one taste had been enough for Alice) sitting before Lady's empty plate. If only Lady or Blossom would stop serving food and sit down for a minute, she could escape from the intolerable hypochondriac. "Tell me," she said, "when did it all start?"

The fish were all eaten, and Blossom began gathering the bones. The moment everyone had been waiting for—the dreadful moment of the main course—could be put off no longer. While Blossom brought around the bowl of steaming polenta into which were stirred a few shreds of chicken and garden vegetables, Lady herself distributed the sausages. A hush fell over the table.

Each of them had a single sausage. Each sausage was about nine inches long and three-quarter inch in diameter. They had been crisped over the fire and came to the table still sizzling.

There is some pork in them, Alice reassured herself. *I probably won't be able to tell the difference.*

Everyone's attention turned to the head of the table. Anderson lifted his knife and fork. Then, fully aware of the solemnity of the moment, he sliced off a piece of hot sausage, put it in his mouth, and began to chew. After what seemed a full minute, he swallowed it.

There, but for the grace of God . . . , Alice thought.

Blossom had turned quite pale, and under the table Alice reached for her hand to lend her strength, though Alice didn't feel an excess of it just then.

"What's everyone waiting for?" Anderson demanded. "There's food on the table."

Alice's attention drifted toward Orville, who was sitting there with knife and fork in hand, and that strange smile of his. He caught Alice's look—and winked at her. Of all things! Or was it *her?*

Orville cut off a piece of the sausage and chewed it consideringly. He smiled beamishly, like a man in a toothpaste ad. "Mrs. Anderson," he announced, "you are a *marvelous* cook. How do you do it? I haven't had a Thanksgiving dinner like this since God knows when."

Alice felt Blossom's fingers relax and pull out of hers. *She's feeling better, now that the worst is over,* Alice thought.

But she was wrong. There was a heavy noise, as when a bag of meal is dropped to the ground, and Mae Stromberg screamed. Blossom had fainted.

He, Buddy, would not have allowed it, much less have originated and insisted upon it, but then very probably he, Buddy, would not have been able to bring the village through those seven hellish years. Primitive, pagan, unprecedented as it was, there *was* a rationale for it.

It. They were all afraid to call it by its right name. Even Buddy, in the inviolable privacy of his own counsel, shied away from the word for it.

Necessity might have been some justification. There was ample precedent (the Donner party, the wreck of the *Medusa*), and Buddy would have had to go no further than this for an excuse—if they had been starving.

Beyond necessity, explanations grew elaborate and rather metaphysical. Thus, metaphysically, in this meal the community was united by a complex bond, the chief of whose elements was complicity in murder, but this complicity was achieved by a ritual as solemn and mysterious as the kiss by which Judas betrayed Christ; it was a sacrament. Mere horror was subsumed into tragedy, and the town's Thanksgiving dinner was the crime and the atonement, so to speak, in one blow.

Thus the theory, but Buddy, in his heart, felt nothing but the horror of it, mere horror, and nothing in his stomach but nausea.

He washed down another steadfast mouthful with the liquorice-flavored alcohol.

Neil, when he had polished off his second sausage, began to tell a dirty joke. They had all, except for Orville and Alice, heard him tell the same joke last Thanksgiving. Orville was the only one to laugh, which made it worse rather than better.

"Where the hell is the deer?" Neil shouted, as though this followed naturally from the punch line.

"What are you talking about?" his father asked. Anderson, when he drank (and today he was almost keeping up to Neil), brooded. In his youth he had had a reputation as a mean fighter after his eighth or ninth beer.

"The *deer,* for Christ's sake! The deer I shot the other day! Aren't we going to have some venison? What the hell kind of Thanksgiving is this?"

"Now, Neil," Greta chided, "you *know* that has to be salted down for the winter. There'll be little enough meat as it is."

"Well, where are the other deer? Three years ago those woods were swarming with deer."

"I've been wondering about that myself," Orville said, and again he was David Niven or perhaps, a little more somberly, James Mason. "Survival is a matter of ecology. That's how I'd explain it. Ecology is the way the different plants and animals live together. That is to say—who eats whom. The deer—and just about everything else, I'm afraid—are becoming extinct."

There was a silent but perceptible gasp from several persons at the table who had thought as much but never dared say so in Anderson's presence.

"God will provide," Anderson interposed darkly.

"Yes, that must be our hope, for Nature alone will not. Just consider what's happened to the soil. This used to be forest soil, podzol. Look at it—" He scooped up a handful of the gray dust on the ground. "Dust. In a couple of years, with no grass or brush to hold it down, every inch of topsoil will be in the lake. Soil is a living thing, it's full of insects, worms—I don't know what all."

"Moles," Neil put in.

"Ah, *moles!*" said Orville, as though that cinched it. "And all those things live on the decaying plants and leaves in the soil—or on each other, the way we do. You've probably noticed that the Plants don't shed their leaves. So, except where we plant crops, the soil is dying. No, it's dead already. And when the soil is dead, plants—*our* plants—will not be able to live in it again. Not the way they used to."

Anderson snorted his contempt for so preposterous a notion.

"But deer don't live underground," Neil objected.

"True—they are herbivores. Herbivores need to eat grass. For a while, I suppose, they must have lived on the young Plants springing up near the lakeshore, or else, like rabbits, they can eat the bark from the older Plants. But either that was an inadequate diet nutritionally, or there wasn't enough to go around, or—"

"Or what?" Anderson demanded.

"Or the wild life is being eliminated the way your cows were last summer, the way Duluth was in August."

"You can't prove it," Neil shouted. "I've seen those piles of ashes in the woods. They don't prove a thing. Not a thing!" He took a long swallow from the jug and stood up, waving his right hand to *show* that it couldn't be proved. He did not estimate the position or inertia of the concrete table very well, so that, coming up against it, he was knocked back to his seat and then drawn by gravity to the ground. He rolled in the gray dirt, groaning. He had hurt himself. He was very drunk. Greta, clucking disapproval, got up from the table to help.

"Leave him lay!" Anderson told her.

"Excuse *me!*" she declaimed, exiting grandly. "Excuse me for living."

"What ashes was he talking about?" Orville asked Anderson.

"I haven't the faintest idea," the old man said. He took a swallow from the jug and washed it around in his mouth. Then he let it trickle down his throat, trying to forget the flavor by concentrating on the sting.

Little Denny Stromberg leaned across the table and asked Alice Nemerov if she was going to eat any more of her sausage. She'd taken only a single bite.

"I think not," Alice replied.

"Can I eat it then?" he asked. His blue-green eyes glowed from the liquor he had been sneaking all through the meal. Otherwise, Alice was sure, his were not the sort of eyes to glow. "Please, huh?"

"Don't mind Denny, Miz Nemerov. He doesn't mean to be *rude*. Do you, sweet?"

"Eat it," Alice said, scraping the cold sausage off on to the boy's plate.

Eat it and be damned! she thought.

Mae had just observed that they had been thirteen at the table. ". . . so if you believe the old superstitions, one of us will die before the year's out," she concluded with a gay little laugh, in which only her husband joined. "Well, I do believe it's getting awfully cold here," she added, raising her eyebrows to show that her words bore more than a single meaning. "Though what can you expect at the end of November?"

Nobody seemed to expect anything.

"Mr. Orville, tell me, are you native to Minnesota? I ask because of your accent. It sounds sort of English, if you know what I mean. Are you an American?"

"Mae—really!" Lady scolded.

"He does talk funny, you know. Denny noticed it too."

"Really?" Orville stared at Mae Stromberg intently, as though to count each frizzled red hair, and with the strangest smile. "That's odd. I was raised all my life in Minneapolis. I suppose it's just the difference between the city and the country."

"And you're a city person at heart, just like our Buddy. I'll bet you wish you were back there right now, eh? I know your kind." She winked lewdly to indicate just what kind that was.

"Mae, for heaven's sake—"

But Denny succeeded where Lady could not in bringing Mrs. Stromberg to a stop. He vomited all over the table. The heavings splashed on to the four women around him—Lady, Blossom, Alice, and his mother—and there was a great commotion as the women tried to escape the danger that was threatening anew on Denny's face. Orville couldn't hold him himself—he laughed. He was joined, fortunately, by Buddy and little Dora, whose mouth was filled with sausage. Even Anderson made a noise that might charitably have been interpreted as laughter.

Buddy excused himself, and Orville rose only a moment later, with more compliments for the cook and a scarcely perceptible gesture in Blossom's direction, which, however, Blossom perceived.

Stromberg took his son off into the woods, but not far enough to prevent the rest of them from hearing the whipping.

Neil was asleep on the ground.

Maryann, Dora, and Anderson were left alone at the table. Maryann had been crying off and on all day. Now, since she too had had something to drink, she started to talk: "Oh, I can remember the time . . ."

"Excuse me," said Anderson, leaving the table, and taking the jug with him.

". . . in the old days," Maryann went on. "And everything was so beautiful then—the turkey and the pumpkin pie—and everybody so happy . . ."

Greta, after quitting the table, had gone roundaboutly to the church. Before vanishing into the dark vestibule, she and Buddy, who had watched her all the while, had exchanged a glance and Buddy had nodded *yes*. When the dinner broke up, he followed her there.

"Hello there, stranger!" Apparently she had settled on this gambit permanently.

"Hello, Greta. You were in high form today."

In the vestibule they were out of the line of sight from the picnic grounds. The floor was reassuringly solid. Greta took the nape of Buddy's neck firmly in her two cold hands and pulled his lips to hers. Their teeth gnashed together, and their tongues renewed an old acquaintance.

When he began to pull her closer, she drew back, laughing softly. Having gained what she wanted, she could afford to tease. Yes, that was the old Greta.

"Wasn't Neil drunk?" she whispered. "Wasn't he just stinko?"

The expression in her eyes was not exactly as he remembered it, and he could not tell, of the body beneath her winter clothes, whether it had changed likewise. It occurred to him to wonder how much *he* had changed, but the desire mounting within him overrode such irrelevancies. Now it was he who kissed her. Slowly, in an embrace, they began to sink to the floor.

"Oh no," she whispered, "don't."

They were on their knees thus, when Anderson entered. He did not say anything for a long time, nor did they rise. A strange, sly look came over Greta's face, and Buddy thought that it had been this, nothing but this, which Greta had hoped for. She had chosen the church for that very reason.

Anderson made a gesture for them to get up, and he allowed Greta to leave, only after spitting in her face.

Was this compassion, that he did not demand the punishment that the law—his own law—exacted of adulterers: that they be stoned? Or was it only parental weakness? Buddy could read nothing in the old man's grimace.

"I came here to pray," he said to his son when they were alone. Then, instead of finishing his sentence, he swung his booted foot hard at him, but too slowly—perhaps it was the liquor—for Buddy twisted aside in time and received the kick safely in his hip.

"Okay, boy, we'll take care of this later," Anderson promised, his voice slurring the words. Then he went into the church to pray.

It seemed that Buddy was no longer to enjoy the position he had inherited last June of being foremost in his father's favor. As he left the church, the first snowflakes of the new season drifted down from the gray sky. Buddy watched them melting on the palm of his hand.

Chapter 7

ADVENT

Gracie the cow lived right there in the commonroom with everybody else. The chickens, likewise, had a corner to themselves, but the pigs were housed in a sty of their own, outside.

For four days, beginning that Thanksgiving, the snow had drifted down slowly, ponderously, like snow settling on the miniature town inside a glass paperweight. Then for one week of bright wintry weather the children went sledging down the old lakeshore. After that the snow came down in earnest, driven by gale winds that made Anderson fear for the walls, bolstered though they were by the high drifts. Three or four times a day the men went outside to wind back the "awning" that formed the roof of the commonroom. As the half of the roof heavy with snow was cleared off and rolled up, the other half emerged from its weathertight cocoon to replace it. Aside from this chore and the care of the pigs, the men were idle during a blizzard. The rest of the work—cooking, weaving, looking after the children and the sick—was for women. Later, when the weather cleared, they could hunt again or, with more hope of success, fish through the ice of the lake. There were also plenty of Plants to chop down.

It was hard to get through these idle days. Drink wasn't allowed in the commonroom (there were enough fights as it was), and poker soon lost its appeal when the money in the pot was no more valuable than the money the children played with at their unending games of Monopoly. There were few books to read, except Anderson's calf-bound Bible (the same that once had graced the lecturn of the Episcopal Church) for indoor space was at a premium. Even if there had been books, it was doubtful that anyone would have read them. Orville might have—he seemed a bookish sort. Buddy would have. And Lady had always read a lot too.

The conversation, such as it was, never rose above the level of griping. For the most part, the men imitated Anderson, who sat immobile on the edge of his bed, chewing the pulp of the Plant. It is questionable, however, whether they spent this time, like Anderson, in thought directed to useful ends. When spring came, all the ideas, the projects, the innovations came from Anderson and no one else.

Now, it appeared, there *was* someone else capable of thought. He, by contrast, preferred to think aloud. To the old man, sitting there listening to Jeremiah Orville, the ideas that were put forth seemed positively irreligious at times. The way he talked about the Plants, for instance—as though they were only a superior laboratory specimen. As though he admired their conquest. Yet he said many things, in almost the same breath, that made good sense. Even when the weather was the subject of conversation (and more often than not it was), Orville had something to say about that.

"I still maintain," Clay Kestner had said (this was on the first day of the bad blizzard, but Clay had been maintaining the same thing for several years), "that it's not the weather getting colder but *us* getting out in the cold more. It's psychosomatical. There ain't no *reason* for the weather to get colder."

"Damn it, Clay," Joel Stromberg replied, shaking his head reprovingly (though it might have been just palsy), "if this winter ain't colder than the winters in the sixties and fifties I'll eat my hat. It used to be that we'd worry whether we was going to have a white Christmas. And I say it's the way the lake has gone down causes it."

"Poppycock!" Clay insisted, not without justice.

Usually no one would have paid any more attention to Clay and Joel than to the wind whinning about the spiky Plants outside, but this time Orville intruded: "You know—there *may* be a reason why it's getting colder. Carbon dioxide."

"What's that got to do with the price of eggs?" Clay quipped.

"Carbon dioxide is what the Plants—any plants—take in to combine with water when they're making their own food. It's also what we—that is, animals—exhale. Since the Plants have come, I suspect that the old balance between the carbon dioxide they take in and the amount we give off has started favoring the Plants. So there's less carbon dioxide in the atmosphere. Now, carbon dioxide is a great absorber of heat. It stores heat from the sun and keeps the air warm. So with less carbon dioxide, there'll be a lot more cold and snow. That's just a theory, of course."

"That's a hell of a theory!"

"I'll agree with you there, Clay, since it's not mine. It's one of the reasons geologists give for the ice ages."

Anderson didn't believe strongly in geology since so much of it went against the Bible, but if what Orville said about carbon dioxide was true, then the worsening of the winters (and they were worse, no one really doubted it) might well have that for a cause. But truce or not, there was something he didn't like in Orville's tone, something more than just the know-it-all attitude of the college grad, which Anderson was used to from Buddy. It was as if these little lectures on the wonders of science (and there had been more than a few) had but a single purpose: to lead them to despair.

But he *did* know more science than anyone else, and Anderson grudgingly respected him for it. If nothing else, he'd stopped Clay and Joel from arguing about the weather, and for that small blessing Anderson could not help but give thanks.

It was not as bad yet as it would become in February and March, but it was very bad: the close quarters, the silly quarrels, the noise, the stench, the abrasion of flesh on flesh and nerve on nerve. It was very bad. It was well nigh intolerable.

Two hundred and fifty people lived in 2,400 square feet, and much of that space was given over to storage. Last winter when there had been almost double the number in the same room, when every day witnessed a new death, every month a new epidemic of the deadly common cold, it had been measurably worse. The more susceptible types—those who couldn't bear up—had run amok, singing and laughing, into the deceiving warmth of the January thaws; these were gone this year. This year the walls were firmly anchored and tightly woven from the start; this year the rationing was not so desperately tight (though there *would* be less meat). Yet for all these improvements, it was still an intolerable way to live and everyone knew it.

The thing that Buddy could not stand, the very worst thing, was the presence of so much flesh. All day it rubbed against him, it displayed itself, it stank in his nostrils. And any of the hundred women in the room, even Blossom, would by the simplest gesture, by the tamest word, trigger his lust. Yet for all the good it did him, he might as well have been watching the bloodless phantasms of a movie. There was simply no place, day or night, in the cramped commonroom for sex. His erotic life was limited to such occasions as he could impose upon Maryann to come with him to visit the freezing outhouse by the pig sty. Maryann, in her seventh month and prone at any time to sniffles, seldom accommodated him.

It did not help that, as long as there was daylight in the room, Buddy could look up from whatever he was doing (or more likely— whatever he wasn't doing) and see, probably no more than twenty feet away, Greta.

More and more, he found himself seeking the refuge of Jeremiah Orville's company. Orville was the sort of person, familiar to Buddy from the university, whom he had always liked much more than they had liked him. Though he never once told a joke in Buddy's hearing, when the man talked—and he talked incessantly—Buddy couldn't keep from laughing. It was like the conversations in books and movies or the way people talked on the old Jack Paar show, people who could take the most commonplace thing and, in the telling, make it funny. Orville never tried to clown; his humor was in the way he looked at things—with a certain, sly irreverence (not so much that someone like Anderson could object), an oblique mockery. You never knew where you stood with him, so that most folks —the authentic grassroots hicks like Neil—were reluctant to get into conversations with him, though they listened gladly. Buddy found himself imitating Orville, using *his* words, pronouncing them *his* way (*gen*-uine instead of genu-*wine*), adopting *his* ideas.

It was a constant source of wonder how much the man *knew*. Buddy, who considered his own education barely sufficient to judge the scope of another person's, considered Orville's encyclopedic.

Buddy fell so thoroughly under the older man's influence that it would not be unjust to say he was infatuated. There were times (for instance, such time as Orville would talk too long with Blossom) when Buddy felt something like jealousy.

He would have been surprised to learn that Blossom felt much the same way when Orville spent undue time with him. It was quite evidently a case of infatuation, of conventional puppy-love.

Even Neil had a good word to say for the newcomer, for one day

Orville had taken him aside and taught him a whole new store of dirty jokes.

The hunters hunted alone; the fishermen fished together. Neil, a hunter, was grateful for the chance to be alone, but the lack of game that December aggravated him almost as much as the shove and clamor of the commonroom. But, the day the blizzard stopped, he found deer tracks cutting right through the still-uncrusted snow of the west cornfield. He followed them four miles, stumbling over his own snow-shoes in his eagerness. The tracks terminated in a concavity of ash and ice. No tracks led away from or approached the area. Neil swore loudly. Then he screamed for a while, not really aware that he was screaming. It let off the pressure.

No use hunting now, he thought, when he began to think again. He decided he would rest for the rest of the day. Rest . . . rest! Ha! He'd have to remember that. With the other hunters and fishermen still out of the commonroom, maybe he'd get a little privacy.

That's what he did—he went home and drank a pot of cruddy liquorice-flavored tea (that's what they called it, tea) and he got to feeling drowsy and hardly knew what he was looking at or what he was thinking (he was looking at Blossom and thinking of her) when all of the sudden Gracie started making an uproar like he'd never heard before. Except he had heard it before: Gracie was calving.

The cow was making grunting noises like a pig. She rolled over on her side and squirmed around in the dirt. This was Gracie's first calf, and she wasn't any too big. Trouble was only to be expected. Neil knotted some rope into a noose and got it over her neck but she was thrashing around so that he couldn't get it over her legs so he let that go. Alice, the nurse, was helping him, but he wished his father was there anyhow. Old Gracie was bellowing like a bull now.

Any cow that goes more than an hour is a sure loss, and even half an hour is bad. Gracie was in pain like that and bellowing for half an hour. She kept squirming backward to try and escape the shooting pains. Neil hauled on the rope to keep her from doing that.

"I can see his head. His head's coming out now," Alice said. She was down on her knees in back of Gracie, trying to spread her wider open.

"If that's all you can see, how do you know it's a he?"

The calf's sex was crucial, and everyone in the commonroom had gathered around to watch the calving. After each bellow of pain, the children shouted their encouragement to Gracie. Then her squirming got worse, while her bellowing quieted. "That's it, that's it!" Alice was calling out, and Neil hauled all the harder against the rope.

"It's a boy!" Alice exclaimed. "Thank God, it *is* a boy!"

Neil laughed at the old woman. "It's a *bull* is what you mean. You city slickers are all alike." He felt good because he hadn't made any mistakes and everything was hunky-dory. So he went over to the barrel and got the top off and dipped himself a drink to celebrate. He asked Alice if she wanted one, but she just looked at him funny-like and said no.

He sat down in the room's single easy chair (Anderson's) and watched the little bull-calf sucking at Gracie's full udder. Gracie hadn't got up. She must have been exhausted by the birthing. Why, if Neil hadn't been around, she probably wouldn't of lived through it probably. The liquorice flavor wasn't so bad once you got used to it. All the women were quiet now, and the children too.

Neil looked at the bull-calf and thought how someday it'd be a big horny bull mounting Gracie—his own mother! *Animals,* he thought foggily, *are just like animals*. But that wasn't it exactly.

He had some more to drink.

When Anderson got home he looked like he'd had a bad day (was the afternoon gone already?), but Neil got up from the warm chair and called out happily: "Hey, Dad, it's a bull!"

Anderson came up, and he looked the way Neil remembered him looking Thanksgiving night, all dark and with that ugly smile (but he hadn't said a word then or later, about Neil drinking too much at dinner), and he hit Neil in the face, he just knocked him right down on the floor.

"You goddamn stupid asshole!" Anderson yelled. "You dumb turd! Don't you know that Gracie's dead? You strangled her to death, you son of a bitch!"

Then he kicked Neil. Then he went over and cut Gracie's neck where the rope was still tight around it. Most of the cold blood went into the basin Lady was holding, but some of it spilled out in the dirt. The calf was pulling at the dead cow's udder, but there wasn't any more milk. Anderson cut the calf's throat too.

It wasn't *his* fault, was it? It was Alice's fault. He hated Alice. He hated his father too. He hated all those bastards who thought they were so goddamn smart. He hated all of them. He hated all of them.

And he cupped his pain in his two hands and tried not to scream from the pain in his hands and the pain in his head, the pain of hating, but maybe he did scream, who knows?

Shortly before dark the snow began to come down again, a perfectly perpendicular descent through the windless air. The only light in the commonroom came from the single hurricane lamp burning in the kitchen alcove where Lady was scouring the well scoured pots. No one spoke. Who dared say how fine the usual mush of cornmeal and rabbit tasted flavored with the blood of cow and calf. It was quiet enough to hear the chickens fussing and clucking in their roosts in the far corner.

When Anderson went outside to direct the butchering and salting down of the carcasses, neither Neil nor Buddy was invited to participate. Buddy sat by the kitchen door on the dirty welcome mat and pretended to read a freshman biology text in the semi-darkness. He had read it through many times before and knew some passages by heart. Neil was sitting by the other door, trying to screw up the courage to go outside and join the butchers.

Of all the townspeople, Buddy was probably the only one who took pleasure in Gracie's death. In the weeks since Thanksgiving, Neil had been winning his way back into his father's favor. Now since Neil himself had so effectively reversed that trend, Buddy reasoned that it would be only a matter of time before he would again enjoy the privileges of his primogeniture. The extinction of the species (were Herefords a species?) was not too high a price to pay.

There was one other who rejoiced at this turn of events, but he was not, either in his own estimation or in theirs, one of the townspeople. Jeremiah Orville had hoped that Gracie or her calf or both might die, for the preservation of the cattle had been one of Anderson's proudest achievements, a token that civilization-as-we-had-known-it was not quite passé and a sign, for those who would see it, that Anderson was truly of the Elect. That the agency that would realize Orville's hopes should be the incompetence of the man's own son afforded Orville an almost aesthetic pleasure: as though some tidy, righteous deity were assisting his revenge, scrupulous that the laws of poetic justice be observed. Orville was happy tonight, and he worked at the butchering with a quiet fury. From time to time, when he could not be seen, he swallowed a gobblet of raw beef—for he was as hungry as any man there. But he would starve willingly, if only he might see Anderson starve before him.

A peculiar noise, a windy sound but not the wind, caught his attention. It seemed familiar, but he couldn't place it. It was a sound that belonged to the city. Joel Stromberg, who was looking after the pigs, shouted: "Ah, hey!—there—whadaya—" Abruptly, Joel was metamorphosed into a pillar of fire.

Orville saw this no more distinctly than he had heard the sound preceding it, but without taking thought he hurled himself over a nearby snowbank. He rolled in the powdery snow till he was out of sight of everything—the carcasses, the other men, the pigsty. Everything but the flames rising from the burning sty. "Mr. Anderson!" he yelled. Terrified lest he lose his intended victim to the fires of the incendiaries, he crawled back to rescue the old man.

Three spherical bodies, each about five feet in diameter, floated just above the snow at the periphery of the flames. The men (with the exception of Anderson, who was crouched behind the flank of the dead cow, aiming his pistol at the nearest sphere) stood watching the blaze, as though bewitched. Spumes of steamy breath drifted from their open mouths.

"Don't waste bullets on armor plate, Mr. Anderson. Come on—they'll fire the commonroom next. We've got to get the people out of there."

"Yes," Anderson agreed, but he did not move. Orville had to pull him away. In that moment of stuporous incapacity, Orville thought he saw in Anderson the seed of what Neil had become.

Orville entered the commonroom first. Since the walls were buttressed with great drifts of snow, none of them was yet aware of the blaze outside. They were, as they had been all evening, leaden with unhappiness. Several had already got into bed.

"Everybody—start getting your clothes on," Orville commanded in a voice as calm as authoritative. "Leave this room as quickly as possible by the kitchen door and run into the woods. Take anything with you that's at hand, but don't waste time looking for things. Don't wait for someone else to catch up. Quickly, now."

As many as had heard Orville looked dumbfounded. It was not for him to be giving orders.

"Quickly," Anderson directed. "And no questions."

They were accustomed to obeying Anderson unquestioningly, but there was still much confusion. Anderson, accompanied by Orville, went directly to the area by the kitchen where his own family was quartered. They were all bundling into their heavy clothes, but Anderson bundled them faster.

Outside there were screams, brief as the whistle of a slaughtered rabbit, as the incendiary devices were turned on their spectators. A man ran into the room, flaming, and fell to the floor dead. The panic began. Anderson, already near the door, commanded respect even in the midst of hysteria and managed to get his family out among the first. Passing through the kitchen, Lady grabbed an empty cooking pot. Blossom was burdened with a basket of laundry, which, proving too heavy, she emptied into the snow. Orville, in his anxiety to see them out of the commonroom safely, took nothing at all. There were no more than fifty people running through the snow when the far corner of the commonroom caught fire. The first flames shot up thirty feet from the roof, then began to climb as they ate into the bags of corn stacked against the walls.

It is hard to run through unpacked snow, just as it is hard to run in knee-deep water: as soon as you acquire momentum, you are apt to tumble forward. Lady and Greta had left the house wearing only straw slippers, and others streamed out the door now in their nightshirts or wrapped in blankets.

The Andersons had almost reached the forest edge when Lady threw aside her cooking pot and exclaimed: *"The Bible! The Bible is back there!"*

No one heard her. She ran toward the burning building. By the time Anderson was aware of his wife's absence, there was no longer any way to stop her. His own scream would not be heard among so many others. The family stopped to watch. "Keep running." Orville shouted at them, but they paid no heed. Most of those who had escaped the house had reached the wood by now.

The flames illuminated the neighborhood of the building for a hundred feet, making the snow shine with an unsteady orange glow upon which the swift, uncertain shadows of the smoke rippled, like the fires of visible darkness.

Lady entered by the kitchen door and did not reemerge. The roof caved in; the walls fell outward, neatly as dominoes. The three spherical bodies could be seen in silhouette to rise higher from the ground. In close formation they began to glide toward the wood, their hum disguised by the crackling of the flames. Within the triangle they defined, the snow melted and bubbled and rose steaming into the air.

"Why would she do a thing like that?" Anderson asked of his daughter, but seeing that she was delicately poised on the brink of hysteria, he took her in one hand and the length of the rope he had taken up from a wheelbarrow outside the house in the other and hurried after the others. Orville and Neil were practically carrying barefoot Greta, who was screaming obscenities in her rich contralto.

Orville was frantic, and yet close behind the frenzy was a sense of exultation and headlong delight that made him want to cheer, as though the conflagration behind them were as innocent and festal as a homecoming game bonfire.

When he shouted *"Hurry on; hurry on!"* it was hard to tell whether he was calling to Anderson and Blossom or to the three incendiaries not far behind them.

Chapter 8

THE WAY DOWN

Maybe *we'll die*, Maryann thought, when they had at last stopped running and she could think. But that was impossible. It was so cold! She wished to heaven she could understand what Anderson was talking about. He'd just said: "We'll have to take inventory." They were all standing around in the snow. It was so cold, and when she'd fallen down she'd got snow inside her coat, under her collar. The snow was still coming down in the dark. She'd catch a cold and then what would she do? Where would she live? And her baby— what about him?

"Maryann?" Anderson asked. *"She's* here, isn't she?"

"Maryann!" Buddy barked impatiently.

"I'm here," she said, snuffling the wet that trickled from her nose.

"Well—what did you bring with you?"

Each of her numb hands (she'd forgotten mittens too) was holding something, but she didn't know what. She held up her hands so she could see what was in them. "Lamps," she said. "The lamps from the kitchen, but one of them is broken. The chimney's smashed." It was only then that she remembered falling on it and cutting her knee.

"Who's got matches?" Orville asked.

Clay Kestner had matches. He lit the good lamp. By its light Anderson took a headcount: "Thirty-one." There was a long silence while each survivor examined the thirty-one faces and tallied his own losses. There were eighteen men, eleven women and two children.

Mae Stromberg began to cry. She'd lost a husband and a daughter, though her son was with her. In the panic Denny had not been able to find the shoe for his left foot, and Mae had pulled him the three miles from the conflagration on one of the children's sledges. Anderson, having concluded the inventory, told Mae to be quiet.

"Maybe there'll be more food back there," Buddy was saying to his father. "Maybe it won't be burned up so bad we can't still eat it."

"I doubt it," Orville said. "Those damn flamethrowers are pretty thorough."

"How long will what we've got last if we ration it?" Buddy asked.

"Till Christmas," Anderson replied curtly.

"If *we* last till Christmas," Orville said. "Those machines are probably scouting the woods now, picking off anyone who got out of the fire. There's also a matter of where we'll spend the night. Nobody thought to bring along tents."

"We'll go back to the old town," Anderson said. "We can stay in the church and tear off the siding for firewood. Does anyone know where we are now? Every goddam Plant in this forest looks like every other goddam Plant."

"I've got a compass," Neil volunteered. "I'll get us there. You just follow me." Off in the distance, there was a scream, a very brief scream. "I think it's that way," Neil said, moving toward the scream.

They formed a broad phalanx with Neil at the head and moved on through the snowy night. Orville pulled Greta along on the sledge, and Buddy carried Denny Stromberg on his back.

"Can I hold your hand?" Maryann asked him. "Mine are just numb."

Buddy let her put her hand in his, and they walked along together for a half-hour in perfect silence. Then he said, "I'm glad you're safe."

"Oh!" It was all she could say. Her nose was dripping like a leaky faucet, and she began to cry too. The tears froze on her cold cheeks. Oh, she was so happy!

They almost walked through the village without realizing it. An inch of snow had blanketed the cold, leveled ashes.

Denny Stromberg was the first to speak. "Where will we go now, Buddy? Where will we sleep?" Buddy didn't answer. Thirty people waited in silence for Anderson, who was kicking the ashes with the toe of his boot, to lead them through this Red Sea.

"We must kneel and pray," he said. "Here, in this church, we must kneel and ask forgiveness for our sins." Anderson knelt in the snow and ashes. "Almighty and merciful God . . ."

A figure came out of the woods, running, stumbling, breathless—a woman in bedclothes with a blanket wrapped shawl-like about her. Falling to her knees in the middle of the group, she could not draw breath to speak. Anderson ceased praying. In the direction from which she had come, the forest glowed faintly, as though, at a distance, a candle were burning in a farmhouse window.

"It's Mrs. Wilks," Alice Nemerov announced, and at the same moment Orville said, "We'd better pray somewhere else. That looks like a new fire over there."

"There *is* nowhere else," Anderson said.

"There must be," Orville insisted. Under the pressure of hours of crisis, he had lost track of his original motive—to save the Andersons for his personal revenge, for slower agonies. His desire was more primary—self-preservation. "If there are no houses left, there must still be some place to hide: a burrow, a cave, a culvert . . ." Something he had said touched the chord of memory. A burrow? A cave?

"A cave! Blossom, a long time ago, when I was sick, you told me you'd been in a cave. You'd never seen a mine, but you'd been in a cave. Was that near here?"

"It's by the lake shore—the old lake shore. Near Stromberg's Resort. It's not far, but I haven't been in it since I was a little girl. I don't know if it's still there."

"How big a cave is it?"

"Very big. At least, I thought so then."

"Could you take us there?"

"I don't know. It's hard enough in the summertime to find your way around through the Plants. All the old landmarks are gone, and with the snow besides . . ."

"Take us there, girl! Now!" Anderson rasped. He was himself again, more or less.

They left the half-naked woman behind them lying in the snow. Not through cruelty: it was simply forgetfulness. When they had gone, the woman looked up and said, "Please." But the people whom she had thought to address were not there. Perhaps they had never been there. She got to her feet and dropped her blanket.

It was very cold. She heard the humming sound again and ran blindly back into the woods, heading in the opposite direction from that which Blossom had taken.

The three incendiary spheres glided to the spot where the woman had lain, quickly converted the blanket there to ash, and moved on after Mrs. Wilks, following the spoor of blood.

Much of the old lake shore was still recognizable under the mantle of snow: the conformation of the rocks, the stairways going down to the water—they even found a post that had once been part of the resort's pier. From the pier Blossom estimated it would be a hundred yards to the cave entrance. She went along the rockface that rose ten feet above the old beach and played the lamplight into likely crevasses. Wherever she directed him, Buddy cleared the snow with a shovel, which, along with an axe, he had rescued from the commonroom. The other searchers scraped off the snow (which had drifted more than a yard deep among the boulders) with their hands, mittened or bare, as luck would have it.

The work went slowly, for Blossom remembered the entrance to the cave as being half-way up the rockface, so that one had to clamber over snowy rocks to be able to dig. Despite the hazard this involved, they did not have time to be careful. Behind the clouds, from which the snow sifted steadily down, there was no moon; the digging went on in near-total darkness. At regular intervals one of them would call a sudden halt to the work and they would stand there straining to hear the telltale hum of their pursuers that someone had thought he'd heard.

Blossom, under the unaccustomed weight of responsibility, became erratic, running from rock to rock. "Here!" she would say, and then, running: "Or here?" She was a good two hundred yards from the old pier, and Buddy began to doubt that there *was* a cave.

If there were not, then surely they had come to an end.

The prospect of death disturbed him most in that he could not grasp the *purpose* of these burnings. If this were an invasion (and even his father could not doubt that now; the Good Lord did not need to build machines to wreak his vengeance), what did the invaders want? Were the Plants themselves the invaders? No, no—

they were only Plants. One had to suppose that the real invaders—the ones inside the incendiary globes (or whoever had built them and put them to work)—wanted the Earth for no other reason than to grow their damn Plants. Was Earth, then, their farm? If so, why had there been no harvest?

It wounded his pride to think that his race, his species, his world was being defeated with such apparent ease. What was worse, what he could not endure was the suspicion that it all meant nothing, that the process of their annihilation was something quite mechanical: that mankind's destroyers were not, in other words, fighting a war but merely spraying the garden.

The opening to the cave was discovered inadvertently—Denny Stromberg fell through it. Without that happy chance, they might well have gone the whole night without finding it, for everyone in their party had passed it by.

The cave went farther back than the lamplight would reach from the entrance, but before the full depth was explored, everyone was inside. All the adults except Anderson, Buddy, and Maryann (all three under five feet six) had to bend over double or even crawl to keep from hitting their heads against the crumbling ceiling. Anderson declared that the moment for silent prayer was at hand, for which Orville was grateful. Huddled next to each other for warmth, their back against the sloping wall of the cave, they tried to recover their sense of identity, of purpose, of touch—whatever senses they had lost in the hours-long stampede through the snow. The lamp was left burning, since Anderson judged that matches were more precious than oil.

After five minutes given over to prayers, Anderson, Buddy, Neil and Orville (though not of the family hierarchy, he *had* been the one to think of the cave—and of more things besides than Anderson cared to reckon) explored the back of the cave. It was big but not so big as they'd hoped, extending some twenty feet to the rear, narrowing continually. At its far end, there was a small el filled with bones.

"Wolves!" Neil declared.

Closer inspection confirmed this with some definiteness, for the skeletons of the wolves themselves were discovered, stripped as clean as the others, topmost on the pile.

"Rats," Neil decided. "Just rats."

To reach the far depth of the cave they had had to squeeze past the gigantic root of a Plant that had broken through the cave wall. Returning from the pile of bones the men examined this, the only other exceptional feature of the cave, with some care. The Plant's root at this level was very little distinguishable from its trunk. To judge from the curvature of the portion exposed in the cave, it was, like the bol of the Plant, some fourteen or fifteen feet in diameter. Near the floor of the cave, the smooth surface of the root was abraded, just as the smooth green trunks were often chewed by hungry rabbits. Here, however, there appeared to be more than a nibble taken out.

Orville stooped to examine it. "Rabbits didn't do this. It's gone right to the heart of the wood." He reached his hand into the dark hole. The outermost layer of wood extended no more than a foot, beyond which his fingers encountered what seemed a tangle of vines —and beyond this (his whole shoulder pressing against the hole), nothing; emptiness; air. "The thing is hollow!"

"Nonsense," Anderson said. He got down beside Orville and thrust his own arm into the hole. "It can't be," he said, feeling that it could be and was.

"Rabbits certainly didn't make *that* hole," Orville insisted.

"Rats," Neil repeated, more than ever confirmed in his judgment. But, as usual, no one paid him any attention.

"It *grows* that way. Like the stem of a dandelion—it's hollow."

"It's dead. Termites must have gotten to it."

"The only dead Plants I've seen, Mr. Anderson, are the ones we've killed. If you don't object, I'd like to see what's down there."

"I don't see what good that could do. You have an unhealthy curiosity about these Plants, young man. I sometimes have the impression that you're more on their side than ours."

"The good it could do," Orville said, half-truthfully (for he dared not yet express his real hope), "is that it may provide a back door to the cave—an escape hatch to the surface in the event that we're followed here."

"He's right about that, you know," Buddy volunteered.

"I don't need your help to make up my mind. *Either* of you," Anderson added when he saw that Neil had begun to smile at this. "You are right again, Jeremiah . . ."

"Just call me Orville, sir. Everyone else does."

Anderson smiled acidly. "Yes. Well. Shall we start to work now? As I recall, one of the men managed to bring a hatchet. Oh, it was

you, Buddy? Bring it here. Meanwhile, you—" (designating Orville)
"—will see that everyone moves to the back of the cave, where
they'll be warmer. And safer perhaps. Also, find some way to block
up the entrance, so the snow will cover it over again. Use your coat
if necessary."

When the opening to the root had been sufficiently enlarged, Anderson thrust the lamp in and squeezed his bony torso through. The
cavity narrowed rapidly overhead, becoming no more than a tangle
of vines; there was little possibility of an exit—at least not without
much hard work. But *below* was an abyss that stretched quite beyond the weak shaft of light from the lamp. The lamp's effectiveness
was further diminished by what seemed to be a network of gauze or
cobweb that filled the hollow of the root. The light passing through
this airy stuff was diffused and softened so that beyond a depth of
fifteen feet one could discern only a formless, pinkish glow.

Anderson swiped at these strands of gauze, and they broke
unresistingly. His calloused hand could not even feel them giving
way.

Anderson squirmed back out of the narrow hole and into the cave
proper. "Well, it won't be any use to escape by. It's solid up above.
It goes *down,* though—farther than I can see. Look for yourself if
you want."

Orville wormed into the hole. He stayed there so long, Anderson
became annoyed. When he reappeared he was almost grinning.
"That's where we'll go, Mr. Anderson. Why, it's perfect!"

"You're crazy," Anderson said matter-of-factly. "We're bad
enough off where we are."

"But the point is—" (And this had been his original, unexpressed
hope.) "—that it will be *warm* down there. Once you get fifty feet
below the surface, it's always a comfortable fifty degrees Fahrenheit.
There's no winter and no summer that deep in the ground. If you
prefer it warmer than that just go down deeper. It warms up one degree for every sixty feet."

"Ah, what are you talking about?" Neil jeered. "That sounds like
a lot of hooey." He didn't like the way Orville—a stranger—was
telling them what to do all the time. He had no *right!*

"It's one thing I should know about, being a mining engineer.
Isn't that why I'm alive, after all?" He let that sink in, then continued calmly: "One of the biggest problems in working deep mines is
keeping them at a bearable temperature. The least we can do is see

how far down it does go. It must be fifty feet at least—that would be only a tenth of its height."

"There's no soil fifty feet down," Anderson objected. "Nothing but rock. Nothing grows in rock."

"Tell that to the Plant. I don't know if it does go that deep, but again I say we should explore. We've a length of rope, and even if we didn't those vines would support any of us. I tested them." He paused before he returned to the clinching argument: "If nothing else, it's a place to hide if those things find their way to us."

His last argument turned out as valid as it had been effective. Buddy had only just gone down by the rope to the first branching off of the secondary roots from the vertical primary root (Buddy had been chosen because he was the lightest of the men), when there was a grating sound at the entrance of the cave, as when children try to fill a glass bottle with sand. One of the spheres, having tracked them to the cave, was now trying to bulldoze its way through the narrow entrance.

"Shoot!" Neil yelled at his father. "Shoot it!" He started to grab for the Python in his father's side holster.

"I don't intend to waste good ammunition on armor plate. Now, get your hands off me and let's start pushing people down that hole."

Orville did not have to prompt any further. There was nothing left for them to do. Not a thing. They were the puppets of necessity now. He stood back from the mêlée and listened as the sphere tried to shove its way into the cave by main force. In some ways, he thought, those spheres were no smarter than a chicken trying to scratch its way through a wire fence that it could walk around. Why not just shoot? Perhaps the three spheres had to be grouped about their target before they could go zap. They were, almost surely, automatons. They directed their own destinies no more than did the animals they were programmed to track down. Orville had no sympathy for the dumb machines and none for their prey. He rather fancied himself at that moment as the puppeteer, until the real puppeteer, necessity, twitched a finger, and Orville went running after his fellow men.

The descent into the root was swift and efficient. The size of the hole insured that no more than one person passed through at a time, but fear insured that that person got through as fast as he could. The unseen (the lamp was below with Buddy) presence of the metal sphere grinding at the ceiling and walls of the cave was a strong motivation to speed.

Anderson made each person strip off his bulky outer clothing and push it through the hole ahead of him. At last only Anderson, Orville, Clay Kestner, Neil and Maryann were left. It was evident that for Clay and Neil (the largest men of the village) and for Maryann, now in her eighth month, the hole would have to be enlarged. Neil chopped at the pulpy wood with frantic haste and much wasted effort. Maryann was eased first through the expanded opening. When she reached her husband, who was astraddle the inverse *v* formed by the divergence of the branch root from the greater taproot, her hands were raw from having slipped down the rope too quickly. As soon as he laid hold of her, all her strength seemed to leave her body. She could not go on. Neil was the next to descend, then Clay Kestner. Together they carried Maryann on into the secondary root.

Anderson called out, "Watch out below!" and a steady rain of objects—foodstuffs, baskets, pots, clothing, the sledge, whatever the people had brought with them from the fire—fell into the abyss, shattering the delicate traceries. Buddy tried to count the seconds between the time they were released and the moment they hit bottom, but after a certain point he could not distinguish between the sounds of the objects ricocheting off the walls of the root and their striking bottom, if any. Anderson descended the rope after the last of the provisions had been dropped down the root.

"How is Orville coming down?" Buddy asked. "Who'll hold the rope for him?"

"I didn't bother to ask. Where is everyone else?"

"Down there . . ." Buddy gestured vaguely into the blackness of the secondary root. The lamp was lighting the main shaft, where the descent was more dangerous. The secondary root diverged at a forty-five degree angle from its parent. The ceiling (for here there could be said to be floor and ceiling) rose to a height of seven feet. The entire surface of the root was a tangle of vines, so that the slope was easy to negotiate. The interior space had been webbed with the same fragile lace, though those who preceded Anderson into the root had broken most of it away.

Orville clambered down on the vines, the end of the rope knotted about his waist in the manner of a mountain climber. An unnecessary precaution, as it proved: the vines—or whatever they were—

held firm. They were almost rigid, in fact, from being so closely knit together.

"Well," said Orville, in a voice grotesque with good cheer, "here's everybody, safe and sound. Shall we go down to the basement, where the groceries are?"

At that moment he felt an almost godlike elation, for he had held Anderson's life in his hands—literally, by a string—and it had been his to decide whether the old man should die just then or suffer yet a little longer. It had not been a difficult choice, but, ah, it had been *his!*

Chapter 9

THE WORM SHALL
FEED SWEETLY

When they had ventured down the branch root a further twenty-five feet (where, as Orville had promised, it was tolerably warm), they reached a sort of crossroads. There were three new branches to choose from, each as commodious as the one through which they had been travelling. Two descended, like proper roots, though veering off perpendicularly to the right and left of their parent; the other shot steeply upward.

"That's strange," Buddy observed. "Roots don't grow up."

"How do you know that's up?" Orville asked.

"Well, look at it. It's *up*. Up is . . . up. It's the opposite of down."

"My point exactly. "We're *looking* up the root, which may be *growing* down to us—from another Plant perhaps."

"You mean this thing could be just one big Plant?" Anderson asked, moving into the circle of lamplight, scowling. He resented each further attribute of the Plant, even those that served his purpose. "All of them linking up together down here this way?"

"There's one sure way to find out, sir—follow it. If it takes us to another primary root—"

"We don't have time to be Boy Scouts. Not until we've found the supplies we dropped down that hole. Will we get to them this way? Or will we have to backtrack and climb down the main root on the rope?"

"I couldn't say. This way is easier, faster and, for the moment, safer. If the roots join up like this regularly, maybe we can find another way back to the main root farther down. So I'd say—"

"I'll say," Anderson said, repossessing, somewhat, his authority. Buddy was sent ahead with the lamp and one end of the rope; the thirty others followed after, Indian file. Anderson and Orville bringing up the rear had only the sounds of the advance party to guide them: both the light and the rope were played out this far back.

But there was a plenitude of sound: the shuffle of feet over the vines, men swearing, Denny Stromberg crying. Every so often Greta inquired of the darkness: "Where are we?" or "Where the hell *are* we?" But that was only one noise among many. There were, already, a few premonitory sneezes, but they went unnoticed. The thirty-one people moving through the root were still rather shell-shocked. The rope they held to was at once their motive and their will.

Anderson kept stumbling on the vines. Orville put an arm around the old man's waist to steady him. Anderson tore it loose angrily. "You think I'm some kind of invalid?" he said. "Get the hell out of here!"

But the next time he stumbled, he went headlong into the rough vines of the floor, scratching his face. Rising, he had a dizzy spell and would have fallen again without Orville's help. Despite himself, he felt a twinge of gratitude for the arm that bore him up. In the darkness, he couldn't see that Orville was smiling.

Their path wound on down through the root, passing two more intersections such as the one above. Both times Buddy turned left, so that their descent described, approximately, a spiral. The hollow of the root gave no sign of diminishing; if anything it had been growing larger for the last few yards. There was no danger of becoming lost, for the shattering of the root's lacy interior blazed an unmistakable trail through the labyrinth.

A commotion at the head of the line brought them to a halt. Anderson and Orville pushed their way to the front.

Buddy handed the lamp to his father. "It's a dead end," he announced. "We'll have to go back the way we came."

The root's hollow was much enlarged at this point, and the cobwebby stuff filling it more condensed. Instead of shattering glassily under the force of Anderson's blow, it tore off in handfuls, like rotted fabric. Anderson pressed one of these pieces between his hands.

Like the pink candy floss at carnivals or like the airiest kind of white bread, it wadded into a little ball less than an inch round.

"We'll push our way through," Anderson announced. He took a step back, then threw his shoulder like a football tackle into the yielding floss. His momentum gave out two and a half yards ahead. Then, because there was nothing solid beneath his feet, he began, slowly, to sink out of sight. Inexorably, under his weight, the candy floss gave way. Buddy stretched his hand forward, and Anderson was able barely to catch hold, fingertips hooked in fingertips. Anderson pulled Buddy into the mire with him. Buddy, falling in a horizontal position, served somewhat as a parachute, and they sank more slowly and came to a stop, safely, some ten feet below.

As they fell, a powerful sweetness, like the odor of rotting fruit, filled the air behind them.

Orville was the first to realize their good fortune. He wadded a mass of the floss to a medium density and bit into it. The Plant's characteristic anise flavor could be discerned, but there was besides a fullness and sweetness, a satisfaction, that was quite new. His tongue recognized it before his mind did and craved another taste. No, not just his tongue—his belly. Every malnourished cell of his body craved more.

"Throw us down the rope," Anderson shouted hoarsely. He was not hurt, but he was shaken.

Instead of playing out the rope, Orville, with a happy, carefree shout, dove into the flossy mass. As he was swallowed into its darkness, he addressed the old man below: "Your prayers have been answered, sir. You've led us across the Red Sea, and now the Lord is feeding us manna. Taste the stuff—taste it! We don't have to worry about those supplies. This is the reason for the Plants. This is their fruit. This is manna from heaven."

In the brief stampede over the edge, Mae Stromberg sprained her ankle. Anderson knew better than to pit his authority against raw hunger. He hesitated to eat the fruit himself, for it could be poisonous, but his body's need strained against an overcautious will. If the rest of them were to be poisoned, he might as well join them.

It tasted good.

Yes, he thought, *it must seem like manna to them.* And even as the sugary floss condensed on his tongue into droplets of honey, he hated the Plant for seeming so much their friend and their deliverer. For making its poison so delicious.

At his feet the lamp burned unnaturally bright. The floor, though hard enough to hold him up, was not rock-solid. He took out his pocket knife, brushed away the matted floss, and cut a slice of this more solid substance from the fruit. It was crisp, like an Idaho potato, and juicy. It had a blander and less acid taste than the floss. He cut out another piece. He could not stop eating.

Around Anderson, out of range of the lamp, the citizens of Tassel (but was there still a Tassel of which they could be said to be citizens?) snuffled and ate like swine at a trough. Most of them did not bother to press the floss into comfortable mouthfuls but pushed it blindly into their mouths, biting their own fingers and gagging in their greedy taste. Strands of the pulp adhered to their clothes and tangled in their hair. It stuck to the lashes of their closed eyes.

An upright figure advanced into the sphere of lamplight. It was Jeremiah Orville. "I'm sorry," he said, "if I started all this. I shouldn't have spoken out of turn. I should have waited for you to say what to do. I wasn't thinking."

"That's all right," Anderson assured him, his mouth full of half-chewed fruit. "It would have happened the same no matter what you did. Or what I did."

Orville sat down beside the older man. "In the morning . . ." he began.

"Morning? It must be morning now." In fact, they had no way to know. The only working timepieces—an alarm clock and two wrist-watches—had been kept in a box in the commonroom for safety. No one escaping the fire had thought to rescue the box.

"Well, when everyone's fed full and they've got some sleep—that's what I meant—then you can set them to work. We've lost a battle, but there's still a war to fight."

Orville's tone was politely optimistic, but Anderson found it oppressive. To have come to sanctuary after a disaster did not erase the memory of the disaster. Indeed, Anderson, now that he had stopped running from it, was only just becoming aware of its magnitude. "What work?" he asked, spitting out the rest of the fruit.

"Whatever work you say, sir. Exploring. Clearing out a space down here to live in. Going back to the main root for the supplies we dropped there. Pretty soon, you might even send a scout back to see if anything can be salvaged from the fire."

Anderson made no reply. Sullenly he recognized that Orville was right. Sullenly he admired his resourcefulness, just as, twenty years earlier, he might have admired an opponent's fighting style in a brawl at Red Fox Tavern. Though to Anderson's taste the style was a little too fancy, you had to give the bastard credit for keeping on his feet.

It was strange, but Anderson's whole body was tensed as though for a fight, as though he *had* been drinking.

Orville was saying something. *"What'd* you say?" Anderson asked in a jeering tone. He hoped it was something that would give him an excuse to smash his face in, the smart punk.

"I said—I'm very sorry about your wife. I can't understand why she did that. I know how you must be feeling."

Anderson's fists unclenched, his jaw grew slack. He felt the pressure of tears behind his eyes, the pressure that had been there all along, but he knew that he could not afford to give in to it. He could not afford the least weakness now.

"Thank you," he said. Then he cut out another large wedge of the solider, more succulent fruit, split it in two, and gave part to Jeremiah Orville. "You've done well tonight," he said. "I will not forget it."

Orville left him to whatever thoughts he had and went looking for Blossom. Anderson, alone, thought of his wife with a stony, dumb grief. He could not understand why she had, as he considered it, committed suicide.

He would never know, no one would know, that she had turned back for his sake. He had not yet taken thought of the Bible that had been left behind, and later, when he would, he would regret it no more nor less than Gracie's death or the hundred other irredeemable losses he had suffered. But Lady had foreseen quite accurately that without that one artifact, in which she herself had had no faith, without the sanction it lent his authority, the old man would be bereft, and that his strength, so long preserved, would soon collapse, like a roof when the timbers have rotted. But she had failed, and her failure would never be understood.

More than one appetite demanded satisfaction that night. A satiety of food produced, in men and women alike, an insatiable hunger for that which the strict code of the commonroom had so long denied them. Here, in warmth and darkness, that code no longer obtained. In its stead, the perfect democracy of the carnival proclaimed itself, and liberty reigned for one brief hour.

Hands brushed, as though by accident, other hands—exactly whose it made little difference. Death had not scrupled to sort out husband and wife, and neither did they. Tongues cleaned away the sweet, sticky film from lips that had done feasting, met other tongues, kissed.

"They're drunk," Alice Nemerov stated unequivocally.

She, Maryann and Blossom sat in a separate cove dug from the pulp of the fruit, listening, trying not to listen. Though each couple tried to observe a decorous silence, the cumulative effect was unmistakable, even to Blossom.

"Drunk? How can that be?" Maryann asked. She did not want to talk, but conversation was the only defense against the voluptuous sounds of the darkness. Talking and listening to Alice talk, she did not have to hear the sighing, the whispers—or wonder which was her husband's.

"We're all drunk, my dears. Drunk on oxygen. Even with this stinking fruit stinking things up, I know an oxygen tent when I smell it."

"I don't smell anything," Maryann said. It was perfectly true: her cold had reached the stage where she couldn't even smell the cloying odor of the fruit.

"I worked in a hospital, didn't I? So I should know. My dears, we're all of us higher than kites."

"High as the flag on the Fourth of July," Blossom put in. She didn't really mind being drunk, if it was like this. Floating. She wanted to sing but sensed that it wasn't the thing to do. Not now. But the song, once begun, kept on inside her head: *I'm in love, I'm in love, I'm in love, I'm in love, I'm in love with a wonderful guy.*

"Sssh!" Alice ssshed.

"Excuse *me!*" Blossom said, with a wee giggle. Perhaps her song had not after all been altogether inside her head. Then, because she knew it was the correct thing to do when tipsy, she hiccoughed a single, graceful hiccough, fingertips pressed delicately to her lips. Then, indelicately, she burped, for there was gas on her stomach.

"Are you all right, my dear?" Alice asked, laying a solicitous hand on Maryann's full womb. "I mean, everything that's happened—"

"Yes. There, you see! He just moved."

The conversation lapsed, and through the breach the assault was renewed. Now it was an angry, persistent sound, like the buzzing of a honeycomb. Maryann shook her head, but the buzzing wouldn't stop. "Oh!" she gasped. "Oh!"

"There, there," Alice soothed.

"Who do you think is with him?" Maryann blurted.

"Why, you're all upset for no reason at all," Blossom said. "He's probably with Daddy and Orville this very minute."

Blossom's obvious conviction almost swayed Maryann. It *was* possible. An hour ago (or less? or more?) Orville had sought out Blossom and explained that he was taking her father (who was naturally very upset) to a more private spot, away from the others. He had found a way into another root, a root that burrowed yet deeper into the earth. Did Blossom want to go there with him? Or perhaps she preferred to stay with the ladies?

Alice had thought that Blossom would prefer to stay with the ladies for the time being. She would join her father later, if he wished her to.

Anderson's departure, and the departure with him of the lamp, had been the cue for all that followed. A month's dammed energy spilled out and covered, for a little while, the face of sorrow, blotted out the too-clear knowledge of their defeat and of an ignominy the features of which were only just becoming apparent.

A hand reached out of the darkness and touched Blossom's thigh. It was Orville's hand! it could be no other. She took the hand and pressed it to her lips.

It was not Orville's hand. She screamed. Instantly, Alice had caught the intruder by the scruff of his neck. He yelped.

"Neil!" she exclaimed. "For pity's sake! That's your sister you're pawing, you idiot! Now, *get!* Go look for Greta. Or, on the other hand, maybe you'd better not."

"You shut up!" Neil bellowed. "You ain't my mother!"

She finally shoved Neil away. Then she laid her head down in Blossom's lap. "Drunk," she scolded sleepily. "Absolutely stoned." Then she began to snore. In a few minutes, Blossom slept too—and dreamed—and woke with a little cry.

"What is it?" Maryann asked.

"Nothing, a dream," Blossom said. "Haven't you gone to sleep yet?"

"I can't." Though it was as quiet as death now, Maryann was still listening. What she feared most was that Neil *would* find his wife. And Buddy. Together.

Buddy woke. It was still dark. It would always be dark now, here. There was a woman beside him, whom he touched, though not to wake her. Assured that she was neither Greta nor Maryann, he gathered his clothes and sidled away. Strands of the sticky pulp caught on his bare back and shoulders and melted there, unpleasantly.

He was still feeling drunk. Drunk and drained. Orville had a word for the feeling—what was it?

Detumescent.

The grainy liquid trickled down his bare skin, made him shiver. But it wasn't that he was cold. Though he was cold, come to think of it.

Crawling forward on hands and knees, he bumbled into another sleeping couple. "Wha?" the woman said. She sounded like Greta. No matter. He crawled elsewhere.

He found a spot where the pulp had not been disturbed and shoved his body into it backward. Once you got used to the sticky feeling, it was quite comfortable: soft, warm, snuggly.

He wanted light: sunlight, lamplight, even the red, unsteady light of last night's burning. Something in the present situation horrified him in a way he did not understand, could not define. It was more than the darkness. He thought about it and as he dropped off to sleep again it came to him:

Worms.

They were worms, crawling through an apple.

Chapter 10

FALLING TO PIECES

"Who's *your* favorite movie star, Blossom?" Greta asked.

"Audrey Hepburn. I only saw her in one movie—when I was nine years old—but she was wonderful in that. Then there weren't any more movies. Daddy never approved, I guess."

"Daddy!" Greta snorted. She tore off a strand of fruit pulp from the space overhead, lowered it lazily into her mouth, mashed it with her tongue against the back of her teeth. Sitting in that pitch-black cavity in the fruit, her listeners could not see her do this, but it was evident from her blurred speech that she was eating again. "And you, Neil? Who's your favorite?"

"Charlton Heston. I used to go to anything with him in it."

"Me too," said Clay Kestner. "Him—and how about Marilyn *Mon*-roe? Any of you fellas old enough to remember old Marilyn *Mon*-roe?"

"Marilyn Monroe was vastly overrated in my opinion," Greta mouthed.

"What do you say about that, Buddy? Hey, Buddy! Is he still here?"

"Yeah, I'm still here. I never saw Marilyn Monroe. She was before my time."

"Oh, you missed something, kid. You really missed something."

"I saw Marilyn Monroe," Neil put in. "She wasn't before my time."

"And you still say Charlton Heston's your favorite?" Clay Kestner had a booming, travelling-salesman's laugh, gutsy and graceless. In former years he had been half-owner of a filling station.

"Oh, I don't know," Neil said nervously.

Greta laughed too, for Clay had begun to tickle her toes. "You're all wet, all of you," she said, still giggling but trying to stop. "I still say that Kim Novak is the greatest actress who ever lived." She had been saying it and saying it for fifteen minutes, and it seemed now that she would say it again.

Buddy was mortally bored. He had thought it would be better to stay behind with the younger set than to go along on another of his father's tedious, purposeless explorations through the labyrinthine roots of the Plants. Now that the supplies had been gathered in, now that they had learned everything about the Plant that there was to learn, there was no point in wandering about. And no point in sitting still. He had not realized till now, till there was nothing to do, what a slave to work and Puritan busy-ness he had become.

He rose, and his hair (cut short now, like everyone else's) brushed against the clinging fruit. The fruit pulp, when it dried and matted in one's hair, was more aggravating than a mosquito bite that couldn't be itched.

"Where are you going?" Greta asked, offended that her audience should desert her in the middle of her analysis of Kim Novak's peculiar charm.

"I've got to throw up," Buddy said. "See you all later."

It was a plausible enough excuse. The fruit, though it nourished them, had minor side effects. They were all, a month later (such was the estimate on which they had agreed), still suffering from diarrhea, gas pains and belly-aches. Buddy almost might have wished he did have to vomit: it would have been something to do.

Worse than the stomach upsets had been the colds. Nearly everyone had suffered from these too, and there had been no remedy but patience, sleep, and a will to recover. In most cases these remedies were sufficient, but three cases of pneumonia had developed, Denny Stromberg among them. Alice Nemerov did what she could do, but as she was the first to confess, she could do nothing.

Buddy climbed up the rope from the tuber into the root proper. Here he had to walk crouched, for the hollow space in the root was only four and a half feet in diameter. Bit by bit over the last month, the party had moved down many hundred feet—to a depth, Orville had estimated, of at least 1,200 feet. Why, the Alworth Building wasn't that high. Not even the Foshay Tower in Minneapolis! At this depth the temperature was a relaxed seventy degrees.

There was a rustling sound close ahead. "Who's that?" Buddy and Maryann asked, almost in unison.

"What are you doing here?" Buddy asked his wife in a surly tone.

"Making more rope—but don't ask me why. It's just something to do. It keeps me busy. I've shredded up some of the vines, and now I'm putting them back together." She laughed weakly. "The vines were probably stronger than my ropes."

"Here, take my hands—show them how to do it."

"You!" When Buddy's hands touched hers, she continued busily knitting so that her fingers would not tremble. "Why would you want to do that?"

"As you say—it's something to do."

She began to guide his clumsy fingers but grew confused trying to keep in mind that his right hand was in her left and vice versa. "Maybe if I sat behind you . . ." she suggested. But as it turned out, she couldn't even close her arms around his chest. Her belly was in the way.

"How is he?" Buddy asked. "Will it be much longer?"

"He's fine. It should be any day now."

It worked out as she had hoped: Buddy sat behind her, his thighs clenched about her spread legs, his hairy arms beneath hers, supporting them like the armrests of a chair. "So teach me," he said.

He was a slow learner, not used to this kind of work, but his slowness only made him a more interesting pupil. They wore away an hour or more before he was ready to start his own rope. When he had finished it, the fibers fell apart like shreds of tobacco sliding out of a beginner's cigarette.

From deep inside the tuber came the music of Greta's laugh, and then Clay's bass-drum accompaniment. Buddy had no desire to rejoin them. He had no desire to go anywhere except back to the surface, its fresh air, its radiance, its changing seasons.

Maryann apparently was having similar thoughts. "Do you suppose it's Ground Hog's Day yet?"

"Oh, I'd say another week. Even if we were up there where we could see whether or not the sun was out, I doubt there'd be any groundhogs left to go looking for their shadows."

"Then Blossom's birthday could be today. We should remind her."

"How old is she now? Thirteen?"

"You better not let her hear that. She's fourteen and very emphatic about it."

Another sound came out of the fruit: a woman's anguished cry. Then a silence, without echoes. Buddy left Maryann on the instant to find out what had caused it. He returned shortly. "It's Mae Stromberg. Her Denny's dead. Alice Nemerov's taking care of her now."

"Pneumonia?"

"That, and he hasn't been able to hold any food."

"Ah, the poor thing."

The Plant was very efficient. In fact, as plants go, it couldn't be beat. It had already proved that. The more you learned about it, the more you had to admire it. If you were the sort to admire such things.

Consider its roots, for instance. They were hollow. The roots of comparable, Earth-evolved plants (a redwood is roughly comparable) are solid and woody throughout. But what for? The bulk of such roots is functionless; in effect, it is so much dead matter. A root's only job is to transport water and minerals up to the leaves and, when they've been synthesized into food, to carry them back down again. To accomplish this, a root must hold itself rigid enough to withstand the constant pressure of the soil and rock around it. All these things the Plant did excellently well—better, considering its dimensions, than the most efficient of Earth's own plants.

The greater open space within the root allowed the passage of more water, more quickly and farther. The tracheids and vessels that conduct water up through an ordinary root do not have a tenth of the capacity of the expansible capillaries that were the cobwebs of the Plant. Similarly, the vines lining the hollow roots could in a single day transport tons of liquid glucose and other materials from the leaves down to the tubers of fruit and the still-growing roots of the lowest levels. These were to the phloem of ordinary plants as an intercontinental pipeline is to a garden hose. The hollow space within the root served a further purpose: it supplied the nethermost regions of the Plant with air. These roots, stretching so far below the airy topsoil, did not have, as other roots would, an independent supply of oxygen. It had to be brought to them. Thus, from the tips of its leaves to the farthest rootcaps, the Plant *breathed*. It was this multifarious capacity for rapid and large-scale transportation that had accounted for the Plant's inordinate rate of growth.

The Plant was economical; it wasted nothing. As its roots sank deeper and thickened, the Plant digested even itself, forming thereby the hollow in which the complex network of capillaries and vines then took shape. The wood that was no longer needed to maintain a rigid exoskeleton was broken down into useful food.

But the fundamental economy of the Plant, its final excellence, consisted in none of these partial features, but rather in the fact that all Plants were one Plant. As certain insects have, by social organization, achieved that which to their individual members would have been impossible, so the separate Plants, by forming a single, indivisible whole, had heightened their effective power exponentially. Materials that were not available to one might be available to another in superfluity. Water, minerals, air, food—all were shared in the spirit of true communism: from each according to his ability, to each according to his need. The resources of an entire continent were at its disposal; it did not want for much.

The mechanism by which the socialization of the individual Plants took place was very simple. As soon as the first branch roots budded from the vertical primary root, they moved by a sort of mutual tropism toward the kindred branch roots of other Plants. When they met, they merged. When they had merged indissolubly, they diverged, seeking still another union at a deeper level. The many became one.

You had to admire the Plant. It was really a very beautiful thing, if you looked at it objectively, as, say, Jeremiah Orville looked at it.

Of course, it had had advantages other Plants hadn't had. It had not had to evolve all by itself. It was also very well cared for.

Even so, there were pests. But that was being looked after. This was, after all, only its first season on Earth.

By the time Anderson, Orville and the other men (those who'd bothered to come) returned from that day's exploration deeper into the Plant, Mae Stromberg had already disappeared. So had her son's corpse. In her last hours with the dying boy, she had not said a word or wept a tear, and when he died there had been only that single maddened outcry. The loss of her husband and daughter she had borne much less calmly; she had felt, perhaps, that she could afford to lose them—could afford, therefore, to grieve for them afterwards. Grieving is a luxury. Now she was left only grief.

There were twenty-nine people, not counting Mae Stromberg. Anderson called for an assembly right away. Of the twenty-nine, only the two women still down with pneumonia and Alice Nemerov were absent.

"I am afraid," Anderson began, after a short prayer, "that we are falling to pieces." There was some coughing and a shuffle of feet. He waited for it to pass, then continued: "I can't blame anyone here for Mae's running off like this. I can't very well blame Mae either. But those of us who have been spared this last blow and guided here by Divine Providence, those of us, that is to say . . ."

He stopped, irretrievably tangled in his own words—something that had been happening to him increasingly of late. He pressed a hand to his forehead and drew a deep breath.

"What I mean to say is this: We can't just lay around eating milk and honey. There is work to be done. We must strengthen ourselves for the trials ahead, and . . . And, that is to say, we must not let ourselves go *soft*.

"Today I have gone down lower into these infernal tunnels, and I found out that the fruit down there is better. Smaller and firmer—there's less of this sugar candy. I also found that there's less of this oxygen, which has been . . . I mean to say that up here we're turning into a bunch of—what was that word?"

"Lotus-eaters," Orville said.

"A bunch of lotus-eaters. Exactly. Now this must *stop*—" He struck his palm with his clenched fist in emphasis.

Greta, who had had her hand up during the latter half of his speech, at last spoke up without waiting for recognition. "May I ask a question?"

"What is it, Greta?"

"*What* work? I just don't see what it is that we've been neglecting."

"Well, we haven't been doing *any* work, girl. That's plain to see."

"That doesn't answer my question."

Anderson was aghast at this effrontery—and from *her*. Two months ago he could have had her stoned as an adulteress—and now the harlot was vaunting her pride and rebellion for everyone to see.

He should have answered her challenge with a blow. He should have quelled that pride by letting it be known, even now, just what she was: a harlot—and with her husband's brother. That he did not return her attack was a weakness, and everyone could see that too.

After a long boding silence, he returned to his speech as though there had been no interruption. "We've got to get the lead out! We can't *lay around* like this. We'll keep on the move from now on. Every day. We won't sit around in one place. We'll *explore*."

"There's nothing *to* explore, Mr. Anderson. And *why* should we move every day? Why not clear out one space that's comfortable and live there? There's enough food in just one of these big potatoes—"

"Enough! That's enough, Greta! I've said all I'm going to. Tomorrow we—"

Greta stood up, but instead of moving forward into the lamplight, she backed away. "It is *not* enough! I've had enough of you. I'm sick and tired of being ordered around like I was a slave. I've had *enough* of it, I'm through! Mae Stromberg did the right thing when she—"

"Sit down, Greta," the old man ordered, his sternness breaking into mere stridency. "Sit down and shut up."

"Not me. Not Greta. Not any more. I'm going. I have had it. From now on, I do as I damn well please, and anyone that wants to come along is welcome."

Anderson drew his pistol and pointed it at the shadowy figure outside of the lamp's full light. "Neil, you tell your wife to sit down. If she don't I'll shoot her. And I'll shoot to kill—by *God* I will!"

"Uh, sit down, Greta," Neil urged.

"You won't shoot me—and do you want to know why you won't shoot me? Because I'm pregnant. You wouldn't kill your own grandchild, now would you? And there's no doubt he *is* your grandchild."

It was a lie, a complete fabrication, but it served its purpose.

"My grandchild?" Anderson echoed, aghast. "My *grandchild!*" He turned his Python on Buddy. His hand trembled—with rage or simply with infirmity, one could not tell.

"It wasn't me," Buddy blurted. "I swear it wasn't me."

Greta had disappeared into the darkness, and three men were scrambling to their feet, eager to follow her. Anderson shot four bullets into the back of one of the men. Then, utterly spent, senseless, he collapsed over the feebly burning lamp. It was extinguished.

The man he had killed was Clay Kestner. The fourth bullet, passing through Clay's chest, had entered the brain of a woman who had leaped up in panic at Anderson's first shot.

There were now twenty-four of them, not counting Greta and the two men who had gone off with her.

Chapter 11

A NATURAL DEATH

Anderson's hair was coming out in handfuls. Maybe it would have at his age in any case, but he blamed it on his diet. The meager supplies rescued from the fire had been rationed out in dribs and drabs, and the little corn that remained now was for Maryann and for seed when they returned to the surface.

He scratched at his flaky scalp and cursed the Plant, but it was a half-hearted curse—as though he were peeved with an employer, instead of at war with an enemy. His hatred had become tainted with gratitude; his strength was quitting him.

More and more he pondered the question of who was to succeed him. It was a weighty question: Anderson was perhaps the last leader in the world—a king almost, undoubtedly a patriarch.

Though generally he believed in primogeniture, he wondered if a difference of only three months might not be construed charitably in favor of the younger son. He refused to think of Neil as a bastard, and he had therefore been obliged to treat the boys as twins—impartially.

There was something to be said for each of them—and not enough for either. Neil was a steady worker, not given to complainings, and strong; he had the instincts of a leader of men, if not all the abilities. However, he was stupid: Anderson could not help but see it. He was also . . . well, disturbed. Just how he was disturbed or why, Anderson did not know, though he suspected that Greta was in some way responsible. Considering this problem, he tended to be vague, to eye it obliquely or as through smoked glass, as we are told to observe an eclipse. He did not want to learn the truth if he could help it.

Buddy, on the other hand, though he possessed many of the qualities lacking in his half-brother, was not to be relied upon. He had proven it when, in the face of his father's sternest disapproval, he had gone to live in Minneapolis; he had proven it conclusively on Thanksgiving Day. When Anderson had found his son in, as he supposed, the very commission of the act, it had become quite clear that Buddy would not succeed to his own high place. Anderson, in passing from early manhood to middle age, had developed an unreasoning horror of adultery. That he had once been adulterate himself and that one of his children was the fruit of such a union did not occur to him now. He would, in fact, have denied it outright—and he would have believed his denial.

For a long time it had seemed that no one could possibly take his place. Therefore, he would have to carry on alone. Each time his sons had shown weaknesses, Anderson had felt a corresponding growth in strength and purpose. Secretly, he had thrived on their failings.

Then Jeremiah Orville had entered the scene. In August, Anderson had been moved by reasons which were obscure and (it now seemed) God-given to spare the man. Today he trembled at his sight —as Saul must have trembled when he first realized that young David would supplant him and his son Jonathan. Anderson tried desperately both to deny this and to accommodate himself to his apparent heir. (He constantly feared that he would, like that earlier king, war against the Lord's anointed and damn himself in the act. Belief in pre-destination has decidedly some disadvantages.) As by degrees, he bent his will to this unpleasant task (for, though he admired Orville, he did not like him); his strength and purpose quitted him by equal degrees. Orville, without even knowing it, was killing him.

It was night. That is to say, they had once again journeyed to exhaustion. As Anderson was the arbiter of what constituted exhaustion, it was evident to everyone that the old man was being worn down: as after the vernal equinox, each day was shorter than the day that had gone before.

The old man scratched at his flaky scalp, and cursed . . . something, he couldn't remember exactly what, and fell asleep without thinking to take a count of heads. Orville, Buddy and Neil each took the count for him. Orville and Buddy both arrived at twenty-four. Neil, somehow, had come up with twenty-six.

"But that's not possible," Buddy pointed out.

Neil was adamant: he had counted twenty-six. "Whadaya think— I can't *count*, for Christ's sake?"

Since Greta's departure, a month or so had gone by. No one was keeping track of the time any longer. Some maintained it was February; others held for March. From the expeditions to the surface they knew only that it was still winter. They needed to know no more than that.

Not everyone went along. Indeed, besides Anderson, his two sons and Orville, there were only three other men. A permanent base of operations was again being maintained for those, like Maryann and Alice, who could not spend the day crawling through the roots. The number of those who deemed themselves incapable had grown daily until there were just as many lotus-eaters as before. Anderson pretended to ignore the situation, fearing to provoke a worse one.

Anderson led the men up by the usual route, which was marked by ropes that Maryann had braided. It was no longer possible for them to find their way about by the Ariadne's thread of broken capillaries, for in their explorations they had broken so many that they had created a labyrinth of their own.

It was near the surface, at about the sixty-degree level, that they came across the rats. At first it was like the humming of a beehive, though higher pitched. The men's first thought was that the incendiaries had at last come down into the roots after them. When they had ventured into the tuber from which the noise was coming, the humming rose to a raspy whine, as though a coloratura's aria were being broadcast at peak volume over a bad public-address system. The solid-seeming darkness beyond the lamp's reach wavered and dissolved to a lighter shade as thousands of rats tumbled over each other to get into the fruit. The walls of the passage were honeycombed with the rats' tunnellings.

"Rats!" Neil exclaimed. "Didn't I say it was rats that gnawed their way through that root up above. Didn't I, huh? Well, here they are. There must be a million of them."

"If there aren't now, there will be before very long." Orville agreed. "I wonder if they're all in this one tuber?"

"What possible difference can it make?" Anderson asked impatiently. "They've left *us* well enough alone, and I for one feel no need to keep them company. They seem content to eat this damn candied apple, and I'm content to let them eat it. They can eat the whole of it, of all of them, for all I care." Sensing that he had gone too far, he said, in a more subdued tone: "There's nothing we can do against an army of rats, in any case. I have only one cartridge left in the revolver. I don't know what I'm saving it for, but I know it isn't for a rat."

"I was thinking of the future, Mr. Anderson. With all this food available and no natural enemies to keep them down, these rats will multiply out of all bounds. They may not threaten our food supply now, but what about six months from now? a year from now?"

"Before the summer has begun, Jeremiah, we won't be living down here. The rats are welcome to it then."

"We'll still be depending on it for food though. It's the only food left—unless you want to breed the rats. Personally, I've never liked the taste. And there's next winter to think about. With the little seed that's left for planting—even if it's still good—we can't possibly get through the winter. I don't like to live like this any more than the next man, but it's a way to survive. The only way, for the time being."

"Ah, that's a lot of hooey!" Neil said in support of his father.

Anderson looked weary, and the lantern, which he had been holding up to examine the perforations of the wall of the passage, sank to his side. "You're right, Jeremiah. As usual." His lips curled in an angry smile, and he swung his bare foot (shoes were too precious to be wasted down here) at one of the rat holes from which two bright eyes had been staring up intently, examining the examiners. "Bastards!" he shouted. "Sons of bitches!" There was a squeal, and a fat, furry ball of ratflesh sailed on a high arc out of range of the lamplight. The whining, which had grown somewhat quieter, rose in volume, answering Anderson's challenge.

Orville put a hand on the old man's shoulder. His whole body was shaking with helpless rage. "Sir . . ." Orville protested. "Please."

"The bastard bit me," Anderson grumbled.

"We can't afford to scatter them now. Our best hope—"

"Half took off my toe," he said, stooping to feel the injury. "The bastard."

"—is to contain them here. To block up all the passages out of this tuber. Otherwise . . ." Orville shrugged. The alternative was clear.

"Then how do *we* get out?" Neil objected smugly.

"Oh, shut up, Neil," Anderson said wearily. "With what," he asked Orville. "We haven't got anything a hungry rat couldn't chew his way through in five minutes."

"We have an axe though. We can weaken the walls of the roots so that they collapse in on themselves. The pressure at this depth is tremendous. The wood must be hard as iron, but if we can chip and scrape enough of it away at the right points, the earth itself will block the passages. Rats can't chew their way through basalt. There's a danger that the cave in will get out of hand, but I think I can see that it won't. A mining engineer usually has to prevent cave-ins, but that's good training for someone who has to produce them."

"I'll let you try. Buddy, go back and get the axe—and anything else with a cutting edge. And send those other lotus-eaters up here. Neil and the rest of you spread out to each of the entrances of this potato and do what you can to keep the rats inside. They don't seem very anxious to leave yet, but they may when the walls start tumbling down. Jeremiah, you come with me and show me what you mean to do. I don't understand why the whole thing isn't going to come down on our heads when we—God damn!"

"What is it?"

"My toe! Damned rat really took a hunk out of it. "Well, we'll show these bastards!"

The extermination of the rats succeeded—if anything, too well. Orville attacked the first root at just the point where it belled outward to become the hard, spherical shell of the fruit. He worked hours, shaving off thin slices of wood, watching for any sign of stress that would give him an opportunity to escape, scraping away a little more, watching. When it came down, there was no warning. Suddenly Orville stood in the midst of thunder. He was lifted off his feet by the shock wave and hurled back into the passage.

The entire tuber had collapsed in upon itself.

Watchers at the other entrances reported no escaped rats, but there had been a fatality: one man, having missed his lunch (Anderson insisted that they eat only three times a day, and then sparingly), stepped into the tuber for a handful of fruit pulp at exactly the wrong moment. He, the fruit pulp and some few thousand rats were now being converted, at a modest, geological pace, into petroleum. A basalt wall of perfect, Euclidean flatness blocked each of the entrances to the tuber; it had come down quickly and neatly as a guillotine.

Anderson, who had not been present to witness the event (shortly after Orville had begun his work, he had had yet another fainting fit; they came more and more frequently of late), was incredulous when it was reported to him. Orville's *ex post facto* explanation did not convince him. "What's Buckminster What's-his-name got to do with anything. I ask a simple question, and you carry on about geographic domes."

"It's only a supposition. The walls of the tuber have to withstand incredible pressures. Buckminster Fuller was an architect—an engineer, if you prefer—who built things so they'd do just that. He designed skeletons, you might say. Designed them so that if the least part was weakened, the whole body would give way. Like when you remove the keystone of an arch—except that they were all keystones."

"This is a fine time to learn about Buckminster Fuller—when a man's been killed."

"I'm sorry, sir. I appreciate that it was my responsibility. I should have given more thought to the matter before rushing ahead."

"It can't be helped now. Go find Alice and bring her here. I'm coming down with a fever—and that ratbite hurts more every minute."

His responsibility indeed! Anderson thought, when Orville had left him. Well, it *would* be his responsibility soon enough. He had better call an assembly while he still had his wits about him and announce it for a fact.

But that would be tantamount to his own abdication. No, he would bide his time.

Meanwhile, he had had a new idea—a way of legitimatizing Orville as his heir: Orville would become Anderson's son—his eldest son—by way of marriage.

But he balked at this step too. Blossom still seemed so young to him—hardly more than a child. Only a few months ago he had seen her with the other children playing jacks on the floor of the commonroom. Marriage? He would talk to Alice Nemerov about it. A woman always knew best about these things. Anderson and Alice were the two oldest survivors. That fact, and the death of Anderson's wife, had forced them willy-nilly into each other's confidence.

While he waited for her, he massaged his little toe. Where it had been bitten it was now numb; the pain was coming from the rest of the foot.

That night when the headcount was taken (Anderson being even less in a condition to do so) Orville and Buddy both came up with a figure of twenty-three. Neil, this time, counted twenty-four.

"He's slow," Buddy joked. "Give him time. He'll catch up with us yet."

Alice Nemerov, R.N., knew Anderson was going to die. Not just because she was a nurse and could recognize gangrene from its unremarkable inception. She had seen him begin to die long before he was bitten by the rat, even before the fainting fits had become a daily occurrence. When an old person is getting ready to die, you can see it all over him, written in neon. But because she *was* a nurse, and because she had come despite herself to like the old man, she tried to do something to keep him alive.

For this reason she had persuaded him to delay speaking to Orville and Blossom about his intentions for them. She led him on from day to day with a carrot of hope. At least it looked like hope.

At first, when the hope had been real, she had tried to suck off the infection, as in snakebite. The only effect was that she had grown nauseous and couldn't eat for two days. Now, half his foot was a dusky, dead blue. Decomposition would set in very quickly, if it had not already begun.

"Why don't you keep sucking off the infection?" Neil asked. He wanted to watch again.

"It wouldn't do any good now. He's dying."

"You could *try*. That's the least you could do." Neil bent down and examined his father's sleeping face. "Is he breathing better now?"

"Sometimes his breath comes very hard. Sometimes he scarcely seems to breathe at all. Neither symptom is out of the ordinary."

"His feet are cold," Neil said critically.

"What do you expect?" Alice snapped at him, past all patience.

"Your father is dying. Don't you understand that? Only an amputation could save him at this point, and in his condition he couldn't survive amputation. He's worn out, an old man. He *wants* to die."

"That's not my fault, is it?" Neil shouted. Anderson woke for a moment at the noise, and Neil went away. His father had changed so much in the last few days that Neil felt awkward with him. It was like being with a stranger.

"The baby—is it a boy or a girl?" His voice was barely audible.

"We don't know yet, Mr. Anderson. It may take another hour. No more than that. Everything is ready. She made the ligatures herself, from scraps of rope. Buddy went up to the surface for a bucket of snow—he says it was a real March blizzard up there—and we've been able to sterilize the knife and wash out a couple of pieces of cotton. It won't be a hospital delivery, but I'm sure it will be all right."

"We must pray."

"*You* must pray, Mr. Anderson. You know I don't hold with those things."

Anderson smiled, and it was not, for a wonder, a really unpleasant expression. Dying seemed to mellow the old man; he had never been nicer than now. "You're just like my wife, just like Lady. She must be in hell for her sins and her scoffing, but hell can't be much worse than this. Somehow, though, I can't imagine her there."

"Judge not lest ye be judged, Mr. Anderson."

"Yes, Lady would always hark on that one too. It was her favorite Scripture."

Buddy interrupted them: "Time now, Alice."

"Go on, go on, don't dally here," Anderson urged. Unnecessarily, for she was already gone, taking the lamp with her. The darkness began to cover him like a woollen blanket, like a comforter.

If it's a boy, Anderson thought, *I can die happy*.

It was a boy.

Anderson was trying to say something. Neil could not make out quite what. He bent his ear closer to the old man's dry lips. He couldn't believe that his father was dying. His father! He didn't like to think about it.

The old man mumbled something. "Try and talk louder," Neil shouted into his good ear. Then to the others standing around:

"Where's the lamp? Where's Alice? She should be here now. What are you all standing around like that for?"

"Alice is with the baby," Blossom whispered. "She said she'd be only another minute."

Then Anderson spoke again, loud enough for Neil but no one else to hear. "Buddy." That was all he said, though he said it several times.

"What'd he say?" Blossom asked.

"He said he wants to talk to me alone. The rest of you, go away and leave us together, huh? Dad's got things he wants to tell me alone."

There were shufflings and sighs as the few people who were not yet sleeping (the waking period having ended many hours ago) walked off into the other areas of the tuber to leave father and son together. Neil strained to hear the least sound that would have meant that one of them remained nearby. In this abysmal darkness, privacy was never a sure thing.

"Buddy ain't here," he said at last, assured that they were alone. "He's with Maryann and the baby. So's Alice. There's some kind of problem about the way it breathes." Neil's throat was dry, and when he tried to make saliva and swallow it, it hurt. *Alice,* he thought angrily, *shouldn't be off somewhere else now.* All people talked about, it seemed to Neil, was the baby, the baby. He was sick of the baby. Did anybody care about *his* baby?

Curiously, Greta's lie had made its most lasting impression on Neil. He believed in it with the most literal, unquestioning faith, just as Maryann believed in Christ's virgin birth. Neil had the ability to brush aside mere, inconvenient facts and considerations of logic like cob-webs. He had even decided that *his* baby's name was to be Neil Junior. That would show old Buddy-boy!

"Then get Orville, will you?" Anderson whispered vexedly. "And bring the others back. I have something to say."

"You can tell it to me, huh? Huh, Dad?"

"Get Orville, I said!" The old man began to cough.

"Okay, okay!" Neil walked some distance from the small hollow in the fruit where his father was lying, counted to a hundred (skipping, in his haste, everything between fifty-nine and seventy), and returned. "Here he is, Dad, just like you said."

Anderson did not think it extraordinary that Orville should not greet him. Everyone, these last days, was mute in his presence, the presence of death. "I should have said this before, Jeremiah," he began, speaking rapidly, afraid that this sudden renewal of strength would desert him before he could finish. "I've waited too long. Though I know you've been expecting it. I could tell by your eyes. So there was no need to—" He broke off, coughing. "Here," (he gestured feebly in the darkness) "take my revolver. There's only one bullet left, but some of them see it as a sort of symbol. It's just as well to let them. There were so many things I wanted to tell you, but there was no time."

Neil had grown more and more agitated during his father's valedictory, and at last he could not contain himself: "What are you talking about, Dad?"

Anderson chuckled. "He doesn't understand yet. Do *you* want to tell him, or shall I?" There was a long silence. "Orville?" Anderson asked in a changed voice.

"Tell me what, Dad? What don't I understand?"

"That Jeremiah Orville is taking over from now on. So bring him here!"

"Dad, you don't mean that." Neil began to chew fretfully on his lower lip. "He ain't an Anderson. He ain't even one of the village. Listen, Dad, I'll tell you what—I'll take over, huh? I'd do a better job than him. Just give me a chance. That's all I ask, just one chance."

Anderson didn't reply. Neil began all over again, in a softer, more persuasive tone. "Dad, you gotta understand—Orville ain't one of us."

"He will be soon enough, you little bastard. Now bring him here."

"What do you mean by that?"

"I mean I'm marrying him to your sister. Now cut out the crap and bring him here. And your sister too. Bring everybody here."

"Dad, you can't mean that, Dad!"

Anderson wouldn't say another word. Neil showed him all the reasons it was impossible for Orville to marry Blossom. Why, Blossom was only twelve years old! She was his sister—Neil's sister! Didn't he undertand that? And who was this Orville character anyhow? He wasn't anybody. They should have killed him long ago, along with the other marauders. Hadn't Neil said so at the time? Neil would kill him now, if Anderson only said the word. How about it?

No matter what arguments Neil offered, the old man just lay there. *Was he dead?* Neil wondered. No, he was still breathing. Neil was in misery.

His keen ears picked up the sounds of others returning. "Leave us alone!" he shouted at them. They went away again, unable to hear Anderson's orders to the contrary.

"We've got to talk this thing over, you and me, Dad," Neil pleaded. Anderson wouldn't say a word, not a word.

With tears in his eyes, Neil did what he had to do. He pinched together the old man's nostrils and held his other hand down tightly over the old man's mouth. He wiggled around a little at first, but he was too weak to put up much of a struggle. When the old man was very, very quiet, Neil took his hands away and felt if he was still breathing.

He wasn't.

Then Neil took the holster and pistol off the old man and strapped it about his own thicker body. It was a sort of symbol.

Shortly afterward Alice came, with the lamp, and felt the dead man's wrist. "When did he die?" she asked.

"Just a minute ago," Neil said. It was hard to understand him, he was crying so. "And he asked me—he told me I should take his place. And he gave me his pistol."

Alice looked at Neil suspiciously. Then she bent over the face of the corpse and studied it attentively under the lamp. There were bruises on the sides of his nose, and his lip was cut and bleeding. Neil was bending over behind her. He couldn't understand where the blood had come from.

"You murdered him." Neil couldn't believe his ears: she had called him *a murderer!*

He hit Alice over the top of the head with the butt of the pistol. Then he wiped away the blood trickling down his father's chin and spread fruit pulp over the cut lip.

More people came. He explained to them that his father was dead, that he, Neil Anderson, was to take over his father's place. He also explained that Alice Nemerov had let his father die when she could have saved him. All her talk about looking after the baby was so much hogwash. It was just as bad as if she'd killed him outright. She would have to be executed, as an example. But not right away. For now they'd just tie her up. And gag her. Neil attended to the gag himself.

They obeyed him. They were accustomed to obeying Anderson, and they had been expecting Neil to take over from him for a long time—for years. Of course, they didn't believe Alice was in any way guilty, but then neither had they believed a lot of things Anderson had told them, and they'd always obeyed him anyhow. Maybe if Buddy had been there, he would have put up more of a fuss. But he was with Maryann and his new-born son, who was still weakly. They didn't dare bring the baby near his grandfather for fear of infection.

Besides, Neil was waving the Python around rather freely. They all knew there was a bullet left, and no one wanted to be the first to start an argument.

When Alice was securely bound, Neil asked where Orville was. Nobody, as it turned out, had seen or heard from him for several minutes.

"Find him and bring him here. Right now. Blossom! Where's Blossom? I saw her here a minute ago." But Blossom too was nowhere to be found.

"She's gotten lost!" Neil exclaimed, in a flash of understanding. "She's lost in the roots. We'll get up a search party. But first, find Orville. No—first help me with this." Neil grabbed up Alice by the shoulders. Somebody else took her feet. She didn't weigh more than a feed-bag, and the nearest taproot where there was a sheer vertical drop wasn't two minutes away. They dropped her down the shaft. They couldn't see how far she fell, because Neil had forgotten to bring the lamp. No doubt, she fell a long, long way.

Now his father was revenged. Now he would look for Orville. There was only one bullet left in his father's Colt Python .357 Magnum. It was for Orville.

But *first* he must find Blossom. She must have run off somewhere when she heard her father was dead. Neil could understand that. The news had upset him too, upset him something terrible.

First, they'd look for Blossom. Then they'd look for Orville. He hoped, how he hoped, that he wouldn't find them together. That would be too awful for words.

Chapter 12

GHOSTS AND MONSTERS

You'd *better hide,* she thought, and that was how she got lost.

Once, when Blossom was seven, her parents had gone to Duluth for the weekend, taking the baby, Jimmie Lee, with them, leaving her alone in the big two-story house on the outskirts of Tassel. It was their eighteenth wedding anniversary. Buddy and Neil, both big boys then, had gone away—one to a dance, the other to a baseball game. For a while she had watched television, then she played with her dolls. The house became very dark, but it was her father's rule never to turn on more than one lamp at a time. Otherwise, you wasted current.

She didn't mind being a *little* scared. There was even something nice about it. So she turned off *all* the lights and pretended the Monster was trying to find her in the dark. Hardly daring to breathe and on the tips of her toes, she found safe hiding places for all her children: Lulu, because she was black anyway, in the coal bin in the basement; Ladybird, behind the cat's basket; Nelly, the oldest, in the waste-basket by Daddy's desk. It got scarier and scarier. The Monster looked everywhere in the living room for her except the one place she was—behind the platform rocker. When he left the living room, Blossom crept up the stairs, keeping close to the wall so they wouldn't creak. But one *did* creak, and the Monster heard it and came gallumphing up the stairs behind her. With an excited shout she ran into the first room and shut the door behind her. It was Neil's bedroom, and the big horned moosehead glowered down at her from his place over the chest of drawers. She had always been afraid of that moose, but she was even more afraid of the Monster, who was out there in the hall, listening at every door to hear if she was inside.

She crept on hands and knees to Neil's closet door, which was ajar. She hid among the smelly old boots and dirty blue jeans. The door to the bedroom creaked open. It was so dark she couldn't see her hand in front of her face, but she could *hear* the Monster snuffling all over. He came to the door of the closet and stopped. He *smelled* she was inside. Blossom's heart almost stopped beating, and she prayed to God and to Jesus that the Monster would go away.

The Monster made a loud terrible noise and threw open the door, and for the very first time Blossom saw what the Monster looked like. She screamed and screamed and screamed.

Neil got home first that night, and he couldn't understand what Blossom was doing in his closet with his dirty blue jeans pulled down over her head, whimpering like she'd been whipped with the strap, and trembling like a robin caught in an April snowstorm. But when he picked her up, her little body became all rigid, and nothing would content her but that she sleep that night in Neil's bed. The next morning she'd come down with a fever, and her parents had to cut their trip short and come home and take care of her. No one ever understood what had happened, for Blossom didn't dare tell them about the Monster, whom *they* couldn't see. Eventually the incident was forgotten. As Blossom grew older, the content of her nightmares underwent a gradual change: the old monsters were no more terrifying now than the moosehead over the chest of drawers.

Darkness, however, is the very stuff of terror, and Blossom, running and creeping through the roots, descending depth after depth, felt the old fear repossess her. Suddenly all the lights in the house had been turned off. The darkness filled itself with monsters, like water pouring into a tub, and she ran down stairs and down hallways looking for a closet to hide in.

All through these last, long days of her father's dying, and even before, Blossom had been too much alone. She had felt that there was something he wanted to say to her but that he wouldn't let himself say it. This restraint humiliated her. She had thought that he did not want her to see him dying, and she had forced herself to stay away. Alice and Maryann, with whom she would customarily have passed her time, had no concern now but the baby. Blossom wanted to help them, but she was too young. She was at that age when one is uncomfortable in the presence of either birth or death. She haunted the fringes of these great events and pitied herself for being excluded from them. She imagined herself dying: how sad they would all be, how sorry they had neglected her!

Even Orville had no time for Blossom. He was either off by himself or at Anderson's side. Only Neil seemed more upset at the old man's death. Whenever Orville's path had crossed Blossom's he looked at her with such deadly intensity that the girl turned away, blushing, and even slightly scared. No longer did she feel she understood him, and this, in a way, made her love him more—and more hopelessly.

But none of these things would have caused her to take flight, except into fantasies. It was only after she had seen the expression on Neil's face, the almost somnambulistic cast to his features, when she had heard him speak her name in that particular tone of voice—it was then that Blossom, like a doe catching scent of a hunter, panicked and began to run: away, into the deeper, sheltering dark.

She ran blindly, and so it was inevitable that she would go over one of the dropoffs into a primary root. It could happen, in the dark, even if you were careful. The void swallowed her whole.

Her bent knees first entered the pulp of the fruit, then her body pitched forward into the soft, yielding floss. She sank deep, deep into it. She landed unhurt, only a few inches away from the broken but still breathing body of Alice Nemerov, R.N.

He had delayed, had Jeremiah Orville, altogether too long. He had meant to revenge, and he had instead assisted. Day by day he had observed Anderson's death, his agony, his humiliation, and he knew that he, Jeremiah Orville, had had nothing to do with them. It was the Plant and mere happenstance that had brought Anderson low.

Orville had stood by, Hamletlike, and said *amen* to Anderson's prayers—had deceived only himself by his subtleties. He had been so greedy that all Anderson's sufferings proceed from himself alone and none from the Plant that he had led the old man and his tribe to a land of milk and honey. And now his enemy lay dying by the merest accident, by an infected bite on a vestigial toe.

Orville brooded, alone, in that deep darkness, and an image, a phantasm, took shape in the vacant air. Each day, the apparition took on greater definition, but he knew even from the first white shimmering that it was Jackie Whythe. But *this* was a Jackie who had never been: younger, lither, sweeter, the very essence of female grace and delicacy.

She made him, by all her familiar wiles, declare his love for her. He swore he loved her, but she was not satisfied, she would not believe him. She made him say it again and again.

She reminded him of the nights they had been together, of the treasures of her young body . . . and the horror of her death. Then she would ask again: *Do you love me?*

I do, I do, he insisted. *I do love you. Can you doubt it?* He was in an agony of desire to possess her once again. He craved a final kiss, the slightest touch, a breath merely, but he was refused.

I am dead, she reminded him, *and you have not revenged me.*

"Who will you have?" he asked aloud, grabbing up the axe, which he had been whetting on the palm of his hand all this while. "Give me the name, and with this same axe . . ."

Blossom, the phantasm whispered eagerly, not without a hint of jealousy. *You've abandoned me for that child. You court an infant.*

No! it was only that I might betray her. It was all for the sake of you.

Then betray her now. Betray her, and I will return to you. Then, only then, will I kiss you. Then, when you touch me, your hand will feel flesh. With those words she disappeared.

In the same instant he knew she had not been real, that this was, quite possibly, the inception of madness. But he did not care. Though she was not real, she was right.

Immediately he went in search of his victim. He found her standing on the edge of a group gathered about her father's corpse. Alice Nemerov was lying bound near the corpse, and Neil Anderson was there too, raving. Orville paid no heed to any of this. Then Blossom, as though sensing his purpose, ran madly into the dark tunnels of the Plant. He followed her. This time he would do what must be done: do it neatly, expeditiously, and with an axe.

Pressing the hard, crisp pulp from the rind of the fruit between her palms, Blossom was able to squeeze out a few oil drops of water. But it was so warm at this depth—eighty degrees or more—that she could hardly hope to revive Alice with it. She began again to massage the old woman's thin hands, her cheeks, the sagging flesh of her arms. Mechanically she repeated the same few words of comfort:

"Alice dear, please . . . *Try* to wake up, try . . . Alice, it's *Blossom.* . . . Alice? . . . It's all right now. . . . Oh, *please!*" At last the old woman seemed to be conscious, for she groaned.

"Are you all right? Alice?"

Alice made a noise verging on speech, which was terminated by a hissing intake of breath. When she did speak, when she could speak, her voice was unnaturally loud and strangely resolute. "My hip. I think . . . yes, it's broken."

"Oh no! Alice! Does it . . . does it hurt?"

"Like hell, my dear."

"Why did he do it? Why did Neil—" Blossom paused; she dared not say what it was that Neil had done. Now that Alice was conscious, her own fear and agitation settled over her again. It was as though she had revived Alice only that she might be able to tell her, Blossom, that the Monster wasn't real, just something she'd imagined.

"Why did he throw me down here? Because, my dear, the bastard murdered your father, and because I knew it and was fool enough to say so. And then, I fancy, he never *has* liked me very much."

Blossom said she would not believe it, that it was absurd. She made Alice tell her how she knew, called for the evidences, refuted them. She made her, suffering as she was, repeat each detail of the story, and still she would not believe it. Her brother had faults, but he was not a murderer.

"He murdered *me,* didn't he?" It was a difficult question to answer.

"But *why* would he do such a thing? Why kill a man who's almost dead? It makes no sense. There was no reason."

"It was on your account, my dear."

Blossom could almost feel the Monster breathing down her neck. "What do you mean?" She grabbed Alice's hand almost angrily. "Why on *my* account?"

"Because he must have found out that your father was intending for you and Jeremiah Orville to be married."

"Daddy intended—I don't understand?"

"He wanted Jeremiah to be the new leader, to take his place. He didn't *want* it, but he saw that it would have to be that way. But he put off telling anyone about it. That was my doing. I told him to wait. I thought it would keep him going. I never thought . . ."

Alice talked on, but Blossom had stopped listening. She understood now what her father had wanted to tell her and why he had hesitated. Grief and shame flooded over her: she had misjudged him; she had left him all those days to suffer alone. And he had only wanted her happiness, the happiness she wanted for herself! If only she could return to beg his forgiveness, to thank him. It was as though Alice, by those few words, had turned on all the lights in the house and restored her father to life.

But Alice's next words dispelled this illusion. "You'd better watch out for him," she said grimly. "You dare not trust him. *Especially* you."

"Oh no, no, you don't understand. I love him. And I think he loves me too."

"Not Orville. Of course he loves you. Any fool can see that. It's Neil you'd better watch out for. He's crazy."

Blossom did not protest this. She knew, better than Alice, though less aware till now, how true this was.

"And part of his craziness has to do with you."

"When the others know what he's done, when I tell them . . ." Blossom did not have to say more than this. When the others knew what Neil had done, he would be killed.

"That's why I told you. So they *would* find out."

"You'll tell them yourself. We've got to get back. *Now*. Here—put your arm around my shoulder." Alice protested, but Blossom would not listen. The old woman was light. Blossom could carry her, if need be.

An agonized cry parted the old woman's lips, and she tore her arm away from Blossom. "No! no, the pain. . . . I can't."

"Then I'll get help."

"What help? Whose help? A doctor? An ambulance? I couldn't help your father recover from a rat bite, and this is—" The sound that intruded upon her speech was more eloquent than any words she might have intended.

For a long while, Blossom bit her lip to keep silent. When she felt Alice was ready to listen, she said, "Then I'll just sit here with you."

"And watch me die? It will take a while. No more than two days, though, and most of the time I'll be making these awful noises. No —that would be no comfort to me. But there is something you can do. If you're strong enough."

"Whatever it is, I'll do it."

"You must promise." Blossom's hand tightened over hers in assurance. "You must do for me what Neil did for your father."

"Murder you? No! Alice, you can't ask me to—"

"My dear, I've done it in my time for those who have asked. Some of them had less reason than I. A hypodermic of air, and the pain is—" She did not, this time, cry out. "—gone. Blossom, I *beg* you."

"Someone may come. We'll make a stretcher."

"Yes, someone may come. Neil may come. Can you imagine what he would do if he finds me still alive?"

"No, he wouldn't—" But immediately she knew he would.

"You *must,* my dear. I'll hold you to your promise. But kiss me first. No, not like that—on the lips."

Blossom's trembling lips pressed against Alice's that were rigid with the effort to hold back the pain. "I love you," she whispered. "I love you like my very own mother."

Then she did what Neil had done. Alice's body twisted away in instinctive, unthinking protest, and Blossom let loose her grip.

"No!" Alice gasped. "Don't torture me—do it!"

Blossom did not let loose this time until the old woman was dead.

The darkness grew darker, and Blossom thought she could hear someone climbing down the vines of the root overhead. There was a loud terrible noise as his body came down into the fruit pulp. Blossom knew what the Monster would look like: he would look like Neil. She screamed and screamed and screamed.

The Monster had an axe.

"Return soon," she begged.

"I will, I promise." Buddy bent down to his wife, missing her lips in the darkness (the lamp, by Neil's authority, was to remain with the corpse) and kissing her nose instead. She giggled girlishly. Then, with an excess of caution, he touched one finger to the tiny arm of his son. "I love you," he said, not bothering to define whether he was addressing her or the infant or perhaps both. He did not know himself. He only knew that despite the terrible events of the last months, and especially of the past hour, his life seemed meaningful in a way that it had not for years. The most somber considerations could not diminish the fullness of his hopes nor dampen the glow of his satisfaction.

In even the worst disaster, in the largest defeats, the machinery of joy keeps on grinding for a lucky few.

Maryann seemed more aware than he that their charmed circle was of very small circumference, for she murmured, "Such a terrible thing."

"What?" Buddy asked. His attention was taken up with Buddy Junior's teeny-tiny toe.

"Alice. I can't understand why he—"

"He's crazy," Buddy said, moving reluctantly outside the circle. "Maybe she called him a name. She has—she *had* a sharp tongue, you know. When he gets back, I'll see that something's done. There's no telling what rotten thing he'll do next. Orville will help, and there are others, too, who've let a word drop. But in the meantime he has a gun and we don't. And the important thing now is to find Blossom."

"Of course. That must come first. It's just that it's such a terrible thing."

"It's a terrible thing," he agreed. He could hear Neil calling to him again. "I have to go now." He began to move away.

"I wish the lamp were here, so I could see you one more time."

"You sound like you don't think I'll return."

"No! Don't say that—even as a joke. You *will* come back. I know you will. But, Buddy—?"

"Maryann?"

"Say it one more time."

"I love you."

"And I love you." When she was quite sure he was gone she added: "I've *always* loved you."

The several members of the descending search party threaded their way through the labyrinth of divergent roots on a single slim rope, braided by Maryann from the fiber of the vines. When any member of the party separated from the main body, he attached the end of his own reel of rope to the communal rope that led back to the tuber where Anderson was lying in state beside the vigilant lamp.

Neil and Buddy descended the farthest along the communal rope. When it gave out, they were at a new intersection of roots. Buddy knotted one end of his rope to the end of the main line and went off to the left. Neil, having done likewise, went to the right, but only for a short distance. Then he sat down and thought, as hard as he could think.

Neil did not trust Buddy. Never had. Now, with their father passed on, wouldn't he have to trust him still less? He thought he was so smart, Buddy did, with that brat of his. Like he was the only man in the world ever had a son. Neil hated his guts for other reasons too—which his mind shied from. It would not do for him to be consciously aware that the presumable Neil Junior, if he existed at all, existed most probably as a result of other seed than his own. That was a thought that he had best not think at all.

Neil was worried. He sensed in several of the men who'd gone out on the search a resistance to his authority, and this resistance seemed strongest in Buddy. A leader can't afford to let his leadership be challenged. Their father had always harped on that. It didn't seem to make any difference to Buddy that Anderson had *wanted* Neil to take over for him. Buddy had always been a wild one, a rebel, an atheist.

That's what he is! Neil thought, astonished at how perfectly the word defined everything dangerous in his brother. *An atheist!* Why hadn't he realized that before?

One way or another, atheists had to be stomped out. Because atheism was like poison in the town reservoir; it was like. . . . But Neil couldn't remember how the rest of it went. It had been a long time since his father had given a good sermon against atheism and the Supreme Court.

On the heels of this perception another new idea came to Neil. It was, for him, a true inspiration, a revelation—almost as though his father's spirit had come down from heaven and whispered it in his ear.

He would tie Buddy's line in a circle!

Then, when Buddy tried to get back, he'd just keep following the rope around and around the circle. Once you grasped the basic concept, it was a very simple idea.

There was one hitch, however, when you thought about it carefully. One part of the circle would be here at this intersection, and Buddy could feel around, maybe, and discover the end of the main line where it was still knotted to Neil's.

But he wouldn't if the circle didn't touch this intersection!

Chuckling to himself, Neil unknotted Buddy's rope and began following Buddy, winding the rope up as he went along. When he figured he'd taken up enough of it, he turned off along a minor branch of the root, unwinding the rope as he crawled along. This small root connected to another equally small, and this to yet another. The roots of the Plant were always circling around on themselves, and if you just keep turning the same direction, you usually came back to the point you started from. And sure enough, Neil soon was back in the larger root, where he caught hold of Buddy's line, stretched taut, a foot off the floor. Buddy was probably not far away.

Neil's trick was working splendidly. Having nearly reached the end of the length of rope, he knotted it to the other end and formed a perfect circle.

Now, Neil thought, with satisfaction, *let him try and find his way back. Let him try and make trouble now! the lousy atheist!*

Neil began to crawl back the way he had come, using Buddy's rope as a guide, laughing all the way. Only then did he notice that there was some kind of funny slime all over his hands and all over his clothing, too.

Chapter 13

CUCKOO, JUG-JUG,
PU-WE, TO-WITTA-WO!

There are people who cannot scream even when the occasion calls emphatically for screaming. Any drill sergeant can tell you of men, good soldiers every other way, who, when they must run forward to plant a bayonet in the guts of a sawdust dummy, cannot let loose with any sort of battle cry—or at best can manage some bloodless imitation, a half-hearted *Kill Kill Kill!* It is not that these man lack the primordial emotions of hatred and bloodlust; they have just become too civilized, too bound in, to experience a pure berserker rage. Perhaps a real battle will bring it out of them; perhaps nothing will.

There are emotions more primordial, more basic to survival, than hatred and bloodlust; but it is the same with them too—they can be stifled, covered over with civilized form and secondary modes of feeling. Only extreme circumstances can release them.

Jeremiah Orville was a very civilized man. The last seven years had liberated him in many ways, but they had not effaced his civilization until very lately, when events had taught him to desire the consummation of his revenge above his own happiness and safety. It was a beginning.

But as he stood beside Blossom, the axe in his hand unseen, himself unseen, hearing these heartrending cries that fear wrenched from her throat, now the more primordial emotion of love overcame him, shattered the civilized Jeremiah, and, dropping the weapon, he fell to his knees and began kissing the young body that was now the most important and beautiful thing in the world.

"Blossom!" he cried with joy. "Oh Blossom! Blossom!" And continued senselessly to repeat her name.

"Jeremiah! You! My God, I thought it was *him!*"

And he, in the same instance: "How could I have loved *her,* a ghost, bodiless, when all this while—Forgive me! Can you ever forgive me?"

She could not understand him. *"Forgive* you!" She laughed and cried, and they said many things to each other then without thinking, without caring to understand any more than the as-yet-unassimilable fact that they were in love.

Passion's highest flights tend to be, if not completely innocent, slow. Orville and Blossom could not enjoy the happiness of gazing hours-long into each other's eyes, but the darkness permitted as much as it denied. They dallied; they delayed. They called each other by the simple, affectionate names of schoolgirl romances (names that had never passed between Orville and Jackie Whythe, who had been given, when Orville's hands moved over her, to cruder expressions—a certain sign of sophistication), and these *sweethearts,* these *darlings* and *my very owns,* seemed to express philosophies of love exact as arithmetic and subtle as music.

Eventually, as they must, a few words of common sense disturbed the perfect solitude of their love, like pebbles thrown in a still pond. "The others must be looking for me," she said. "I have to tell them about something."

"Yes, I know—I was listening up above as Alice spoke to you."

"Then you know that Daddy wanted this. He was going to say so when—"

"Yes, I know."

"And Neil—"

"I know that too. But you needn't worry about him now." He kissed the soft, drooping lobe of her ear. "Let's not speak of it though. Later, we'll do what we have to do."

She pushed Orville away from her. "No, Jeremiah. Listen—let's go away somewhere. Away from them and all their hating and jealousy. Somewhere where they'll never find us. We can be like Adam and Eve and think of new names for all the animals. There's the whole world—" She did not say any more, for she realized that there *was* the whole world. She stretched out a hand to draw Orville back to her—and to push the world aside for a little longer—but instead of Orville's living flesh her hand encountered Alice's fractured hip.

A voice, not Orville's, called her name. "Not *yet*," she whispered. "It can't end *now*."

"It won't end," he promised, helping her to her feet. "We have our whole life ahead of us. A lifetime lasts forever. At my age, I should know."

She laughed. Then, for the whole world to hear, she shouted: "We're down here. Go away, whoever you are. We'll find our way back by ourselves."

But Buddy had already found them, entering the tuber by a side passage. "Who's that with you?" he asked. "Orville, is it you? I should knock your block off for pulling a stunt like this. Don't you know the old man is dead? What a hell of a time to elope!"

"No, Buddy, you don't understand. It's all right—Orville and I are in love."

"Yeah, I understand that all right. He and I'll have a talk about that—in private. I only hope I got here before he could put your *love* to the test. For Christ's sake, Orville—this girl is only fourteen! She's young enough to be your daughter. The way you're going at it, she's young enough to be your *grand*daughter."

"Buddy! It's not like that at all," Blossom protested. "It's what father *wanted* for us. He said to Alice and then—"

Buddy, moving forward with their voices as a guide, stumbled over the nurse's dead body. "What in hell!"

"That's Alice. If you'd only *listen*—" Blossom broke into tears in which frustration mingled with sorrow.

"Sit down," Orville said, "and shut up for a minute. You've been jumping to the wrong conclusions, and there are a lot of things you don't know. No—don't argue, man, *listen!*"

"The question, then, is not what should be done in Neil's case, but who's to do it." Orville concluded. "I don't think I should have to bear that responsibility, nor that you should either. Personally, I've never liked your father's high-handed way of being judge, jury, and law all by himself. It's an honor to have been nominated as his successor, but an honor I'd rather decline. This is a matter for the community to act on."

"Agreed. I know that if *I* did . . . what has to be done, they'd say it was for personal reasons. And it just wouldn't be true. I don't want anything he's got. Not any more. In fact, the only thing I want right now is to go back and see Maryann and my son again."

"Then the thing to do is to set about finding the others. Blossom and I can stay out of the way until the matter has been settled. Neil can be king for a day, but he'll have to sleep sometime, and that will be time enough to depose him."

"Fine. We'll go now—but not back along my rope. It would be too easy to run into Neil that way. If we climb up the vines of the root that you came down, there'll be no danger of our crossing his path."

"If Blossom's up to it, I'm agreeable."

"Jeremiah, you strange old man, I can climb up those things twice as fast as any thirty-five-year-old, two-hundred-pound grandfather."

Buddy heard what he supposed was a kiss and pursed his lips in disapproval. Though he agreed in theory with all that Orville had said in his own and Blossom's defense—that times had changed, that early marriage was now positively to be preferred to the old way, that Orville (this had been Blossom's argument) was certainly the most eligible of the survivors, and that they had Anderson's posthumous blessings on their union—despite all these cogent reasons, Buddy could not help feeling a certain distaste for the whole thing. *She's still a child,* he told himself, and against this, to him, incontrovertible fact all their reasonings seemed as specious as the proofs that Achilles can never pass the tortoise in their endless footrace.

But he swallowed his distaste, as a child swallows some loathed vegetable in order to go outside and do something more important. "Let's shove off," he said.

To return to the primary root down which Blossom and Orville had dropped it was necessary to detour back along the way Buddy had come and then angle up along a branch root so narrow that even crawling through it was arduous.

But this was only a foretaste of the difficulties they faced in climbing the vertical root. The vines by which they hoped to ascend were covered over with a thin film of slime; the hand could not grip them firmly enough to keep from slipping. Only at the nodal points, where the vines fed into each other, forming a sort of stirrup (like the system of roots, these vines were forever joining and rejoining,) could one purchase a secure hold, and there was not always certain to be another such nodal intersection of vines within grasping distance overhead. They had continually to backtrack and reascend along a different network of vines. Even more frustrating was that their feet (though bare, they were not prehensile) were constantly slipping out of these makeshift stirrups. It was like trying to climb a greased rope ladder with rungs missing.

"What's to be gained killing ourselves?" Buddy asked rhetorically, after having come within one slippery fingerhold of doing exactly this for himself. "I don't know where this slop is coming from, but it doesn't seem to be letting up. The higher we go, the more likely we are to break our necks if we fall. Why not go back along my rope after all? It's not that likely we'll run into Neil, and if we do, we don't have to let on that we know anything he wouldn't want us to. I'd rather risk five, ten minutes with him than another hundred yards up this greased chimney."

This seemed a sensible course, and they returned to the tuber. The descent was easy as sliding down a firepole.

Following Buddy's line up a mild slope, they noticed that here too the vines were slimed and slippery beneath their bare feet. Feeling down beneath the layer of vines, Orville discovered that a rivulet of the slime was flowing down the slope.

"What is it, do you suppose?" Buddy wondered.

"I think the springtime has come at last," Orville replied.

"And this is the sap—of course! I recognize the feel of it now—and the smell—Oh, don't I know that smell!"

"Springtime!" Blossom said. "We'll be able to return to the surface!"

Happiness is contagious (and wasn't there every reason for a young man newly in love to be happy in any case?), and Orville quoted part of a poem he remembered:

> "Spring, the sweet Spring, is the year's pleasant
>   king;
> Then blooms each thing, then maids dance in a
>   ring,
> Cold doth not sting, the pretty birds do sing,
> Cuckoo, jug-jug, pu-wee, to-witta-wo!"

"What a lovely poem!" she said, catching hold of his hand and squeezing.

"What a lot of nonsense!" Buddy said. *"Cuckoo, jug-jug, pu-we, to-witta-wo!"*

The three of them laughed gaily. The sun seemed to be shining on them already, and nothing was needed to make them laugh again but that one of them repeat the silly old Elizabethan words.

Some two thousand feet above their heads, the reviving land basked under the bright influence of the sun, which had indeed passed the equinox. Even before the last patches of snow had melted from the southern sides of boulders, the leaves of the great Plants unfurled to receive the light and began without further ado to set about their work as though October were only yesterday.

Except for the noise of the leaves snapping open (and that was over in a day,) it was a silent spring. There were no birds to sing.

The leaves spoke hungrily to the stems, drained dry to last out the freezing northern winter, and the stems spoke to the roots, where the solute-bearing sap, which the leaves needed to make new food, began to boil up through myriad capillaries. Where these capillaries had been broken by the passage of man, the sap oozed forth and spread over the vines that lined the hollows of the roots. As more and more sap poured through the arteries of the awakening Plant, the thin sap formed little rivulets, which, merging with other rivulets, became little streams, and these streams ran down to flood the lowest depths of the roots. When they flowed into hollows in which the capillaries were still intact, they were reabsorbed, but elsewhere the levels of these streams rose higher and higher, flooding the roots, like sewers in a sudden March thaw.

Now the tubers of the fruit, which had been forming for years, took on a fine, autumnal richness. The airy floss at their cores, receiving their final supplies of food from the leaves above, thickened to the consistency of whipped egg white.

In both hemispheres, the Plant was coming to the end of a long season, and now, at regular intervals over the green earth, there descended from the spring skies gleaming spheres so immense that each one, landing, crushed several of the Plants under its ponderous bulk. Viewed from the proper distance, the landscape would have resembled a bed of clover overspread with grey basketballs.

These grey basketballs basked a few hours in the sun, then extruded, from the apertures at their bases, hundreds of exploratory cilia, each of which moved toward a nearby Plant and with tidy, effective little drill bits, began to bore down through the woody stem into the hollow of the root below. When a satisfactory passage had been opened, the cilium was drawn back into the gray basketball.

The harvest was being prepared.

Neil had gone three times about the circle of rope he had fashioned to trap Buddy, and he was beginning, dully, to sense that he had been caught in his own snare (though *how* it had happened he did not yet understand.) Then, as he had feared, Buddy could be heard returning along the root. Blossom and Orville were with him, all of them laughing! At him? He had to hide, but there was nowhere to hide, and he didn't want to hide from Blossom anyhow. So he said, "Uh, hi." They stopped laughing.

"What are you doing *here?*" Buddy asked.

"Well, you see, uh . . . This rope here, it keeps. . . . No, that's not it, either." The more he talked, the more confused he became, and the more impatient Buddy.

"Oh, never mind then. Come along. I've found Blossom. And Orville too. Let's round up the others now. It's spring. Haven't you noticed the slime—Hey—what's this?" He found the point where the end of his own rope was knotted to its own middle. "This surely isn't the intersection where we left each other. I'd remember if I'd gone down any root as small as this."

Neil didn't know what to do. He wanted to hit his snoopy brother over the head, that's what he *wanted* to do, and shoot Orville, just blast his brains out. But he sensed that this had better be done away from Blossom, who might not understand. Then too, when you're lost the most important thing is to get home safe. When you're home safe, things won't seem so muddled as when you're lost.

A whispered conversation was going on among Buddy, Orville and Blossom. Then Buddy said: "Neil, did you—?"

"No! I don't know how . . . it just must of *happened!* It's not *my* fault!"

"Well, you dumb clod!" Buddy began to laugh. "Why, if you had to saw a limb off a tree, I swear you'd sit on the wrong side to do it. You've tied my line in a circle, haven't you?"

"No, Buddy, honest to God! Like I said, I don't know how—"

"And you didn't bring your own line along so you could get back. Oh, Neil, how do you do it? How do you always find a way?"

Orville and Blossom joined Buddy's laughter. "Oh, *Neil!*" Blossom cried out. "Oh, *Neil!*"

That made Neil feel good, to hear Blossom say his name like that, and he began to laugh along with everybody else. The joke was on him!

Surprisingly, it seemed that Buddy and Orville weren't going to make a big stink. Maybe they knew what was good for them!

"It seems we'll have to find our way back as best we can," Orville said with a sigh, when they were all done laughing. "Neil, would you like to lead the way?"

"No," Neil said, somber again and touching the Python in his holster for assurance. "No, I'll be the leader, but I'll bring up the rear."

An hour later they had come up against a dead end, and they knew they were thoroughly lost. It was no longer possible to shatter the capillaries with a wave of one's arm. They were swollen with sap and resilient. It would have been no more difficult to crawl through a honeycomb than through the unopened hollows. They were compelled therefore to stay strictly within the bounds of path already blazed. Thanks to Anderson's explorations, there were quite enough of these. Quite too many.

Orville summed up their situation. "It's back to the sub-basement, my dears. We'll have to take another elevator to get to the ground floor."

"Wha'd you say?" Neil asked.

"I said—"

"I heard what you said! And I don't want you to use that word again, understood? You remember who's leader here, huh?"

"What word, Neil?" Blossom asked.

"My dears!" Neil screamed. Neil had always been able to scream when he felt the occasion called for it. He was not overcivilized, and the primordial was very close to the surface of his mind. It seemed to grow closer all the time.

Chapter 14

THE WAY UP

The quiet, which for months had been absolute, was broken by the trickling of the sap. It was a sound like the sound of water in early spring, flowing through the town gutters underneath unmelted banks of snow.

While they rested they did not speak, for the most innocuous statements could throw Neil into a state of hysterical excitement. Naturally, they knew better than mention Anderson or Alice, but why, when Buddy began to worry out loud about his wife and son, should Neil complain that he was "selfish," that all he thought about was sex? When Orville spoke of their predicament and speculated (with more good cheer than he felt) on their chances of reaching the surface, Neil thought they were blaming him. Silence seemed altogether the best policy, but Neil could not endure more than a few moments of silence either. Then he would start to complain: "If only we'd brought down the lamp, we wouldn't be having any trouble now." Or, remembering one of his father's favorite themes: "Why do I have to do the thinking for everybody? Why is that?"

Or he would whistle. His favorite tunes were the *Beer-Barrel Polka, Red River Valley, Donkey Serenade* (which he accompanied percussively with the popping of his cheeks), and the theme from *Exodus*. Once he had started any of these, he could go on perpetuum mobile for the duration of the time they rested. It wouldn't have been so bad if he'd been able to stay in the same key for eight bars running.

It was hardest for Buddy. Blossom and Orville had each other. In the darkness they would hold each other's hands, while Neil ground out the tune one more time around, like a diligent monkey; they could even kiss, quietly.

Here there was neither north nor south, east nor west; there was only up and down. There were no measurable units of distance, only rough estimates of temperature and depth, and their only measure of elapsed time was the time it took their bodies to drop, too exhausted to continue without another rest.

They never knew whether they were at the periphery or near the heart of labyrinth. They might ascend, through channels already opened, to within a few hundred feet—or even ten—of the surface only to find themselves at a dead end. It was necessary not simply to find a way up but to find *the* way up. It was hard to make Neil understand why this was so. When Blossom had explained it to him, he had seemed to agree, but later when Orville brought up the subject again, the argument started all over.

They were soaked through with their own sweat and with the sap, which in the least steep roots reached levels of four and five inches. After hours of climbing they were at a height where the heat was not so overwhelming (the lower depths felt like a sauna), and the air seemed to be gas again. Orville estimated the temperature as seventy-five, which placed them a probable fifteen hundred feet from the surface. Ordinarily, over a known route, they could have climbed that height in little more than three hours. Now it might very well take days.

Orville had hoped that the flow of sap would abate as they reached higher levels; instead it was worsening. Where did it all come from? The logistics of the Plant's water supply was something he had never stopped to consider. Well, he couldn't stop now either.

You couldn't just grab hold of a vine and haul yourself up the slope; you had to make your hand into a sort of hook and slip it into a stirrup. You couldn't just reach back and help the next person up after you; you had to grapple the two hooks together. So it was always the hands that hurt worst and were first to give out. You'd hang there and feel them letting loose, and you'd hope that you wouldn't slide back with the sap too far. Once you let go, it wasn't so bad—you'd slide along soft and easy if the slope wasn't too steep, or else shoot down like a toboggan, until you came up against someone or something with a bump, and then you had to get your hooks bent back into shape and start clawing your way back up through the slime. But you knew your body could go a long way yet, and you hoped that would be far enough.

They might have been climbing twelve or twice twelve hours. They had eaten and rested a few times, but they had not slept. They had not slept, in fact, since before the night of Anderson's dying and Maryann's delivery. Now it must be night again. Their minds were leaden with the necessity for sleep.

"Absolute necessity," Orville repeated.

Neil objected. This was just going to be a resting period. He feared that if he went to sleep first, they would take away his gun. They weren't to be trusted. But if he just sat here and let his body *relax* . . . dogtired, that's what he. . . .

He was the first to sleep after all, and they didn't take his gun. They didn't care. They didn't want his gun: they only wanted to sleep.

Neil's repertoire of dreams was no larger than his stock of songs. First he dreamed his baseball dream. Then he was walking up the stairs of the old house in town. Then he dreamed of Blossom. Then he dreamed his baseball dream again, except this time it was different: when he opened the closet door, his father was the first baseman. Blood spurted from the deep cleft of the first baseman's mitt, which opened and closed, opened and closed, in the dead man's hand. But otherwise the dreams were just the same as always.

The next day, after an hour or so, the hurt went out of their hands, and it was the stickiness that was hardest to endure. Their clothes clung to their straining limbs or hung loose and heavy like skins that could not be sloughed off. "We'd move faster," Orville said, "if we weren't weighted down with these denim jackets."

Somewhat later, since it appeared that the idea was not going to come to Neil of itself, Buddy added, "If we knotted our jackets together, sleeve to sleeve, and used them for rope, we could climb faster."

"Yeah," Neil said, "but you're forgetting there's a lady with us."

"Oh, don't bother about *me*," Blossom protested.

"Just our jackets, Neil. It wouldn't be any different than going swimming."

"No!" The strident tone was creeping into his voice again. "It wouldn't be *right!*" There was no use arguing with him once he had made up his mind. He was their leader.

The next time they stopped to rest and eat, the sap was raining down on them in great globs, like the water-drops that announce a summer thunderstorm. The central stream of sap flowing through the root was now well over their ankles. As soon as they were not quite sopping wet, their clothes stuck to them like suits of adhesive tape. They could move freely only when they were drenched.

"I can't stand it any longer," Blossom said, beginning to cry. "I can't *stand* it."

"There now, Miss Anderson. Chin up! Tally-ho! Remember the Titanic!"

"Stand what?" Neil asked.

"These clothes," she said. And indeed that was a part of what she couldn't stand.

"Oh, I guess she's right," Neil said, as uncomfortable as the others. "It can't hurt if we just take off our jackets. Hand them to me, and I'll knot the sleeves together."

"Good idea!" Orville said. They all handed their jackets to Neil.

"Blossom!" he said. "I didn't mean *you*. It isn't right." She didn't say anything. Neil sort of giggled. "Well, if that's the way you want it," he said.

The stuff gushed from the small opening above as from a burst water main. Quite properly, it could not be called sap. It was more like water. For a while they were happy because it cleaned them off. But it was cold, too cold.

The roots, as they ascended through them, had been growing smaller instead of larger. To get through them now they had to crawl on hands and knees, and even so they could scrape their heads on the ceiling if they weren't careful. The water was up to their elbows.

"I think," Orville said cautiously, "that we're coming up underneath Lake Superior. This much water can't be coming from spring thaws." He waited for Neil to protest. Then, still more cautiously: "I think we'll have to go back the way we came. Let's hope we have better luck a second time."

The reason Neil had not protested was that he had not heard. Orville's voice had been drowned out by the roar of the water, which acres and acres of thirsty Plants were siphoning from the lake bottom. Orville explained his theory several times over when they had backed off to a quieter spot. Then Blossom tried.

"Neil, look, it's very simple—the only way away from the lake is *down*. Because if we try to move along at *this* level, we can as easily be going east—farther on into the lake—as west—away from it. If we had the lamp, we could use your compass, but we don't have the lamp. We might just go along north or south and follow the shore. There's no telling how much area beneath the lake Daddy explored last winter. We just have to go *down*. Do you understand?"

Orville took advantage of this occasion to have some private words with Buddy: "What the hell—let's leave him here if he doesn't want to go with us. It'll be his own fault if he drowns."

"No," said Buddy, "that wouldn't be *right*. I want to do this by the book."

"Okay, I'll go," Neil told Blossom, "but I think it's a lot of hooey. I'm only agreeing for your sake. Remember that."

Down: the sap was in spate. It jostled their bodies together or tore them apart as casually as flood waters bearing off the trees of the riverbank. Strong currents dashed them against the walls of the root wherever the curves were too sharp to too steep. Days of climbing were retraced in minutes.

Deeper down: the stream became less chill, grew thicker, like pudding coming to a boil. But its pace did not slacken. It was like going down a ski trail on a piece of cardboard. At least they need not worry about repeating their mistake: it was no longer possible to move "upstream" toward the lake.

At this depth there were now whole stretches where the hot sap filled the entire hollow of the root. Hoarding a lungful of air, Orville (who was the first to test any new passage) followed the current resistlessly and hoped. There had always been some branch root feeding into the flooded root from above, too small to ascend through perhaps but large enough to butt one's head into for a breath of air. But the next time, of course, there might not be such an opening. There might only be a dead end.

That fear—that the current was leading them down a blind alley —absorbed their whole attention. More and more often their bodies were swept into entangling networks of the sap-swollen capillaries that lined the unexplored passages. Once Orville was caught in such a net where the root had split abruptly in two. Buddy and Blossom, next behind, found him there, his legs moving only as the current moved them. His head had struck against the hard wedge separating the two branches of the root. He was unconscious, perhaps drowned.

They hauled at his pants leg, and his pants slid right off his narrow hips. Then they each took a foot and pulled him out. A short distance away they found an area where the root, sloping gently upward, was only half-filled with sap. Buddy embraced Orville in a bear hug and began squeezing the water out of his lungs rhythmically. Then Blossom tried mouth-to-mouth respiration, which she'd learned in Red Cross swimming classes.

"What are you doing?" Neil asked. Unfamiliar sounds made him nervous.

"She's giving Orville artificial respiration," Buddy answered testily. "He half-drowned back there."

Neil reached out fingers to confirm this. The fingers came between Orville's mouth and Blossom's, then clamped down tightly over Orville's. "You're *kissing* him!"

"Neil!" Blossom screamed. She tried to tear away her brother's fingers, but even desperation did not lend her sufficient strength. One can only be desperate so long, and she'd passed that limit long ago. "You'll kill him!"

Buddy struck a blow in the direction he supposed Neil to be, but it glanced off Orville's shoulder. Neil began to drag Orville's body away.

"He doesn't have pants on either," Neil fretted.

"They come off when we were pulling him out. We told you that, remember?"

The sudden deprivation of oxygen, coming after their efforts at revival, proved to be exactly the stimulus Orville required—he came to.

When the body he was carrying began to stir, Neil let go abruptly, spooked. He had thought Orville was dead, or very nearly.

Buddy and Neil then had a long debate on the propriety of nudity (both in the particular case of Orville and in general) under the present, exceptional circumstances. The argument was mainly a pretext on Buddy's part to give Orville a chance to regain his strength. "Do you want to get back to the surface," Buddy asked, "or do you want to stay down here and be drowned?"

"No!" Neil said, yet once more. "It isn't right. *No!*"

"You've got to *choose*. Which is it?" Buddy was pleased to discover that he could play on Neil's fears as easily as on a harmonica.

"Because if we're going to go *up,* we'll have to go up together, and we'll need some kind of rope."

"We *had* a rope."

"And you lost it, Neil."

"I didn't. I did not. I—"

"Well, you were the last one who had a hold on it, and now it's gone. Now we need another rope. Of course, if you don't *care* about getting back. . . . Or if you think you'll do better on your own . . ."

Eventually Neil agreed. "But Blossom ain't going to touch him, understand? She's my sister, and I ain't going to have it. *Understand?*"

"Neil, you don't have to worry about anything of that sort till we're all home safe," Buddy temporized. "Nobody's going to—"

"And they better not speak to each other either. 'Cause I say so, and what I say *goes.* Blossom, you go on ahead of me, and Buddy behind. Orville goes last."

Neil, naked now except for belt and holster, knotted the legs of their several trousers together, and they set off, each with a grip on the line. The water was deep and so hot their skin seemed to be coming off their bones, like a chicken that boils too long. The current was weakening, however, and they moved more slowly.

Soon they had found a root angling upward from which the trickle of water was not much worse than when they'd first noticed it—how many days ago? Wearily, almost mechanically, they began to climb again.

Blossom remembered a song from nursery school days about a spider washed down a water spout by the rain:

> *Out came the sun and dried away the rain,*
> *And the inky-dinky spider be-gan to climb again.*

She began to laugh, as she had laughed at the strange words of Jeremiah's poem, but this time she couldn't stop laughing, despite how much the laughter hurt.

Of them all, Buddy was the most upset by this, for he could remember the winter before, in the commonroom, and the people who had run out into the thawing snow, laughing and singing, never to return. Blossom's laughter was not unlike theirs.

The root at this point opened on to a tuber of fruit, and they decided to rest and eat. Orville tried to calm Blossom, but Neil told him to shut up. The pulp, which was now semi-liquid, dropped down on their heads and shoulders like the droppings of huge, diarrhoetic birds.

Neil was torn between his desire to go away where the noise of his sister's laughter wouldn't disturb him and an equally strong desire to stay close at hand and protect her. He compromised, removing to a middle distance, where he lay on his back, not intending to go to sleep, just to rest his body . . .

His head came down on the handle of the axe that Jeremiah had dropped there. He let out a little cry, which nobody noticed. They were all of them so tired. He sat for a long time, thinking very hard, his eyes crossing with the effect, though you couldn't see anything in that uncompromising dark.

The softened fruit pulp continued to fall from overhead and spatter on their bodies and on the floor with little crepitant sounds, like the sounds of children's kisses.

Chapter 15

BLOOD AND LIQUORICE

His hand touched her dead body. Buddy thought at first it was his father's corpse, but then he remembered how he had once already stumbled across that same cold body, and delight displaced terror: there *was* a way back! This was the thread that led out of the labyrinth. He traced his steps back to Orville and Blossom.

"Is Neil asleep?" he asked.

"He's stopped whistling," Orville said. "He's either asleep or dead."

Buddy told them his news. ". . . and so, you see, that means we can go back the way we tried to in the first place. Up the shaft. It was a mistake, our turning back when we did."

"Here we are, come full circle. The only difference now," Orville observed, "is that we've got Neil with us. Perhaps we'd do best to ignore that difference and leave him behind. We can go now."

"I thought we'd agreed to let the *others* decide what to do with Neil."

"We won't be doing away with him. We'll be leaving him in almost exactly the same place we found him—caught in the trap he meant for you. Besides, we can leave Alice's body in his way, and he can figure out for himself that the way back is up the shaft he threw her down."

"Not my half-brother. Not Neil. He'd only get scared if he found her body. As for figuring his way back, you might as well expect him to discover the Pythagorean theorem all by himself. Hell, I'll bet if you tried to explain that to him, he wouldn't believe it."

Blossom, who had been listening to all this rather dazedly, began to shiver, as the tension which her body had sustained so long began to drain away. It was like the time she'd gone swimming in the lake in April; her flesh trembled, yet at the same time she felt strangely rigid. Then her body, naked and taut, was suddenly pressed against Orville's, and she did not know if he had come to her or she to him. "Oh, darling, we'll go back! We *will*—after all! Oh, my very own!"

Neil's voice shrilled in the darkness: "I heard that!"

Though she could hear Neil gallumphing forward, Blossom sustained the kiss desperately. Her fingers tightened into Orville's arms, grappled in the wiry muscles. Her body strained forward as his tried to pull away. Then a hand closed around her mouth and another around her shoulder and pulled her roughly away from Orville, but she didn't care. She was still giddy with the high, maenad happiness of those who are reckless in their love.

"I suppose you were giving him some more artificial respiration?" Neil sneered. It was, perhaps, his first authentic joke.

"I was kissing him," Blossom replied proudly. "We're in love."

"I forbid you to kiss him!" Neil screamed. "I forbid you to be in love, I forbid you!"

"Neil, let go of me." But his hands only shifted to secure a better grip and closed tighter.

"You, *you*—Jeremiah Orville! I'm going to *git* you. Yeah, I've been on to you right along. You fooled a lot of people, but you never fooled me. I knew what you was up to. I saw the way you looked at Blossom. Well, you ain't going to get her. What you're going to get is a bullet in your head."

"Neil, let go—you're hurting me."

"Neil," Buddy said in a low, reasoning tone, the tone one adopts with frightened animals, "that girl is your sister. You're talking like he stole your girl. She's your *sister*."

"She is not."

"What in hell do you mean by that?"

"I mean I don't care!"

"You filth."

"Orville, was that you? Why don't you come here, Orville? I ain't going to let Blossom go. You're going to have to come and rescue her. Orville?"

He jerked Blossom's arms behind her back and circled the slender wrists with his left hand. When she struggled, he twisted her arms up painfully or cuffed her with his free hand. When she seemed pacified, he unsnapped the leather flap of the holster and took out his Python, as one removes jewelery from a giftbox, lovingly. "Come here, Orville, and git what I got for you."

"Be careful. He does have a gun," Buddy said. "He has father's."

Buddy's voice came more from the right than Neil had expected. He shifted his weight, but he wasn't really worried, because he had a gun and they didn't.

"I know," Orville said.

A little to the left. The space inside this tuber was long and narrow, too narrow for them to circle around to either side of him.

"I got something for you too, Buddy, if you think you're going to move in when your buddy's brains are blown out. I got me an axe." He chirruped an ugly laugh. "Hey! that's a joke: Buddy . . . buddy, get it?"

"Your jokes stink, Neil. If you want to improve your personality, you shouldn't make jokes."

"This is just between me and Orville, Buddy. You go away, or . . . or I'll chop your head off, that's what I'll do."

"Yeah! With what, with your big front teeth?"

"Buddy," Orville cautioned, "he *may* have the axe. I brought it down here with me." Fortunately no one thought to ask why.

"Neil, let *go* now. Let go—or I'll never speak to you again. If you stop acting this way, we can all go right up and forget this happened."

"No, you don't understand, Blossom. You're not safe yet." His body leaned forward until his lips were touching her shoulders. They rested there a moment, uncertain what to do. Then his tongue began to lick away the fruit pulp with which her whole body was slimed. She managed not to scream.

"When you're safe, I'll let you go, I promise. Then you can be my queen. There'll be just the two of us and the whole world. We'll go to Florida, where it never snows, the two of us." He spoke with unnatural eloquence, for he had stopped thinking too closely about what he said, and the words left his lips uncensored by the faulty mechanisms of consciousness. It was another triumph for the primordial. "We'll lay on the beach, and you can sing songs while I whistle. But not yet, little lady. Not until you're safe. Soon."

Buddy and Orville seemed to have stopped moving forward. All was quiet except for the plops of the ripe fruit. Neil's blood surged with the raw delight that comes from inducing fear in another animal. *They're afraid of me!* he thought. *Afraid of my gun!* The weight of the pistol in his hand, the way his fingers curved around it, the way one of them pressed against the trigger, afforded him pleasure more richly gratifying than his lips had known touching his sister's body.

They *were* afraid of him. They could hear his hard breathing and Blossom's theatrical whimpering (which she maintained, like a foghorn, just so that they might hear it and gauge their distance), and they hung back. They had too much contempt for Neil to be ready to risk their lives desperately against his. Surely there was some way to trick him—to make *him* take the gamble.

Perhaps, Buddy reasoned, if he became angry enough, he would do something foolish—squander his single bullet on a noise in the dark or at least loose his grip on Blossom, which must by now be wearying. "Neil," he whispered, "everybody knows about you. Alice told everyone what you did."

"Alice is dead," Neil scoffed.

"Her ghost," Buddy hissed. "Her ghost is down here looking for you. On account of what you did to her."

"Ah, that's a lot of hooey. I don't believe in no ghosts."

"And on account of what you did to Father. That was a terrible thing to do, Neil. He must be awful angry with you. He must be looking for you, too. And he won't need a lamp to find you with."

"I didn't do *nothing!*"

"Father knows better than that. Alice knows better, doesn't she? We all do. That's how you got the pistol, Neil. You killed him to get it. Killed your own father. How does it feel to do something like that? Tell us. What did he say at the very last moment?"

"Shut up! shut up! shut up!" When he heard Buddy begin to talk again, he set up the same shrill chant backing away meanwhile from the voice that seemed to be drawing nearer to him.

Then it was quiet again, and that was worse. Neil began to fill the quiet with his own words: "I didn't kill him. Why would I want to do that? He loved me more than he loved anybody else, cause I was the one that always stuck by him. I never ran away, no matter how much I wanted to. We were pals, Dad and me. When he died—"

"When you *murdered* him—"

"That's right—when I murdered him, he said, "Now you're the leader, Neil." And he gave me his gun. "That bullet's for Orville," he says. "Yes, Dad," I said, "I'll do anything you say." We were always pals, Dad and me. I *had* to kill him, you can see that, can't you? Why, he would have married off Blossom to Orville. He said so. 'Dad,' says I, 'you gotta understand—Orville ain't one of us!' Oh, I explained it very careful, but he just lay there and wouldn't say a thing. He was dead. But nobody else cared. Everbody hated him except me. We were pals, Dad and me. Pals."

It was evident, to Orville, that Buddy's strategem was failing of its desired effect. Neil was past the point where he could be shaken. He was over the edge.

While Neil spoke. Orville moved forward, crouched, his right hand exploring the air before him, tentative as a mouse's whisker. If Neil had not been holding Blossom, or if he had not had a gun, it would have been a simple matter of running in low and tackling. Now it was necessary, for his own sake but more especially for Blossom's, either to disarm him or to make sure that his shot went wild.

To judge by his voice, Neil could not be far off. He swung his hand around in a slow arc, and it encountered not the gun, not Neil, but Blossom's thigh. She did not betray her surprise by the slightest flinch. Now it would be easy to wrench the gun from Neil's hand. Orville's hand stretched up and to the left: it should be right about *here*.

The metal of the gun barrel touched Orville's forehead. The weapon made such perfect contact that Orville could feel the hollow bore, concave within a distinct circlet of cool metal.

Neil pulled the trigger. There was a clicking sound. He pulled the trigger again. Nothing.

Days of immersion in the sap had effectually dampened the gunpowder.

Neil did not understand, then or ever, *why* the gun had failed him, but after another hollow *click,* he was aware that it had. Orville's fist came up for his solar plexus and glanced off his rib cage. As Neil toppled backward, the hand holding the pistol struck down with full force where he supposed Orville's head must be. The gunbutt struck against something hard. Orville made a noise.

Lucky—Neil was lucky. He struck down again and hit something soft. No noise. Orville's body was limp at his feet. Blossom had gotten away, but he didn't mind so much about that now.

He pulled out the axe from his gun belt, where it had been hanging, the head flat against his stomach, the handle crossing his left thigh.

"You stay away, Buddy, you hear? I still got me an axe."

Then he jumped on Orville's belly and his chest, but it was no good without shoes on, so he sat down on his belly and began hitting him in the face with his fists. Neil was beside himself. He laughed—oh, how he laughed!

But even so he stopped at intervals to take a few swipes at the darkness with the axe. "Whoop-pee!" he yelled. "Whoop-pee!"

Someone was screaming. Blossom.

The hard part was to keep Blossom from rushing right back into the thick of it. She just wouldn't listen.

"No!" Buddy said. "You'd get yourself killed. You don't know what to do. Listen—stop screaming and listen!" He shook her. She quieted. "I can get Orville away from him, so let *me* do it. Meanwhile, you go up the shaft the way we went before. Along the detour. Do you remember the way?"

"Yes." Dully.

"You'll do that?"

"Yes. But you've got to get Jeremiah away from him."

"Then I'll expect to see you up there. Go on now."

Buddy picked up Alice's rigid and festering corpse, which had been already in his hands when Orville had rushed in like a fool and spoiled everything. He lugged it a few feet in the direction of Neil's voice, stopped, grappled the old woman's body to his chest like a suit of armor. "Oooow," he moaned.

"Buddy," Neil shouted, standing, hoisting the axe, "you go away."

But Buddy only went on making the same silly moans and groans that children make playing ghost on a summer night or in the dark attic.

"You can't scare me," Neil said. "I ain't scared of the dark."

"It isn't me, I swear," Buddy said calmly. "It's Alice's ghost. She's coming to get you. Can't you tell by the smell it isn't me?"

"Ah, that's a lot of hooey," Neil retorted. The moaning started up again. He was uncertain whether to return to Orville or go after Buddy. "Stop it," he yelled, "I don't like that noise."

He could smell it! It was the way his father had smelled when he was dying!

Buddy's aim was good. The corpse struck Neil fullforce across his body. A stiff hand grabbed at his eyes and wiped across his mouth, tearing his lip. He toppled, waving the axe wildly. The corpse made an awful screaming sound. Neil screamed too. Maybe it was just all one scream, Neil's and the corpse's together. Someone was trying to pull the axe away! Neil pulled back. He rolled over and over again and got to his feet. He still had the axe. He swung it.

Instead of Orville, there was someone else underneath his feet. He felt the rigid face, the long hair, the puffy arms. It was Alice. She wasn't tied, and the gag was out of her mouth.

Someone was screaming. Neil.

He screamed all the while he hacked apart the dead woman's body. The head came off with one stroke of the axe. He split the skull with another. Again and again he buried the axehead into her torso, but that wouldn't seem to come apart. Once the axe slipped and struck his ankle a glancing blow. He fell over, and the dismembered body squished under him like rotten fruit. He began to tear it to pieces with his hands. When there was no more possibility that it would haunt him again, he stood up, breathing heavily, and called out not without a certain reverence: "Blossom?"

I'm right here.

Ah, he knew she would stay behind, he knew it! "And the others?" he asked.

They've gone away. They told me to go away too, but I didn't. I stayed behind.

"Why did you do that, Blossom?"

Because I love you.

"I love you too, Blossom. I always have. Since you were just a little kid."

I know. We'll go away together. Her voice singsonged, lulled him, rocked his tired mind like a cradle. *Someplace far away where nobody can find us. Florida. We'll live together, just the two of us, like Adam and Eve, and think of new names for all the animals.* Her voice grew stronger, clearer, and more beautiful. *We'll sail on a raft down the Mississippi. Just the two of us. Night and day.*

"Oh," said Neil, overcome with this vision. He began to walk towards the beautiful strong voice. "Oh, go on." He was walking in a circle.

I'll be the queen and you'll be my king, and there won't be any-body else in the world.

His hand touched her hand. His hand trembled.

Kiss me, she said. *Isn't that what you've always wanted?*

"Yes." His lips sought her lips. "Oh yes."

But her head, and therefore her lips, were not where one would have expected it to be. It was not attached to her neck. At last he found her head a few feet away. The lips that he kissed tasted of blood and liquorice.

And for a few days, he satisfied the years' pent-up lusts on the head of Alice Nemerov, R.N.

Chapter 16

HOME SAFE

Sometimes distance is the best cure, and if you want to recuperate you keep on going. Besides, if you stopped, you couldn't be sure of starting up again. Not that they had that much choice—they *had* to keep going up. So they went up.

It was easier this time. Perhaps it was just the contrast between a sure thing (sure if they didn't slip, but that sort of danger hardly stimulated their adrenals at this point) and the distinct if unacknowledged presence of death that had burdened these last few days, so that their ascent was also a resurrection.

There was only one anxiety now, and it was Buddy's. Then even this was dissipated, for after less than an hour of climbing they had reached the level of their home base, and Maryann was waiting there. The lamp was burning so they could see again, and the sight of each other, mired as they were, bruised, bleeding, brought tears to their eyes and made them laugh like children at a birthday party. The baby was all right, they were all right, everything was all right.

"Do you want to go up to the surface now? Or do you want to rest?"

"Now," Buddy said.

"Rest," said Orville. He had just discovered that his nose was broken. It had always been such a good nose too—straight and thin, a proud nose. "Does it look awful?" he asked Blossom.

She shook her head sadly and kissed his nose, but she wouldn't say anything. She hadn't said a word since the thing that had happened down there. Orville tried to return her kiss, but she averted her head.

Buddy and Maryann went away so they could be by themselves. "He seems so much bigger," Buddy remarked, dandling Buddy Junior. "How long have we been gone?"

"Three days and three nights. They were long days, because I couldn't sleep. The others have already gone up to the surface. They wouldn't wait. But I knew you'd be back. You promised me. Remember?"

"Mmm," he said, and kissed her hand.

"Greta's come back," Maryann said.

"That makes no difference to me. Not any more."

"It was on your account that she came back. She told me so. She says she can't live without you."

"She's got her nerve—saying that to you."

"She's . . . changed. You'll see. She's not back in the same tuber where I was waiting, but in the one next above. Come, I'll bring you to her."

"You sound like you *want* me to take up with Greta again."

"I only want what you want, Buddy. You say that Neil is dead. If you want to make her your second wife, I won't stop you . . . if that's what you want."

"That's not what I want, dammit! And the next time I say I love you, you'd better believe me. Okay?"

"Okay," she said in her teeniest, church-mouse voice. There was even the suggestion of small laughter, stifled. "But you'd better see her anyhow. Because you'll have to think of some way of getting her back to the surface. Mae Stromberg is back too, but she's already gone up with the rest of them. She's sort of crazy now. She was still carrying her Denny around with her—what's left of Denny. Bones mostly. This is the tuber. Greta's over at the other end. I'll stay back here with the lamp. She prefers the dark."

Buddy smelled a rat. Soon, advancing through the tuber, he smelled something much worse. Driving through a town in southern Minnesota in pea-canning season once, he had smelt something like this—a outhouse gone sour. "Greta?" he said.

"Buddy, is that you, Buddy?" It was surely her voice that replied, but its timber had altered subtly. There was no crispness to the *d*'s, and the initial *B* had a sputtering sound. "How are you, Buddy? Don't come any closer than you are! I—" There was a gasping sound, and when Greta began to speak again, she burbled, like a child who tries to talk with his mouth full of milk. "—shill lub you. I wan oo be yours. Forgib me. We can begin all over again—like Adamb and Ebe—jus us oo."

"What's wrong with you?" he asked. "Are you sick?"

"No. I—" A sound of violent gargling. "—I'm just a little hungry. I get that way now and again. Maryann brings me my food here, but she won't ever bring me enough. Buddy, *she's trying to starve me!*"

"Maryann," Buddy called. "Bring the light here."

"No, don't!" Greta shouted. "You've got to answer my question first, Buddy. There's nothing standing between us now. Maryann told me that if you wanted—No—go away! The light hurts my eyes." There was a slopping, sucking sound, as when one moves too suddenly in a full bathtub, and the air was roiled, releasing new tides of fetor.

Maryann handed her husband the dimly burning lamp, which he held over the sty into which the huge bulk of Greta Anderson had sunk of its own great weight. Her bloated body had lost any distinctively human features: it was an uncomplicated mass of flaccid fat. The contours of her face were obscured by folds of loose flesh like a watercolor portrait that has been left out of doors in a rainstorm. Now this face began to move from side to side, setting the flesh into a jellylike commotion—a gesture of negation, as far as one could judge.

"She doesn't move any more," Maryann explained, "and she's too heavy to lift. The others found her when they were looking for Blossom, and they pulled her this far with ropes. I told them to leave her here, cause she needs someone to look after her. I bring her all her food. It's a full-time job."

The commotion of flesh at their feet became more agitated, and there seemed almost to be an expression on the face. Hatred, perhaps. Then an aperture opened in the center of the face, a mouth, and Greta's voice said, "Go away, you *disgush* me!"

Before they had left, the figure at their feet was already stuffing handfuls of the syrupy fruit pulp into the cavity in the center of its face.

While the men and Blossom rested, Maryann rigged a sort of harness and even succeeded, over loud protests, in cinching it about Greta. Maryann fetched another heaping portion of swill using the laundry basket that had been rescued from the commonroom fire. If this wasn't done for Greta at hourly intervals, she would begin to take up handfuls of the surrounding filth and stuff her gullet full of it. She no longer seemed to be aware of the difference, but Maryann was, and it was largely for her own sake that she kept the basket replenished. After Greta had downed sufficient of the fruit pulp, she was usually good, as now, for a few moments of conversation, and Maryann had been grateful for this during the long, dark hours of waiting. As Greta had often observed during these sober interludes: "The worst part is the boredom. That's what got me into my *condition*."

Now, however, she was pursuing a less weighty subject: "There was another movie, I can't remember the name now, where she was poor and had this funny accent, and Laurence Harvey was a medical student who fell in love with her. Or else it was Rock Hudson. She had him right in the palm of her hand, she did. He'd have done anything she said. I can't remember how that one ended, but there was another one I liked better, with James Stewart—remember him?— where she lived in this beautiful mansion in San Francisco. Oh, you should have seen the dresses she had. And such lovely hair! She must have been the most beautiful woman in the world. And she fell down from a tower at the end. I *think* that's how it ended."

"You must have seen just about every movie Kim Novak ever made," Maryann said placidly while the baby nursed at her breast.

"Well, if there was any I missed, I never heard about them. I wish you'd loosen these ropes." But Maryann never replied to her complaints. "There was one where she was a witch, but not, you know, old-fashioned. She had an apartment right on Park Avenue or someplace like that. And the most beautiful Siamese cat."

"Yes, I think you've told me about that one already."

"Well, why don't you ever contribute to the conversation? I must have told you about every movie I've ever seen by now."

"I never saw many movies."

"Do you suppose she's still alive?"

"Who—Kim Novak? No, I don't suppose so. We may be the very last ones. That's what Orville says."

"I'm hungry again."

"You just ate. Can't you wait till Buddy is finished nursing?"

"I'm *hungry,* I tell you! Do you think I *like* this?"

"Oh, all right," Maryann took up the basket by its one remaining handle and went off to a more wholesome section of the tuber. Filled, the basket weighed twenty pounds or more.

When she could no longer hear Maryann nearby, Greta burst into tears. "Oh, God, I *hate* this! I hate *her!* Oh, I'm so *hungry!*" Her tongue ached to be covered with beloved, liquorice-flavored slop, as a three-pack smoker's tongue craves nicotine on a morning when he has no cigarettes.

She was not able to wait for Maryann's return. When she had driven away the worst of her hunger, she stopped cramming the stuff in her mouth and moaned aloud in the darkness. "Oh Ga, how I hay myself! *Myself,* thas who I hay!"

They had hauled Greta a long way, only stopping to rest when they had reached the uppermost tuber in which they had spent the first night of their subterranean winter. The relative coolness at this height was a welcome relief from the steamy heat below. Greta's silence was an even more welcome contrast. All during the ascent she had complained that the harness was strangling her, that she was caught in the vines and they were pulling her apart, that she was hungry. As they passed through each successive tuber, Greta would stuff the pulp into her mouth at a prodigious rate.

Orville estimated that she weighed four hundred pounds. "Oh, more than that," Buddy said. "You're being kind."

They would never have been able to get her as far as they had, if the sap coating the hollow of the roots had not been such an effective lubricant. The problem now was how to hoist her up the last thirty, vertical feet of the primary root. Buddy suggested a system of pulleys, but Orville feared that the ropes at their disposal might not be able to support Greta's full weight. "And even if they can how will we get her out through that hole? In December, Maryann was barely able to squeeze in through it."

"One of us will have to go back for the axe."

"Now? Not *this* one of us—not when we're this close to the sunlight. I say let's leave her here where there's food ready at hand for her and go up the rest of the way ourselves. Later is time enough to be Good Samaritans."

"Buddy, what's that sound?" Maryann asked. It was not like Maryann to interrupt.

They listened, and even before they heard it, they feared what it might be, what it was. A low grating sound—a whine—a rasp not so loud a noise as the metal sphere had made trying to push its way into the cave, because, for one thing, it was farther away, and for another, it did not seem to be having the same difficulty purchasing entrance. The whine grew louder; then a vast flushing ensued, as when a swimming pool begins to drain.

Whatever it was, it was now in the tuber with them.

With a fury sudden as their terror, a wind sprang up and bowled them to their knees. Tides of liquid fruit rose from the floor and walls and dropped from the ceiling; the wind swept off the crest of each successive wave and carried it toward the far end of the tuber, like the superfluous suds that spill out of an automatic washer. All that could be seen in the lamplight were white flashes of the blowing froth. Maryann clutched her child to her breast convulsively, after a blast of wind had almost lifted him from her arms. Assisted by Buddy, leaning into the wind, she made her way to the sanctuary of a root that branched off from the tuber. There they were sheltered from the worst effects of the gale, which seemed to howl still more fiercely now.

It was left to Orville to attempt Greta's rescue, but it was a hopeless task. Even under ordinary circumstances, it was difficult to pull her weight across the slippery floor of the fruit; alone, against the wind, he could not budge her. In fact, she seemed to be moving into the vortex with the pulp of the fruit. After a third quixotic attempt, he surrendered willingly to Blossom's mute entreaties and they joined Buddy and Maryann in the root.

Greta's ponderous weight slid forward with the other matter of the fruit. Miraculously, the lamp which had been entrusted to her during the rest period was still burning. Indeed it burned brighter than before.

Though her vision was beginning to flicker like badly spliced film, she was certain in the last moments of consciousness that she could see the great, palipant maw of the thing, a brilliant rosy orange that could only be called Pango Peach and, superimposed over it, a grille of scintillating Cinderella Red. The grille seemed to grow at an alarming pace. Then she felt the whole mass of her being swept up in the whirlwind, and for a brief, weightless moment she was young again, and then she spattered over the grille like a cellophane bag of water dropped from a great height.

In the root they heard the popping sound distinctly. Maryann crossed herself, and Buddy mumbled something.

"What'd you say?" Orville shouted, for the tempest had reached its height, and even here in the root they were clinging to the vines to keep from being sucked back into the tuber.

"I said there'll be worms in the cider tonight," Buddy shouted back.

"What?"

"Worms!"

The rasping sound, which had ceased or been inaudible during the storm, was renewed, and as abruptly as the wind had sprung up, it died. When the rasping sound had diminished to a reassuring level, the five of them returned to the tuber. Even without the lantern, the change was evident: the floor was several feet lower than it had been; voices echoed from the surfaces, which were hard as rock; even the thick rind of the fruit had been scraped loose. In the center of this larger space, at about the level of their heads, a large tube or pipeline stretched from the upper root opening to the lower. The tube was warm to the touch and was in constant movement—down.

"That was some vacuum cleaner," Orville said. "It scoured this place as clean as a whistle. There's not enough left here to feed a mouse."

"The harvesters have come," Buddy said. "You didn't think they'd plant all these potatoes and leave them to rot, did you?"

"Well, we better go up to the surface and see what Farmer MacGregor looks like."

But they were strangely reluctant to leave the dry tuber. An elegiac mood had settled over them. "Poor Greta," Blossom said.

They all felt better when the simple memorial had been pronounced. Greta was dead, and the whole old world seemed to have died in her person. They knew that the world to which they would now ascend would not be the same as the one they'd left behind.

> *Behold even to the moon, and it shineth not;*
> *yea, the stars are not pure in his sight.*
> *How must less man, that is a worm? and the*
> *son of man, which is a worm?*

Job 25:5–6

Epilogue

THE EXTINCTION
OF THE SPECIES

Just as a worm passing through an apple may suppose that the
apple, its substance and quality, consists merely of those few elements which have passed through his own meager body, while in
fact his whole being is enveloped in the fruit and his passage has
scarcely diminished it, so Buddy and Maryann and their child, Blossom and Orville, emerging from the earth after a long passage
through the labyrinthine windings of their own, purely human evils,
were not aware of the all-pervading presence of the larger evil that
lies without, which we call reality. There is evil everywhere, but we
can only see what is in front of our noses, only remember what has
passed through our bellies.

The gray basketballs, pumped full of the pulp of the fruit, had
risen from an earth that was no longer green. Then, like primitives
clearing their lands, the machines that served the alien farmers
turned that earth into a pyre. The towering stalks of the great Plants
were consumed, and the sight had all the grandeur of a civilization
falling to ruins. The few humans who remained retreated into the
earth one more time. When they reemerged, the pall that hung over
the scorched earth made them welcome the total eclipse of night.

Then a wind moved in from the lake, and the pall thinned to reveal the heavy cumulus above. The rains came. The pure water
cleared the skies and washed the months' encrustations from their
bodies and soaked into the black earth.

Out came the sun and dried the rain, and their bodies gloried in its tenuous April warmth. Though the earth was black, the sky was blue, and at night there were stars—Deneb, Vega, Altair—brighter than anyone had remembered. Vega, particularly, shone bright. In the false dawn, a sliver of moon rose in the east, later the sky would lighten, and once more the sun would rise.

It all seemed very beautiful to them, for they believed that the natural order of things—that is to say, their order—was being restored.

There were expeditions down into the roots to search out traces of fruit that the harvesters had overlooked. Such traces were rare, but they existed; by rationing out these scraps of rind sparingly, they might hope to survive the summer at least. For the time being, there was also the water and weeds in the lake, and as soon as it became warmer, they planned to make their way down along the Mississippi, to the warm southlands. There was also the hope that the ocean would still be fruitful.

The lake was dead. All along the fire-blackened shore, shoals of stinking fish were heaped memorially. But that the ocean might be in the same condition—that was unthinkable.

Their chief hope was that the earth had survived. Somewhere there must be seeds sprouting in the warm soil, survivors like themselves, from whose flowering the earth might be made green again.

But their cardinal hope without which all hopes else were vain, was that the Plant had had its season, long though it had been, and that that season was over. The armored spheres had left with the rape of a planet, the fires had burned over the stubble, and the land would now wake from the nightmare of that second alien creation. That was their hope.

Then everywhere the land was covered with a carpet of the richest green. The rains that had washed the sky clean of the smoke of the burning had also borne the billion spores of the second planting. Like all hybrids, the Plant was sterile, and could not reproduce itself. A new crop had to be planted every spring.

In two days the Plants were already ankle-deep.

The survivors spread out over the flat green uniformity of the plain resembled the figures in a Renaissance print illustrating the properties of perspective. The nearest three figures in the middle distance, comprised a sort of Holy Family, though moving closer, one could not help but note that their features were touched by some other emotion than quiet happiness. The woman sitting on the ground was, in fact, weeping bitterly, and the man on his knees behind her, his hands planted on her shoulders as though to comfort her, was barely able to restrain his own tears. Their attention was fixed upon the thin child in her arms, who was futilely pulling at her dry breast.

A little farther on was another figure—or should we say two?—without any iconographic parallel, unless we allow this to be a Niobe sorrowing for her children. However, Niobe is usually depicted alone or in the prospect of all fourteen children; this woman was holding the skeleton of a single child in her arms. The child had been about ten years of age when it died. The woman's red hair was a shocking contrast to the green everywhere about her.

Almost at the horizon one could make out the figures of a man and a woman, nude, hand in hand, smiling. Certainly these were Adam and Eve before the Fall, though they appeared rather more thin than they are usually represented. Also, they were rather ill-matched with respect to age: he was forty if he was a day; she was barely into her teens. They were walking south, and occasionally they would speak to each other.

The woman, for instance, might turn her head to the man and say. "You never told us who your favorite actor is." And the man would reply. "David Niven, I always liked David Niven." Then how beautifully they would smile!

But these figures were very, very small. The landscape dominated them entirely. It was green and level and it seemed of infinite extent. Vast though it was, Nature—or Art—had expended little imagination upon it. Even viewed closely, it presented a most monotonous aspect. In any square foot of ground, a hundred seedlings grew, each exactly like every other, none prepossessing.

Nature is prodigal. Of a hundred seedlings only one or two would survive; of a hundred species, only one or two.

Not, however, man.

THE PUPPIES
OF TERRA

Being a True and Faithful Account of the
Great Upheavals of 2037; with Portraits
of Many of the Principals Involved; as
well as Reflections by the Author on the
Nature of Art, Revolution & Theology

For Olex and Valkyrie,
for Precious and Anathema,
for Sheba and Elf
    and good dogs everywhere.

CONTENTS

'I am His Highness' dog at Kew;
Pray tell me, sir, whose dog are you?

—Alexander Pope
On the Collar of a Dog

Chapter 1

*In which I am born, and my father is done in
by Dingoes.*

My name is White Fang, though of course that is not really my
name. My name is really Dennis White, now. I like the old name
better; it is more in keeping with the image I have of myself. But
perhaps such an attitude is just a hangover from the time I was a
pet. Some people would say that once you've been a pet, once
you've grown used to the Leash, you're never quite human again—
in the sense of being free. I don't know about that. Of course, it *is*
more fun to be Leashed, but one can learn not to want it so badly. I
did. And this, in one sense, is the story of how I did it.

As a puppy . . .

But already I have made a botch of it! For will not most of my
readers resent such a phrase? Puppies, Pets, Masters, Leashes: the
old way of speaking has come to have almost the force of obscenity
among the zealous. And who in these times dares not to be among
the zealous?

Yet, how am I to tell the story of my life as a pet without using a
pet's language, without adopting his attitudes? Surely the time must
come to an end when every politician and philosopher must conceal
himself behind the mask of a bare-bones, know-nothing prose. And
am I then required to tell White Fang's story from the point of view
of a Dingo? No! The memoirs of a member of Louis XVI's court
could not be set down in the rough accents of a *sansculotte*—and *I*
must be allowed to write of White Fang as White Fang would have

written of himself. For the time being, let us leave Dennis White in abeyance—and let me say, without more preamble, that *as a puppy* I was uncommonly happy.

How could it have been otherwise? I was raised in the best kennels of the Solar System. My young body was sportive, and so it sported. My education ranged freely through the full scope of human knowledge, and yet I was never forced beyond my inclinations. I enjoyed the company of my own kind as well as the inestimable pleasures of the Leash. Lastly, I was conscious from earliest childhood of possessing the finest pedigree. My father Tennyson White was a major artist, perhaps *the* major artist, in a society that valued art above all things else. No little bit of that glory rubbed off on his bloodline. Later, in adolescence, a father's fame may cramp the expanding ego, but *then* it was enough to know that one was as valuable a pet as there could be. It made me feel *secure*. In what else does happiness consist than in this: a sense of one's own value? Not in freedom, surely. For I have known that state, oh very well, and I can assure you that it is far less happy. Had I been free in my childhood, I would almost certainly have been wretched.

Actually, when I speak of my childhood as being so idyllic, I refer chiefly to my first seven years, for shortly after my seventh birthday I was orphaned—that is to say, the Dingoes made away with my father, while Motherlove simply committed Pluto and myself to care of the Shroeder Kennel and vanished into outer space. Thus even at the age of seven I might have been said to be free, and it was a condition I bitterly resented, thinking of it simply as neglect. Now, of course, I can see that the Shroeder Kennel, by contrast to what we call "the human condition", is truly Paradise. Then I only had the moons of Jupiter to judge by. But I see I am making something of a jumble of this. Perhaps it would be better to set about this in a more chronological fashion.

Let me make a narrative of this.

To begin my life with the beginning of my life, as David Copperfield does, I record that I was born on a Sunday afternoon in the year of Our Lord 2017, on Ganymede, the fourth moon of Jupiter. At my father's behest a gigantic thunderclap accompanied my birth, attended with quite a smart display of meteors and artificial comets. These natural wonders were succeeded by a Masque written by my father and set to a reconstituted Vivaldi cantata, in which various of the bitches of the kennel took the parts of my fairy godmothers. The eleven fairies portrayed were Trustworthy, Loyal, Helpful, Friendly, Courteous, Kind, Obedient, Cheerful, Thrifty, Brave, and Clean. Each presented me with a little token emblematic of the spiritual gift she was bequeathing to me, but my father had somehow neglected to invite the twelfth fairy, Reverence, with fateful consequences for my character.

In speaking of my "earliest memories", I encounter difficulties, for I cannot be sure at this late date which of my seeming memories are indeed mine and which are borrowed from Motherlove, Pluto, or whichever other brain my Master may have happened to pick for me. For instance, I have a distinct recollection of Daddy (excuse me, but that is the name I know him by; he has no other) looking yearningly into my eyes as he declaimed a poem, which I also remember clearly though I dare not here repeat it. I think it is one of the Earl of Rochester's. Daddy is wearing a shirt in the Byronic style, with billowing sleeves and a soft, expansive collar. His tights are of black velvet, with silver piping. His thin hair, blonde almost to whiteness, hangs down to his shoulders. His eyes are the deep blue of a Martian sky, and their blue is heightened by contrast to the extreme pallor of his skin. Like his use of clothes and his broad *A*, the pallor is sheer affectation. He might have been tan for the asking.

Now surely this is not *my* memory. Perhaps it is Motherlove's, though she claimed, when I recited the poem for her, that she'd never heard such a thing in her life (attempting all the while not to giggle). It could have been the memory of any of a dozen bitches on Ganymede, for since Daddy was the kennel's prize possession he was encouraged to bestow his favors liberally. From the number of pedigreed descendants who could legitimately claim paternity from him it seems evident that Daddy cooperated with this policy. I have never met (and now I never shall meet) *all* my half-brothers and half-sisters.

Another memory that is more likely to have been mine is of Daddy from a vantage point of about three feet from the ground. He is conventionally nude this time and laughing to bust a gut. I can't remember the joke. This must have been one of my last memories of him, for behind him I can make out the vivid green of a Terran meadow and the light that plays across his body can only be the light of the sun as it shines on our home planet, no more nor less.

Even foreshortened I can see that Daddy had then the body of an athlete—but so had everyone else under the Mastery. Daddy was really quite modest in his somatic tastes, tending toward the Cellini side of the scale, while the majority favored a more Michelangelesque style.

Of my mother, Clea Melbourne Clift, I have *more* memories but none so distinct. She had a type of classic handsomeness over which time could not exercise his cruel authority: a noble brow; an unimpeachable nose; lips that might have been sculpted of marble, so perfect was their articulation. Indeed, from the tip of her toe to the highest-piled lock of her perfectly composed hair, there was something about Clea Clift that suggested the work of a stonemason. Clea was such a stickler for *form*. She always wanted me and Pluto to call her "Clea" or better, "Miss Clift", and would become incensed if we ventured to use, in moments of unconsidered fondness, the simpler "Mom", or Daddy's slightly joking "Motherlove". Had we been French, I daresay she would have insisted upon the formal *vous* and forbidden the familiar *tu*. Like so many women of her generation, the first to grow up under the Mastery, Clea was something of a bluestocking and very jealous of her independence. For Clea to have married and taken on the name of White, renowned though that name was and proud as she might be otherwise to be associated with it, would have been in contradiction to the first article of her faith: the sexes must be equal in all things.

Pluto and I didn't know quite how we were to behave around Clea. She didn't want us to think of her as a mother, but more as a sort of friend of the family. A distant friend. She interested herself but little in our education, limiting her attentions to serving us up with little snippets of history and culture-lore. The legend of van Gogh's ear seemed to possess a special attraction to her for some reason, and she related it to me in my comfy force-field gravity-pulse cradle in a dozen variant forms, in which, successively, the character of van Gogh himself grew more and more peripheral while that of his "girlfriend" became of central importance. All I can recall of van Gogh's girlfriend now, however, was that she had, like Motherlove, a classic nose and the ability to drive men mad with love.

It was Clea's distinction to have been the first puppy born on Ganymede, which was at that time and for decades after the premier kennel of the Solar System. Daddy only came to Ganymede after the success of his novel, *A Dog's Life,* when he was thirty-three years old. Daddy says that at first Clea Melbourne Clift would have nothing to do with him. Only when it appeared that his literary reputation was not to wane after a season of notoriety, and more important, that Clea's aloofness had served only to open up the field to candidates who would otherwise have stood little chance against Clea's superior charms—only then did she relent. Too late. A month sooner, and she might have constrained Daddy to monogamy, as he had sometimes offered; as it was, she was lucky to win the position of "first wife." Their romance resembled that of *Romeo and Juliet,* in the respect that the lovers' misfortunes arose from their having failed, by ever so small a margin, to synchronize their watches.

From the very first they quarreled. I can remember in particular one night (a very crucial one for this tale, for it was the night upon which its narrator was conceived) when the several causes of their rupture had come to a head all at once. Daddy had been taking his duties as a stud more seriously than usual and was consequently not giving Clea all the attention she felt was her due. Moreover, he had happened to make disparaging remarks upon Clea's interpretation of some Schubert *Lieder.* (Have I mentioned that Clea was a singer? No? Then let me at once make it clear that her voice was not her prime attraction, or—for Daddy—any at all.)

Throughout the argument I seem to see Clea's lovely face—usually a delicate tint of rose, but now flushed an angry red—so I presume that this memory originated in Daddy's mind; certainly its *timbre,* the pervading irony, the sense that everything he says is "in quotes," is his. But perhaps the whole scene is no more than a transparently Oedipal dream disguising itself as a borrowed "memory." Or worse, what if truth and fancy, event and wish, have become inextricably tangled, beyond the power of even a Tiresias to unknot them?

Well then, I must use a sword and just hack away . . .

The scent of jasmine. The smoothness of Clea's skin beneath my hand. Everything bathed in the pink glow of a desert twilight. "Now, Clea," I can hear my voice saying, "we've been through all this before. I have to do these things for the sake of the kennel—to keep the standard up. You can understand that. Why—it should make you *proud.*"

She moves away and veils her beauty, like a startled squid, in sworls of inky mist. "Bother the kennel!" she whines. "If you really loved me as much as you say, you wouldn't want to be off every night . . ."

"That's just it, Clea my loveliest bitch, I *don't* want to be away from you. But it's my duty, my vocation."

"And tonight, just because our Master's given you the go-ahead . . ."

"Isn't that a good reason? Don't you want another son?"

"But . . ."

"And don't you want the very best possible son [Meaning me] that you can possibly have? Well then, Clea my lovely, tonight's the night. Be reasonable, darling."

"Oh, reason!" she says, with highest disdain. "You'll always be right, if you use reason as an argument." But already the black mists about her were beginning to disperse.

"If you won't be persuaded logically, let me show you what I mean." Daddy's mind calls for its Master, and in the same instant the meshes of the Leash close around his and Clea's mind, linking them in telepathic bondage. Argument is no longer possible; reason is subdued; only the Vision persists and that Vision is of me, of White Fang, the son who will be theirs, the form potential in the chromosomatic patterns that their Master, a renowned breeder, had selected from the trillions of possible permutations and combinations available to him during the several months past.

I must say it is a good likeness, this Vision. The face is mine as surely as the one I see every day in my bathroom mirror. Truly, I am now missing one or two of the teeth that the model White Fang flashes in a smile, and I have a little scar on my left cheek (it is only evident when I blush) which the prophecy did not include. But these discrepancies are the work of environment, not heredity. The body is as excellently put together as one might hope, though here again environment has been making itself felt (I eat too much). Splendid hind quarters and a handsome torso. The head is smallish, according to the classic prescription, but well compact with intelligence for all that. And of course, a flawless character. Trustworthy, Loyal, Helpful, Friendly . . .

"Oh, all right," Clea sighs.

I—or rather, Daddy—kisses her, and there I had better bring this particular reminiscence to an end.

Of my first visit to Earth in 2024 I have only the fuzziest recollection, for here I must fall back on my own mnemonic resources.

My chief impression seems to have been of sunlight, the authentic, inimitable sunlight of Earth. Organs that have evolved under particular conditions will naturally be more comfortable where those conditions obtain, and thus no substitute, however artful, can provide just those balances of color and intensity, those alternations of night and day, summer and winter, hazy and clear, that our very cells will recognize, demand, and crave. Though born on Ganymede, I knew from the first that Earth was my home.

But I did not like it. In this certainly I was influenced by the example of my Motherlove, for whom every day away from the civilized life of Jupiter was a torment of boredom. "There is nothing to do," she would lament, when Daddy had returned from his afternoon jaunts about the countryside. "There's nothing to see, and nothing to listen to. I'm going out of my mind."

"It won't be much longer now, Clea my loveliest. Besides, this is good for you. Being out here in the country, off your Leash and on your own, develops self-reliance and initiative.

"—self-reliance and initiative!" Clea said with a stamp of her gold-slippered foot. "I want my Leash. But it's not me I'm worried about. It's the boys. It's been weeks since White Fang and Pluto have had any lessons. They're running around these woods like a couple of wild Indians. Like Dingoes! What if they were captured! They'd be eaten alive."

"Nonsense. You'd think this were Borneo or Cuba, the way you go on. There aren't any Dingoes in the United States of America in the year 2024. This is a civilized country."

"What about those people you said you met the other day—what was their name? The Nelsons. They were Dingoes."

"They were just poor honest country folk trying to scratch a living out of the dirt. Once you get through to them, they're very friendly."

"I think it's disgusting!" Clea said, stretching out in the little gravity-pocket of the Prefab that our Master has left behind so that we would not be utterly without the amenities. "Talking with them. Eating their dirty food. You could catch a disease."

"Then I'd call up the Shroeder Kennel and be cured. Really, this part of Minnesota is just as civilized as anything on Ganymede. I like it here. If I had my way . . ."

"If you had your way, we'd all become Dingoes! The Shroeder Kennel—don't talk to me about the Shroeder Kennel! Have you been there? Have you seen the way the pets are treated on Earth?"

"Not to the Shroeder Kennel exactly, but . . ."

"Well, *I* have, and I can tell you it's barbaric. Those poor pets live like animals. It's like something before the Mastery. They all run around unleashed, in this awful sunlight, out-of-doors, among all these loathsome vegetables . . ."

"It's only grass, my love."

"It's disgusting. You're disgusting to want to live here. Why you wanted to bring me and the children to this living hell, I'll never comprehend."

"I've explained to you a dozen times—my work requires it. I can't even begin the sequel until I've recaptured the feeling of the place— the sense of being stranded here, of being without hope, of being mortal . . ."

Motherlove gave a little gasp of horror and covered her ears. The idea of mortality—even the word—was too depressing. She went to the medicine dispenser and dialed for a skyrocket, a mildly euphoric beverage derived from LSD. In a little while she was hallucinating happily in her own little pocket of gravity. Pluto and I wanted some drugs too, but Daddy promised us he'd read us a chapter from *A Dog's Life* instead.

My father Tennyson White belonged to the first generation of humans to grow up away from the planet Earth. Born in 1980, just ten years after the first manifestations, Daddy had been abandoned on the steps of a power station. His first Master had been more interested in botanical specimens than in caring for foundlings, and so his early education had been erratic. Even so, it was such an education as no human had ever had before—with the possible exception of John Stuart Mill—and one feels that Mill did pay a rather steep price for his education. But with a Master assisting, one can be as polymathematical as one would like. Language and science, music and gymnastics—anything that requires more of competence and familiarity than of creative insight—can become "second nature" with no more effort than it would take to read a novel by, for instance, George Eliot.

At the age of three Daddy was sold or traded or somehow exchanged (just how the Masters arrange these matters among themselves none of their pets have ever been given to understand; when asked, the Masters make an analogy to the gold standard—but who has ever understood the gold standard?) and transported to the asteroid Ceres, where his abilities were cultivated to the full by one of the first truly great breeders. In fact, it was largely due to the successes of the Master of Ceres that the study and breeding of *homo sapiens* gradually usurped the attention of all Masters involved in Terran problems. Whether we are to be grateful to the Masters of Ceres for this is not within my province to judge. I only wish to make it clear that, from the age of three to the age of twenty, Daddy could not have wanted a better Master or more thorough cultivation.

Then at the age of twenty it was discovered that Daddy had leukemia. Though it was easily within the competence of his Master to have cured him of this wasting disease (what was *not* within their competence, after all?), nothing was done. As his Master explained to Daddy, as he lay there in his sickbed, it was considered *unsporting* to tamper with basic genetic materials, as any permanent cure would have required. Daddy protested and was assured that his case was being debated in the highest councils of the Mastery, but that it would be an indeterminate time before any decision could be reached. Meanwhile Daddy was shipped back to Earth, much as a piece of inferior merchandise might be returned to the factory. There, in an inferior, overpopulated, and understaffed hospital in Northeastern Minnesota, haunted by the knowledge that his life or death was nothing but a sporting proposition to the Masters, he conceived of his great novel, *A Dog's Life*. He began writing it the same day his Master announced to him that his leukemia was going to be cured and that he would be allowed to return to his home on Ceres.

A Dog's Life was an epoch-making book—like Luther's Bible, or *Das Kapital,* or *Uncle Tom's Cabin*. Even the Masters read and admired it. Tennyson White received the Nobel Prize, was elected to the French Academy, and was the first man to hold two seats in the American Congress—he was the senior senator from Arizona and the representative from the Ninth District in Minnesota. More than any other person, it was he who effected the reconciliation of men and their Masters. And it was just for that reason that the Dingoes —the small element of the population that still resisted the sovereignty of the Master—had marked him for vengeance. It was from *A Dog's Life,* in fact, that they had taken their name.

The wonder of that novel is that it's told entirely from a dog's point of view—a *real* dog, a canine of the Industrial Revolution. The realistic surface is never distorted by the demands of the allegory, and yet . . . And yet, no one has ever surpassed Daddy in depicting their essential and unfathomable alienness. As Woof to Mr. Manglesnatch, so man to his Master. The analogy is almost infinitely extensible.

Before *A Dog's Life*, the Dingoes (this is still the most convenient name to use when discussing the various dissident elements prior to 2037, for though they went by any number of names—Republicans, Baptists, Harvard Club, B'nai B'rith, etc.—they never could come together on a good brand name to sell revolution) had used such words as "kennel," "leash" and even "pet" as invectives. Daddy's book rather turned the tables. It gave them the old one-two-transvaluation-of-all-values-sockeroo punch, as it were. Thus, it became a point of pride to be a pet; to be domesticated was self-evidently a superior state than to be wild. One has only to observe the difference between a greyhound and a wolf, a clever dachshund and a vulgar Dingo, to see why the Masters are innately our . . . Masters.

There were other, more trifling consequences of the book's vogue. Everyone who read it, everyone who was anyone, began to name his children after famous dogs. There hasn't been a generation of puppies with stranger names since the Pilgrim Fathers went off the deep end back in the seventeenth century. To mention only those who have gone on to win fame on their own: Ladadog, Bobby Greyfriars, Little Sheba, Rintintin, Beautiful Joe, Snoopy and See Spot Run.

The reason that Daddy had returned to Earth yet once again, despite the unhappy associations one would have expected him to have from his last sojourn there, was that after a slight hiatus he was at work on a new novel that was to be a sequel to *A Dog's Life*. His work proceeded in absolute privacy, a privacy that even in the most self-transcendent moments of being Leashed he would not allow his Master to intrude upon. For this would have been to cast doubt upon the value of the work as an authentic *human* creation.

The days of his research project passed into weeks, the weeks into months. Motherlove grew more and more vocal in her boredom, and since Daddy was not usually about during the day for her to complain to, it fell upon Pluto and myself to bear witness to her wrongs and play endless rubbers of three-handed bridge with her. It was not a very gratifying occupation for two boys our age (I was seven; Pluto, ten), and we tried to be out of her way whenever possible. We spent the daylight hours roaming the woods and exploring the innumerable lakeshores and riverbanks of the area. It was impossible to get lost, for we had a homing device that could instruct us how to retrace our every step. We observed none of the cautions that Motherlove was always inventing for us, and I'm sure that if we had been lucky enough to meet any Dingo children we would have been delighted to befriend them and join their wild games. Pluto and I were quite sick of each other by this time. Partly it was the difference in age; partly the isolation (in two months almost anyone becomes unendurable). I also think that a fundamental antipathy between Pluto and myself extends right down to the core of pineal glands (which organ, Descartes tells us, is the residence of the soul).

And so it came about quite naturally that it should be Pluto and I who discovered the car—his late-vintage Volkswagen—overturned and just beginning to smolder as we got there. The windshield was shattered into opacity with buckshot, and the driver's seat was dark with blood. Even as we watched the automobile caught fire, and we had to back away.

It did not take a woodsman to follow the spoor of Daddy's blood to the edge of the forest. Apparently he was still alive then, for there are evidences of a struggle all along the path into the wood. Once or twice we called his name aloud, but the woods remained as silent as death. Is there a better analogy?

It was another day before the search party from Shroeder Kennel found the traces of the pyre. The ashes were scattered all about the meadow. The Master of the Shroeder Kennel identified the bloodstains on the edge of the clearing as Daddy's and Daddy's alone, and the ear that they found nailed to the oak tree was likewise identified beyond the shadow of a doubt. The severed ear was given to Clea. It was perhaps exactly what she'd always wanted of Daddy. She had a special locket made to contain it—a sort of reliquary.

As for the bulk of him, one could assume that the Dingoes would have been thorough in disposing of the remains. It was popularly believed (and I'm not sure myself that it isn't true) that the Masters could have resurrected a body from utter hamburger.

A monument was built to him on the site of the murder. It was a statue of Woof and Mr. Manglesnatch. Beneath the bronze figures was a plaque with the inscription:

TENNYSON WHITE
1980–2024
A Martyr to the Spirit of Domestication

There was, as well, a quotation from his novel: "Ah, what bliss there is in servitude!" The monument was later disfigured by Dingoes in ways too hideous to be recalled.

Chapter 2

*In which I am neglected shamefully by my
Master, and I bloody my brother's nose.*

The Masters: let me say a few words about the Masters.

Perhaps my dear readers will tell me that there is no need for me
to put in *my* two-cents' worth on a topic so threadbare and tired as
the Mastery. It is considered good form these days to leave the subject alone, just as in the third and fourth centuries A.D. one did not
bring up the subject of the Trinity with strangers. Whether the Son
was of *one* substance with the Father, or of *like* substance, or
perhaps of only *similar* substance was a matter best left to each man's
private conscience. The analogy extends farther than I first intended,
for the Masters *were* our gods and though now their altars have
been overturned, there is still something a little holy (or unholy,
which is almost the same thing) about their empty shrines and tem-
ples. When gods die, they become demons and are then, if anything,
more troublesome than before.

But since most of the figures involved in the present controversies
on the essential nature of the Masters had not had the benefit, as I
have, of direct experience of them, I can justly claim a sort of
apostolic authority—a distinction that few of the controversialists
will begrudge me, I am sure.

As nearly as we can know them, the Masters can be said to be a
pure electromagnetic phenomenon—formed of a "substance" that
cannot be called either "matter" or "energy" but which nonetheless
displays a *potentiality* for either. No, that isn't quite right, since I've

not mentioned the neutrino. The neutrino is a sub-atomic particle that has a mass of 0, a charge of 0, and a spin of $+\frac{1}{2}$. Well, the Masters, according to the best authority (theirs), can be identified more or less exactly (it depends on a few other things) with that spin.

As a direct consequence of these wonderful properties, the power of the Masters approached (should I not rather say "approaches"?) cosmic proportions, and their knowledge approached omniscience They were not quite infinite, but then what is? Considered simply as a field of force (or as a potentiality for such) they were, corporately, of a scope and dimension equal at least to the magnetic field of the Earth. Beside them mankind is insignificant and laughable— or so it often seemed in *those* days. Like Jehovah in his earlier, more anthropomorphic days, it was no problem at all for them to take over the management of Earth from us. They were, if not altogether omnipotent, potent enough for all *our* purposes and, presumably, for most of theirs.

In the strictest sense of the word, the Masters were unaccountable. One could only accept them, reverence them, and hope for the best.

The best that one could hope for was the Leash. Despite the hundreds of volumes written about it, the Leash has always eluded description: the tides of knowledge that sweep through the mind; the sense of being in communion with the most transcendental forces, of being a spoke from the hub about which the universe is spinning; the total *certainty* that it affords; the ecstasy and the consuming love. Naturally it didn't always reach those proportions. Sometimes it was no more than a mild, diffuse sense of well-being—just the absence of anxiety. But if the Leash had never been more than a tranquilizer it could never have bound man as firmly as it did and made his love his servitude.

What was the Leash then, in *fact?*

First let me say what it was not. It was not a "telepathic link" with the Masters, any more than the tug of a leather leash on the jeweled collar of a poodle is *speech*. It was the Masters' means of communicating with us, truly—but they could communicate no more to us than our minds were capable of receiving, and I can assure you that the depths of the Masters will never be fathomed by even the best of *our* divers.

The Leash was simply their *touch*. Those floods of ecstasy it brought were nothing more than the Masters' way of tugging on our collar. A touch of their hand could transmute a human nervous system from gross lead to gleaming gold, or scramble a brain into idiocy with, literally, the speed of lightning, but it could not, without changing the nature of the beast, make a man something he was not. They could not, in short, raise us up to their own level.

Desirable as the Leash was, one could not coerce it. Like the state of grace, it came as a gift or not at all. How often a pet was Leashed and the intensity of the bond depended upon the whim or good will of one's master. And here I must clear up another popular misconception: all Masters are *not* alike. They have discrete and individual personalities, as any pet who has had more than a single Master can tell you. Some of them seemed to be deeply concerned for their pets' well-being. (How large this interest loomed in the whole framework of any Master's life can never be known, for *all* that a pet can know about his Master is what sort of interest he takes in pets.) Others simply put them into a kennel and let them languish there, scarcely ever bothering to Leash them and put them through their paces. Such a master was the Master of the Shroeder Kennel.

Pluto and I were placed in the Shroeder Kennel within a week of our father's assassination. Clea told us that it would be only for a little while and then she would be back for us. Perhaps she meant it, but I have always felt that her deed was very much on a par with that of Hansel and Gretel's stepmother. Clea surely knew the sort of place the Shroeder Kennel was, for we had heard her complain about it to our poor father. Daddy, we were sure, would never have left us in such a joyless place. But Clea, now that Daddy was out of the picture, now that the glamor was gone, simply didn't give a damn for the two puppies he had given her.

In a purely physical sense, we were well cared for, I'll grant that. The Shroeder Kennel (named for a little town that had once occupied that site, of which it had been said, in the days before the Mastery, that you could throw a frozen turd from one end of town to the other without much experience as a pitcher) had an excellent gymnasium, warm and cold pools, indoor tennis and golf courses, good robotic instruction in all sports, and the kennel rations were prepared with that exquisite simplicity that only the most refined tastes can command. Our rooms, both public and private, were spacious, airy, and bright. The central architectural feature of the Kennel, the jewel for which all else was but the setting, was a reconstruction, perfect in every detail, of the Cathedral of St. John the Divine in

New York City. (*Why?* I have always wondered. *Why that? Why not Notre Dame, Salisbury, the Frauenkirche?*) The reconstituted cathedral was set amid acres of English landscape gardening and playing fields. Naturalness was everywhere the style of the thing, and it was no less natural for being adjusted, indoors and outdoors alike, to our convenience. Thus, in the summer the air was filtered and cooled, and in the winter the dome that encompassed the kennel heated us and added extra hours of sunlight and warmth to the brief northern days. The dome delimiting the kennel was fully a mile in diameter, and within its bounds our comforts were secure against the enmity of the Dingoes.

It would have been an ideal existence—if only our Master had truly cared for us.

Motherlove left us at the gate of the Shroeder Kennel at sunset of an autumn afternoon. Outside the dome, the ground was sere and the tree branches already denuded; within, the grass was a perpetual midsummer green, and though the leaves of the trees still crimsoned and fell, they did so in graceful sequence so that there was never a preponderance of decay. Motherlove blew us a parting kiss; then, wreathed in baroque spires of golden light, like an irradiated Bernini Madonna, she ascended into the clear blue sky of October. As her figure diminished to a pinpoint and vanished, we felt our Leashes fall away (for no Master's influence can extend beyond a dozen or so miles) and our minds stood naked in an alien world—a world that, having just been the scene of our father's bloody death, we could not suppose to be friendly.

In the middle distance we could make out the spire of the cathedral, and, supposing it to be the administrative center, we made our way toward it along a neatly graveled path that circled a field where a gymnastic competition was in progress. Five youths were running pell-mell along a dirt track in a race so evenly contested that none of them could hold the lead more than a few meters at a time. A distance away other young men hurled the discus and javelin, while dispersed over the grass at regular intervals, like polka dots, pairs of wrestlers strained against each other, groaning with effort. Each of these gymnasts was blond, deeply-tanned, and constructed according to the specification that Michelangelo had developed for his "David." Neither Pluto nor I were of a mind to disarrange so splendid a grouping of figures in a landscape by asking our way from them, any more than we would have thought to disturb a display of china figurines on the mantel of a house we were visiting for the first time. We pressed on cheerlessly to St. John's.

The Master of Ganymede from whom Pluto and I had received our earliest education had not been an enthusiastic archaeologist, so there had been few reconstructions on Ganymede other than a purely utilitarian sort—a scaled-down version of Hampton Court, a couple of Palladian villas, that sort of thing. Nothing monumental. Our first impression of St. John the Divine was out of proportion, therefore, to anything but its proportions. It is a vulgar building, but it is an incredibly *big* building. With my chin hanging slack and my heart pumping at double-time, I stretched out my hand to touch the torus at the base of one of the gigantic columns at the rear of the nave. It was cool and tingly, reminding me that what here seemed to be stone was in fact much less substantial: an immensely strong force-field with a skin of matter only one molecule thick. It was this stagey method of construction (let me assure you, though, that the illusion was perfect, the stagecraft consummate) that made "Architecture" a matter of such indifference to the Masters. Under such conditions munificence was taken for granted, and taste became the sole consideration.

Though it was empty, there was something about the cathedral that made Pluto and me wish to stay there. The sheer magnitude of the place seemed to put our little problems into perspective. What could *we* possibly matter beneath a ceiling as high as all that? It is the size of the gods, and nothing else, that endears them to their worshippers. The best god is simply the biggest.

(Forgive me, dear reader, these little wanderings from the true path of narrative. Theology is my special vice, but I must learn to keep a tighter rein on it.)

Shortly after we had entered the cathedral, a solitary worshipper came in behind us: a young lady of indeterminate age (I would have guessed eighteen, and I would have been wrong), wearing clothes of a most improbable cut, and a complexion so white that a geisha might have envied her. She blessed herself at the front, then walked down the center aisle with such a deal of swaying and unsteadiness that one feared, despite the voluminous base provided by her hoop skirt, that she would topple at every step. Her black hair was done up in an artful and complicated style and was surmounted by a bonnet of even greater complications—a construction of cloth, flowers, jewels, and papier-mâché that seemed to vie with the high altar for the attention of the faithful. It seemed a shame that there was no one but Pluto and myself present to admire it. When this mirror of fashion had reached the foremost pew of the nave, she genuflected (I thought she had really toppled then), entered, and knelt in an attitude of devotion, reading from a little black book she had taken from her reticule.

We approached respectfully, wondering if it was right to come into such a building unclothed. It was my first intimation of guilt, and I did not like it.

Pluto reached a timid hand out to pull at her puffy sleeve for attention, and the woman (one could see she was not *such* a young lady after all) turned a cold eye upon us. "What is it? Can't you see I'm reading? Why don't you go bother a robot? That's what they're for. Well, don't just stand there gaping. What is it you want? Speak up!"

"Please, Miss," Pluto stammered, "we're the new puppies, and we don't know where to go."

"Go to a robot, of course. Do *I* look like a robot? Does this" (gesturing with her little black book at the vast spaces of the cathedral) "look like a schoolroom?"

"Could you take us to a robot, please? Because we're lost, you know."

"Bother!" the woman exclaimed.

From the first, you can see, there was something daunting about Roxanna Proust, as though the very melancholy in which she wrapped herself up were an actively aggressive force. She was at almost all times *steeped* in emotion. She didn't seem to care what flavor it was either, just as long as she got lots of it. Even before we had interrupted her, she had been crying into her book, and, as she scolded us, there were still two tears trembling in the corners of her dark eyes. The skin thereabouts was scrunched into a great delta of wrinkles, as though from the pressure of squeezing out the tears. She had a prominent nose in profile, with a good cutting edge to it, and a small, slightly recessed chin that would tremble in moments of stress; that is, usually. She wore quantities of jewelry, especially rings, with the idea that an opulence of ornament would compensate for the general spareness of her own person. Yet for all this, she did give one the impression of a sort of beauty, a rare and highly frangible sort.

Pluto broke under the pressure and began crying . . . not, I suspect, without a certain childish cunning. "B-but we're *lost!* We're orphans. We're all alone!

Roxanna's delta of wrinkles narrowed under the pressure of a thought, "What did you say your names were?"

"My name's Pluto, and he's White Fang. He's my little brother."

"Your *last* name, child!"

"White."

"Your father was Tennyson White? *The* Tennyson White?" Pluto nodded. Roxanna made a sound rather like a bird of prey swooping down on a field mouse. "You poor dear darlings!" Even as this cry echoed and reechoed in the cathedral vaults, Roxanna laid down her book and caught up Pluto and myself into the dark, ample folds of her dress, as if she were netting us. "Why didn't you *say* so? Oh my little pets! My loves!"

With such endearments and as many others as she knew, she led Pluto and myself out of the cathedral. Only when we got to the bronze doors did she remember her little black book. She regarded the two of us a moment calculatingly, then pointed a heavily bejeweled forefinger at me: "You! Run back and fetch my book, will you? That's a good dog."

I was only too eager to please her and at the same time escape a little while from a presence that was, like a room in which a bottle of perfume has been broken, a little overpowering.

When I had found Roxanna's book, I opened it to the title page out of curiosity and discovered it was not, as I had imagined, a prayerbook, but something in French that I'd never heard of called *A La Recherche du Temps Perdu* (Volume V: *La Prisonnière*) by somebody called Marcel Proust.

Aside from the robots and teaching machines that looked after us, it was chiefly Roxanna Proust who undertook the responsibility of our education. *Faute de mieux. Tant pis.* Roxanna taught us French, reading long passages to us from her favorite author (from whom she had appropriated her surname). Even now, when I wish, I can close my eyes and hear her voice again, shrill with didacticism: "Proust! Proust is the great spirit of our age! No one but Proust has seen so profoundly into the depths, the veritable *abysses,* of the human character. No one! Only Marcel Proust!" I sometimes wondered if she had read any other book in her life besides the

Remembrance of Things Past. She taught us German by reading a German translation of Proust. She taught us the history of literature by comparing all other authors to Proust. (There was no comparison.) If she could have taught us mathematics by reading Proust, she would have done that too.

She despised all other novelists, with but one exception: Daddy. "He did have a certain degree of literary skill," she had informed us shortly after our arrival. "I'm sure that if he had been able to continue, he would have learned to profit from Proust's example."

It is possible that Roxanna's attentions were not entirely due to her selfless concern for the development of our literary taste. She was only too well aware that her talents were not widely appreciated at the Shroeder Kennel, where the emphasis was so much on athletics. She languished in the intellectual night of Shroeder, much as Chekhov's Three Sisters languished in the provinces, always dreaming of that wonderful, never-to-be day when they would go to Moscow. Roxanna's Moscow was the asteroids, and she was hopeful that Pluto and I, sons of the eminent Tennyson White, would get her there more readily than her own rather limited attainments and a pedigree she blushed even to mention. (Roxanna had been born on a nearby farm to a family with the unhappy name of Skunk).

It was an eclectic education, but there was no one else about with even a fraction of Roxanna's talent, special as it was. Most of the pets at Shroeder lived their lives between the gymnasium and the boudoir. For my own part, I'll confess that I spent more time exercising and playing games than I did in the education booths or at Roxanna's feet. Without the intellectual stimulation and aid of the Leash, literature has not been my natural inclination.

Pluto was different. Pluto loved to read, and he sucked right up to the Skunk Lady (as she was generally known at Shroeder). Under her guidance he began to write. Not surprisingly his first style (at age ten) was very derivative of Proust. The next year he began to sound more like Joyce, and by the time he was pushing thirteen he came into his own.

That was a red-letter day in Pluto's life—the day he found his own style—and I remember how he came running across the playing field to drag me away from a rough session of gymnochess. I was a bit peeved, since White was winning, but I liked to humor Pluto in these things, since he had almost no other audience at Shroeder and I knew he was lonely.

He wouldn't read *Ceremony* (the title of his work) to me out-of-doors, but insisted that I come to the Cathedral, which was empty every day but Sunday, the one day when our Master would gather his pets together and give them an hour on the Leash of full-pressure beatitude. Once in the cathedral, Pluto put on what he called "vestments," oddments of clothing he scraped together from the theatrical wardrobes, and insisted I do the same.

"This is going to be a ceremony," Pluto informed me in a whisper. "So you have to fold your hands together like this and not say anything till I'm done with it." He lighted a candle and threw on a tape of organ fugues that sounded peculiarly hollow here, since the walls lacked the acoustical properties of real stone. Candle in hand, he marched up the steps to the pulpit in time to the music, where in an uneven adolescent baritone, he began to declaim from *Ceremony*.

"*Ceremony*. Part One: Worship of the Muse. First, an oration composed by Plutonium Keats White, Ahem! Art! Art is a thing of futile beauty. It has no part in our lives, or very little, and it is as unsuitable at moments of great stress as it is silly on occasions of state. It has an affinity to death. Its greatness is the greatness of a king resigned to his fate. It is defeatist. It is not the sort of thing you would inculcate in children, for"—and here he stared down at me in his gravest manner—"it might kill them in too large a dosage. Art is the way we delay our departure, but it is no way to start the day."

He seemed to have finished, and I clapped—rather mildly, I'm afraid. "It's nothing like Proust," I assured him. "And I don't think you could say Joyce influenced it very much either."

"Quiet! That was only Part One. Part Two is called 'The Sacrifice,' and for that part you can have to get down on your knees and hold out your hands so I can tie them together."

I laughed, thinking he was making a joke."

"On your knees, you little son of a bitch!" he screamed at me.

I cannot say what my reply was to this strange demand, except to suggest that I had first discovered the expression in a novel by J. D. Salinger.

It is difficult to say which of us was responsible for the fight. Pluto *did* come storming down the pulpit in what was for him a beserker rage. He *did* strike the first blow. But all this while I continued to shout "(Salinger)!" at him, and he could claim to having been provoked.

Pluto was thirteen, I a mere ten; Pluto was quite five feet tall, I only a bit over four. But Pluto was a creampuff, and my three years of gymnastics made the contest almost even. He kicked and bit and flailed about and made some really splendid loud noises, but before I'd even warmed to the task he was in retreat. I managed to put a good rip in his foolish "vestment" and dyed it a noble red with the blood from his noble nose. At last he admitted that everything I'd said about him was true, and I let him get up from the floor.

He ran straight to the power station to signal our Master on the emergency switch, something no other pet had ever dared to do, since the Master of Shroeder didn't like to be bothered—I am amazed—to this day I am amazed—that it was I who was punished and not Pluto. He *started* the fight.

A bloody nose! What is so dreadful about a bloody nose?

It was not a dire punishment. In some ways it was scarcely a punishment at all. It was just done to guarantee that I would be less inclined to shed blood in the future. I was conditioned, irrevocably, to respond to the sight of blood, be it ever so small a gout, with nausea and vomiting, succeeded by fainting. In all my years as a pet, my conditioning was never put to the test, but later there would be occasions, bloody occasions . . .

But I am getting ahead of myself. Everything in due order.

Chapter 3

*In which I meet Darling, Julie, and fly away
to Swan Lake.*

I have always considered that my adult life began at the age of ten.
Before that age my memory can only reconstruct a chronology of
events from a few key images. Everything is suppositive, as it were.
But from age ten on, I can remember whole days exactly as they
happened.

The whole day I would take most pleasure in remembering is the
Fourth of October, 2027, a Wednesday. On Wednesdays in good
weather Roxanna would take Pluto and me out into the country, beyond the dome of the kennel. We drove along the dusty country
roads in a special little cart operated by solar tap and covered with
an invisible but nonetheless reassuring bubbleshield so strong that
not even the Masters themselves could break through it once it was
switched on. Not that we had to worry about such an eventuality
(we would have been only too happy if a Master would break in
and Leash us), but the Dingoes had become more and more of a
nuisance since the incident three years before of my father's assassination. Several pets visiting Earth for their pleasure had been done
away with in similar ways, with nothing left to bury but ashes. In
half an hour we would arrive at a deserted farm, where, in the shade
of over-burdened apple trees, we would pursue our studies or, if
Roxanna felt indulgent toward us, explore the old farm buildings,
and rusting machinery. We never went into the house itself though.

The aura of Dingoes still clung to it, and in any case Roxanna had absolutely forbidden it.

Only years later did Roxanna admit to us what we had known all along—that this had been her parents' farm, abandoned during the Great Collapse of 2003, when the economy of those humans who were still holding out against the Mastery fell completely into ruin. The Skunks (their name was still legible on the mailbox) had volunteered themselves and their children for the nearest kennel—Shroeder, as it happened. The children had been accepted, but the parents had been judged unfit and sent away, as by that time most older Volunteers were. The Masters had no more need of wild pets (who could never be perfectly domesticated), for now they were breeding their own and (so it seemed to us pets) doing a better job of it than Man ever had.

It was principally from kennel rejects like the Skunks that the society of Dingoes, as we know it today, has evolved, and this no doubt accounts for the scent of sour grapes that clings to so many of them and even, a little, to Roxanna—as I think I've already pointed out.

It was late in the afternoon, and Roxanna, tired of reading, was fanning herself with a perfumed handkerchief and reminiscing to Pluto about her country childhood and how different the world had been then. She told about her father's drinking bouts on Saturday nights and how he would come back home and *beat* Roxanna's poor mother terribly. She had never witnessed these beatings, but she had heard them and assured us they were terrible. For Pluto and myself, such tales confirmed our worst imaginings about the Dingoes. I, having but recently bloodied my brother's nose, was *persona non grata* and accordingly I had gone up into the branches of the apple tree, higher than Pluto dared climb, to work problems in calculus, which I had just began to study. Suddenly there appeared as in a vision, suspended in the air before me almost near enough to touch, a girl of about my own age. Wisps of heliotrope spiraled about her bare, sunbronzed body, and her white hair gleamed in the dying sunlight as though it were itself luminescent.

"Hello," she said. "My name is Darling, Julie. Darling is my last name, but you can call me Julie if you like. Don't you want to play with me?"

I couldn't reply. I was stunned—as much by her loveliness (yes, I was only ten, but children are not insensible of these things; perhaps not so insensible as *we* are) as by the shock of meeting a stranger in those unlikely circumstances.

She took a step toward me, smiling (Darling, Julie has always had the loveliest, cheek-dimpling smile), and I realized what would have been immediately evident to any well-brought-up pet: that it was her Master's unseen presence that supported her. For him, anti-gravity would be a moment's improvisation. But our Master's neglect had made even such commonplaces as flight seem rare and wonderful to us.

"Aren't you Leashed?" she asked, seeing that I hesitated to step off my branch and meet her halfway.

"No—none of us are."

By this time Roxanna and Pluto had become aware of our visitor, but since they were a good ten feet below Julie and me, it was awkward for them to join the conversation. It was awkward for me, for that matter, but I blustered on.

"Would you like an apple?" I asked, picking one from the abundance about me and offering it to her. She stretched forth her hand, then with a guilty look drew it back.

"My Master thinks I'd best not," she explained. "He says that sort of food is for Dingoes. *You're* not a Dingo, are you?"

"Oh no!" I blushed, and Julie laughed.

"Well, you look like a Dingo to me." I should have realized at once that this was all teasing, for there could be no serious doubt of our domestication. Dingoes wear clothing, and pets (who never have to be ashamed of their bodies) only dress for the theater or a pageant or (like Roxanna) out of perversity. "If you're not a Dingo, why don't you step off that silly old tree branch and prove it?"

From the first I've always behaved like a fool for Darling, Julie. I did just as she suggested and began falling, in obedience to Newton's laws, directly toward Roxanna. Then, with a funny little internal somersault, I felt myself caught up in the anti-gravity belt supporting Julie. Julie swooped down, giggling, and caught hold of my hand, and in the same moment I felt the meshes of the Leash close over my mind. Beneath us, Roxanna had fainted. Pluto was trying to revive her. Each time he slapped her face, she groaned deliciously.

"What a silly game," Julie commented. Then, letting go my hand, she leaped into the accommodating air to a height of thirty feet and hung there, secure as a ping-pong ball suspended by a jet of air.

"Try and catch me!" she shouted, and then sailed off on a long parabola that ended behind the sagging roof of the old barn.

"What about me?" Pluto protested. "I want to fly too."

"You're probably too old, but I'll ask her," I promised. Then I flew off to catch Julie, and Pluto saw no more of me or Julie for a good two hours. She led me quite a chase, high into the clouds, skimming the branches of the nearby scrub woods, skipping like stones over the smooth waters of Lake Superior. We were both delightfully exhausted before she let me catch her.

When I had caught my breath back, I asked her what kennel she came from.

"Oh, it's a new kennel out in the asteroids. You've probably never heard of it. Not *yet*," she added patriotically.

"And what are you doing *here?* I mean, the Skunk farm isn't really a crossroads. Why come to Earth at all, if you've got a nice kennel in the asteroids?"

"Well, my Master needs more stock, and he brought me along to help him choose. Things are cheaper on Earth and my Master has to count his pennies. That's what he tells me anyhow. As far as *I'm* concerned," she finished loyally. "I'd rather live at Swan Lake than anywhere else in the universe."

I wanted to say that I felt exactly the same way, but instead I put in a good word for Shroeder's rugby field and tennis courts.

Julie suddenly grew dejected. "Oh dear, then you won't want to come back with us! I'd been hoping so much . . ."

"Ask me. Don't jump to conclusions."

"Will you come back to Swan Lake with me? Please!"

Her Master's voice resonated in my mind, echoing Julie's plea: *Will you?*

Her Master? No—now he was mine! I didn't have to answer Julie's question for our Master conveyed my happy assent to her mind. Her own delight bounced back like a well-returned ball in a friendly game of tennis.

"What about my brother? You'll want him too, won't you?" (It's amazing how accomplished a hypocrite one can be at ten years of age.)

"Well, naturally! After all, you're both Whites."

I was more than a little shocked. Aside from *Uncle Tom's Cabin,* I had never come across examples of race prejudice. "Some of my best friends—" I began indignantly.

"Oh, not that kind of White, silly! *Tennyson* White. The most famous novelist in the last fifty years. And you're his sons. The only ones, I might add, who haven't been snapped up by top kennels. I wouldn't say a word against Shroeder, you understand, but I really think you can do better. Why, the two of you are worth all the other pets in that kennel taken together!"

Now, of course, I realize that that kind of talk is undemocratic and subversive, but then my tender mind, depraved by the false values of the Mastery, was flattered by such a compliment. I even thanked Julie for it.

"I've told you my name. But you haven't told me yours."

"White Fang," I said, still swollen with pride.

"Fang, White. That's a funny name. I don't see you as 'Fang, White,' at all. I think I'll call you Cuddles instead."

I should have objected then and there, but I was anxious lest I offend her and lose my ticket to the asteroids. And that's how it happened that, for the next ten years of my life, I was known as Cuddles to all my friends.

When Julie and I returned to the Skunk farmhouse, we found that Roxanna and Pluto had tired of waiting for us and returned to the kennel in their bubbletank. Julie and I took a direct route, skimming the treetops of the twilit woods, protected against the chill of the October evening by our Master's thoughtfulness.

Within a few minutes of our return, Julie's Master had negotiated the transfer of myself and Pluto from the Shroeder Kennel to Swan Lake. Roxanna protested that he could not interrupt our literary studies at this crucial point. We must either remain at Shroeder or she must be allowed to accompany us to the asteroids. I leave it to the reader to imagine which course Roxanna had in mind. But to all her pleadings and threats, the Master of Swan Lake was coldly indifferent. Roxanna's pedigree was worthless; her physical person possessed an at-best-problematical beauty; her literary attainments extended no farther than her appreciation of Proust, an author for whom the Master of Swan Lake had the lowest regard. Roxanna cried; she fainted; she tore her hair. It was all to no avail. At last, when Pluto had gathered together all his scraps of poetry, and we were ready to go, Roxanna bade us farewell with a curse.

The trip to the asteroids was made that night as we slept. What means our new Master employed to transport us, I could not say.

Nothing so crude as a spaceship. The Master's technology was a spur-of-the-moment thing, and I will admit, for my own part, that mechanical engineering isn't really that interesting to me.

We woke to the subdued luminescence of kennel walls that we had known all our lives. The walls shifted to livelier color schemes in response to the quickening neural patterns of our waking minds. For a moment I feared that we were still back at Shroeder.

But there was this difference: instead of the relentless drag of Earth gravity, a gentle gravitational pulse, a relaxed ebb-and-flow, seemed to issue from my own heart.

I felt the Leash of my new Master close more tightly over my mind (for the next ten years it would never entirely desert me, even in sleep), and I smiled and whispered my thanks to Him for having brought me away.

Julie was awake now too, and with a wave of her arm and a flourish of synthetic horn-music, the walls of the kennel dissolved, and I beheld the boundless, glowing landscape of the asteroids.

I gasped.

It is yours, said a voice in my head that would soon come to seem as familiar as my own.

Hand in hand, Julie and I sailed out over this phantasmagoric playground, and the spheres of heaven played their music for us. Exotic blossoms exploded like Roman candles, discharging hoards of rich perfume. Colors wreathed us in abstract, joyous patterns, as the two of us bounded and tumbled through the shifting fields of gravity, like starlings caught in a dynamo.

Chapter 4

In which I am perfectly happy.

It was paradise. What more can I say?

Oh, I know that's cheating. I know I have to *try*. But consider the immensity of the task; consider how many better men than I have tried and failed. Milton's heaven is a bore; his Eden, though nice enough at first glance, has a deadly sameness about it. Dante did rather better, but even so most of his admirers find it more difficult to soar through his Empyrean than to climb the steep side of Purgatory or slough through Hell's mires. On the whole, Heaven is best left in the hands of the gods.

Let me begin, then, with something easy, like geography . . .

Swan Lake was composed of twelve smallish asteroids, which our Master had artfully woven into a sort of celestial clockwork. The interwoven trajectories of the twelve asteroids had been determined with such niceness that the whole configuration—from twelve o'clock to twelve o'clock, as it were—came full circle once every hundred years. It was thereby possible with just a glance at the sky to determine the year, the month, the day of the week, and—within a few minutes—the hour, providing of course that one could remember the code. The largest of these asteroids, Tchaikovsky, was a scant ten miles in diameter, and the least, Milhaud, was a tawdry rock not five thousand feet from pole to pole. The main kennels and all permanent installations of any size were on Tchaikovsky, but any pet could travel freely to the other asteroids along broad slipstreams, or—if he was feeling his oats—just by jumping, since the gravity was a piddling .03 that of Earth anywhere outside the kennel proper. The kennels themselves were all gravitized at a comfortable .85 just as they had been at Shroeder.

Swan Lake, though done up in better taste than other kennels I have known, was built along the usual lines. The walls, the floors, all the elements of construction were force-fields wrapped in microscopically thin layers of stuff—atoms, molecules, that sort of thing. The only permanent feature in any room was a console that any pet knew how to operate. This console controlled temperature, humidity, wind velocity, illumination, fog effects, gravity and dimensions. The dimensional control was extremely complex, and only a professional architect of long experience (or a Master) knew all its ins and outs. Most of us contented ourselves with a selection from the thousand or so presettings: Louis Sixième, Barnyard, Dracula's Castle, Whale-belly, Sahara, Seraglio Steamroom, etc. There was a special dial that controlled the degree of realism or stylization of any of these scenes, and one could produce some very uncanny effects by, for instance, demanding a totally abstract Bronx Renaissance living room or an ultrarealistic Pleistocene swamp. And the effects one could get by *spinning* the dial . . . !

No more! I can't stand remembering these things. The happiness—

Stoicism, White Fang old boy, stoicism!

Actually, Julie and I spent most of our time out-of-doors, dashing in and out among the asteroids. The ten asteroids intermediate in size between Tchaikovsky and Milhaud were, in descending order: Stravinsky, Adam, Pugno, Prokofiev, Delibes, Chopin, Glazunov, Offenbach, Glière and Nabokov.

As my readers may have gathered from this list, the Master of Swan Lake was something of a balletomane. For each of his asteroids was named after a composer of notable music for the ballet —or, a slight but telling distinction, of music for notable ballets. In fact, *all* of Swan Lake had been fashioned, all the pets had been gathered there, to serve this single passion of our Master, which was, I hasten to add, our passion too, our entire purpose, and our highest happiness next to the Leash itself.

Oh, hell, I should never have started to try to explain! I might have known I'd end up like this, muttering dithyrambs.

I was explaining a little ways back, how Julie and I would go sailing out among the asteroids. Now such times as we did this, we were dancing. In fact all the time we were at Swan Lake, all those ten years, we never stopped dancing. And as we would soar past any one of the asteroids, our passage would trigger a recording—a miniaturized electronic orchestra, actually—that would play the single composition of that composer which most suited our velocity, trajectory, idiorhythmic motion, and mood. It could also improvise transitions from and to any piece of music in the repertoire of any of the other asteroids. These transitions were often the most amazing passages of all (imagine a collaboration between Offenbach and Stravinsky!), which encouraged us never to linger overlong in one vicinity but to be ever flitting about like will-o'-the-wisps.

There were other machines that served the same purpose as a crew of stagehands, managing the lights, providing props, laying scenes when the music demanded something more specific than fireworks . . .

And machines that released scents that were harmonized with the other elements synaesthetically . . .

Yes, and finally there was *us*—Julie and me and the other pets. The *ensemble*. It was on our account that Swan Lake had been put together, so that our revels never would be ended, so that we would have music wherever we'd go. I say we *danced,* but that will not convey to most of my readers just what we did. For the average Dingo, dancing is just an exercise preliminary to mating. It provides a release of certain powerful tensions along socially approved channels. When *we* danced, it was nothing so crude as that. Everything we did, everything a person *could* do, became part of our dance: our dinners, our lovemaking, our most secret thoughts, and our silliest jokes. The dance integrated all these disparate elements into an aesthetic whole; it ordered the randomness of life into immense tapestries. Not *Art for Art's Sake,* but *Life for Art's Sake* was our motto.

How am I to explain this to Dingoes? There was nothing *wasted.* I think that's the important thing. Not a word or thought or glance between two persons but that there was a deeper meaning to it. It fit, just as in a piece of music that observes the canons each chord has its place in the melodic succession.

Here again was the old Romantic idea of a synthesis of the arts: the same that inspired Wagner's Bayreuth or Diaghilev's *Ballets Russes.* But the Master of Swan Lake had resources to accomplish what those men fumbled for—and his chief resource necessarily was his dearly beloved pets—us. He pampered us, he coddled us, he got us into trim. Not only physical trim (even the most negligent Master would see to that); more even than *mental* trim. In fact, too much acuity could be a disadvantage. Daddy's Masters on Ceres and Ganymede had developed their pets' intellects more than *our* Master altogether approved. There had always been something over-refined about that first generation of pets. Pope somewhere says of Shakespeare that he was an "unpolished diamond." Well, what might not Shakespeare have said of Pope? The important thing, as we saw it, was not to be witty and cultivated and bright, but to be *sincere*. We of the second generation found our parents' style dry, over-intellectual, unbecomingly ironic. We wanted to simplify, and since the material of our art was our own lives, we simplified ourselves. Like Young Werther, we cultivated a certain willful naïveté. Not only did we make a dance of our lives, but we turned the simplest statements —a "thank you" or a "by your leave"—into a sort of rhapsody.

It was certainly paradise, but what would *not* have been paradise with Darling, Julie there? It is nice to have a Master, but it is necessary to have a mate—as Woof observes somewhere in *A Dog's Life*.

How to speak of her? Putting Julie "into words" is like sculpting in quicksilver. There was nothing constant about her, nothing you could call *hers*. The color of her hair changed from day to day; her eyes were blue or brown or hazel, as the mood came upon her; her figure might be lithe as a nymphette or buxom as a Rubens. It all depended on the rôle she had to play.

For Julie essentially was an actress. I have seen her dance the major rôles in the classical repertoire; I have seen her improvise; when I've been Leashed with her I've looked into the furthest recesses of her charming mind. And never have I glimpsed even a hint of the real, the quintessential Julie—unless it was an infinite capacity for pretending. She was Juliet and Lucrezia Borgia in equal measure; she was both acts of *Giselle;* she was Odette and Odile, the black swan and the white swan too. She was whoever it might occur to her that she might be. And she was lovely.

We were only sixteen, Julie and I, when our first child was born to us. The High Mass that celebrated Petite's christening was based on the standard Roman model and set, sweetly, to Mother Goose melodies. My brother Pluto officiated at the ceremony and delivered a sermon in verse of his own composition in honor of the occasion.

Since all of us present at the ceremony were in telepathic rapport with him, our appreciation of the sermon was equal exactly to Pluto's (who admired it greatly), but I have had a chance recently to reexamine his verses with more dispassion, and I wonder . . .

But let my readers judge for themselves. The following is Pluto's sermon in its entirety. It is meant to be read under bright lights with a slight scent of musk, as of a diaper pail opened briefly in the nearby room. Like most work he was turning out at that time, it should be delivered in a loud voice with something of a Gregorian chant:

> Scrumptious ornament,
> Bubbling liquid joy!
> Thing, thing, energy, energy, thing!
>
> Dearly beloved, let us pray.
> Let us bump-dee bump-dee play!
> Petite jeune fille, jolie et bonne!
>
> Mr. Wopsle, Lady Flutter,
> Caracas Venezuela O!
> Thing, thing, energy, energy, thing!
>
> Amalgamation, splendid event
> To celebrate beserk the little girl:
> Petite jeune fille, joile et bonne, hélas!

Considering that this was how our little Petite got her start in life, I think she's done pretty well.

I should explain at once, since the subject has intruded itself here, that there was nothing promiscuous about Swan Lake. The hearth was sacred to us, the marriage bed a shrine. In this we differed from the cynical libertinism of our forebears—not through any want of libido, but really from an excess of it. For us monogamy was a continually passionate state. Anything else would have been less. Moreover, our Master did have fixed ideas on the subject of organic breeding (as he called it), and perhaps he sometimes assisted our natural inclination to monogamy by weeding out adulterous thoughts from our minds' neat gardens in order to further these policies of his and, incidentally, to keep the prices up.

It may be, as contemporary critics have suggested, that the New Domesticity of the Twenties and Thirties was a highly artificial condition—a fashion if not merely a fad. But cannot the same charge be brought against Victorian sentimentality? Against the Moslem purdah? Against all institutions whatever? The difference between a folkway and a fashion is one of degree, not of kind.

What I mean to establish by all this is the simple fact that though we lived in Swan Lake ten years, we were always true to each other, Julie to me and me to Darling, Julie. And if anyone ever dares insinuate anything to the contrary, he will have to answer to me for it— and I shall accept no answer slighter than the forfeit of his life.

It was paradise.

Really, my dear readers, it was *almost* paradise. Illness and pain were banished from our lives, and it may have been (for I know of no instances to disprove it) that so long as we stayed Leashed, death too had lost its sting. Women no longer brought forth children in sorrow, nor did men eat their bread salted by the sweat of their brows. Our happiness did not degenerate into boredom, and our pleasures were never dampened by an aftertaste of guilt.

Paradise has a considerable flaw, however, from the narrative point of view. It is anti-dramatic. Perfection doesn't make a good yarn, because it doesn't have to *go* anywhere. Perfection is happy right where it is. So there isn't much for me to tell you about Swan Lake, except : *I liked it.*

I liked it; for ten years that was the story of my life.

And so here we are in the year 2037 already, time having flown. By angle of declination between Glazunov and Chopin I can see that it was August. We were in a large marble courtyard, where Julie was teaching four-year-old Petite to pirouette. The sky flickered violently, and an obbligato of hunting horns announced visitors from outer space. At the console, I called up a triumphal arch from the willing ground so that our guests might enter in style. I turned the gravity up to a more formal 1.05, and poor little Petite went into a tailspin and plopped down to the floor, dismayed and giggling.

The horns quieted, and an anguished metallic din split the air, as of an anvil being struck—but no, it was only a pet striding forward through the arch. He wore armor in the Attic manner, very leathery and crusted with gauds, and his face was hidden behind a grotesque iron mask. Gaily waving a mace-and-chain, he shouted his greeting aloud to us above the anvil-clamor of his footsteps: *"Hoi-ho! Hoi-ho!"* The richness of his perfect *Heldentenor* voice made the ringing of the anvils seem the merest trill of violins. Only a few feet away from us he released the mace-and-chain, which went spinning straight up over our heads and at the top of its arc burst into fireworks, at which instant our visitor gripped my forearm with his right hand. A gesture I would have reciprocated, except that the casing of leather and iron about his massive wrist was too thick to afford me any sort of purchase. With his free hand he doffed the iron helmet and peering up (for as we stood, toe to toe, my eyes were at the level of the Medusa graven on his breastplate) I could behold the blond hair and the blue eyes of Wagner's Seigfried.

"Hi there!" I said friendlily. Darling, Julie echoed my greeting, while Petite, ever the show-off, tried to execute another pirouette under 1.05 gravity and fell on her inevitable ass.

"I am St. Bernard of Titan," the visitor said, rending the air. "All just and godly men are my friends, but villains tremble at my name."

"I'm glad to hear it. My name is White Fang, and this is my wife —Darling, Julie, and that at your feet is our daughter Petite. We all bid you welcome to Swan Lake, St. Bernard."

Now a softer music filled the air (the Venusberg music from *Tannhäuser,* I believe) and St. Bernard, turning to face the arch, lowered himself reverently to one knee. A shimmering golden light formed in the center of the arch, and within this lambency, like a diamond set in a gold chalice, appeared a woman of beauty to rival the gods."

My mother.

"Motherlove!" I exclaimed. "That is to say—Clea! What a surprise!"

"Yes, *isn't* it? How long has it been now? Thirteen years? Fourteen? You're not even a puppy any more—and who is *this?"* (It was Petite, who was shyly bent double and peering at Clea through the archway of her legs.) "Am I a grandmother! Fancy that! You'd never know by *looking* at me, would you? I still look as *young* as on the day your father first met me."

Though this was true, the years had not been without their effect in other ways. Certain tics of character had reached a mature growth, chiefly an unawareness of other people that bordered on autism. Thus, she breezed right on with her soliloquy, oblivious of my attempts to introduce Julie to her.

"And *speaking* of your father, I assume you've already met my *new* companion?" By the solicitous manner in which she laid her hand on St. Bernard's leathern thigh, she robbed that "companion" of whatever sense it might have had of the euphemistic. "It was he who insisted that we stop by at Swan Lake. I was reluctant, since it is hardly a *major* attraction. *Nothing* on the order of Titan, which is positively another Bayreuth! You may be interested to know that St. Bernard is our *leading* Titanic tenor. You've no doubt heard of his *Lohengrin,* and as for *The Ring* . . ."

"Actually, Clea," I broke in determinedly, "we're not such great Wagner fanciers here, you know. Our Master inclines more to the French and Russian end of the spect . . ."

"As I was *saying,* St. Bernard said we *had* to stop by, so he could meet you and Pluto—Pluto is somewhere about too, no?—because, you see, St. Bernard happens to be your *brother."*

"But—Motherlove . . . isn't that rather . . . ? I mean, if he's my *brother,* then isn't this a matter of—if you'll excuse the expression—inbreeding?"

St. Bernard's hand reached for the battleaxe hanging at his side, but Clea stopped him.

"Nonsense, White Fang! He bears no relation to *me* whatever. Shame on you, for making such a suggestion! You know your father sired several *hundred* children. St. Bernard was his son by Sieglinde of Titan *years* before I ever met Tennyson White. I suppose, if you want to pick nits, you could say that St. Bernard is your *half*-brother. But he's no more related to *me* than his father was—or, rather, that is his relation precisely."

I made a slight bow in acknowledgment of this unexpected bond, but St. Bernard, not content with small gestures, came gallumphing forward to clasp me in a half-brotherly, titanic embrace, which I sidestepped by sitting down quickly at the console. "A feast!" I declared. "This definitely calls for feasting and song."

I vanished the arch and dialed for an Anglo-Saxon Banquet Hall, moderately stylized, with an Automatic Tumbler. Julie quickly whisked herself into a few yards of brocade and a high-peaked hat, and I got into something suitable in cloth-of-gold. Pluto was called for and arrived in short order in a cardinal's gowns. St. Bernard, a true and reverent knight, had to get back down on one knee to kiss the cardinal's ring.

"Mead!" I shouted to the robots in attendance (all done up, appropriately, in fustian). "Roast boar! Venison! Hecatomb of roast beef!"

"*Hecatombs* is anachronistic, Cuddles," Julie advised.

"Well then, if you're such a hot-shot Medievalist, *you* order!" Which she did—and in Old High German at that. As she told me later, though, our Master helped with irregular verbs. When she finished, Petite added her own postscriptive request in English for butter brickle ice cream.

While we sipped before-dinner meads, the Automatic Tumbler tumbled and a Robo-Jester came around to the table and made deliciously bad jokes, which St. Bernard seemed to think as jolly as they had been on opening night a thousand years ago. Maybe it was the mead. Alcohol-wise the stuff was perfectly innocuous, but our Masters supplied through our Leashes the exact degree of inebriation that each of us was aiming at. Clea filled us in on her missing thirteen years (and they were just about what one would suppose they'd been, judging by their effect on her: the style of Titan—Clea's style—was very Wagnerian, very passionate, and very, very *big*); then Pluto gave an account of our neglect and redemption, which I don't think Clea heard because St. Bernard was tickling her all the while. After the fish course, some partridges, and a suckling pig with truffles, Clea and St. Bernard sang the second act of *Tristan und Isolde* for our benefit. Julie, to escape listening to it, went blotto on her Leash.

This done, and much mead later, St. Bernard proposed to give an exhibition of his skill at axe-throwing. They have this whole Middle Ages bit on Titan. We upended the oaken dining table and painted a human figure on it as a target. St. Bernard insisted that we make wagers against him. I did have my doubts as to how well he would do, since he was having difficulties just remaining upright at that point—but every axe sank into the wood right where he told it to. Petite was clamorous with admiration.

"*Hoi-ho*, Maedchen! Does the sport please you?" St. Bernard lifted Petite to his shoulder. "Would you like to join it?" She nodded, smiling, eyes aglow.

"Now, see here, St. Bernard—enough's enough! If you're getting delusions of singing *William Tell,* I can assure you it isn't in my daughter's repertoire."

"Oh, let him have his way, or he'll get into a pet," Clea advised.

"It's exactly because I'm afraid he shall get into a pet with that axe of his—that I worry. If you have so much confidence in him, Motherlove, why don't you let him use *you* as a target?"

"I have, many times. It's terribly dull. I mean, you just stand there. I wish you hadn't gotten him so loaded. He always gets this way when he's had more than he can handle. Next he'll be sentimental. I hate that!"

St. Bernard, meanwhile, had posed Petite before the dining table and gone back twenty paces to take aim. The blade of the axe he was using was fully a third of the total length of my daughter.

"Stop, madman!" I screamed, but too late—already the axe was hurtling at Petite, seeming to wobble as it turned end over end about its center of gravity. I rushed forward, as though to catch it in flight . . .

There now, good fellow, be comforted! Your Master is watching and he won't let anything ill betide. Calmly, calmly.

If I had not had so much mead myself, I would not have needed the Leash's reminder. For what could there ever be to worry about at Swan Lake with my Master ever watching over me?

When St. Bernard had finished his demonstration to Petite's and his own immense satisfaction, I stepped up to the board and pulled out the axes. "Now," I said airily, "let me show you how we throw axes at Swan Lake. Julie, step up here!"

Julie, who had been sailing through heaven at the end of her Leash until this moment, came to with a start of real fear. "Cuddles, are you out of your *mind?* I will not!" But quickly her features assumed a milder expression, and I knew that our Master had whispered his reassurances to her. She took her place before the target.

I opened my demonstration with an axe that sliced neatly between Julie's legs, rending the thick brocade of her gown. Then I threw one underhand that snapped off the peak of her cap. Then several perfect throws as I stood with my back turned to Julie. St. Bernard gasped at the daring of the feat. I concluded my show of skill by spinning an axe not end over end but *sideways,* rotating about the shaft like a top.

I bowed to St. Bernard's thunderous applause. "Thank you," I said, as much for my Master's assistance as for St. Bernard's applause.

"But you are *wonderful!* You are a genius! Now I am proud that you are my brother. Come, we must make it a solemn union—we must swear eternal brotherhood in blood. *Blutbruderschaft!* With these words St. Bernard removed the leathern bracelet binding his right wrist and sliced across the exposed flesh with a jeweled dagger. "Now you," he said, handing me the bloody instrument. "We will mix our blood, and then to the end of time . . ."

St. Bernard was interrupted by my rather copious heavings (it had been a large feast), which I regret to say was the only thing I contributed to be mixed with his blood. I remember only his first oaths (*"Wotan! Fricka!"* etc.), for as soon as my stomach was emptied out I fainted dead away.

When I woke, I found myself moving through outer space. Pluto had been kind enough to explain to St. Bernard my peculiar infirmity (though failing to mention his own part in that story), and St. Bernard had insisted, as a sort of reparation, that we all accompany himself and Clea on their trip to Earth. Pluto and Julie had demurred, for they were even less inclined to the Wagnerian than I, but our Master, surprisingly, had overridden them. So we had set forth, the eight of us (six pets, two Masters) immediately, and in no time at all we were on Earth. The morning sun was glittering with immoderate intensity on the waters of Lake Superior, and there again in the middle distance was the cathedral tower of St. John the Divine.

Can it be that I shall never again enjoy the easy pleasures of that time? That I shall never, never again see Swan Lake and fly about among the familiar asteroids? And can it be that this exile has been my free choice! O ye Heavens, when I remember you—as I do now —too clearly, too dearly, all the force of my will melts away and I long only to be returned to you. Nothing, nothing on Earth can rival, and very little has the power even to suggest, the illimitable resources of the Master's pleasure domes. Oh, nothing!

It was paradise—and it is quite, quite gone.

Chapter 5

In which the worst happens.

As soon as her feet touched Earth, Darling, Julie fell into one of her sentimental moods and begged our Master to take us out to the Skunk farm, where she had first met me. I seconded her request, less from sentiment than out of a need to escape the presence of St. Bernard (who had somehow got hold of the notion that he was in the neighborhood of the Black Forest). Our Master, as usual, indulged our whim.

While Petite ran off to explore the dark wood (which was in its way every bit as realistic as anything one could produce on the console), Julie and I sat in the lightest of Leashes and marveled at the changes that time had wrought not only in ourselves (for we had, after all, passed from puppyhood to maturity in the meantime, and the gleeful shouts of our own dear pup were ringing in our ears) but also in the scene about us. The roof of the barn had fallen in, and in the orchard and surrounding meadows, saplings had taken root and were flourishing. Julie gloried in all this decay, just as the young ladies of the eighteenth century must have gloried in the built-to-order ruins of the Gothic Revival. So great was her passion for returning to the past that she begged our Master to be unleashed!"

"Please!" she whined. "Just this once. I feel so aloof, so anachronistic, out here in a Leash. I want to see what wilderness tastes like."

Our Master pretended to ignore her.

"Pretty please," she whined more loudly, though it had become more of a bark by now.

A voice in my head (and in Julie's too, of course) soothed: *There, now, gently. What's this, my darlings, my dears, my very own pets? Why should you wish to throw off your nice Leashes? Why, you're hardly Leashed at all! Do you want to turn into Dingoes?*

"Yes!" Julie replied. "Just for this one afternoon I *want* to be a Dingo."

I was shocked. Yet I must admit that at the same time I was a little excited. It had been so long since I had been without a Leash that so primitive an idea appealed to me. There is always a certain morbid pleasure in putting on the uniform of one's enemy, of becoming, as it were, a double-agent.

If I unleash you, there's no way for you to call me back. You'll just have to wait till I come back for you.

"That's all right," Julie assured him. "We won't set foot off the farm."

I'll return in the morning, little one. Wait for me.

"Oh, we will, we will," Julie and I promised antiphonally.

"Me, too," Petite demanded, having returned from her explorations, prompt to her Master's bidding.

And then he was gone, and our minds slipped from their Leashes and into such a tumble and whirlwind of thought that none of us could speak for several minutes. Leashed, one can keep more thoughts simultaneously before consciousness, and with the Leash off we had to learn to think more slowly than in linear sequence.

A more vivid pink flushed Julie's cheek, and her eyes were sparkling with a sudden, unaccustomed brilliance. I realized that this was probably the first time in her life as a pet—in her whole life, that is—that she had been entirely off her Leash. She was probably feeling tipsy. I was, and I was no stranger to the experience.

"Hello, Earthling," she said. Her voice seemed different, sharper and quicker. She plucked an apple from the branches overhead and polished it on her velvety skin.

"You shouldn't eat that, if you recall," I warned. "There may be germs."

"I know." She bit into it, then, repressing her laughter, offered the rest of the apple to me. It was rather an obvious literary reference, but I could see no reason to refuse the apple on that account.

I took a large bite out of it. When I saw the other half of the worm that remained in the apple, I brought our little morality play to an abrupt conclusion. It was Julie who found the old pump and got it working. The wellwater had a distinctly rusty flavor, but it was at least preferable to the taste lingering in my mouth. Then, with my head in Julie's lap and her fingers tousling my hair, I went to sleep, though it was the middle of the day.

When I woke the heat of the afternoon sun was touching me at every pore, and I was damp with sweat. The wind made an *irregular* sound in the trees around us, and from the branches overhead, a crow cried hoarsely and took to the air. I watched its clumsy trajectory with an amusement somehow tinged with uneasiness. *This* was what it was like to be mortal.

"We're getting sunburnt," Julie observed placidly. "I think we should go into the house."

"That would be trespassing," I pointed out, recalling how Roxanna had laid the house under her interdict.

"So much the better," said Julie, for whom the romance of being a Dingo for a day had not yet worn off.

In the farmhouse, dusty strands of adhesive—cobwebs—hung from ceilings, and the creaking floor was littered with paper that time had peeled from the walls. In one of the upstairs rooms, Julie found closets and drawers of mildewed clothing, including some cotton dresses that would have been the right size for a ten-year-old. It was hard to think of Roxanna ever being that small—or that poor. I felt vaguely guilty to have opened up this window on her past, and when one of the dresses, rotten with age, came apart in my hands, a little spooky too. I took Julie into another of the upstairs rooms, which contained a broad, cushioned apparatus, raised about a yard off the floor. The cushion smelled awfully.

"Cuddles, look—a bed! A real one! Why, an antique like this would be worth a fortune in the asteroids."

"I suppose so," I replied. "If they could get the smell out of it."

"Beds must decay—like clothing."

I sat down on the edge of the bed, and it bounced with a creaking, metallic sound, much like the sound made by the pump outside. Julie laughed and jumped onto the bed beside me. It groaned, and the groan deepened to a rasp, and the rasp snapped. Julie went right on laughing as the bed collapsed to the floor. Looking at her sprawled out beside me on that quaint apparatus, I became aware of a feeling that I had never experienced before. For, though we had known each other intimately for years, I had never felt quite this urgently desirous of Julie. Undoubtedly this too was a consequence of being unleashed.

"Julie," I said, "I'm going to bite you."

"Grrr," she growled playfully.

"Arf," I replied.

"Me too, me too!" Petite cried, bounding into the room. She very quickly found herself outside again, digging a hole in the garden in which to bury her uncle Pluto. Before the afternoon was passed, there were holes for Clea and St. Bernard and the entire absentee Skunk family.

Julie is my Darling, Julie is my Darling.

The three of us spent the night in the farmhouse amid creakings and groanings of old wood and ominous scurryings in the walls. Petite slept in a little crib that must once have been Roxanna's. We were up with the sun and went, shivering, directly out of doors to wait beneath the apple trees. We were cold and we were hungry, and swarms of hostile, buzzing insects rose from the dew-drenched grass to settle on our raw skins and feed on our blood. I killed three or four, but the senseless things continued to attack us oblivious to their danger. Even in the darkest ages of Shroeder, we pets had not been subjected to such strenuous discomforts. I began to see the utilitarian value of clothing and wished wistfully for my cloth-of-gold suit of yesterday's feasting.

The sun had risen nearly to noonday, when Julie finally turned to me and asked: "What do you suppose is wrong, Cuddles?"

It was useless by now to pretend that nothing was amiss, but I could only answer her question with a look of dismay. Perhaps we were being punished for asking to be unleashed. Perhaps, impossible as such a thought was, our Master had forgotten us. Perhaps . . .

But how could a pet presume to interpret his Master's actions? Especially such irresponsible, inconceivable, and thoughtless ways as leaving three pedigreed pets—one the merest puppy—defenseless in an alien world among Dingoes!

When our hunger grew extreme, we gorged on apples, cherries, and sour plums, not even bothering to look for wormholes. Through that afternoon and into the night we waited for our Master's return, until at last the chill and darkness of the night forced us into the house.

The next morning was spent in more useless waiting, though this time we had the prudence to wear clothing—pants and jackets of rough blue cloth and rubberized boots. Almost everything else had rotted beyond salvage. Our Master did not return.

"Julie," I said at last (having sent Petite off to pick blueberries so that she might be spared for as long as possible the knowledge of her changed condition), "we're on our own. Our Master has abandoned us. He doesn't want us anymore." Julie began to cry, not making much noise about it, but the tears rolled down her cheeks in a steady stream faster than I could kiss them away.

But for all that, I must confess that Julie adapted to our abandoned state more readily than I. She enjoyed the challenges of that archaic, Dingo-like existence. No doubt she was aided by her sense of make-believe. Every day while I went to a high hill in the vicinity to call, hopelessly and to no apparent effect, to our Master, Julie made believe to fix up the farmhouse. She cleared the floors, dusted, washed, aired out the musty furniture and decaying mattresses, and experimented with the interesting new vegetables that grew among the weeds of a forgotten garden. (Carrots, by the bye, are very good boiled in rusty water with a little dirt thrown in for seasoning.) After the first week my visits to the hillside became less frequent. I was convinced that our Master would never return to us. The thought of such cruelty and indifference—after all those years at Swan Lake—passed quite beyond belief.

Helping Julie at odd jobs around the farm, I began to have a certain respect for the pre-Mastery technology of Earth. I discovered and repaired one mechanism that was especially useful: a rough stone wheel three feet in diameter and three inches thick that was set into rotary motion by a foot pedal. By holding a piece of metal to the revolving wheel, the machine could be made to give off sparks, and these in turn ignited dry scraps of wood. The fire thus produced could be conserved in various ingenious engines in the farmhouse. Fire has an immense utility, but since I assume my readers are familiar with it, I will not make my digression any longer. I only mention in passing that on the night of my discovery Julie, sitting by me in front of a roaring log fire, looked at me with real *admiration!* A look that I returned—for she was very lovely in the firelight, lovelier than she had ever been before, it seemed. The firelight softened the contours of her face, until I was aware only of her relaxed, easy smile and the brightness of her eyes, a brightness that did not need to borrow its brilliance from the fire but seemed to issue from her very being.

"Prometheus," she whispered.

"My own Pandora," I returned, and a scrap of old verse popped into my mind, at once comforting and terrible in its implications. I recited it to Julie in a low voice:

> Your courteous lights in vain you waste,
> Since Julianna here is come;
> For she my mind has so displaced,
> That I shall never find my home.

Julie shivered theatrically. "Cuddles," she said, "we've *got* to find our own way home."

"Don't call me Cuddles," I said in, for me, a rough manner. "If you won't call me White Fang, stick to Prometheus."

Day followed day with no sign of our Master's return. The longer we stayed at the farm, the more inevitable discovery became. On my trips to the hillside I had sometimes noticed clouds of dust rising from the country roads, and, though I was careful to keep under cover and off the roads, I knew that luck alone and merely luck had prevented our capture so far. My imagination recoiled from what would become of us if we were to fall into the hands of Dingoes. I had only to behold my father's defaced monument (which I passed by every day on the way to my hilltop) to be reminded of his terrible fate and it was not a memory to inspire confidence.

Therefore I determined that Julie, Petite and I must find our way to Shroeder Kennel on foot, where, though we might not be so happy as we had been in the asteroids, we would at least be secure. But I had no idea how to get there. Years ago when we had driven with Roxanna to the Skunk farmhouse, the robot-driver had taken a circuitous route, in a vaguely southwesterly direction, which I had never troubled to learn. In any case, it was not wise to walk along the roads.

I renewed my treks through the nearby woods, searching for a vantage from which I could see the cathedral tower or some other signpost back to civilization. At last, a sign was given to me: a hill rose on the other side of a marsh; on the crest of that hill was an electric power line!

Where there was electricity there, surely, would be Masters.

In 1970 when the Masters had first manifested themselves to mankind, they had insisted that they be given complete authority over all electric plants, dams, dynamos, and radio and television stations. Without in any way interfering with their utility from a human standpoint (indeed, they effected major improvements), the Masters transformed this pre-existent network into a sort of electromagnetic pleasure spa.

In time, of course, their additions and refinements exceeded mere human need or comprehension. What do the cows know of the Muzak playing in their dairybarn, except that it makes them feel good? Human labor could manufacture devices according to the Masters' specification that human understanding would never be able to fathom. But even human labor became obsolete as the Masters—in themselves, a virtually unlimited power supply—stayed on and took things over, setting automatons to do the dirty work, freeing man from the drudgery of the commonplace that had been his perennial complaint. Freeing, at least, those who would accept such freedom—who would, in short, agree to become pets.

Although in many respects the Masters' innovations had superseded the primitive technology of the 1970's, they still maintained (largely for the benefit of ungrateful Dingoes) a modified system of electric power lines, lacing the entire world in arcane geometrical patterns that only the Masters could understand—or maintain.

It was to these high-tension lines that the Masters came to bathe and exercise, and so it was to the power lines that I would take my family. Even if there was no way to reach the Masters as they flowed back and forth in the wires overhead, we could follow the lines to some generator or powerhouse, perhaps the one that adjoined Shroeder, perhaps another elsewhere, for kennels were invariably located near power stations.

Once we reached the power line, it would be safe journeying. No Dingo would dare trespass into the very heart of the Masters' domain.

I rushed to the farm jubilantly, Julie was drawing water at the pump. "Don't run through the garden, Cuddles," she called to me. "We'll need those tomatoes for the winter ahead."

"It makes . . . no difference . . . any more . . . Darling, Julie!" I had run a long way, and breath came hard. "I *found* them! . . . We can go now . . . home again, home again . . . jiggety-jog!"

Stumbling up to Julie I gave her a quick kiss and upended the bucket of water over my head, shuddering deliciously. The cold water seemed to stun every nerve ending into a happy numbness. It felt marvelous—almost like the Leash. Julie stood dumbfounded. I kissed her again.

"You beast, you're soaking wet!"

Clothing does have its inconveniences, the chief of which (once one is used to the discomfort) is absorbency.

"Julie, I found them! I have. We're practically home already." And I explained about the power line and what it meant.

Julie looked meditative. "Well, I guess that means we'll have to leave the farm now."

"Have to! Mastery, Julie, aren't you anxious to be away from here?"

"I don't know. It was coming to seem like our own kennel. It was so nice, so private. And I haven't *started* to learn to cook. Do you know what Petite brought home today? Eggs! We can . . ."

"You want to stay in this wilderness with Dingoes on all sides? Never to be Leashed again? And in this archaic, stinking, ruinous, dirty, foul . . ." Julie began to cry piteously, and I relented, conscious that I had rather overstated the case. "It *would* have been every bit that horrible without you. It *was* nice, Julie, but only on your account. If we go back, I'm sure our Master will let you continue learning to cook. And he'll rig up a much better kitchen than you have here. With an *electric* stove." She brightened, and I pressed my point. "But you know we have to go back. Our Leashes need us. If we stayed here, we'd become no better than Dingoes."

"I suppose you're right. I suppose."

"That's the spirit! Now, how soon can we be ready? You fix something to carry food in. Blankets would do, and at night we'll be able to keep warm. And see if you can't find some shoes that will fit Petite. If we start out early tomorrow, I don't expect we'll spend a night in the open, but just in case . . ."

While Julie improvised knapsacks, I went to the toolshed. There was an ancient weapon there that circumstances had made me uniquely equipped (as it then seemed) to handle—an axe. Not in the flaring Medieval style of St. Bernard's, but lethal enough in its modest way to slice through any number of Dingoes. I found that it was more difficult to throw the thing at a target than it had been at Swan Lake, because the sharp edge of the wedge was as often as not facing in the wrong direction at the moment of impact. However, wielding it by hand I was able to break up armloads of kindling from the broken rafters of the barn. Take that! And that! What ho! What havoc!

Grimly I refined upon the murderous properties of my weapon. I had noticed that the spark-producing machine would put a fine edge on metal that was held against it at the proper angle. After patient experimentation, I had so sharpened the iron blade that the merest touch of it would sliver flesh. Now, I thought, *let* the Dingoes come!

We set off before noon. Though Petite, still believing it was all a game, was amused and talkative, neither of her parents were in such high spirits. Julie was wistful and melancholic at leaving the farm (though she agreed we had no other choice), and I was nervous and apprehensive. From the hill from which I had espied the power line, we struck out into a wood of scrub pine, birch, and balsam. In the woods there was no way to estimate our progress. The sun can be used as a compass and even, in a rough way, as a clock, but it is no speedometer at all. We walked, and when it seemed that we had walked twice, three times the distance to the power line, we kept on walking. Julie became petulant; I became angry. Then she grew angry and I sulked. But always while we were walking. The brush caught at our pants' legs and the mud at the edge of the marshes about which we were forced to detour sucked at our boots. And we walked. Petite, riding pickaback on my shoulders, was having a world of fun slapping the mosquitoes that landed on my forehead. And still we walked.

The sun, striated by long, low, wispy clouds, hung huge and crimson at the horizon behind us; before us a pale sliver of moon peeped over the crest of a hill—and on the hill, black against the indigo of the sky, stood the power line.

Julie dropped her pack and ran up the hill. "Masters!" she cried. "Masters, we've come! Leash us. Make us yours again. Bring us home."

The power line stood stark and immobile, wires swaying gently in the breeze. Julie embraced the wooden pole and screamed at the unhearing wires: "Master, your pets have come back to you. We love you! MASTER!"

"They don't hear you," I said softly. "If they could hear you, they would come."

Julie stood up, squaring her shoulders bravely, and joined me where I had remained at the foot of the hill. There were no tears in her eyes. But her lips were pressed together in a mirthless, unbecoming smile. "I hate them," she pronounced clearly. "With my whole being, I hate them!" Then she fell into my arms in a dead faint.

Petite stayed awake to keep me company through the early hours of the evening. We listened to the nightsounds of animals and birds and tried to guess what they were. At about nine o'clock by the moon, a complete and utter silence enveloped the land.

"Now that's strange," I observed.

"What's strange, Papa?"

"That when the crickets are quiet, there's no sound at all. Not a scrap. Aren't wires supposed to *hum?* To make some small noise? These don't. I think they may be dead."

"Dead?" echoed Petite. "Are the Masters dead? Will the Dingoes eat us now? Will they let me go to the bathroom first? Because when I get scared . . ."

"No, Pete sweet. The *wires* are dead, not the Masters. The Masters will never die. Don't you remember what I told you the other day about God?"

"But that was *God.*"

"Same difference, darling. Now you go to sleep. Your Papa was just thinking aloud and your Mommy was only pretending to be afraid. You know Mommy likes to pretend."

"But why didn't God come down from the electric poles when Mommy asked?"

"Maybe this line isn't in use, honey. Maybe it's broken. Tomorrow we're going to walk down the line and find out. Anyhow I was probably wrong about the noise. That could be just a superstition that wires hum, and only Dingoes are superstitious. The Masters probably can't hear us through all the insulation on the wires. What would they be listening for way out here, anyhow? We'll find our way to a nice kennel tomorrow, Petite, don't you worry."

Petite fell asleep then, but I could not. Great shafts of light streamed from the northern horizon. They glowed whitely in the black sky, dimming the stars as they shot out, dissolved, reformed.

The Northern Lights. Aurora Borealis.

It was there especially that the Masters loved to play and relax. They felt at home among the electrons of the Van Allen belt, and where it curved in to touch the Earth's atmosphere at the magnetic poles they followed it, controlling the ionization of the air, structuring those pillars of light that men have always wondered at to conform to the elaborate rules of their supravisual geometry. These shifting patterns were the supreme delight of the Masters, and it was precisely because Earth, of all the planets in the solar system, possessed the strongest Van Allen belt that they had originally been drawn to this planet. They had only bothered to concern themselves with mankind after a number of nuclear explosions had been set off in the Van Allen belt in the 1960's.

The aurora that night was incredibly beautiful, and so I knew that the Masters were still on Earth, living and flaming for their pets— their poor, lost maltreated pets—to see.

But it was a cold flame and very remote. I drew small comfort from it.

"Your courteous lights in vain you waste," I muttered.

Julie, who has always been a light sleeper, stirred. "I'm sorry," she mumbled, probably too sleepy still to remember why she was supposed to be sorry.

"It's all right. We'll find them tomorrow," I said, "and tomorrow and tomorrow." Julie smiled and slid by imperceptible degrees back into sleep.

The next day we followed the lines to the north. They ran along beside an old asphalt road, scarred with fissures and upheavals, but still easier to travel than the rank brush on either side. We moved slower since I had found that my knees would no longer support the double burden of a knapsack and Petite, and we were obliged to match our pace against hers.

A faded sign gave the distance to Shroeder as twelve miles. Using the road (for the wires overhead were sufficient protection, as we thought, against the Dingoes), we could hope to reach the kennel by midafternoon. Regularly we passed deserted farmhouses set back from the road and, twice, the road widened and the ruins of houses were set closer together: a town. Here the wires would branch off in all directions, but the main power line followed its single course toward Shroeder. The poles were of rough pine, stained to reddish-brown by creosote, one just like another, until . . .

Julie noticed it as we were on the outskirts of Shroeder. Running up and down the poles were thin silvery lines that glinted metallically in the sunlight. On closer inspection these lines could be

seen to form vertical chains of decorative elements in simple, repeating patterns. One common design consisted of overlapping circles linked in series by straight lines, so:

Another was a single zigzag pattern:

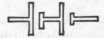

The most frequent design resembled a circuiting diagram of dry
cells in series:

In fact they were all circuiting diagrams.

It was too crude decoratively and such nonsense from any other
viewpoint that I knew it could not be the work of the Masters. There
was something barbaric about these markings that smelt of Dingoes!

But what Dingo would dare approach this near the sanctuary of
the Masters? The Kennel must be only a few hundred yards off. I
began to have misgivings about our security. Before I could properly
begin to savor this danger, another, and graver, had presented itself.

"Cuddles!" Julie screamed. "Gods and Masters, look! The
power station!"

I scooped up Petite and was at Julie's side instantly. A cyclone
fence that ran some hundred feet along the road prevented our entrance to the power station, but it made no difference, for it was
nothing but a rubble heap now. I-beams, gnarled and twisted like
the limbs of denuded oaks, showed in gruesome silhouette against
the light blue of the summer sky. The pylons that had fed the high-
tension wires into the substation lay on the ground like metal
Goliaths, quite dead. The wires that had led out from the station
had been snapped and hung inert from the top of the cyclone fence,
where now and again a breeze would stir them. All, all defunct.

"It's been *bombed*," I said, "and that's impossible."

"The Dingoes?" Petite asked.

"I daresay. But how *could* they?"

It made no sense. So primitive an attack as this could not succeed against the Mastery when the whole rich arsenal of twentieth-century science had failed. Oh, the nuclear blasts in the Van Allen belt had *annoyed* them, but I doubted then and I doubt now whether man has it in his power actually to kill one of the Masters.

How could it be done? How do you fight something without dimensions, without even known equations that might give some symbolic approximation of their character? Not, surely, by bombing minor power stations here and there; not even by bombing all of them. As well hope to kill a lion with a thistle. The Masters transcended mere technology.

Inside the fence, from somewhere in the tangle of gutted machinery, there was a moan. A woman's voice reiterated the single word: Masters, Masters . . ."

"That's no Dingo," Julie said. "Some poor pet is caught in there. Cuddles, do you realize this means all the pets have been abandoned?"

"Hush! You'll only make Petite cry with talk like that."

We made our way through a hole in the fence sheared open by a falling pylon. Kneeling a few feet from that hole, her face turned away from us, was the moaning woman. She was using the blasted crossbeam of the pylon as a sort of *prie-dieu*. Her hair, though tangled and dirty, still showed traces of domestication. She was decently naked, but her flesh was discolored by bruises and her legs were badly scratched. Confronted with this pathetic ruin of a once-handsome pet, I realized for the first time how terribly *wild* Julie looked: dressed in the most vulgar clothes, her hair wound up in a practical but inartistic bun and knotted with strips of cloth, her lovely feet encased in clumsy rubber boots. We must have looked like Dingoes.

The poor woman stopped moaning and turned to confront us. By slow degrees her expression changed from despair to blank amazement. "Father!" she said, aghast.

"Roxanna!" I exclaimed. "Is it you?"

Chapter 6

*In which I defend a woman's honor, and with
what dire consequence.*

It was nobody else. She was rather thinner now than she had been;
time had encroached upon her beauty to that degree that one could
not, with the best will in the world, mistake her for eighteen—or
even for twenty-eight. But her nose and her glance and her intelligence—these were still as sharp as they had ever been. No doubt
of it, this was Roxanna Proust, née Skunk.

Roxanna, for her part, was not as readily convinced that, quite
contrary to being her father, I was only her little White Fang, her
former disciple, grown now to a man's estate.

"But those clothes . . ." she insisted. "I'd know that jacket anywhere, with the missing bottom button. And those boots with the red
circles around the rim. And a week's growth of beard. It's my father
to the life!"

Out of courtesy I removed my jacket, but I was reluctant to
remove my pants for some reason. Perhaps clothes are the cause of
modesty, rather than, as Genesis would have it, the other way
around. Briefly as I could, I explained to Roxanna how our Master
had brought us to the farm and from there deserted us, and how we
had to take clothes from the farmhouse to make our journey—her
parents' clothes, as it happened.

"And Pluto and your mother—you say they came with you?"
Roxanna asked, scrunching up those shrewd wrinkles of hers inquir-
ingly. "Where are *they* now?"

"I was hoping *you* might know, Roxanna. I thought Pluto might have seen fit to pay you a visit. I know that he sends you each new book he does."

"No. No, it must not have occurred to him. This is the first I've heard of your being here. But what"—her expression underwent a subtle change, as though she had begun to make calculations—"a delightful surprise it is!"

Here the conversation lapsed awkwardly, for Julie and I did not wish to show ourselves boorishly concerned only with our own problems when Roxanna herself was in such evident distress, and Roxanna for her part seemed to be occupied with some private debate.

"Have you read *The Prayers for Investments?*" Julie asked after this embarrassing silence. "All Swan Lake is certain it's Pluto's best thing to date. They say his new ceremonies are absolutely *compulsive.*"

"I started it, but I couldn't seem to . . . make much sense of it. So often, I find that . . . these modern writers, as I've observed . . . although Proust, however . . ." She trailed off vaguely and began absentmindedly to rub her bony, bare thighs. I noticed that her skin was covered with small black-and-blue marks, chiefly on her thighs and lower torso. The marks were too tiny to have resulted from blows, too numerous to be accidental.

She sighed deeply, a sign expressive of more than the grinding ennui of life at Shroeder, of more than even the loss of her Master. It was an inexpressibly sad sound, yet at the same time perversely pleasurable. "The brute!" she whispered, not for our ears. "The filthy, f—brute!"

Then, as though this had all occurred in one mighty parenthesis, she returned to her earlier theme. "If the truth be known, I read much less of late than once I did. Even Proust, even he, doesn't have the same—whatever it was he did have. No, not even Proust . . ." This speech, too, died away in a whisper, so that by the end it was not quite certain whether the last word was *Proust* or a repetition of *the brute.* "And then, of course, there's been this revolution. And it's hard to concentrate on reading, with a revolution going on all about one."

"Ah yes," I said, "the revolution. Would you tell us something about that?"

Roxanna's account was none too clear, having been assembled

from eavesdropped conversations and uninformed conjectures. Even the word *revolution* proved to be misleading. Further, her whole account was interlarded with such a quantity of sighs and imprecations, laments and curses, that a full transcription would be an excess of verisimilitude. Therefore, I've written here not the garbled story Roxanna told us that afternoon but the facts as they were later to be established by the courts and newspapers.

July had been a month of unusual sunspot activity. The Masters, anticipating the dynamic auroral displays that follow such periods, had flocked to Earth—many, like our Master, bringing their pets with them. Shortly after our arrival, during the afternoon that Julie and I had been unleashed, a solar prominence of extraordinary intensity had erupted from the center of a sunspot cluster and knocked the Masters out of commission.

It was like a house that's been totally electrified. Everything was plugged in: the refrigerators, the stove, the air conditioner, the iron, the toaster, the coffeepot, the floodlights, the television and the model railroad in the basement. When BLAT! lightning strikes, and there's one hell of a short-circuit. Lights out, tubes popped, wires fused, motors dead. The Masters weren't dead, of course. They're made of stronger stuff than toasters. But while they convalesced . . .

Roxanna herself had been spared the worst of it, since she'd been sitting on the cathedral steps when the lights went out. But she'd seen it happen. In a flash (literally, a flash) the entire kennel—walls, floors, even the stores of food and sporting equipment—had disappeared. It was as though they had existed only as an idea in the mind of God, and then God had gone off and forgotten that idea. Pets who had been soaring along slipstreams in the vast spaces of the gymnasium soared now in vaster spaces. Everyone who had been in the upper floors of the kennel buildings suddenly found himself plunging down to the ground, overpowered by Earth's gravity, accelerating. For the fortunate, like Roxanna, it had meant only a sore behind or a sprained ankle. Others died.

The carnage had been terrible. The Shroeder Kennel, what was left of it, was thrown into panic. But the worst was still before them. The Dingoes, quicker to realize what had happened than the distracted pets, had overrun the breeding farms and kennels everywhere. In the first fire of insurrectionary excitement, they were ruthless. Puppies were taken from their mothers, to be raised in the dens of Dingoes; the men, any who resisted, were ruthlessly slaughtered before the eyes of their mates, and the poor bitches . . . Well, what would one expect of Dingoes?

At this point Roxanna broke into tears, quite unable to carry on with even the semblance of a chronology. "Oh, the brute!" she wailed. "Oh, you've no idea how I *hate* him! When he saw me that night, he had two of his minions take me to his tent, and then—it was so awful! The things I was forced to do! The abasement! Oh, I could *poison* him! The brute! But he doesn't give me a chance. Oh, when I think . . . If you only *knew* . . ." As this diatribe continued, Roxanna's hands rubbed ever more frenziedly across the scant flesh of her thighs, dark with a multitude of those curious pinpoint bruises. "Remember, when I told you, years and years ago, about my parents? How my father would go into town on Saturday night and return all tanked up? The beatings he gave my poor mother? How I would listen at the register upstairs? How I wanted to *see* them! But now I know! Because *he's* just the same. Another brute. A vicious, ignorant, smelling, loutish *brute!*"

All in all, it took Roxanna the better part of an hour to tell this story, for she had a way of breaking into passionate denunciations or veering off into a digression that would have been the delight of any admirer of *Tristram Shandy*. For my own part, I am inclined to be more straightforward. In fact, her divagations began to distress me considerably as soon as I realized that the vicinity was still swarming with armed Dingoes, and that Roxanna was living at Shroeder in bondage to the chief of them. Bruno Schwarzkopf!

"Roxanna," I said, trying to raise her to her feet, "Julie and I are going to help you *escape* from him. We'll take you back to the farm. No one will look there. But we'd better start right away. We've wasted too much time sitting about and talking to no purpose."

"It's too late," Roxanna said with a sigh in which the resignation was not unmixed with a certain self-satisfaction. "It's already too late."

Too long allegiance to the authority of Proust had finally taken its toll on Roxanna's character, and though I may anticipate my story by mentioning the word here, I should like to say it this once and have done: Roxanna, sadly, was something of a masochist.

"Roxanna," I said, more firmly now, "you *must* come with us."

"Get your own bitch, Mister," came a good-natured bellow of a voice from not too far away. With a sinking heart I faced the in-

truder, a red-faced, bow-legged, asymmetrical knot of flesh in khakis
crusted with mud and grease. He stood on the other side of the
fence, arms akimbo, exposing several ill-formed, decay-blackened
teeth in the sort of grin I have since been told is "well-meaning."
Though not much more than five feet tall, his chest and arms
seemed thick almost to deformity. He held what looked like a glass
fishing rod in one meaty hand.

"The name's Schwarzkopf, Mister. Bruno Schwarzkopf, and I'm
the head of the RIC in these parts. We're repatriating these damned
pets. Now, come on home, Rocky old girl. You know what I told
you about sniffing up to other dogs." He laughed, rather the way a
bull would laugh, if bulls laughed.

So this was a Dingo! This wretched, misformed runt. All these
years of dread—and now at the moment of confrontation it was
nothing much worse than a genetic prank. I allowed my just wrath
to swell luxuriously. "You are not Roxanna's Master, and she is not
going with you."

"The hell you say!"

"Please," Roxanna implored. "I must go to him now." But her
body didn't protest; she was limp with fear. I pushed her behind me
and picked up my axe from the ground. *That* should send him running, I thought confidently.

His smile broadened. "What's with you, pal? Are you some kind
of goddamned pet? Or what?"

"Dingo!" I said, eloquent with contempt. "Defend yourself!"

Bruno reached a hand behind his back and made adjustments on
an apparatus strapped there. It was the size of one of our knapsacks.
Then he climbed through the hole in the fence, brandishing the long,
flexible pole.

"Axes!" he scoffed. "The next thing you know, somone's going
to invent the bow and arrow.

I advanced toward the Dingo, who stood within the fence now,
my axe at the ready and murder in my heart, as they say. With my
left hand I held to the metal frame of the fallen pylon, using it as a
crutch. My knees were very weak, which I am told is not unusual in
such circumstances.

Bruno flicked the end of the glass fishing rod against the pylon.
There was a spark, and my mind reeled.

I was sitting on the ground. I could see Bruno's black-toothed grin above me between white flashes of unconsciousness. I swung at his face wildly. The axe hit the pylon with a dull *thunk*.

He flicked the pole at me again. It touched my left leg at the knee. The shock tore through my body and wrenched a cry from my lips.

"Good stuff, huh, Jack? Great for the circulation. If you're interested in mechanical things, it's real easy to make. It's a prod pole. Prod poles are meant for cattle, but they work even better on smaller animals."

He flicked it again, tracing a line of pain across my neck. I screamed in agony—I couldn't help it.

"The fishpole was my idea. Handles easier this way."

He let the tip of the pole play over my right arm. Every shred of consciousness that remained to me was in my hand. I clenched the axe handle until the pain in my hand was worse than the flashes of pain that tore through my whole body—until there was no consciousness left.

When I woke—seconds later? minutes? I don't know—I could hear Roxanna's hysterical laughter. Bruno had finished with her. Julie's voice, pitched so high that I could hardly recognize it, was saying *Stay away!* and then, still more shrilly, *Stay away from my daughter!*

There was a sparkling sound, and Petite's scream. "White Fang!" Julie called. "Oh, Mastery—*White Fang!*"

She had called me *that!* Not Cuddles, not Prometheus. But White Fang!

I sprang to my feet, and the axe was just part of my hand now. I felt, as never before, even when I was Leashed, totally alive and aware, absolutely sure of myself. My body was a living flame. Wow!

Bruno had ceased to torment Petite and had caught hold of Julie. He heard me scrambling over the wreckage of the station and turned around just in time for the axe to come crashing down across his chest.

I hadn't meant to draw blood. I didn't dare to. I had only wanted to smash the power pack strapped on his back.

There was a terrible gush of blood from the chest wound, thick and winy. The axe in my hand was covered with blood. It was horrible. I had never seen anyone bleeding like this before, never. It was a hundredfold worse than the injuries I'd done Pluto or St. Bernard.

It was horrible! The blood.

Convulsed with vomiting, I collapsed onto Bruno's fallen body. The last thing I remember was Roxanna's tear-streaked face as she rushed forward to take the fallen Dingo in her arms.

In these days of P(BLAT)eril and P(BLAT)ossibility . . . Whenever the speaker enunciated a *P,* the public address system erupted into a horrible crepitant noise: *P(BLAT)!*

The crowd roared.

Hands tied, feet bound, I wiggled up in the back seat for a better view. We were moving down a city street at no more than five miles per hour through such a concentration of Dingoes that my immediate response was to wish myself unconscious again, the smell was so terrific.

Yes—P(BLAT)ossibility!   Another   oP(BLAT)ortunity   to hoP(BLAT)e once more—for the Inductance Corps! P(BLAT)rovidence has ordained it, and . . .

The speaker's voice (which issued from a metal horn on the hood of the jeep) was drowned by the swelling anthem that the swarm of Dingoes about us raised and that the resonating masses further along the parade route caught up and amplified:

> Diode! Triode!
> Highest Cathode!
> Charge our hearts with a hundred amps!
> Guard our ohms and light our camps
> With the burning of your lamps!
> As we chant this ode
> To Victory,
> Be thou still our goad
> To Victory!
> Guide us on the road
> To Victory!
> Hurray!

Though Julie was in the back seat with me, an armed Dingo sat between us and discouraged our conversation with little pokes of his rifle butt. I was able to pantomime the question that concerned me most: "Petite?" But Julie could only give an anguished shrug and shake her head in reply.

"Where are we going?" I asked the Dingo guard. He answered with his rifle butt against my lower ribs. "Where are we now?" The rifle butt seemed not to know. I retired into a philosophic silence.

At the end of the anthem the loudspeaker renewed its own patriotic cacophony: *But we must grasp this oP(BLAT)ortunity! Only B(BLAT)lood and sweat and toil and tears can P(BLAT)ay the P(BLAT)rice that history demands of us . . .*

A woman rushed from the frenzied crowd through which the jeep was bulldozing its way. She threw a bouquet into my face and followed it as well as she could with herself. "Give 'em hell, boy!" she shouted between kisses. "Give 'em hell!" she was still screaming as the men in khaki were dragging her away. I had the distinct feeling that had she known me for what I was—a pet—she would have been less friendly, though perhaps no less demonstrative. Fortunately, the driver of the jeep, a Major of the so-called Inductance Corps, had had the foresight to wrap me in his overcoat, which offered almost as effective protection as invisibility.

The parade terminated at a makeshift airport, once a city park, where a Ford Trimotor was warming its engine at the end of a rough gravel runway. As our jeep pulled up to the plane, we could see a stretcher being loaded into the cabin under Roxanna's fretful supervision.

"You brute!" she called out above the hiccoughing of the plane's motors, as soon as she caught sight of me. When Bruno was stowed aboard and we were being led on at gunpoint, Roxanna developed her theme with more imagination. "Axe-murderer! Fiend! Judas! They've got your number *now,* boy! They'll take care of you! I only wish I could do it with my own two hands. But I did what I could— I told them who you were—who your father was. Tennyson White! You should have seen the faces they made! And now they're going to do for you what they did for him—and for the Manglesnatch statue. Ha!" The driver of the jeep began pulling her back. "Send me his ear, officer. And hers too. And their bones: I'll grind their bones to make my bread!"

When we were at last safely (so to speak) aboard the plane and the hatch was closed, the guard assured us it would be nothing so awful as Roxanna had suggested. "You'd think we wasn't civilized, the way she talks. Hanging's the worst that can happen, you know. We've got a gallows out front of the courthouse in St. Paul can hang *five* at a time. Christ almighty, you should see that! Oh, sweet Jesus!

But don't you believe any of her bull about cutting folks up in pieces. There ain't none of *that* . . . any more."

"Could you tell me, please," I asked of him (for he seemed to be in a better mood now than he'd been in the jeep), "where my daughter is?"

"The little girl? That lady back there's taking care of her. She asked to be the foster-mother, and so . . ."

"Petite! With that ogress? No!" Julie struggled against her bonds, while the plane began to taxi down the runway. "You have to stop this machine. I must have my daughter back!" When the plane was off the ground, even Julie could see the futility of further complaint.

The declining sun, scarcely five degrees above the horizon, was visible through the right-hand windows of the cabin, so I knew we were flying south. It seemed probable that so minuscule an aircraft could accomplish only a few hundred miles without having to touch down for fuel. I knew there were important kennels in that direction —Anoka, St. Cloud, etc.—but I had never paid any attention to the geography of the Dingoes' settlements. But the guard had mentioned one city—"St. Paul."

"What will happen when we get to St. Paul?" I asked. "Will we be released then? Or held in a dungeon?"

The guard laughed. He didn't bother to explain the joke.

"Shall I be tried in court? I demand a jury of my peers! I'm innocent. Julie witnessed it. I didn't mean to . . ."

As though in reproof, the guard walked to the front of the small cabin to examine Bruno. I was left to stare out the window at the laboring propellers and wish desperately for a Master to assist them at their rustic task.

The guard was called up front to confer with the pilot, and I tried to comfort Julie with hollow reassurances. It was almost a relief when the erratic behavior of the plane (how can the air be *bumpy?*) took our attention from the longer-range anxieties and focused it on the existential moment, now. The guard returned to announce that the left-hand propeller had failed and the right-hand was going. The plane was losing altitude (though I couldn't understand how he knew that, since it was perfectly dark and there was no way to judge). I had to help him jettison various complicated metal do-jiggers out the open hatch. The plane (we were told) regained altitude, but it continued to make arhythmic gaspings and grindings. The guard made us get into parachutes and showed us how they worked. One only had to jump, count ten, pull the little ring out, and wait to see if it would work.

"Have you ever done it?" I asked the guard as we stood looking out the open hatch at the black nothingness below.

"Yeah, once. It was no picnic."

"But it did work? It *usually* works?"

"Yeah. The danger isn't so much in its not opening. It's how you land. You can break a leg easy, and if you get caught in a bad wind—"

"Good-bye, Darling, Julie!" I shouted. "Wait for me. I'll rescue you as soon as I possibly can."

And then I was falling, the plane wasn't above me, only its fading noise. The stars vanished as I fell through cloudbanks. I counted to five, and I *couldn't* think what came next, so I pulled the string, the chute opened, the strap across my chest tightened and pulled me upright, and for a couple of minutes I had nothing to do but swing back and forth lazily in my lattice of straps and regret my hasty derring-do. For all I knew I was over an ocean!

Landing, I knocked my coccyx against some intractable concrete and twisted my ankle. All about me the floodlights switched on, and voices shouted contradictory orders.

"An excellent landing, sir. An as-*ton*-ishing landing, I would say. I hope you're quite all right?" The man who addressed me was wearing an overcoat similar to my own. He had great white Franz-Josef moustaches and supported himself on an ornately carved walking stick. I had never seen so wrinkled a face, except in reproductions of Rembrandts.

"Oh, quite," I replied. "Whom do I have the honor of addressing?"

His hand came up in a stiff salute. "Captain Frangle, sir. I'm commander of this here peniten-itentiary, sir."

"Peniten-itentiary?"

"Well, that's what we used to call it. What's the word now? There's so many new words for things, I tend to forget one here and one there. Repatriation center—that's it! For the goddamned pets, you know."

Chapter 7

In which I stand in debt to N. Gogol.

Let us say nothing of frying pans and fires. Let us say nothing of probabilities. To have parachuted smackdab into the middle of the enemy's camp (and the neatest bomb could not have dropped on its target more truly than I had, by blind chance) is an event so deficient in probability that only the incontrovertible fact of its having happened can ease my embarrassment in relating it. In fiction such a coincidence would be inexcusable; in *history* these things happen all the time.

So, to return to *la chose véritable* . . .

"You have been," I asked, hesitatingly, "expecting me?"

Captain Frangle twirled a moustache craftily. "There have been rumors . . . a word dropped here, and a word there . . . Nothing you can put your finger on, you understand . . . nothing explicit, but nevertheless."

"Rumors, you say? Exactly what sort of rumors?"

"Oh—*vague* rumors, sir! Extremely vague and indistinct. Almost unbelievable, but nevertheless . . ." And the Captain winked knowingly.

"Nevertheless?" I insisted.

"What I meant to say was—nevertheless, here you are, you see. Which shows, I think, that there must have been something in the rumors after all. Then again, perhaps not. Far be it from *me* to say, one way or the other. You would certainly know better than *I*, Major. He trailed off into a laugh of consummate self-deprecation.

Then, turning to two of his underlings who had been gathering up the folds of the parachute, he bade them hurry up with their work— in quite opposite tones.

Now fortunately I was at that time well enough acquainted with "The Inspector General," that splendid comedy by the Russian master, Nikolai Gogol, to suspect a certain congruence between the situation of Gogol's hero and my own plight. The eagle on the shoulder of my borrowed overcoat had apparently deceived Captain Frangle into thinking I was his superior officer; it also seemed that he had been anticipating the visit of a senior officer—and not with relish. For the time being I could hope to keep up the bluff, but it was not an imposture that could be maintained indoors, for beneath my overcoat and rubber boots I was naked as Laocoön.

"A cup of coffee, Major? Or if you prefer something more . . . spirited? Eh? Something to bring color to the cheek and a smile to . . . Eh? That is to say, if you don't *object* to a glass . . . or two? Eh? All the while, Captain Frangle was edging toward a lighted doorway at the corner of the compound.

"A few questions first, Captain, if you don't mind."

"By all means, sir! Abso-*lute*-ly! We've nothing to hide from *you*, sir. Our hearts . . . and our hands . . . are as open for your inspections as if . . . and, if you wish, our pocket-books, too! Only joking, you understand, but feel free, Major. Make yourself right at home in our little penitentiary here."

"How many officers are here beside yourself? And how many guards?"

"Officers? Well, Lieutenant Mosely, of course. Good man, Mosely. You've already met him, I think, when you were at the Shroeder evacuation."

"Oh yes, *Mosely*. Where *is* Mosely?"

"He was in the shower when you landed. I suppose he's getting dressed. He should be out here any minute now. And you might count Palmino. He's only a warrant officer, but he runs the radio shack and keeps the generator working for us. We couldn't get on very well without Palmino, I'm afraid. Though he's not really a gentleman . . . not like you and me, Major. And then there's Doc Quilty and the Reverend Captain. The Reverend Captain will probably want to discuss a matter of religion with you, sir. About these goddamned pets. You see, *he* thinks they should all be Baptists . . . now, understand, I have nothing *against* Baptists . . . some of my best friends are . . . you know? But the shock—that's what I object to . . . all that *current!* I mean . . ."

"Later, Captain. How many guards?"

"No doubt you've seen my last memo on that subject. There is nothing to add. The situation has only become worse: desertions, betrayal, sabotage . . . I need guards to guard the guards, and that's a fact. You see, now that the shouting's over, now that the monotony's setting in again, all the volunteers are . . . you know? And only the regulars—the old Corps members, like myself . . ."

"I didn't ask for excuses, Captain. Only for a number."

"Hundred and twenty. Less. I think. You see, sir, I can explain, if . . ."

"A hundred and twenty? For how many pets?"

"I'm not sure of the exact number. It changes all the time. I don't understand. But this prison was never meant to accommodate . . ."

"Captain! The number!" This in my most peremptory tone.

"Thirteen thousand, sir. Give or take a few hundred."

"One guard for every hundred pets! How do you keep them under control?"

"Oh, that's no problem. I could probably get by with ten guards if I had to. They're only pets, after all. It's not as if . . . I mean, they aren't like *us*. They don't seem quite . . . what is the word . . . *human?* They know their place, and they keep in it. And then, you know, they're in pretty poor spirits, thinking that their Masters have sold them back to us for slaves."

"Slaves! The Masters? But that isn't so?"

"Of course, it isn't *lit*-erally true, but how are *they* to know? Eh?" Captain Frangle had recovered some of his earlier bounciness now that the worst of the interrogation seemed to be over, and he began edging back toward the open doorway.

"Captain Frangle, I did not give you permission to leave me!"

"No sir! I only thought . . . that is, wouldn't *you* be more comfortable?"

"Don't concern yourself with my comfort, Mister! I am interested solely in the management of this repatriation center. Or should I say *mis*management? I suspect, Captain . . . I suspect . . ."

Captain Frangle had come tremblingly to attention, and he listened to my improvised diatribe with visible dread. "Suspect, sir? May I ask what? May I ask . . . who?

"Ha! Do you think I shall reveal *that* so easily? It would make it

altogether too easy for you, sir. Or, if not for you, then for whoever
has been . . . responsible . . . for these crimes."

"Not me! No, you've been misinformed about . . . The petty cash
is short, perhaps, I don't know . . . I would have to examine . . . it
may take *days* . . . and another thing, I have my own way of bookkeeping . . . a safer way, I must explain it to you first . . ."

"*First,* Captain, I would like you to assemble *all* the guards in this
compound. Where I can see them. See that Lieutenant What's-His-
Name looks after that."

"Lieutenant Mosely."

"Him, yes. And I wish the barracks and rooms to be left in *exactly* the condition they're in now. The men will assemble here in
their *shorts*. And in stocking feet. The officers as well. See to it,
Captain!"

While Captain Frangle roused up those few guards who had not
already been roused by the news of my so-sudden arrival, I withdrew into the shadows and deliberated my next steps. When all
guards and the four other officers were present in ranks before me, I
had Captain Frangle show me to the door of the barracks.

"Mosely's room is in this building?"

"The next floor up, sir. His name is on the door."

"And *your* room, Captain?"

"I have the third floor to myself. I must explain . . . before you
go up there . . . that not everything you may find up there is what
you would call, in the strict sense, mine. I'm holding some articles in
safekeeping for friends in town . . . citizens who were afraid of the
anarchists, the vandals, you understand how it's been . . ."

"You will return to your men, Captain Frangle, and see that they
remain at attention. I do not tolerate laxity. There will be no conversations out there, not even among the officers."

"Just as you say, sir."

"Before you go, Captain—your uniform. Leave it on that . . ."
What was the word? I couldn't remember the word! ". . . on that
. . . thing there."

"The bunk, you mean? But, Major, consider my position—my
dignity. What will the men think if they see me out there in my dirty
. . . that is to say, in the same state they're in?"

"Perhaps you're right."

"Oh, thank you, Major, I knew you'd understand." Captain Frangle began to leave, but once more I brought him up short.

"I didn't give permission to go, Captain. I must still insist on a complete inspection. But you may submit to it *here* instead of in the presence of your men. I expect to find you undressed by the time I've returned from my inspection upstairs." With these words (which guaranteed that, for the time being, the Captain would not have any opportunity to converse with Mosely or anyone else who might have regarded my imposture with a keener eye) I turned my back on the Captain and went up a spiral staircase to the next floor.

Lieutenant Mosley's room showed a pedantic respect for military punctilio. The walls were daubed the same drab olive as the metal bedposts and wall locker. The uniforms inside the locker were arrayed as if for an inspection. After assuring myself of complete privacy, I took down his best dress uniform and pulled on the trousers. The Lieutenant, fortunately, had a good figure, and the pants fit reasonably well. His shirt proved to be a little loose at the collar, but I was able to correct that by tightening the tie.

The tie! That was nearly the death of my whole scheme. I had never worn a tie in my life, and if I had, I certainly would not have been obliged to tie it myself. I tried to improvise a knot or two, but nothing I could manage bore any resemblance to what I had seen about Frangle's neck. Desperately I emptied out Mosely's footlocker, hoping there might be a preknotted tie there. Instead, I found his Manual of Arms, where on page 58 there are instructions for the approved military four-in-hand. As the alarm clock on the window sill ticked off the minutes, I fumbled with the maddening piece of silk. At last it passed muster (Lax muster.) By then I was in such a state of frazzlement that I nearly forgot to remove the silver bars from the shoulders of Mosely's jacket and replace them with the gold oak leaf from the overcoat I had been wearing. Then I tried to squeeze into Mosely's parade shoes.

No go. They were sizes too small. I tried in the next room. (*Capt. C. Quilty, M.D.,* the placard on the door announced.) Quilty's shoes, though nowhere near so well polished, fit snugly. I left Mosely's shoes in Quilty's locker to cover up my theft.

As a finishing touch, I retrieved a ragged copy of *G.I. Jokes* from the tumble of personal items that had fallen out of the footlocker. Then, smartly turned out in dress uniform, I returned to the dismantled, dismayed Captain Frangle on the floor below.

"I've found what I sought, Captain. You may dress and accompany me back to the compound."

Outside Captain Frangle was able to obtain silence (and they were supposed to be at attention!) by lifting one hand. After he'd given them appropriate hell, I had him place Lieutenant Mosely under arrest. His hands were cuffed, his feet shackled, and his mouth securely gagged.

"I have in my right hand," I then announced in my stagiest voice, "evidence that this man, known to you as Mosely, is in reality an imposter, a spy, an agent and a tool of the Mastery. The High Command first grew suspicious of him at Shroeder, when he was seen to go alone into the bombed power station there . . ." A gasp went up among the men. "Captain, do you have a stone wheel—or something equally suitable for starting a fire!"

"I have a cigarette lighter."

"Set this so-called 'jokebook' on fire, please. What harm has been done cannot be undone, but the enemy shall not receive *this* report, at least. Pray God we have stopped their plot in time."

While the jokebook burned, Lieutenant Mosely struggled against his bonds and went: *Mmmph! Mmmph! Nn! Nn! Mmmmph!*

"Captain, I presume you have a cell where this man may be kept to await trial in solitary confinement?"

"We do, but there are ten pets locked in there now. We're filled up . . . right to the brim, as I explained before, but of course . . . if you say . . ."

"Put the pets elsewhere. Mosely is to be kept strictly incommunicado. He will receive bread and water twice a day—under my personal supervision. The man is known to be devilishly persuasive. We can't take chances. As for his room, I shall take that for myself. There may be other documents secreted there."

"Yes, sir. Will that be all, sir? May I release the men?"

"Not just yet. I must see Mosely put away, and then I'd like you to accompany me on a tour of the prison itself. If I wait till tomorrow the whole point of this inspection may have been lost. I trust you take my meaning, Captain?"

"Perfectly," the old man assured me. "Like crystal." But truth to tell, he did look a bit puzzled.

It was easy enough to put it in terms he *did* understand. "And *then,* my good Captain, you may explain your system of bookkeeping." Which Frangle understood perfectly, like crystal.

Such is the wonder of military discipline that the guards remained at attention out in the compound until two A.M. and were quiet as churchmice all the while. Meanwhile I dined (the best meal I'd had since coming to Earth and the most heartily appreciated of my life), then with Frangle at my side took a leisurely tour of the prison. It was . . .

Unspeakable: the crowding; close, fetid air; inadequate sanitary facilities. Since the meager electric current produced by the prison's own emergency generators was required for the operation of the security system, the only light in the cellblock was what leaked in through the barred windows. The place was as gloomy as the Dark Ages. Miseries heaped upon miseries, tier upon tier. And this was only a *single* cellblock!

"How many more are there of these?"

"Besides this, nine."

After I'd gone past only a few of the cells, playing the beam of a flashlight over those sad heaps of still-proud bodies (so much finer than the ramshackle flesh of the guards standing outside), meeting their anguished, pleading gazes, I felt the bottom drop out. Pity consumed me, and rage seemed close behind. Often, the puppies, less perfectly in control, would come to the bars and stretch out their little hands for food. Captain Frangle would slap them away with an indignant bellow. I am ashamed to say that I tolerated his behavior, for I was still afraid he would construe my humanitarian impulses as being un-Dingolike, and begin to suspect . . .

"Oh sir," one of the puppies begged, "can't you spare a scrap of food? For pity's sake, sir, some food!"

"Food? You'll get food, you little sonofabitch! You'll taste this *fist* if you don't lie back down there. Food? If you're hungry you have only your father to blame—if you know who *that* is. There's plenty enough food outside these walls for them as are willing to gather it up."

This seemed to exceed the reasonable limits of abuse, and I said as much.

"But it *is* their fault, Major, if you'll forgive my saying so. We've sent out work parties of hundreds of men to take in the harvests from the abandoned farms around here. It's August, and that food is rotting away. The birds are eating it up, but these goddamned pets are so goddamned lazy they won't lift their hands to feed their mouths."

Though this seemed not quite credible, I determined to consult a calmer authority—if I ever had the time.

Time—that was the difficulty! For though I did feel obliged to exert the full force of my spurious but nonetheless potent authority for the welfare and (if possible) the freedom of these thirteen thousand pets, I knew that each new hour I spent with Frangle only made my discovery that much more inevitable. My mask was slipping, slipping . . .

But—if I could release them that very night, I would not only have done the prisoners a service but would myself benefit by their escape, for their very numbers would act as a smokescreen to conceal my own departure.

"I intend to examine all ten cellblocks, Captain, but you needn't accompany me. Just give me the keys. The ones for the individual cells, as well as those for the cellblocks."

"Impossible, Major. We don't use keys, you know. Everything is done by electricity. You can't beat that, you know . . . *electricity!*" He seemed to lay special importance upon this notion, and I nodded sagely. Encouraged, he went on: "Electricity is man's most powerful servant. It is the doorway to tomorrow. It's another Aladdin's Lamp. I love electricity, and electricity loves me."

"Fine. I love it too. But who's the electrician here—the man who *can* open the doors? I want to get this inspection over with."

"We don't have an electrician—in the strict sense. Palmino—the warrant officer—he does that sort of thing for us—in an amateur sort of way. Nothing very refined about him, you understand, but he keeps it running."

"Let me see the switchbox that controls the cells—and send Palmino to meet me there. You, meanwhile, can put the time to use ordering your books."

Frangle grasped my hand with speechless gratitude. He didn't need speech, for he had just slipped me five hundred-dollar bills in the Dingo currency. I put the bribe in my pocket, and tears sprang to the eyes of Captain Frangle.

The man who came into the radio shack had a head of black hair so thick with dirt and oil that it looked like an engine component. His swarthy skin was corrugated by decades of acne, and his narrow eyes, magnified by thick glasses, glistened with rheum. He was short; he was overweight; he was ill-proportioned. He was, in short, exactly my idea of a Dingo.

The Dingo saluted smartly. "Major Jones? Warrant-Officer Palmino reporting for duty, as ordered, sir."

I returned what I hoped was a convincing salute, but I boggled in replying to him. By what title should an officer address a warrant officer? There were whole worlds of protocol I was still innocent of. I had got through the bit with Frangle by piecing together faded memories of novels and Von Stroheim movies. Slipping, slipping . . .

"Very well, Palmino," I replied, turning away from him, simulating absentmindedness. "I wish all the cellblocks to be opened. And then all the cells themselves. For my inspection. Immediately." I turned to leave.

"I'm afraid that can't be done, Major Jones. They can only be opened in sequence. That's S.O.P." Then, as though in mockery. "Standard operating procedure, you know."

"My orders override standard procedure, Palmino. You will obey my orders."

The Dingo laughed aloud. "I don't think so, sir. If I may make a suggestion, sir, I think you will obey mine." Palmino took a pistol from the drawer of his desk and pointed the end with a hole in it at me.

The show was over, obviously. The mask was off. "How . . ."

"There were a dozen signs, sir—easily a dozen. Though I *have* been admiring the way you ride right over them. With me helping out, it will be a lot easier now."

"Helping out?"

"Don't interrupt me, sir," he commanded meekly. "I was just telling you how I figured it all out. First, there was an announcement over the radio here that a pet had escaped from an airplane flying from Duluth to St. Paul—" (*So* I thought, *that's where Julie will be!*) "—which pet was said to be last seen wearing a major's overcoat. That was a very suggestive clue to me, sir. The report came over the air a few moments after you'd landed. I put two and two together."

"Helping me, you say?"

"And *then* observed that you had about two inches of skin showing between the hem of your coat and the top of your boots, whereas when you came out of the barracks you was wearing what appeared to me to be Lieutenant Mosely's parade uniform. *Ah-ha!* I said to myself, *there's something fishy going on!"*

"I have money, if that's what you want . . ."

"Finally, when I came in here I addressed you as Major *Jones,* if you recall. Whereas the name of the Major we've been expecting is

Worthington. When you didn't object to being called *Jones,* everything seemed to fit together. Like the pieces of a jigsaw. It all came to me in a flash."

"Five hundred dollars?"

"You didn't *listen!* You pets are all alike—snobs! You think you're so much better than we are, and you're not worth the bullets it would take to kill you. If I didn't need you to help me, I'd like to . . . I'd make you live in *my* body for a while. That would show you!" Palmino's eyes grew rheumier; his pistol trembled with emotion.

"What is it you want of me? Practically speaking, that is."

"I want to be a pet."

"I'm sure we all do. All thirteen thousand of us. But the Masters have gone. They've deserted us."

"They'll return. We'll wait for them. Here."

"That's fine for you, but I can't stay on indefinitely. When the real Major Worthington arrives—"

"We'll see he has a good funeral. Mosely, too. I never did like that bastard Mosely. And Frangle—you're going to start putting the screws on Frangle. Oh, we'll have fun while we wait, sir, let me tell you. There are about five thousand bee-*yoo*-tiful bitches in those cells, sir. Five thousand—goddamn!"

"Really, Palmino, if you want to become a pet, you're going about it in the wrong way. I appreciate your cooperation, but no Master would tolerate the kind of actions you have in mind."

"So? When they get me, they can reform my character. I won't object to that. I'd probably like myself a lot better then. They can cure my acne and deepen my voice. They can give me 20-20 vision and fill me brimful with hormones and sweet charity. I'm willing. But meanwhile I'll enjoy myself."

"I need time to think about this. By myself."

"Take fifteen minutes. But remember—if you don't go along *with* me, you'll be going against me. In which case, Captain Frangle will learn all about Major *Jones*. Think about it—but don't think you can do with me like you did with Mosely—because I've already told four of the guards—friends of mine—which way the wind is blowing. And I don't intend to let you know *which* four. But you go right ahead and think about it."

I went to Mosely's room. The window above the bed was not barred, and it was a negligible fifteen-foot drop from the ledge. No one would observe me, since the guards were still assembled at attention in the compound. It would be a simple matter to escape across the fields and hide out in other abandoned farmhouses as I worked my way south to St. Paul and Darling, Julie. What purpose, after all, could I expect to serve by releasing these thousands of prisoners? What had they that was worth escaping *to?* Why should they risk their lives? The Masters' return was, as Palmino had pointed out, their only hope, and the Masters would not be much hindered by prison walls.

I was perched on the window ledge, ready to leap, my feet dangling down over the rough stones, when I heard, distantly, a tenor voice, ineffably sad, a voice that could have melted even so adamantine a heart as Palmino's with its melancholy refrain:

> *A! che la morte ognora è tarde nel venir*
> *a chi desia, a chi desia morir!*

(Which I would translate roughly thus:

> *Ah! how tardily death draws nigh*
> *to he who, to he who desires to die!*)

It was the last act of *Il Trovatore!* It was St. Bernard!

St. Bernard's voice was joined by Clea's faltering soprano. It is unreasonable, I know—it was madness—but I decided that moment that, willy-nilly, I would have to stay. My mother had thought nothing of deserting *me* when I was the merest pup, but my conscience would not be eased by that. I would have to rescue Motherlove from the Dingoes.

Chapter 8

*In which we may witness some of the sad
consequences of domestication.*

"And these," Doctor Quilty explained, waving a pudgy hand at certain rude upheavals of unfenestrated brick, "are the ovens."

"They're very big," I commented blandly. (Wanting very much to add—*And ugly*. But one of the first lessons Palmino had given me was to steer clear of aesthetic judgments. The average Dingo was too much at home with ugliness to notice any but the most awful examples.)

"We used to use gas, but that was before the manufacturer who supplied it to us went out of business. A pity too . . . gas is much more efficient. But the whole chemical industry is gone now—or going. For which we have the Masters to blame. All these years of free power have sapped our technological strength. Fortunately, Frangle was able to have the ovens converted."

"To what? Electricity?"

The Doctor laughed nervously, as at a particularly gauche joke. "Hardly! We burn logs. You'd be surprised the temperatures one can build up that way. The problem is getting these goddamned pets to go out and cut down the trees. Without lots of firewood, we can't work the ovens to capacity."

"What is their capacity?"

"I'm told that working all the ovens around the clock they can turn out twenty thousand units. But of course we don't work all around the clock. And since it's the goddamned, lazy pets who have to do all the heavy work, we don't come anywhere near capacity even in the ovens that are working. Talk about feet-dragging!"

"How many *do* you do, then?"

"No more than five hundred. That's a good day. You can see that that doesn't come anywhere near our needs. Ideally, this should be a profit-making proposition."

"Selling the ash as fertilizer, you mean?"

"Say, that's an angle that never occurred to me! We've just been dumping the ashes till now. Would you like to *see* the operation? Are you interested in that sort of thing?"

"By all means, Doctor. Lead the way."

"It's just around . . . Oh! Just a second, please, Major. My feet! there's something wrong with them these last few days. They've been swelling up . . . I don't understand it."

"Perhaps," I suggested with a small laugh, "it's not your feet at all. Perhaps your shoes are growing smaller?"

Doctor Quilty smiled wanly in reply, as he loosened his laces. A fat man, Doctor Quilty: even so slight an effort as stooping over his shoes caused him to be flushed and short of breath. His sad flesh drooped in dewlaps from his face and forearms, and his great belly was an edifying reminder of man's immemorial bondage to gravity and death.

Limping, Quilty led me around the corner of the building, where we could see teams of dispirited pets hauling sawn-up logs from stacks outside the main gate of the prison and restacking them again within the gate. The whole operation, involving nearly fifty pets, was being supervised by only one drowsy guard.

"Look at them!" Quilty said scornfully. "They don't put any more muscle into the job than a bunch of women would. With their bodies, you'd think they'd at least be able to lift logs."

"Could it be their morale? Perhaps if they were working . . . somewhere else . . . at some other sort of work? Maybe they're *depressed* by the ovens."

"No, take my word for it, they'd do the same half-assed job no matter what kind of work you set them to. And in any case, why should this sort of work depress them? I don't understand you, Major."

I colored, mortified at having to become so explicit. It seemed gruesome. "Wouldn't they show more spirit, if they were working

. . . more in their own interest? Or at least not so entirely *against* it?"

"But what could be more in their own interest than *this?* Where else do you think their *food* comes from?"

"Surely, Doctor, you don't mean to say that . . . that these ovens supply . . ."

"Every loaf of bread in this prison, Major. Yes sir, we're set up to be completely self-sufficient. And we would be too, if these god-damned pets would show some backbone!"

"Oh, *that* kind of oven! Well, then there must be some other sort of reason, I suppose, for their apathy. Perhaps they're not interested in baking any more bread than they can eat themselves. Rather like the Little Red Hen, if you've read that story."

"Can't say I have, Major, not being as much of a reader as I'd like to be. But the point is—they won't even bake that much. There are pets in the cellblocks who are starving, while these curs won't get themselves into a sweat unless you take a whip to them. They just don't have any sense of the consequences of their own actions. They want to be fed, but they won't take the trouble of feeding themselves. That's almost what it amounts to."

"Surely you're exaggerating, Doctor."

"It's hard to believe at first, I know. Take another case in point: the other day they sent out two hundred, men and women, to dig up potatoes, turnips, and such from the old field hereabouts. Well, those two hundred pets returned from their day's work with no more than ten pounds of potatoes *per capita*. That's Latin, you know. We doctors are obliged to learn Latin. Two thousand pounds of potatoes to feed to thirteen thousand prisoners! And you can't tell me they're not hungry, because, damn it, they're starving!"

"It must be something in their background," I theorized, incautiously. (Palmino had been very explicit on just that point: "A Major should *never* express an opinion that someone else might think original.") "They've come to expect their food to be handed to them outright. And they've grown to feel a positive antipathy for any sort of work. That's understandable."

"*I* don't pretend to understand it," Quilty said, shaking his head and setting the folds of his chin into swaying motion. "Everybody has to work—that's life."

"Well, *workers*—of course *they* have to work. But perhaps the pets—the goddamned pets, I should say—have an attitude more like our own, Doctor. Perhaps they think of themselves—however mis-guidedly—as officers and gentlemen."

"Do you think doctoring isn't *work?*" Quilty asked, wonderstruck. "There are few nastier jobs, to *my* mind, than poking around in other people's pustules and looking down their throats and sticking your finger up their *pons assinorum!*"

"You're right, Doctor. Absolutely—but still don't you think there's an essential difference between ourselves and common la-borers? As you point out, work is demeaning, and if a person could possibly get by without doing any . . ."

"De-*mean*-ing? I didn't say that! I *love* my work, Major. I *need* it. I couldn't get through one week without it. But that doesn't mean I have to pretend it's any bed of roses. It's a job, the same as any other, and it has its bad points the same as . . . Major? Major, is something wrong? Are you ill? Your face is so . . ."

My sudden pallor had betrayed the emotion that had overcome me: fear. Only a few yards away and looking directly, intently at me was St. Bernard. He had been among the members of the log-hauling crew. Smiling, but still uncertain, he began walking toward me.

"Back in line there!" the guard bellowed. St. Bernard paid no at-tention.

"White Fang! *Brüderlein, bist du's?*" His arms closed about me in a brotherly embrace of irresistible force.

"Help! Guard!" I shouted. "Arrest this madman! Get him off me! Throw him into prison, into solitary!"

St. Bernard's friendly features clouded with perplexity. As the guard pulled him away, I tried, with a mime show of winks and gri-maces, to tell him that he had nothing to fear.

"If you want this guy in solitary, shall I put Mosely someplace else?" the guard demanded.

"No! Leave Mosely alone. Surely you can find *someplace* to stick this one till I have a chance to cross-examine him. I know—lock him in *my* room and post a guard outside the door. And—" (whis-pering in the guard's ear) "—don't be too rough with him. I want him fresh when I get to him. Then I'll by-god make him wish he'd attacked somebody else.

"Goddamned pets." I grumbled, returning to Quilty, whose bewil-derment might at any moment, I feared, change to suspicion. "I think they must all be *crazy.*"

Which seemed a pretty weak explanation for that last episode with St. Bernard, but happily it contented Quilty. He even waxed enthusiastic. "Insanity—that's exactly my theory, Major! If you had the time, there's a case I've been studying which I'd like you to see. The most extreme example of its type. The classic symptoms of psychosis. A *beautiful* compulsion neurosis. It would only take a moment. Then, if you wanted to, we could come back to see the ovens."

"Take me to Bedlam, Doctor. Let's see *all* your lunatics. A day of watching madmen should be much more entertaining than a peek into the ovens."

"Splendid. But let us walk more slowly, if you please, Major. My feet seem to hurt more every minute."

I should explain somewhere along here that, though this was my third day at the St. Cloud Women's Reformatory (such had been its purpose only a short time before and such has become its purpose again), I had not attempted in the interim to make contact with St. Bernard or Clea. Until such time as I could effect their rescue it would have been an empty—and a dangerous—gesture to have disclosed my presence to them. Dangerous, because it was quite probable that Palmino would learn of their special significance to me and thus have additional resources for blackmail—or betrayal. I dreaded to think to what actions his cruel and lascivious nature would lead him were he to discover Clea was my mother! Already it had taken all my persuasive gifts to make him spare Mosely's life, and, even so, I could not prevent Palmino's nightly interrogations of the unfortunate lieutenant (for which the general opinion held me responsible), though the piteous nocturnal cries arising from the solitary cell caused me to weep tears as I waited out the torturous hours concealed in the radio shack.

I tried as much as possible to escape Palmino's baleful influence by spending my time with the other officers—either exercising a restraining influence upon Captain Frangle's avarice, or accompanying the Reverend Captain or Doctor Quilty as they went about their rounds, baptizing and healing. Between those two men, the latter was more to my taste, a favoritism that Quilty reciprocated.

"Like you, I'm a skeptic. *Cogito, ergo sum.* I doubt, therefore I am. That's Descartes." Quilty had made this declaration in the middle of a discussion of the Reverend Captain's rather roughshod missionary tactics. "I believe, with the immortal Sigmund Freud, in the power of reason. I don't suppose that you military men get to study much about psychology? All that depth stuff must be a *terra incognita* to you guys."

"Unless you'd count military strategy in that category, I guess I haven't studied much psychology." That, I felt sure, was exactly the sort of thing a genuine Major would say.

"Yes . . . Well, that's a very special branch of the subject. Along more general lines, however, you've probably read very little except *The Life of Man*. You must know that by heart though—eh, Major?"

"Oh . . ." (I'd never heard of the book) ". . . *parts*. Other parts I only remember vaguely, indistinctly."

"You're probably surprised to hear me speak of it as a book of psychology—and yet it's one of the profoundest examinations of the subject ever written by the pen of man. Yet it's also eminently practical."

"I've never heard it expressed quite this way, Doctor. Do go on."

"You know where he says: 'When the gods are malign, men worship at the feet of demons.' Now the Reverend Captain would probably interpret that in a strictly religious sense—and of course he would not be entirely wrong. But those words also express an important psychological insight. Oh, my feet!"

"What's wrong?"

"Nothing, only a twinge. I was just trying to make a point, and that is—what the Reverend Captain calls baptism is actually a venerable therapeutic tool in the history of psychology. I'll bet you didn't know that, did you?"

"Actually, no."

"Yes. We psychologists used to call it shock treatment.

"Here they are, Major. The nuts—in this whole cellblock you won't find anything else. And these, I should point out, are only the worst, the most hopeless cases. 'Autism' is the technical word that we psychologists use to describe their condition."

"I like it. It's far more restful here than in the other cellblocks. It rather reminds me of a beehive—that humming sound."

"It's so restful that we don't even have to use guards for this building. They sit like that all day long, mumbling their sick nonsense, or listening to other sick nonsense from somebody else. Impossible to understand them. They eat a bit of porridge in the morning and drink a bowl of broth at night—and even that has to be put in their hands. Otherwise they'd just sit there and starve to death. Pets!"

"How do you explain their condition, Doctor?"

"Insanity, that's *my* theory. The shock of S-Day—" (this was the Dingoes' name for the day on which the sunspots had blown the Masters' fuseboxes) "—was a traumatic experience for them. Consequently, they retreated into themselves until . . ." (the Doctor finished his sentence with a sweeping gesture that included all five tiers of cells) ". . . . *this* happened."

"Of course," he continued, in a somewhat chastened tone, "it's only a *theory*."

"It seems quite sound to me, Doctor. I wouldn't apologize."

"Do you like it? Come then, I want to show you my most interesting patient. This one is for the textbooks. If only Professor Freud were alive today! How he would have enjoyed this one!"

We climbed up a metal staircase to the third tier of cells and down a long corridor that took us farther and farther from what little sunlight sneaked into the building through the dirty skylights. There, standing in the center of a group of puppies and young dogs who were attentive to the point of being hypnotized, swaying in time to the incantatory rhythms of his own speech, was my brother Pluto. I recognized what he was reciting immediately: it was *A Prayer for Investments* from his latest Book of Ceremonies. This brief work is meant to be sung by two antiphonal choirs of fifty voices each, supported by chamber orchestras. While the Celebrant dresses (or "invests") himself in the three "sacred" articles of clothing. It can be an awesome spectacle, but in these reduced circumstances it could inspire only pathos or derision. For an alb Pluto had a begrimed undershirt; his chasuble was a floursack stolen from the bakery; his ring was a rusty bolt. Yet for all the ridiculousness of his appearance, Pluto was not entirely a figure of fun. The nobility of the prayer itself—which I transcribe from memory—went far to redeem him:

A Prayer of Investments

(Investment of the Alb)

Pure white suds
Lemon yellow
The black krater
Bone white salve

(Investment of the Chasuble)

Colorful gown
Trimmed with yellow lace
Colorful gown
Laced with silver

(Investment of the Ring)

Navy blue buttons
Soft black pus
Dark gold ochre
Blacky black black

"You see what I mean?" Quilty said, digging at my ribs with his soft elbow. "He's as nutty as peanut butter. They all are."

"Actually, he seems remarkably unchanged."

"How's that! You've seen this fellow somewhere before? When?"

I was rescued from the necessity of having to seal up this new breach in my defenses by the timely arrival of two guards who were conducting the shadowy figure of a manacled bitch. "I'm sorry, Major," one guard said, "but orders came in over the short wave to let this woman look around for her son. The both of them is ordered to be transported to St. Paul."

"That's him," the bitch said, pointing. "That's my son Pluto."

So Roxanna had finally got around to reporting the probability of my brother and mother being among the captive pets! I had dreaded this moment.

"Exactly!" I rasped in my most Dingo-like tones. "I have been expecting something like this. Before they are sent off, I had better give them a preliminary interrogation. Take them to my chamber, where the other prisoner is already. I shall be there immediately."

Clea, though but ill-acquainted with the timbre of my voice, stepped forward to peer at me in the gloom, but I turned my back on her abruptly. "Take them away! There is no time to spare!"

When the four of us—St. Bernard and Clea, Pluto and myself—were together in the quarters of the unfortunate Lieutenant Mosely, I explained to them, as well as I could how I had come to be in my present, so-convenient position. Only Pluto received my story calmly and without repeated protests and expressions of incredulity—and I suspect this was because he wasn't really listening to me at all, but to the sweeter voices of his own superior, interior world.

"Impossible!" Clea declared firmly. "You can't expect us to believe such a fairy tale. Parachuting right into the prison compound in the middle of the night! In a major's overcoat! Tell me another!"

"But if he says so, Clea," St. Bernard protested, "it must be true. White Fang wouldn't lie to a bloodbrother."

"The problem isn't whether you care to believe me—but how we are to escape. You dare not let them transport you to St. Paul. It is the capital of the Dingoes. Your best safety was to lose yourself among the millions of other abandoned pets. How was it that you let them find you out, Clea?"

"They came around calling for me and Pluto by name. They said the Masters were taking us back. I didn't know if I could believe them, but it seemed that anything would be better than this hellhole. So I spoke up before someone else got the same idea."

"I've already made some escape plans," St. Bernard volunteered. "Is it safe for me to speak of them aloud in this room? Yes? How about digging a tunnel? Under the wall. When I was down in the basement of the bakery I saw that it had a dirt floor. *Dirt*—that eliminates half of the difficulty from the start. Imagine tunneling through stone! Now, if we start the tunnel there and dig west . . ."

"But it's over a hundred yards from there to the wall!"

"So much the better! They'll expect us to start somewhere else. I figure with two men working all through the night, the tunnel can be done in a month."

"A month!" Clea scoffed. "But *I'm* to be carted off *tonight!*"

"Hm! That puts things in a different light. Well, in that case, I have a *second* plan. Here, let me demonstrate . . ." He ripped the bedsheets off the bunk and began shredding them into long strips. "We'll knot these strips together—into a rope ladder—like this. Now here, White Fang, you take this end—and I'll take this end. Now, pull! That's it! Harder! Oops!

"Hm. Does anyone know a better knot?"

"What do you need a rope ladder for?" I asked. It was only a fifteen-foot drop from the window of my room, after all, as St. Bernard must have been well aware after spending the last few hours confined there.

"I thought you and I could take care of the guards at the south-west tower—the one with the nice crenelations—and then we'd climb the stairs to the tops, and then use the rope ladder to climb down."

"But I can just order the guards to let us go up to the top."

"So much the better. Our only problem in that case is making sure the knots will hold. Is a square knot over-and-under and under-and-over or under-and-over and over-and-under? I can never get it straight."

"But we don't have to go to the top of the tower, St. Bernard. If it were just a simple matter of getting out of the prison, we could *jump* from the window of this room."

"You mean you won't need a rope ladder *at all?*" He sounded terribly hurt.

"Finding a way out of the prison is not the entire problem, St. Bernard. Think of the thousands of other pets I'll be leaving in Frangle's hands. What will become of them? Yes, and there's the little matter of eluding Palmino, who's on to my masquerade. I have every reason to believe that he has my least actions closely observed. And he will do his utmost to keep me here, for it's only through me that he possesses a large degree of power here, or hopes of a life in the asteroids hereafter. The problem, then, is not so much escaping from this prison as from him. Palmino—that's the *real* problem."

"Thank you, Major Jones, but it isn't the case any more." said Palmino, stepping into the room, brandishing that little pistol of his. The real problem is escaping *with* him."

"Would you introduce your friend, White Fang?" Clea asked loftily.

"Mother, this is Warrant Officer Palmino. Officer Palmino, this is my mother, Miss Clea Melbourne Clift." Clea offered her hand to Palmino, who received it with his pistol-hand. With a deft motion Motherlove wrenched the pistol from Palmino.

"Now, apologize to my son, young man, for this *rude* interruption, and *pray,* explain yourself more fully."

"I'm sorry. Okay? And you're going to be sorry too. Because they're on to us. I've intercepted radio messages. They're arriving tonight *en masse.*"

"Who? Why? How?"

"The troops from Shroeder and from Fargo. Even a contingent from the capital. They must know you're here, running the operation. You see, there's something I didn't have a chance to tell you. It sort of slipped my mind. Yesterday afternoon Major Worthington showed up for that inspection. The sentry saw him—and as luck would have it, he was one of my men. He fired—"

"But I told you I wouldn't allow that! I can't afford to be involved in *murder*. Things are bad enough already."

"It wasn't murder. The way I see it, it was self-defense. Anyhow, as it happens, it doesn't make any difference what you want to call it, because the sentry had bad aim and Worthington was only wounded. He escaped. He told the Inductance Corps, and they're coming to lay siege to the prison."

"Then it's all over! You botched it! We're through!"

"No—wait till I've explained everything. We're saved, maybe. I've been radioing to the Masters, and . . ."

"Do they still use radios here?" St. Bernard asked. "I've heard some charming transcriptions of the old radio programs. Do you know *The Green Hornet*? Thrilling stuff. But I'm surprised to hear that the Masters listen to the Dingoes' programs."

"It was more like an SOS than a program that I sent out. I've been calling for help ever since Worthington got away. After all, it can't make much difference if it's intercepted."

"Did you contact them? That's the important thing."

"I *think so*. I contacted *someone*. But how can I tell who it is? It's all in Morse. Anyhow, I went under the assumption that it was them. We bargained all morning before we reached an agreement. I said I'd help all the pets get out of the prison, and they promised to let me and four friends come along with the pets and live in a kennel. So now it's only a matter of assembling all the pets around Needlepoint Hill at twelve tonight."

"Why do we have to take them outside the prison? That sounds like a trick."

"It has something to do with the field of potential. It's stronger in places that come to a point. Thirteen thousand pets would weigh a good two thousand tons, and the Masters say they're still weak from S-Day. Do you think we should trust them?"

"Unless you're ready to withstand a siege, it looks like we'll have to. But how are we going to get thirteen thousand pets out the gates by twelve tonight? What explanation could we possibly give Frangle for it? There must be limits to the man's credulity."

"I don't know," Palmino said, shaking his greasy, black curls in perplexity. "I thought we might send some of the pets out on work details with *my* guards, and the others could sneak out this window. One at a time. Unobtrusively, sort of."

"The others?" The thirteen *thousand* others?"

"It's sticky," Palmino agreed, digging his fingers into his hair. "It's really sticky."

Pluto, who had till this time given no impression of being aware of the matters under discussion, suddenly arose from the corner in which he had been sitting in Gandhi-like self-absorption, and, raising the bolt bedizened forefinger, announced in magistral tones:

"Now here's my plan . . ."

Chapter 9

*In which we may witness Salami, and almost
everybody escapes.*

The great escape plot almost foundered at its launching, due to
Pluto's artsy-fartsy insistence on arena staging.

"Theatre-in-the-round, my good God!" I exclaimed. "These are
Dingoes, not Elizabethans, boy. The groundlings, the Great Un-
washed, the stinking rabble that doesn't know the difference between a Holbein and a hole in the ground. What did Bizet say when
he sat down to write the Toreador Song? He said, if they want
merde, I'll give them merde. This is Mass Culture. You're in Hollywood now. Remember it."

"But a proscenium arch! It's . . . it's indecent! *Hamlet* had arena
staging. It was good enough for Marlowe; it was good enough for
Jonson; it was good enough for Shakespeare; and it's good enough
for me."

"Amen, brother!" said Clea, clapping her hands.

"They used a proscenium arch at Bayreuth," St. Bernard ventured
timidly. Logical discourse was not his element.

"And if it was good enough for Wagner, it should be good enough
for us," I said, grateful for whatever allies. "Illusion—that's the
ticket! People like to be fooled. Besides, if we don't have a big old
painted backdrop, how will we get everyone out the gate? This isn't
art for art's sake, but for ours."

"Philistine!" Pluto growled. "Have it your way tonight, but if we
ever get this show out of the provinces . . ."

"Once we're in Swan Lake, I wash my hands of it. But for tonight, we'd better move. Clea, start the ladies sewing up costumes and rehearsing the production numbers. Remember, sex is everything. And they've got to fill up a lot of time, so don't let them have anything until they're screaming for it—and then give them half. Palmino, you've got an exodus to organize and a set to pound together. Don't fuss over the style, but make sure the backdrop is opaque. Pluto, you can start helping St. Bernard with his lines."

"But they aren't written yet."

"Too late, too late. Give him his lines now and write them when you get to Swan Lake. That was Shakespeare's way. For my own part, I'll be the rest of the day at least convincing Frangle that *Salami's* going to be the solution to his morale problem."

"Not salami," Pluto protested, "—*Salome!*"

"*Salami,*" I said sternly. "Remember—you're in Hollywood now."

"*Salami?*" Captain Frangle asked, giving a bewildered twist to his moustaches. "For my part—that is to say, speaking unofficially—I think it could be very, uh, beautiful . . . is that the word? The Bible and all, yes—but nevertheless."

"Nevertheless, Captain?"

"Nevertheless, the men, you know. The men are a crude sort, generally speaking. Not that I wouldn't enjoy a, uh, what is the word . . . a little culture? . . . myself, you know, but nevertheless."

"Oh, as for the men, I can assure you there won't be anything highbrow about this production. You know the story of *Salami,* of course?"

"Of course. That is to say . . . if you could refresh my memory . . ."

"By all means." And I told him the story, more or less as it appears in Matthew and Mark and Wilde and Hofmannsthal—and in the Rita Hayworth movie that had given Pluto his inspiration. Thank heaven for the film archives at the Shroeder Kennel! Pluto had altered the traditional story somewhat in the interests of heightened vulgarity.

"And all that is in the Bible?" Frangle asked, at the conclusion of my tale.

"Even as I have said."

"And they're going to do that on *stage*—here?"

"As I've been given to understand, five hundred or more of the

most beautiful bitches in the penitentiary are rehearsing the roles of
the harem slaves. *Salami* herself is a vision of such chaste purity that
words are inadequate."

"It might be a very rewarding experience at that. Eh, Major? I've
always held that religious education is essential to the moral well-being of an army. Wasn't it Napoleon who said an army travels on its
soul? Too many commanders these days are willing to let spiritual
matters go to hell."

"I never thought you were one, Captain Frangle."

Frangle smiled and adjusted one moustache to an expression of
modest self-satisfaction and the other to randy anticipation. "When
does the fun begin?"

"At nine-thirty, Captain. Promptly at nine-thirty."

Promptly at nine-forty-five, the curtain rose and one hundred and
fourteen guards and three officers of the St. Cloud Repatriation Center gasped as one man as they caught their first view of Herod's Palace in Galilee, brilliantly illuminated by the four searchlights which
had been taken down from the prison watchtowers. The backdrop
represented an infinite perspective of lotus columns and gothic
vaulted roofs, of gilded caryatids and marble pylons, of niches and
cornices and ogive windows looking out upon still vaster Babylonian
perspectives—a mural that had been the corporate achievement of
two hundred and several pets—and looked it. The composition
flowed freely from style to style, from Poussin to Chirico and thence
to Constable, as naturally as a spring brook babbles over a bed of
boulders. Every square inch glowed with a disquietingly gemlike
light, since the paint was still fresh and sticky.

The orchestra struck up the overture—a hastily reconstituted version of the *Tales of the Vienna Woods,* which had, despite itself, a
rather oriental character, due to our instruments: water pipes and
water xylophones, garbage can tympani, and a string section of
barbed wire and bedsprings.

When the effect of these spendors began to dim, Pluto, in sacerdo-
tal robes and a long false gray beard, came centerstage and declaimed, in his most magistral tone: "And Behold!"

And behold, the chorus lines of Herod's wives and concubines
came marching in from stage right and stage left, respectively, one
thousand strong. They overflowed the stage and filled the courtyard.
Not Solomon in all his glory had it so good.

"And behold, it came to pass in those days that Herod was Tetrarch of Galilee. Even Herod Antipasto—"

Herod Antipasto, with a Falstaffian gut, size 15 shoes, a putty
nose, and long, gray moustaches not unlike the Captain's, entered at
the end of the chorus line, hiking up his fancy robes and kicking his
hairy legs, blithely out of time with the orchestra's galop, and
pinching occasional asses to the loud delight of his audience.

"Now Herod was a cruel king who liked nothing better than his
brother's wife, Herodias Antipasto—unless it was his brother's
wife's daughter, Salami Antipasto." Enter Herodias, swinging her
boa. Enter Salami, in a sedan chair borne by eight Nubians. For the
time being, Salami kept her beauty dimmed behind the curtains of
the sedan chair, only peeking out briefly to wink in my direction.
Frangle, sitting beside me, exclaimed: "Did you see that? Did you
see how she looked right *at* me?"

"Now it came to pass in those days, even then, that Herod, Tetrarch of Galilee, had a big party, and he invited *everybody*. He invited the Romans and their wives . . ." Enter the Romans and their
wives. "The Egyptians and their wives." Who entered. "The Nubians
and their wives." And many more, each doing the characteristic national striptease. But somehow, no matter how many Herod invited,
the courtyard never seemed to get any more crowded.

When everyone had got to the party at last, Pluto assumed a
gloomy tone: "But Herod had forgotten to invite one person to his
big party, and that person found out that he'd been left out in the
cold, and he was very angry, and behold he was called the Baptist,
even St. Bernard."

Enter the aforementioned, with much clashing of garbage cans. St.
Bernard sang the Toreador Song from *Carmen,* with new lyrics that
expressed his pique at not receiving an invitation and also scolds the
Tetrarch for marrying his brother's wife. This accomplished, he
joined Motherlove, as Salami, in the love duet from *La Bohème.*

"And behold, Herod waxed hot with anger, and he ordered his
henchmen to put the Baptist down in the dungeon, and behold St.
Bernard the Baptist slew three hundred soldiers with the jawbone of
an ass!"

And sure enough, behold—for twenty minutes St. Bernard lay
about him, scattering the dead on all sides. The stage swarmed with
litter bearers and nurses and fresh replacements. It had scarcely
been cleared stage right, before St. Bernard had reaped a new

harvest stage left—and singing all the while. It was a wonderful fight, and the groundlings loved it, but the odds were against him, and at last he was caught and hauled away. To celebrate Herod's victory, a thousand new dancing girls trooped in to the strains of the Triumphal March from *Aida*.

Pluto's narration went on to describe how Salami and the Baptist were passionately in love with each other, but that Herod was determined to keep them apart because he loved Salami himself. Salami, hoping to save her lover, goes to her mother Herodias, who persuades her daughter (and this is the part that Pluto lifted from the Rita Hayworth movie) to dance the *Dance of the Seven Veils* for the Tetrarch, who has promised her any favor in return. Salami thinks the favor will be St. Bernard's release, but bad old Herodias asks for his head on a silver salver instead. What a plot! At least, that's what was supposed to have happened, but at the point when there was to have been the big scene between the Antipastos, man and wife, a ballet of slave girls was interpolated. Pluto was gesturing frantically for me to come backstage. Excusing myself to Frangle, Quilty, and the Reverend Captain, I left my front-row center seat and went to see what was amiss.

"Herod has deserted!" Clea announced in dire tone, exhibiting the castoff costume. "He couldn't wait to run off to Needlepoint Hill with the Egyptians."

"Are all the pets gone now?" I asked. Unnecessarily, for I could see the steady streams of prisoners still hurrying out the gate under the supervision of Palmino and his four friends—who had volunteered to miss the stage show and man the lookout towers that night. Many of the pets ran right from the wings into the departing throng as soon as their business on stage was completed.

"Only six thousand are out," Pluto confessed. "We're ten minutes behind schedule because of the late curtain, but we're catching up. The problem is Herod. We forgot to assign an understudy, and nobody knows the part."

"Somebody has to go on—that much is obvious. I don't care who you pick."

"We thought . . ." St. Bernard began hesitatingly. ". . . that *you* might."

"You see, my darling, the other pets really have no idea of what we're about," Clea explained. "It's easy enough for the girls to go out there and do a little belly dance, but the actor doing Herod was beside himself with the pain of the *vulgarity*. And we thought that since you've come to know the Dingoes so well . . ."

"But they've come to know *me* so well too!"

"But with this big tummy and the false moustache and a putty nose and a little rouge and mascara, they won't. Please, White Fang, don't be difficult. We can't make those poor slave girls dance all night." Clea took advantage of the time to prepare me for the rôle, and by the end of her entreaty I was more fit to go on as Herod than to return to my seat in front, so I gave in. Besides, as Pluto had known very well, I love amateur theatricals.

My first scene, with Herodias, was easy to ad-lib. The bargain was struck by which Salami was to do her bit and St. Bernard was to have his head taken off. Then I settled back to watch, having no other business during the dance than to scramble out on all fours and pick up each of the seven veils as Motherlove let them fall, then bay like a wolf in appreciation. In all fairness I must say that her dance merited no less.

The first veil, for instance, revealed Motherlove's arms—as graceful and ivory a pair as ever clasped a Tetrarch's neck, hands like two doves, tipped with long almond nails that even the cruel regimen of prison life had not spoiled.

The second veil uncovered Motherlove's classic nose and sculpted lips, parted, as the veil fell, in a taunting and suggestive smile, more exciting than many another woman's kiss.

Motherlove spent as much time over the third veil as if she had been undoing the Gordian knot, and when it at last fell, the audience and I broke into a roar of approval. Motherlove's legs were long, firm, and elegantly muscled. When they moved in time to the crash of the cymbals and squeal of strings, one seemed to feel that the science of anatomy held no more mysteries. Such a feeling, however, was premature.

The orchestra had grown steadily quieter throughout the dance, the tempo slower. As each veil fell, a group of musicians quit their seats at the side of the stage and went behind the backdrop where they joined the escaping throng. The noise of the exodus became perceptible as the music quietened, but Motherlove commanded the guards' attention with queenly authority, to say the least.

The fourth veil bared her swanlike neck and creamy shoulders to the vulgar view; the fifth revealed her midriff. The lithe bare belly rolled and pulled taut, then stretched out at length, making the delicately-convoluted navel peek forth from its little hollow of flesh.

The arms moved violently with the music, clapping, swinging up above the highpiled hair and chopping down in counterpoint to the musician's beat. The music slowed to the consistency of honey. Motherlove's almond fingers touched the hem of the sixth veil.

"Take it off!" the guards chanted. "Take it off! Take it off!" The Tetrarch was limping in circles about the stage, while Captain Frangle had leapt to his feet and was chewing at his moustaches in an agony of concupiscence. Eventually, after a long season of doubt, she took it off. Ah, then what treasures did the Tetrarch's court behold! The two breasts were like two young roes that are twins, which feed among the lilies.

One veil remained, and one musician—Pluto, who played a flute. Motherlove loosened the knot at her hip, but she did not let the veil drop. She lifted it, she lowered it, she moved it laterally—but she did not let it drop. Of a sudden the flute broke off, and Pluto stepped forward to resume his rôle as narrator. "And behold . . ." he sang out.

"Behold! Behold!" the audience shouted in agreement.

". . . the Baptist broke from his bonds and escaped the dungeon of the Tetrarch, and he was at hand to spare the modesty of the Princess Salami from the lustful gaze of Herod." St. Bernard carried in a heavy wooden screen, which unfolded into six sections. The Princess Salami concealed herself modestly behind this screen, one end of which butted against the wing on stage left.

"Off with his head" I, as the Tetrarch, roared.

"Off with his head!" the audience clamored. One of them, Frangle himself, favoring more direct action, rushed at the screen to tear it down. St. Bernard ran downstage to prevent him but tripped over his own loincloth. Only I, Herod Antipasto, could stay Frangle's lewd intent.

Grasping him roughly by the lapels of his uniform I began dragging him back to his seat but Frangle was not to be persuaded even by superior strength. He bit and clawed and tore and grabbed at Herod's moustaches . . .

"Major Worthington!" he exclaimed. "What are you about?"

Fortunately the audience was making enough noise to drown out Frangle's cry of recognition. St. Bernard assisted me in dragging the Captain behind the screen, and together we assisted the Captain to become unconscious. As each of the articles of his clothing was thrown out from behind the screen for their inspection, the guards' laughter grew louder. At last, when the inert officer was carried away in full sight on a stretcher the house came down.

Which bit of extempore business concluded, we returned with relief to the script.

"Desist, villainous Antipasto!" declaimed St. Bernard, in his best Verdian style.

"Nay, prepare to meet thy death, fool," I replied, "for I shall see the precious ruby beneath that final veil or die in the attempt."

"Help, help," said Clea peeking out from behind the screen.

"Off with his head!" the guards began again to chant, drowning out the noise that the last pets were making in their escape.

I whipped out the tipped fencing foil from the sheath at my side and laid on. Though my swordsmanship was no better than might have been expected from a bumbling, fat, old Tetrarch, luck was so far on my side that St. Bernard was unable to despatch me with the same ease with which he'd disposed of the previous three hundred soldiers. Then, by a clever strategem, I made him circle about so that I was between him and the screen. Then I bolted toward Salami. With a shriek Clea started running away, pressing her single remaining veil (rather larger now than it had been) to her bosom and private parts. She was hindered from running too far ahead of my by the fact that the tip of my foil had become tangled in the corner of this garment. In this manner we circled the courtyard thrice, pursued by St. Bernard, who was still tripping over his loincloth and therefore could never quite catch up. The credit for all this choreography must go to Pluto.

At last Motherlove regained the sanctuary of the screen. A mist comes before my eyes and my throat tightens as I am forced again to recall the sight of my mother's cheerful smile and the friendly wave of her hand as she departed into the wings, and thence backstage. Her rôle was at an end, and she was to follow the rest of the pets now to Needlepoint Hill. Never, never more to see her! How lovely she was in those last moments! How hard to believe that she has left the Earth and me irredeemably behind!

But there was not time then to appreciate the ineffableness of that moment, for St. Bernard was laying on thick and fast, switching my padded sides and rump with his lath broadsword. Howling inanely and flailing my foil, I ran about the stage. After a few circuits thus, I ran out at the wings stage left and circled the backdrop that I might reenter on the right. Only Palmino and his four cohorts were left backstage now. The pets were all out. It lacked but fifteen minutes of midnight.

Around the courtyard, back and forth across the stage, then a quick dash behind the screen (where the audience still supposed Clea to be cowering) to catch hold of one end of a trick "veil," which when pulled out to its full length exceeded the measurements of the stage twice over. But the jokes were wearing thin. Our audience was demanding St. Bernard's head ever more loudly. Huggermugger can only go so far.

Then St. Bernard, hoping to liven the performance, struck me one blow that didn't land on the padding but on me. With a cry of authentic pain, I tumbled backward into Herod's Palace. Samson, in the house of the Philistines, did not enjoy so instant a success. Tremors passed through the eclectic canvas, and there was a minatory, splitting sound. St. Bernard pulled me away before it all came down on my head.

Like the rending of the temple veil, Herod's Palace split neatly down the central seam and fell to the right and to the left, leaving in full view the gaping gates through which the pets had departed. But they did not gape quite so much as I would have liked, and they gaped less every second, as Palmino and his four companions pushed them closed. Pluto's plan had called for the gate to be closed and locked, but only after St. Bernard and I were outside. We rushed forward too late to prevent the outer bolt from sliding into place. Palmino had double-crossed us.

The guards that had comprised the audience of *Salami* did not take in the full extent of the deception that had been perpetrated upon them quickly enough to prevent St. Bernard and me from dashing to the barracks' door. When they did realize that all the other pets had escaped out the gate, the main body of them forgot the two of us entirely and battered at the locked portal. A contingent of five, however, did pursue us into the barracks and challenged us to stop. Since they were off duty and unarmed, we could afford to ignore their challenge.

It would have been an easy matter then to go up the stairs to Mosley's room and out the unbarred window and on up to Needlepoint Hill, except that—unfortunately—I tripped.

The five guards were all over me, but St. Bernard flew to my rescue and beat them back with his stick of lath. Which, however, broke off at the hilt. Scrambling to my feet, I tore off my putty nose and false moustaches and ordered the guards to come to attention. "If you dare lift your hand against me, I'll have you court-martialed!"

"Jesus Christ, it's the Major!"

They stood uncertain whether to advance upon us or obey my command, allowing St. Bernard opportunity to pick up a packed foot locker from beside one of the bunks and to hurl it at them. Bonk! Oof! Thud! Great Scott!

We rushed up the stairs and into Mosley's room. St. Bernard was out at the window almost the moment he was in at the door, and I would have followed as quickly after, but for my costume. I was stuffed too abundantly to go through.

"Hurry!" St. Bernard warned, pointing to the distant figures of the last pets gathering around Needlepoint Hill, about which a nimbus of roseate light seemed to be settling. "The Masters are there now."

I had taken off half my uniform extricating myself from my costume, and I was out on the windowledge. Too late! All about us were the armies of the Dingoes!

The soldiers closed in around St. Bernard, and I threw him my foil for his defense. He warred against their electric prods bravely, but it was a hopeless contest from the first. The guards of the penitentiary were pounding on the door at my back.

An officer, his arm in a sling (the original Major Worthington?), addressed me through a megaphone. "Better jump down from that ledge, White Fang. We have orders to take you alive. The guards in that prison do not."

In the distance, on the crest of Needlepoint Hill, the first of the redeemed pets began ascending into the skies. Soon the heavens were filled with their glorious, glowing bodies. A golden light of overwhelming beauty flooded the scene so that even the Dingo soldiers had to turn to admire it. It reminded me of . . . something I could not, quite, put my finger on.

St. Bernard could however: "The Last Judgment!"

The Masters were taking back their pets in exactly the manner that Michelangelo had laid out for them six centuries before on the walls of the Sistine Chapel.

The door gave behind me, and I jumped into captivity.

Chapter 10

In which an execution is executed, followed by
a controversy.

The scene is the prison of the Dingoes—not the teeming, raucous
tumble of St. Cloud (which had been, for all its squalor and in-
spissated misery, redeemed by the sheer bulk of the humanity
packed within its walls)—not that, but a high and solitary chamber,
aseptically white, odorless, soundless, sightless, boding. I say *solitary,*
but I was not alone. St. Bernard was confined in the same cell with
me, but his state so mirrored my own that his companionship merely
deepened my sense of being cut off, alone, doomed. Had there been
a throng in that room with us, it would have been just the same—for
in the courts of death all men are alone. Friends never come to
stand beside a gallows.

The gallows . . .

No, let me for a while yet skirt that subject. Let's talk about . . .

St. Bernard. St. Bernard was even more cast down than I. At least,
his gloom was more tangible. Losing first the support of his Leash
and then the solace of his beloved Clea (and the latter, through
the agency of the contemptible Dingoes), his will had become de-
elasticized. He no longer reacted against his environment; he did not
plan new escapes; he didn't even sing.

My only diversion from anxious speculation (and I shall leave it
to my readers' imagination to develop the subject that preoccupied
me) was looking down from the cell's single window at the semi-
deserted streets below. The fivefold gallows in the foreground,

though it did not inspire confidence, identified our prison as the St. Paul Courthouse that my guard on the airplane had referred to so admiringly. The platform of the gallows was raised a dozen feet above street-level, and the main shaft that supported the cross-trees . . .

We'll return to that subject. For now, let us focus our attention on that prospect beyond the gallows. All day long, civilian Dingoes passed by the Courthouse—the women in long, ungainly dresses and the men in unseasonably heavy suits—but their behavior was so unremittingly dull (mostly, they just marched, left-right, left-right, left-right, in long, slow, straight lines) that I soon grew tired of observing them and began instead to count the cars that went by.

This wasn't so boring as you might think, for the various trucks, jeeps and tractors still in use among the Dingoes (rarely, if ever, did one see an ordinary car) presented a beautiful study in comparative ruination. Roaring and sputtering, spewing out black clouds of noxious gas, bouncing along the potholed road at their top speed of fifteen miles per hour, the procession of antique machines was worthy of the genius of Rintintin. (For those unacquainted with this work, an explanation: Rintintin of Eros is the greatest contemporary sculptor of mechanism. I was present at the premier—and only—performance of the reknowned "Death of a Helicopter," an event that I shall always treasure in my memory and which I would describe at length except for the fear that it would be out of keeping at this moment.)

These machines were usually of an official nature, and those same insignia that I had seen scrawled on the telephone poles outside of Shroeder were painted on the sides of the trucks or on banners that streamed from the jeeps' antennae. I was reminded of the heraldic devices of some crusading army: Resistor statant, sable on a field of gules; diode dormant on a quartered field, ermine and vert.

I would also give a little account of the architecture of the Dingoes, but the truth is I didn't pay it much attention. Most of the time I looked at the gallows. The architecture of a gallows is very simple.

After two days in this limbo, I received my first visitor. It was Julie, but a Julie so altered in appearance that I thought at first she was a Dingo spy in disguise. (Prison does develop one's paranoid tendencies.) She was wearing a high-necked, long-sleeved, floor-length dress in the Dingo style and her beautiful hair was concealed by an

ungainly cork helmet such as I had seen on several persons passing
below my window.

"Julie!" I exclaimed. "What have they done to you?"

"I've been repatriated." She wasn't able to raise her eyes to look
into mine, and her whole manner was one of unnatural constraint.
No doubt, this could be accounted for by the presence of the armed
guard who was watching us from the open doorway.

"You mean they've forced you to . . ."

"Nobody's forced me to do anything. I just decided to become a
Dingo. They're really much nicer than we thought they'd be. They're
not *all* like Bruno. And even he's not so bad once you get to know
him."

"My God, Julie! Have you no shame?"

"Oh, don't be upset. That's not what I meant. Bruno's too much
in love with Roxanna to think of bothering me. Besides, he's still
laid up in a hospital bed.

"That isn't what I meant."

But Julie went blithely on. "They're going to get married as soon
as he's out of the hospital. Isn't that wonderful? On the airplane
coming here, after you jumped out and *deserted* me, Bruno was de-
lirious and he told me all about himself. I can't say I understood
much of it. But do you realize that he actually *likes* you? He does.
There he was all bandaged up, lying on the stretcher, and all of us
thinking the plane was going to crash any minute, and he said: "I
wasn't smashed like that since God knows when. Good man! We'll
get along—White Fang and me. I thought it was just the delirium,
but he was serious. He wants you to visit him and Roxanna as soon
as you can. I explained that that might not be soon."

"If at all."

"That's what Roxanna suggested. And she didn't seem at all upset
by the idea. She's still very angry with you for hurting Bruno."

"But I was trying to protect her!"

The story that Julie at last unfolded, in her rather scattery way,
was this: Roxanna, when she had seen me strike Bruno with the axe,
suddenly was made aware that she was in love with her tormentor.
Her new-found love was every bit as passionate as the hatred she
had expressed only minutes before. In the heat of the moment, she
had been almost angry enough to use my axe on me, but Julie and
the Dingoes who had been drawn to the scene had been able to stop
her. Since then she had pursued her vengeance more deviously.

"And Petite," I asked, "what did she do to Petite?"

"Oh, it wasn't at all what I'd feared. She just read to her from this propaganda-book that all the Dingoes like. It's called *The Life of Man*. She convinced Petite that it's very naughty to be a pet, but the first thing Petite asked when she saw me again was 'Where's my Leash?' She can't adjust to the idea that she'll never have it again."

"Julie, don't say that. Of course she'll have it again. We all will. Haven't you heard about Needlepoint Hill? Pluto and Clea are probably already back on Swan Lake or Titan, and in one week more, or two weeks . . ."

The mention of his home brought a profound groan from the lips of St. Bernard: *"Gott! welch Dunkel hier!"*

Julie pressed her forefinger to her lips anxiously. "Hush! We aren't allowed to mention that. It's a sore point with the Dingoes."

"What are they going to do with us, Julie?" I whispered.

She shook her head sadly, avoiding my intent gaze. "I can't talk about that," she said. "They forbade it. And anyhow, I don't know." Somehow, though, I didn't believe her.

Julie spent the rest of her visit trying to justify the haste with which she had allowed the Dingoes to repatriate her, and since she had no apparent excuse but expediency, it was rather hard going.

At last I interrupted her: "Julie, please don't take on about it. I quite understand that you've had to disassociate yourself from me. Heaven only knows what they intend to do with me, but there's no reason for you needlessly sharing in that fate. Perhaps they mean to use me as a hostage; perhaps they mean something worse. In either case you're lucky to be rid of me." I was just beginning to hit my stride, and I would soon have brought myself to the point of tears, when Julie started to giggle.

To giggle! She tittered and snorted and snuffled like someone who can't keep a joke, and she left the room bent double with the pain of holding back her laughter.

Hysteria, of course. It was a very sad thing to see the girl you love in such a condition and to be unable to help. But I didn't think too long about that, since it was even sadder to think of me in my condition.

Shortly after Julie left, a guard came to our cell to ask what we would like for our last meal.

It was sundown, and from the windows of the cell I could see that a large crowd of spectators had already gathered about the base of the gallows. At ten o'clock a guard came to remove the two trays of untouched food (he wolfed down the choicest bits of the steak before he went out into the corridor), and then a chaplain informed us apathetically that we could confess to him if we wished.

"I only confess to my Master, thank you," St. Bernard informed him. Now that the ceremony of our execution was well under way St. Bernard was able to pull himself together: he knew the rôle he was expected to play.

Our cell began to fill with guards. I was commanded to come away from the window, and my hands were bound behind my back. St. Bernard submitted to his bonds peacefully.

"I'm sorry that you find yourself in this situation on my account, St. Bernard. I didn't want it to end this way—for either of us."

"Shaddup!" said the guard. "You ain't supposed to talk any more."

St. Bernard smiled: "Oh, there's no need for you to be sorry, *Brüderlein*. For my own part, I have but one regret: I regret that I have but one life to give for the Mastery."

"Shaddup you! Whyntya shaddup when I say shaddup?"

We were escorted by some dozen Dingoes to the main entrance of the courthouse, where we were met by the officer in charge of this execution. He bowed to us curtly and smiled a thin—but not unhappy—smile.

"Lieutenant Mosely!" I exclaimed. "What a surprise, sir!"

Without, a solemn tattoo was begun, the doors were swung open, and the crowd screamed its approbation.

"Now," St. Bernard shouted above the din, "more than ever does it seem rich to die."

Despite this noble affirmation he seemed no more eager than I to mount the thirteen steps to the gallows. We were stationed in our places—each in the middle of a rectangle distinctly demarcated from the other boards of the platform. When I jiggled my weight, I could feel the trapdoor wobble. On the whole, I stood very still.

The chaplain approached us a last time. "Did you wish to make a last statement?"

"Yes," said St. Bernard. "I know not what course others may choose, but as for myself—Give me liberty or give me death!"

"And you?"

"I'm willing to compromise. Give me something somewhere in between. How about a stay of execution? How about a trial? I'm being denied my rights as a United States citizen!"

"God damn the United States!" St. Bernard cried. "I hope that I may never see nor hear of the United States again!"

"What a *terrible* thing to say!" the chaplain scolded. "It would serve you right if that's just what happened to you."

It was not, however, to be St. Bernard's fate, for the band assembled in front of the gallows chose that moment to strike up the National Anthem. The men in the crowd took off their caps, and the women quieted. St. Bernard sang the words aloud in his wonderful tenor voice. It was a rare last opportunity.

Lieutenant Mosely came forward and offered blindfolds. I refused, but St. Bernard accepted gratefully. With the black cloth over his eyes, he looked handsomer and more pathetic than ever. There was an ominous silence, interrupted by a rapturous outburst from one of the Dingo women in the front row of spectators: "Cut off their balls! Cut off their balls first!"

Pursing my lips at this demonstration of poor taste, I glanced down at the bloodthirsty creature who had expressed these sentiments—and imagine my surprise when I saw she was the same woman who had showered me with flowers and kisses during the parade in Duluth! Perhaps I was mistaken though; perhaps she was only of the same physical type. A guard hushed her before the last riffle of drums.

Mosely lifted his hand.

St. Bernard rose to the occasion: "It is a far, far better thing that I do, than I have ever done; it is a far, far better rest that I go to, than I have ever known."

Mosely lowered his right hand.

St. Bernard dropped.

"But what about me?" I asked, even as the tears of pity rolled down my cheeks. Poor, poor St. Bernard!

"You've got your stay of execution," Mosely informed me glumly. "There's someone who wants to see you first. You're going there now."

"Fine—but would you take the noose off first? Ah, that's much better."

I could not see where the limousine was taking me, for the curtains were drawn about all the windows in the back seat, but within minutes I found myself in a large and largely vacant underground parking area. Then, after a labyrinth of staircases, corridors, guards and passwords, I was at last left alone before an imposing mahogany desk. The desk and all the appointments of the room testified to the consequence of their possessor. In a subsistence economy like the Dingoes, luxury is a potent symbol.

My attention was especially drawn to the portrait that hung over the desk. Done in the mock-primitive style popular in the sixties of the last century, it slyly exaggerated those features of the subject which were most suggestive of the raw and barbarous. His stomach, though monumental in itself, was seen from a perspective that magnified its bulk. The face was crudely colored, particularly the nose, which was a florid, alcoholic crimson. The violet-tinged lips were at once cynical and voluptuary. The picture was the perfect archetype of the Dingo.

Yet perhaps not perfect—for the eyes shone with an intelligence and good will that seemed to contradict the overall impression of brutishness. This one dissonance added to the archetype that touch of *individual* life which only the best portraitists have ever been able to achieve.

I was still engaged in studying this painting (and, really, it had the strangest fascination for me) when its original stepped into the room and came forward to shake my hand.

"Sorry to have kept you waiting, but my time hasn't been my own ever since that damned sunspot."

When he had left off shaking my hand, he did not immediately release it, but, keeping it still tightly clasped, looked me over appraisingly.

"You'll have to get rid of that name of yours, you know. 'White Fang' just won't do now. We Dingoes—as you call us—don't like those doggish names. Your proper name is Dennis White, isn't it? Well, Dennis, welcome to the revolution."

"Thank you, but . . ."

"But who am I? I'm the Grand High Diode. As far as you're concerned, you may think of me as a vice-president. The Diode is second only to the Cathode Himself. Are you interested in politics?"

"Pets don't have to be. We're free."

"Ah, freedom!" The Grand High Diode made an expansive gesture, then plopped into the seat behind the desk. "Your Master takes care of everything for you and leaves you so perfectly free. Except that you can't taste anything from the good-and-evil tree, why there's nothing that isn't allowed you."

He glowered at me dramatically, and I had time to compare the portrait with the portrayed. Even the man's wild, white locks seemed to be tumbled about his head according to the same formula that the painter had used to guide his brushstrokes. My admiration for him (the painter, not the portrayed) grew by leaps and bounds.

"The Masters appeared two-thirds of a century ago. In that time *human* civilization has virtually disappeared. Our political institutions are in a shambles; our economy is little more than bartering now; there are practically no artists left."

"Among you Dingoes, perhaps not. But under the Mastery, civilization is flourishing as never before in man's history. If you're going to talk about civilization, the Dingoes haven't a leg to stand on."

"Cows were never more civilized than when we bred them."

I smiled. "Word-games. But I can play them just as well."

"If you'd rather not argue . . ."

"I'd *rather* argue. I'd rather do anything that keeps me from returning to the gallows. It was a most distasteful experience."

"Perhaps you can avoid the gallows altogether. Perhaps, Dennis, I can convince you to become a Dingo?" The man's thick, violet lips distended in a wolfish grin. His eyes, which were, like the eyes in the portrait, vivid with intelligence, glittered with a strange sort of mirth.

I tried my best to temper my natural disdain with a quaver of doubt. "Isn't it rather late to join? I should think that most of the carnage must be over by now. Aren't you nearly ready for defeat?"

"We'll probably be defeated, but a good revolutionary can't let *that* worry him. A battle that isn't against the odds would hardly be a battle at all. The carnage, I'll admit, is unfortunate."

"And unjustifiable as well. Poor St. Bernard had done nothing to justify—"

"Then I won't bother to justify it. Dirty hands is one of the prices you pay in becoming a man again."

"Are you fighting this revolution just so you can feel guilty about it?"

"For that—and for the chance to be our own Masters. Guilt and sweat and black bread are all part of being human. Domestic animals are always bred to the point that they become helpless in the state of nature. The Masters have been breeding men."

"And doing a better job of it than man ever did. Look at the results."

"That, I might point out, is exactly the view a dachshund would take."

"Then let me put in a good word for dachshunds. I prefer them to wolves. I prefer them to Dingoes."

"*Do you?* Don't make up your mind too quickly—or it may cost you your head. And, with this threat, my incredible inquisitor began to chuckle. His chuckle became a pronounced laugh, and the laugh grew to a roar. It occurred to me that the gleam in his eyes might as well have been madness as intelligence.

Suddenly I was overcome by a desire just to have done. "My mind is made up," I announced calmly, when he had stopped laughing.

"Then you'll make a declaration?" Apparently, he had taken the exact opposite of the meaning I had intended.

"Why should you care which side I'm on?" I demanded angrily.

"Because a statement from you—from the son of Tennyson White —with the strength of that name behind it—would be invaluable in the cause of freedom.

Very deliberately I approached the mahogany desk where the man was sitting, wreathed in a fatuous smile, and very deliberately I raised my hand and struck him full in the face.

Instantly the room was filled with guards who pinioned my arms behind my back. The man behind the desk began, again, to chuckle.

"You beast!" I shouted. "You Dingo! You have the conscience to kidnap and murder my father, and then you *dare* ask me to make you a declaration of support. I can't believe . . . If you think that . . ." I went on raving in this vein for some little while. And as I raved that incredible man lay sprawled on the top of his desk and laughed until he had lost his breath.

"White Fang," he managed at last to say. "That is to say— Dennis, my dear boy, excuse me. Perhaps I've carried this a little too far. But you see . . ." And now he swept aside the thick white locks from the *stub of his right ear.* "*I* am your father and not murdered in the least."

Chapter 11

In which I commit myself to the Philosophy of Dingoism.

The next week went by at a pace that would have been nightmarish if I hadn't been so giddily, busily happy. First off, I married Julie once again—this time in accordance with the rites of the Dingoes. Daddy explained that in some matters—marriage most especially— the Dingoes could be as great sticklers for ceremony as my brother Pluto. Darling, Julie entered into the spirit of things with enthusiastic atavism, and I suspect now that part of Daddy's insistence had had its origin in my once-again-newlywed bride. Still, it was a wellwrought ceremony, which even Pluto might have approved. Hymen's candle never burned brighter than on the day that our hands were joined over the glowing vacuum tube on the altar of the renovated power station.

We had our first quarrel as newlyweds an hour afterward, when Julie told me that she'd known about Daddy and the ordeal he was preparing for me on the day she had come to visit me in the courthouse jail. But the quarrel ended as soon as Julie had pointed out that, since I'd passed the test so well, I had no cause for anger. I hate to think what might have happened however, if I'd agreed to make the "declaration" that Daddy had proposed.

The moment I had dreaded most—when I should have to inform Daddy that the pet who had been executed with me was also his son —passed by without ruffling his considerable equanimity. He had known all the while, through Julie, and he had gone right ahead and ordered the execution, in order, so he claimed, to set me a sobering example of man's mortality and the likely price of rebellion.

"But your own son!" I protested. "What bond is stronger than between father and son?"

"Yes, I'm sure that's all very true—though that bond is somewhat attenuated when one has had hundreds of sons. But consider, Dennis—he was committing incest. So, even exclusive of his political crimes, which are great . . ."

"Daddy—you're smiling that certain way again. I suspect there's a trick up your sleeve."

"Come see a movie, Dennis. If I told you, you wouldn't perhaps, believe."

The film showed four pallbearers (by their physiques and nakedness one could tell they were pets) supporting a pallet upon which the corpse of St. Bernard had been composed. They were climbing the twisty path to Needlepoint Hill. Reaching the summit, they laid down their burden and watched as a nimbus of golden light formed above the dead body: St. Bernard's Master had been summoned back to the hill.

The fingers trembled—and there is nothing to which I can compare the beauty of that moment unless it be the "Creation of Adam" panel in the Sistine Chapel—the eyelids fluttered (telephoto lens now) and opened. St. Bernard, gloriously resurrected, began to sing Beethoven's Ninth. Then, slowly, the five bodies rose into the air, caroling their joy. With such a happy ending, I couldn't hold the charade of the execution against Daddy.

From the first Julie and I were celebrities among the Dingoes. At a steady succession of lunches, dinners, and dances, we played the parts of refugees from the "tyranny of the Masters, grateful for this new-found freedom." That's a quote from the speech that Daddy wrote for me to deliver on such occasions. It always draws applause. Dingoes have no taste.

While I acted my rôle as a model revolutionary, I carried on another drama inwardly. Had it been merely a contest between filial piety and my loyalty to the Masters, I would not have hesitated long, for filial piety is negligible when for seventeen years one has presumed one's father dead.

But mine had been no ordinary father. He had been Tennyson

White; and he had written *A Dog's Life.* Now I discovered there was a sequel to that book.

I read through *The Life of Man* in one sitting of fifteen hours' duration. It was one of the most shattering experiences of my life. In fact, right at this moment, I can't remember any others comparable.

Anyone who's read it realizes the difficulty one faces trying to describe *The Life of Man.* It's got a little of everything: satire, polemic, melodrama, farce. After the classic unity of *A Dog's Life,* the sequel strikes at one's sensibilities like a jet of water from a high-pressure hose. It begins with the same high and dry irony, the same subdued wit, but gradually—it's hard to say just when—the viewpoint shifts. Scenes from the first novel are repeated *verbatim,* but now its pleasantries have become horrors. Allegory gives way to a brutal, damning realism, and every word of it seemed an accusation aimed directly at me. After the first reading, I had no more distinct memory of it than I would have had of a hammer blow. And so I entirely overlooked the fact that *The Life of Man* is autobiography from first to last.

As I have earlier noted, my father Tennyson White belonged to the first generation of humans to grow up away from the planet Earth. He had had an exemplary upbringing on Ceres; then, when it was discovered he had leukemia, he was relegated to a second-rate Earthside hospital while the Masters argued the "sporting proposition" of his fate. It was then that he lost his faith in the Mastery, and it was then that he drew up the outlines for *both* his great novels. It was then too that Daddy contacted the leaders of the Dingoes and mapped out with their aid a program for revolution. *A Dog's Life* was to be the overture to that program.

Many authors have been accused of corrupting youth and debasing the moral coinage of their times. Probably none has ever set about so deliberately as Daddy. His novel was a time-bomb disguised as an Easter egg and planted right in the middle of the Masters' basket; it was a Trojan horse; it was a slow-working acid that nibbled at the minds of the pets—just a mild, aesthetic tickle at first, then it worked in deeper, an abrasive that scarred them with guilt. For men, in the last analysis, are not meant to be domestic animals.

Those who stood the acid-test of that novel managed to escape to Earth and join the Dingoes (feigning, like Daddy, to having been butchered). Those who didn't (and sadly, these were by far the majority) stayed with the Masters and incorporated the monstrous satire of *A Dog's Life* into the fabric of their daily lives. They became dogs.

A decade after the publication of *A Dog's Life,* Daddy effected his own escape to Earth. He managed to prevent the Master of Ganymede from realizing his intentions, then or later, by deliberately jumbling his true feelings and firm purpose among the welter of fictional ideas that were forever teeming in his fertile fancy. He further deceived his Master by surrounding this "plot" with such lustreless or unpleasant images (the ear, for instance) that his Master never encouraged him to cultivate this train of thought—nor examined it himself with more than cursory attention.

Daddy's autobiography makes no mention of the fact that he left his two sons (to mention only Pluto and me) behind when he went over to the Dingoes, and he refuses to talk about it still. I have always suspected that he doubted, if only slightly, whether he was doing the right thing in leaving the Masters. It was a large enough doubt that he was willing to let us decide for ourselves whether we wished to become Dingoes or remain Leashed.

In 2024 Earth was swarming with refugees from the Mastery, and the revolutionary movement—the Revolutionary Inductance Corps, or RIC—was getting on its feet. (Naturally, the *Dingoes* didn't call themselves "Dingoes.") Daddy's next task was more difficult, for he had to forge an army from the unorganized mass of apathetic Dingoes who had never left Earth. *The Life of Man* accomplished part of this purpose, for it showed the Dingoes what they were: an amorphous mass of discontent, without program or purpose; a race that had taken the first step towards its own extinction.

But the Dingoes were not such novel-readers as the pets. Only the more thoughtful read this second novel—and they didn't need to. Daddy gradually came to see that no amount of literature would spark the tinder of the Dingoes into a revolutionary firebrand.

And so it was—and now we leave Daddy's autobiography and enter the sphere of raw history—that my father invented a mythology.

The Dingoes were ripe for one. Ever since the first Manifestation in the '70's, organized religion had become quite disorganized. The Master bore too close a resemblance to mankind's favorite gods, and men of religious or mystical sensibilities were among the first to volunteer for the kennels, where they could contemplate the very-nearly-divine nature of the Masters without any of the usual discomforts of the ascetic life. The Dingoes, on the other hand, found it difficult to venerate gods who so much resembled their sworn enemies.

Daddy realized that under these conditions the Dingoes might accept a "religion" of demonology and sympathetic magic. When the gods are malign men turn to jujus and totems.

But wax dolls and devil masks would no longer do, for the first law of sympathetic magic is that "Like produces like." The Masters were electromagnetic phenomena: then what better talisman than a dry cell? In any elementary physics text, there was a wealth of arcane lore, hieratic symbols, and even battle cries. Children were taught Kirchoff's laws in their cradles, and revolutionaries wore cork helmets to ward off the Masters—since cork was a good insulator. It was nonsense, but it was effective nonsense. The Revolutionary Inductance Corps won an overwhelming majority in the council of the Dingoes on the slogan: ELECT RIC. Daddy became Diode in the revolutionary government, next in authority to the High Cathode himself. Everyone was ready to begin the revolution, and no one had the least idea how to go about it.

Which goes to show that it's good to be prepared, because that was when the providential support short-circuited the Masters. The leaders of the Dingoes had managed to take credit for their own good luck, but now a month had passed since S-Day, and gradually the Masters were reasserting their old claims to dominion. Electric light and power were back on (though the Dingoes refused to use them); the kennels were back in place beneath their force-field domes; the captured pets were being systematically repossessed, the most imposing demonstration of this having been the massive escape from Needlepoint Hill. In a very short time the Mastery would be established stronger than ever, unless the Dingoes found a way to stop them.

Cork helmets may be good for morale, but in a real contest I'd as soon defend myself with a popgun. If the Dingoes had made any serious plans, Daddy wasn't telling me about them.

Daddy, Julie, and I had been waiting in the lobby of the St. Paul Hotel for fifteen minutes, and in all that time we hadn't seen one room clerk or bellboy. There weren't even any guests, for Earth had become so depopulated during the Mastery that a roof and a bed were always easy to come by. What you couldn't find anywhere was labor. Even the best hotels and restaurants were self-service.

Finally Bruno and Rocky (for this had come to seem a better name for her than Roxanna) finished dressing and came down to the lobby. Bruno was wearing an unpressed cotton suit and a bowling shirt open at the neck, so that a little bit of the bandage about his chest peeped out. Rocky was dressed to kill; Darling, Julie looked as staid as a nun by comparison. But when you're only twenty years old you don't have to try as hard as when you're thirty-eight.

We exchanged pleasantries, decided on a restaurant, and went out to Daddy's car—and thus began the ghastliest evening of my life.

Bruno was returning to his post in Duluth the next day, and we'd been unable to put him off any longer. For weeks he'd been insisting that the five of us—the two Schwarzkopfs and the three Whites—"make a night of it." I felt guilty toward Bruno, and at that time I hadn't yet learned to live with a guilty conscience. I gave in.

I should have been suspicious of overtures of friendship from a man I'd nearly murdered, or I might have simply supposed that, like most Dingoes, Bruno was chiefly interested in making my father's acquaintance. However, his first overture had come before he knew my father was Tennyson White, and so it was hard to doubt his sincerity. I decided that he was only mad.

If I felt guilty and awkward toward Bruno, I can't imagine how Rocky felt toward me. When she revealed my identity to the Dingoes, she couldn't have known that my father was the second-in-command of their forces—not, as she had supposed, their archenemy. Only initiated members of the RIC knew who their leaders were, and his novel, *The Life of Man,* which had won her over to the Dingo viewpoint (to the degree that Bruno hadn't accomplished this purpose), had been published pseudonymously. She had intended to see me executed; instead she had saved my life. Now we were sitting next to each other in the back seat of Daddy's limousine, talking about old times. When we got out, she managed to bring her spiked heel down on my instep with lethal accuracy, and once, in the middle of dinner, smiling brightly and chattering all the while, she kicked me square in the shin, underneath the tablecloth.

The meal wouldn't have gone beyond the main course if it hadn't been that almost all of Rocky's remarks went over Bruno's head. He was dauntlessly ebullient, and when he started to talk, he could go on indefinitely. To shut off Rocky (who couldn't hear enough about our wedding; she was *so* glad that dear little Petite wasn't a bastard any more, I questioned Bruno about his childhood, which had been spectacularly awful—or so it seemed to me. For the majority of Dingoes, life is one long battle: against the world, against their families, against their teachers, and against the decay of their own minds and bodies. No wonder Bruno was the aggressive lout that he was. But knowing this didn't make me like him any better.

When the dinner was done and I thought we might make our escape, Bruno brought out an envelope from his coat-pocket and announced, as though he really expected us to be pleased, that he had five tickets for the fight.

"What fight?" I asked.

"The boxing match at the armory. Kelly Broughan's there tonight, so it should be worth seeing. I bet you don't see many good fights out there in the asteroids, do you?"

"No," I said in defeated tones. "None at all."

"There are some beautiful gymnastic competitions though," Julie put in. "And fencing, though no one is ever *hurt*."

Bruno's laugh was the bellow of a wounded bull. *Gymnastics* was a good joke; *beautiful* was even better. "You're a card, Julie. Dennis, that girl's a card."

Rocky's eyes gleamed wickedly, intent upon prey. "Dennis, you really must come, seeing that you're such a little scrapper yourself. And you too, Mr. White. You look worn out. A man in your position needs diversions now and then."

"What the hell," Daddy said, "let's all go! And afterwards we'll watch the fireworks."

"Oh, I love fireworks," Julie said with forced cheer.

We got up from the table with one accord. Bruno and Rocky were as happy as two children. Julie and I were glum. But Daddy . . .

Daddy was in so profound an abyss of depression and defeat that he was quite literally unaware of most of what was going on around him. He knew, as we did not, that the Masters had presented their ultimatum to the Dingoes that day. It had been decided that mankind could not be entrusted with its own affairs. All men were henceforth to be put in kennels; there would be no more distinction between Dingoes and pets. The High Cathode had been thrown into a panic by this threat, and it had been determined, despite Daddy's pleading to the contrary, that the Dingoes would shoot their wad that evening.

The Dingoes' wad—as Daddy knew, and as they apparently did not—wasn't worth a plugged nickel. All they had was atom bombs.

Whether it was because Bruno knew the gate-attendant or because Daddy was with us, I don't know, but our general-admission tickets got us seats at ringside. The audience in the smoky indoors stadium made the crowd at the parade sound like a bevy of tranquilized sheep. One woman near us (and I am *convinced* that it was the same who had kissed me in Duluth and cursed me at the gallows) was screaming: *"Murder him! Murder the m——!"* And the fight hadn't even begun!

A bell rang. Two men, modestly nude except for colored briefs, approached each other, moving their arms in nervous rhythms, circling about warily. One (in red trunks) lashed out at the other with his left hand, a feint to the stomach. With his right hand, he swung at the other man's face. There was a cracking sound as his naked fist connected with his opponent's cheekbone. The crowd began to scream.

Blood spurted from the man's nose. I averted my eyes. Bruno, in his element, added his distinctive bellow to the uproar. Rocky watched me closely, treasuring my every blanch and wince. Daddy looked bored, and Julie kept her eyes shut through the whole thing. I should have done the same, but when I heard another *thunk* of bone on flesh and a loud crash, curiosity overcame my finer feelings and I looked back into the ring. The man in red trunks was lying on his back, his expressionless face a scant few inches from my own. The blood flowed from his nose and flooded the sockets of his eyes. Rocky was shrieking with pleasure, but Bruno, who felt an allegiance for the fighter in red trunks shouted, "Get up, you bum!"

I rose from my seat, mumbling apologies, and found my way outside, where I was discreetly sick in a hedge across the street from the Armory. Though I felt weak, I knew that I did not have to faint. The Masters' conditioning was wearing off!

The hedge bordered on a park which had been allowed to go to seed. Through the thick summer foliage I could see the glint of moonlit water. I strolled down the hillside to the pond's edge.

Down there, the din of the stadium melted into the other night sounds: the croaking of the frogs, the rustle of poplar leaves, the rippling water. It was quiet and Earthlike.

A full moon shone overhead, like the echo of a thousand poems. All the Earthbound poets who had stolen the fire of their lyrics from the moon, age after age! It had passed them by, oblivious of histories, and it would pass me by in time. That's the way that things should be, I thought. The leaves should fall in autumn, snow in winter, grass springs up in spring, and the summer is brief.

I knew then that I belonged to the Earth, and my spirit dilated with happiness. It wasn't quite the right time to be happy—but there it was. Julie and the moon were part of it, but it was also the frogs croaking, the poplars, the stadium; Daddy, cynical, aspiring, even defeated; partly too, it was Bruno and Roxanna, if only because they were so vital. These things melted into my memory of the farmhouse, and it seemed that I could smell the winy smell of apples rotting in the grass.

The sky was growing brighter and brighter. The moon . . .

But was it the moon? A cloud of mist had gathered above the pond and it glowed until the full moon was almost blotted out behind it.

The Meshes of the Leash closed over my mind, and a voice inside my head purred kindly: *White Fang, good boy! It's all right now. We heard your call* . . . (But I hadn't called! It was just that I had been so happy!) . . . *and now I've come. Your Master has come back at last for you.*

I cried out then, a simple cry of pain. To be taken away now! Only a few days before I had cried for the lack of this voice, and now—"NO!"

There, it soothed, *there, there, there. Has it been bad? Has it been that very bad? Those terrible Dingoes have captured you, but it won't happen again. There, there.*

The Leash began gently to stroke the sensory areas of the cortex: soft fur wrapped me, scented with musk. Faint ripples of harp-music (or was that only the water of the pond?) sounded behind my Master's voice, which poured forth comforting words, like salve spread over a wound.

Then, with a sudden pang, I remembered Daddy. (*Don't think of your poor father*, the Leash bade.)

He was waiting for me. Julie was waiting for me. The Dingoes were waiting for me. (*We'll get Julie back too. Now, don't you worry yourself any more about those nasty Dingoes. Soon there won't be any Dingoes, ever, ever at all.*

Desperately I tried not to think—or at least to keep my thoughts so scrambled that I would not betray the things I knew. But it was exactly this effort that focused my thoughts on the forbidden objects.

I tried to think of nonsense, of poetry, of the moon, dim behind the glowing air. But the Leash, sensing my resistance, closed tighter around my mind, and cut through my thin web of camouflage. It shuffled through my memory as though it were a deck of cards, and it stopped (there was just time enough for me to catch the images then) to examine images of my father with particular attention.

There was, on the very edge of my perception, a sound: *Ourrp*. Which was repeated: *Ourrp*. It was not a sound my Leash would make. The harp-music quavered for a moment, becoming a prosaic ripple of water. I concentrated on that single sound, straining against my Leash.

"What is that sound?" I asked my Master. To answer me he had to stop sorting through my memories. *Nothing. It's nothing. Don't think about it. Listen to the beautiful music, why don't you? Think of your father.*

Whatever was making the sound seemed to be down in the grass. I could see clearly in the wash of light from the nimbus above me. I parted the grass at my feet, and I saw the beastly thing.

Don't think about it!

The front half of a frog projected from the distended jaws of a water snake. The snake, seeing me, writhed, pulling his victim into the denser grass.

Again the Leash bade me not to look at this thing, and, truly, I did not want to. It was so horrible, but I could not help myself.

The frog had stretched his front legs to the side to prevent the last swallow that would end him. Meanwhile, the back half of him was being digested. He emitted another melancholy *Ourrp*.

Horrible, I thought, *Oh, horrible, horrible, horrible!*

Stop this. You . . . must . . . stop . . .

The snake lashed his body, wriggling slowly backwards. The frog's front feet grasped at sprigs of grass. His *Ourrp* had grown quite weak. In the failing light, I almost lost sight of the struggle in the shadow of the tall grass. I bent closer.

In the moon's light I could see a thin line of white froth about the snake's gaping jaws.

Chapter 12

In which I am more or less responsible for
saving the World.

The cloud of light disappeared. My Master had left, and I could hear Daddy calling my name. I ran back up to the street. He was there with Julie.

"Mastery!" Julie said. "You shouldn't have run off like that. We came out and saw a light over the lake, and I was sure they'd carried you off."

"They almost did. My Master was there, and I was in my Leash. But then I slipped out of it—and he went away. Just disappeared. I don't understand it. Are you all right, Daddy?"

I had asked because he was visibly shaking with excitement. "Oh, quite, quite," he said, paying scant attention. "I'm thinking though."

"He had an idea," Julie explained. "Right after you ran out of the stadium. I guess this is what happens when he has ideas."

Bruno pulled up beside us in the limousine and honked, not because we hadn't seen him, but just for the sake of honking. We got into the back seat and the car tore off down the street at a speed that it could not have hit for the last half century.

"Rocky's making the calls you told her to, sir," Bruno announced.

"Fine. Now, Dennis, what was this about your Master?"

I explained what had happened, concluding with an account of the frog and the snake. Not that I thought it relevant, but it had impressed me.

"And while you were watching that, your Master just faded away?"

"Yes. If he'd kept at me much longer, he'd have learned everything he was looking for. I couldn't have stood out against him. So why did he go?"

"One more question: what did you feel about that frog? Precisely."

"It was ugly. I felt . . . disgusted."

"Was it anything like the way you felt at the fight tonight?"

"The fight was worse in a way. The snake was worse another way."

"But both induced similar feelings: a sense of ugliness, then disgust and nausea?"

"Yes."

"Then those are the weapons we'll fight them with. Dennis, my boy, before this night is over, you will be a hero of the revolution."

"Don't I deserve an explanation? Or does the revolution require ignorant heroes?"

"When you left the fight earlier you looked so distressed that I was a bit amused. Dennis is such an esthete still, I thought. And then I remembered the old saw: *Like master, like man.* Turn it around, and it's the formula for our weapon. *Like man, like Master!* The Masters are nothing but their own pets, writ large. They're esthetes, every last one of them. And *we're* their favorite art-form. A human brain is the clay they work in. They order our minds just the way they order the Northern Lights. That's why they prefer an intelligent, educated pet to an undeveloped Dingo. The Dingoes are lumpy clay, warped canvas, faulty marble, verse that doesn't scan."

"They must feel about Dingoes the way I do about Salvador Dali," Julie said. She always wanted to argue about Dali with me, since she knows I like him despite my better judgment.

"Or the way I feel about prize fights," I suggested.

"Or any experience," Daddy concluded, "that offends the esthetic sensibilities. They can't stand ugliness."

We were silent for a while, considering this. Except Bruno. "Give yourself time, Dennis. You'll get so you enjoy the fights. Kelly just wasn't in form tonight, that's all."

Before I could answer, the limousine was sailing down a concrete ramp into a brightly-lit garage. "The hospital," Bruno announced.

A man in a white robe approached us. "Everything is in readiness, Mr. White. As soon as we received your call, we set to work."

"The radiomen are here too?"

"They're working with our own technicians already. And Mrs. Schwarzkopf said she'd join her husband directly."

A terrible light suddenly kindled the night sky outside the garage.

"The Masters!" I cried in terror.

"Damnation, the bombs!" Daddy exclaimed. "I forgot all about them. Dennis, go with the doctor and do what he says. I have to call up RIC headquarters and tell them to stop the bombings."

"What are they trying to hit?"

"They're trying to land one in the Van Allen belt. I tried to tell them it wouldn't do any good. They tried that in 1972, and it didn't accomplish a thing. But they were getting desperate, and I couldn't suggest any better plan. But now it would knock out radio communications, and we're going to be needing them. Bruno, Julie— wait in the car for me."

A team of doctors led me down the long enamel-white corridors to a room filled with a complicated array of electronic and surgical equipment. The doctor-in-chief indicated that I was to lie down on an uncomfortable metal pallet. When I had done so, two steel bars were clamped on either side of my head. The doctor held a rubber mask over my mouth and nose.

"Breathe deeply," he commanded.

The anesthetic worked quickly.

Daddy was yelling at the doctor when I woke up. "Did you *have* to use an anesthetic? We don't have time to waste on daintinesses."

"The placement of the electrodes is a very delicate operation. He should be awake in any moment."

"He is awake," I said.

The doctor rushed over to my pallet. "Don't move your head," he warned. Rather unnecessarily, it seemed, for my head was still clamped in the steel vice, although I was now propped up into a sitting position.

"How are you feeling?" Daddy asked.

"Miserable."

"That's *fine*. Now, listen—the machine behind you . . . ("Don't look" the doctor interrupted.) ". . . is an electroencephalograph. It records brain waves."

The doctor broke in again: "There are electrodes in six different areas. I've tried to explain to your father that we're uncertain where perceptions of an esthetic nature are centered. What is the relationship between pleasure and beauty, for instance? Little work has been done since . . ."

"Later, doctor, later. Now what I want Dennis to do is suffer. Actually, it's White Fang who must do the suffering. White Fang must drown in misery. I've already arranged some suitable entertainments, but you should tell me right now if there's anything especially distasteful to you that we might send off for. Some little phobia all your own."

"Please—explain what this is all about."

"Your electroencephalograms are being taken to every radio station in the city. The wave patterns will be amplified and broadcast over AM and FM, radio and TV. Every station in the country—in the world is standing by to pick them up. Tomorrow night we'll give the Masters a concert like they've never heard before."

A man in workclothes brought in a blackboard and handed it to Daddy.

"Doctor, you have better fingernails than I do. Rub them over this slate." It made an intolerable noise, which the doctor kept up for a solid minute.

"How does the graph look?" Daddy asked.

"Largest responses in the sensory areas. But fairly generalized elsewhere, especially during the first twenty seconds."

"Well, there's lots more coming. Look at these pictures, Dennis. Examine the details." He showed me illustrations from an encyclopedia of pathology that I will refrain from describing here. The people in the pictures were beyond the reach of medicine. Beyond the reach, even, of sympathy. They were ordered in an ascending degree of horribleness, concluding with a large colorplate of . . . "Take these away!"

"The response is stronger now and well sustained. Good definition."

Daddy passed a vial of formaldehyde beneath my nose. It smelt awfully. Actually, it was more of a bottle than a vial. In it—

I screamed.

"Excellent," the doctor said. "Really alarming curves for that."

"Bring in the band," said Daddy.

A crew of four men with musical instruments I was unfamiliar with (they were, I've since learned, electric guitar, musical saw, accordion and tuba) entered the room. They were dressed in outlandish costumes: glorified working-clothes in garish colors garnished with all sorts of leather and metal accessories. On their heads were ridiculous, flaring bonnets.

"Extraordinary!" the doctor said. "He's already responding."

They began—well, they began to *sing*. It was like singing. Their untuned instruments blasted out a stupid *One*-two-three, *One*-two-three, repeating melody, which they accompanied with strident screams of "Roll out the bare-ul."

When I thought that this new attack on my sensibilities had reached the threshold of tolerance, Daddy, who had been watching me intently, leaped up and began to slam his feet on the floor and join them in that awful song.

Daddy has a terrible voice when he sings. It *rasps*.

But his voice was the least awfulness; it was his behavior that was so mortifying. I wanted to turn my head away, but the vice held it fast. For a man of such natural dignity to so debase himself, and that man my own father!

This was, of course, just the response Daddy was looking for.

When they had finished their gross display, I begged for a moment's reprieve. Daddy dismissed the band and returned the accordion player his cowboy hat.

"Don't work him too hard, until we have some idea of his breaking point," the doctor advised. "Besides, I'd like to see the intern, if you'll excuse me. Those photographs gave me an idea: there are some patients in the hospital . . ."

"Have *you* thought of anything, Dennis?"

"In a way, yes. Is Bruno still around?"

"He should be downstairs."

"If he were to tell me about the things he enjoys—the very worst things—in the long run he might think of more horrors than you. They seem to come naturally to him."

"Good idea. I'll send for him."

"Rocky too, if she's down there. I remember how she watched me at the boxing match. She'd be able to help you quite a lot."

As Daddy went out of the room, the doctor returned, escorting a caravan of wheelchairs and litters. Photographs are no equivalent for the real thing.

It went on that way for four hours, and every minute seemed worse than the one before. Bruno had a limitless imagination, especially when it was abetted by alcohol and his wife. He told me about his favorite fights to begin with. He told me what he liked to do with pets—and what he *would* like to do if he had the time. Then he discoursed on the mysteries of love, a subject on which Rocky too was eloquent.

After two hours of these and other pleasures, I asked to have some coffee. Rocky left for it and returned with a steaming mug from which I took one greedy swallow before I realized it was not coffee. Rocky had remembered my peculiar attitude toward blood.

When I had been revived with smelling salts, Daddy brought in more entertainers. They had come to the hospital directly after their last fight at the Armory. For some reason, most of what happened after that point I can no longer remember.

We were out on the tile terrace of the hospital, Daddy, Julie, and I. Below us the Mississippi was a pool of utter blackness and unknown extent. It was an hour after sunset, and the moon had not yet risen. The only light came from the North, where the great auroral floodlights swept out from the horizon across the constellations of the north.

"Five minutes," Daddy announced nervously.

In five minutes, radio stations all over the world would begin to broadcast my performance of the night before. I had heard an aural equivalent of my electroencephalograms, and I wasn't worried. In a war based on esthetics, that recording was a Doomsday machine.

"Does your head still hurt?" Julie asked, brushing a feather-light hand over my bandages.

"Only when I try to remember last night."

"Let me kiss the hurt away."

"Three minutes," Daddy announced, "and stop that. You're making me nervous."

Julie straightened her blouse, which was made of some wonderful, sheer, crinkly nylon. I had really begun to admire some of the uses of clothing.

We watched the aurora. All over the city, lights had been turned off. Everyone, the whole world, was watching the aurora.

"What will you do now that you're High Cathode?" Julie asked, to make the time pass.

"In a few minutes the revolution should be over," Daddy replied. "I don't think I'd like administrative work. Not after this."

"You're going to resign?"

"As soon as they let me. I've got the itch to paint some more. Did you know that I paint? I did that self-portrait that's over my desk. I think it's pretty good, but I should be able to do better. In any case, it's traditional for retired generals to paint. And then I might do my memoirs. I've picked a title for them: *The Esthetic Revolution.*"

"Or *Viva Dingo!*" Julie suggested.

"Ten seconds," I announced.

We watched the northern skyline. The aurora was a curtain of bluish light across which bands and streamers of intense whiteness danced and played.

At first you couldn't notice any difference. The spectacle glimmered with the same rare beauty that has belonged to it from time immemorial, but tonight its beauty was that of a somber *Dies Irae*, played just for us.

Then one of the white bands that was shooting up from the horizon disappeared, like an electric light being switched off. It seemed unnaturally abrupt, but I couldn't be sure.

For a long while nothing more happened. But when five of the arcing lights snapped out of the sky at the same moment, I knew that the Masters were beginning their exodus.

"Elephantiasis, I'll bet."

"What's that, Dennis?"

"The last picture in the bunch you showed me. I remember it very clearly."

The auroral display was less bright by half when they came to the hillbilly band. I turned on the radio just to be sure. Through all the blasts and shrieks and whistles of my neural patterns, there was an unmistakeable rhythm of *Ooom*pah-pah, *Ooom*-pah-pah.

When the broadcast came to Rocky's unspeakable potion, there was a tremendous blast across the heavens. For an instant the entire sky was stained white. The white faded. The aurora was only a dim blue-white shadow in the north. There was hardly a trace of beauty in it. It flickered meaninglessly in random patterns.

The Masters had left Earth. They couldn't stand the barking.